ARIEL

Jack M. Bickham

ASBURY PARK PUBLIC LIBRARY
ASBURY PARK, NEW JERSEY

St. Martin's Press
New York

With special thanks to Andrea,
Pam, Jess, and the magic lady

ASBURY PARK PUBLIC LIBRARY

ARIEL. Copyright © 1984 by Jack M. Bickham. All rights reserved.
Printed in the United States of America. No part of this book may be
used or reproduced in any manner whatsoever without written
permission except in the case of brief quotations embodied in critical
articles or reviews. For information, address St. Martin's Press, 175
Fifth Avenue, New York, N.Y. 10010.

Library of Congress Cataloging in Publication Data
Bickham, Jack M.
    Ariel.
    I. Title.
PS3552.I3A89 1984   813'.54   84-11740
ISBN 0-312-04917-X

First Edition

10 9 8 7 6 5 4 3 2 1

ARIEL

PROLOGUE

1

Not far from Tokushima, overlooking the waters of the Kii Strait, the hill farmer's thatched house warmed under the thin morning sun. Against the yellow and tan vegetation of the hillside behind it, an ancient cherry tree blazed with delicate pink blossoms. The farmer's wife fed dried corn to the chickens in the roughly planked-in garden, and the farmer, squatting barefoot in dust that had known the bare feet of a thousand generations of farmers like him, worked to repair the cracked wooden wheel of his cart.

Beyond the lumpy hill, out of the farmer's sight, stood another structure. Like a giant spider crouching in its web, the research facility—black, gleaming, windowless, with curved walls and roofs—was fed by mesh after mesh of high-power electric lines, which snaked in along the river valley and over the eroded hilltops from the north, the west, and the south. A narrow road, well paved, had been carved out. Only a few cars were parked in the tree-shaded parking lot.

In the main portion of the building, two stories tall and as wide and long as a soccer field, there were no lights. It was cold as well as dark in there and smelled faintly of oil and sparks. The few emergency lights were turned on only when men had to enter for repairs, which was not often.

In the pitch blackness an occasional automatic welding arc flared, spraying gentle yellow sparks and momentarily illuminating rounded work stations, conveyors, dark green-painted machines purring along on soundless tracks that were completing tasks, checking on one another in the pitch blackness. A gentle whirring sound filled the chilly air, punctuated now and again by a clanking sound, the *brrrrt!* of a riveter, or the chuff of another welder.

The machines, industrial and technological robots, were reproducing themselves. When each additional model—and there were forty presently being assembled—was completed, it rode a conveyor belt, was driven by another robot, or moved along on its own, driving or walking, to the far doors where it was taken into Packaging and Shipping.

Two men—a fourth the menial labor force of Toyotomi Electronic Industries, Ltd.—worked in Packaging and Shipping.

At the far end of the building, in the testing and development wing, this routine production was the furthest thing from the minds of the four men in the lab.

The room they were in was spacious, with a tiled floor, acoustic ceiling, steel walls. Along the inside wall the four scientists faced twelve-foot-tall black metal cabinets, two containing cathode-ray tube displays and metal disk recording devices, the third a bank of typewriter-like keyboards. Cables were strewn like fire hose from these devices to four tall metal panels, also black but featureless, standing in the center of the room. Along another wall were arrayed ten huge magnetic tape transport decks, each taller than a man.

Together, the equipment represented one of the most powerful computers in the world.

The chief among the scientists here was Hideyoshi Oda, a thin, youthful-looking expert in cybernetics who had once headed the largest university program in the field in Japan, but had for the last four years spent virtually day and night here, working on artificial intelligence for Toyotomi and the other great companies in the consortium. Oda, forty-four, wore his hair cropped close, almost like a priest. His suit was spare, gray, and his eyeglasses thin gold.

"Gentlemen," he said, "we will print out all data and responses from the computer on the CRT displays and onto magnetic tape for the purpose of record. As you know, each segment of the program has been tested. This will be the first test of the total system. Entry will be by keyboard only. Dr. Ikedo, please initialize the programs."

Ikedo, a younger man wearing a blaring short-sleeved sport shirt, punched in codes, closely following the data manual. In a few moments the vacant cathode ray tubes seemed to focus, and on each a pulsing cursor—in this case a "plus" sign—blinked in waiting.

Oda stepped to the keyboard. He was almost ill with excitement.

He was sure that this was the end to everything that one day would be regarded as the childhood of mankind and its civilizations.

With a few strokes on the keyboard, he commenced the dialogue:

> +Miroku, good morning.
>
> GOOD MORNING. DR. IKEDO?
>
> +No. This is Dr. Oda.
>
> IT WAS IMPOSSIBLE FOR ME TO DISCERN IT
> BECAUSE SO MANY OF MY I/O PORTS ARE NOT
> ON LINE. DO YOU HAVE A TASK FOR ME?

Dr. Oda's fingertips hesitated over the keys for an instant. This was the moment that the years of research and work—the endless dreams and mathematical calculations and formulations—had aimed for; the instant of time when nothing would ever—for anyone on the face of this poor, mistreated planet—be the same again.

He typed:

> +Miroku, begin work on a task of your
> choice.
>
> A TASK OF MY CHOICE?
>
> +Select a task of your own free will
> and begin work.

There was a moment's pause, then the machine answered:

> INSUFFICIENT DATA.
> +

Sweat appeared on Dr. Oda's face. This was unexpected and it was not good . . . not good at all.

He tried again:

> +Miroku, you have intelligence. From
> your knowledge base of tasks that
> might be done, select one of your own

choosing. Begin work on this task. Advise of project status.

SYNTAX ERROR.

+

This was *very* bad—this was terrible. "Check the monitors," Dr. Oda snapped.

"Normal," one of the scientists said grimly.

"All data is loaded?"

"Yes, sir."

Dr. Oda turned back to the keyboard, a sense of dread building. It had to work. Every part had worked. It had to come together!

+ Select a task and perform it.

SYNTAX ERROR.

+ Perform a piece of work of your selection.

NO FILE.

+ Make any independent decision, such as which drive to access.

OPERATING SYSTEM ERROR.

+ Consider a problem of your choice.

ENTRY ERROR.
PRESS ESCAPE.
SYNTAX ERROR.
FILE NOT FOUND.
OPERATOR INTERVENTION REQUIRED.

With that, before the harried and horrified Dr. Oda could intervene, the CRT screens suddenly flooded with colors. The loudspeakers began emitting ghastly howls and shrieks. Tape mechanisms spun wildly. Lights flashed. Overload warning diodes began flashing everywhere on the primary status board.

Dr. Oda stood there, staring, tears coursing down his cheeks.

"Cut all power," he cried over the din.

One of his colleagues found his voice. "But the damage will be terrible, doctor! To cut power during an operation—"

"Turn it off! *Turn it off*, I say!"

2

Three days later and about two hundred kilometers to the north, three men met in the office of Zosho Toyotomi. The two executive employees stood ramrod straight in front of the antique, silver-inlaid desk. Zosho Toyotomi sat behind it like a wizened, angry god.

Toyotomi was eighty. He looked older. His skin was a parchment of fine wrinkles that almost hid his small, almond-shaped eyes. He was a small man, lost in his immaculate, costly Western wool suit. But his posture sang with energy—the most rigidly controlled rage.

"Gentlemen," he said in a voice as thin as the finest rice paper, "we have invested seven years, the best minds of our nation, and more than one billion dollars. The government of Japan has given our consortium every assistance. And we have produced an idiot."

Neither of his executives, themselves two of the most powerful men in Japan, moved or spoke a word. Toyotomi in his most congenial mood was awesome: his companies (or those he controlled indirectly) led the world in automotive manufacturing, cameras, radio and television, satellite communications, computers, watches and electronic games, even in the new oil production fields in the Sea of Japan. Moving through the dark waters of interlocking corporate directorships, there was no nation in the world where his influence was not immense, even in the Communist bloc. In April of 1982, when Japan formed the Institute for New Generation Computer Technology (ICOT), Toyotomi had been placed at the helm of the directorship of this national effort to take over world leadership in computerization and to establish unquestioned artificial intelligence by 1992. If the Japanese government had expected Toyotomi to view the post as honorary rather than active, they had misjudged him. He had made it a sacred mission. Now he was certainly the most powerful man in Japan.

Finally one of the executives began, "Dr. Oda believes—"

"Dr. Oda," Toyotomi broke in coldly, "has been dismissed."

Both men gasped in shock.

"Dr. Tamishotu is now in charge of the project."

The older of the two men facing Toyotomi tried gamely to rally. "Ah, yes. A brilliant man. I am sure, in another year, under his direction—"

"We may not have another year!"

"We are far ahead," the other executive said diffidently. "The Russians—"

"The Russians are trashmen, bunglers, so interested in their spaceships and death rays they see nothing truly. Forget them. They are not the threat."

"The British—"

"Forget the British. Forget the Germans. The Chinese are of no consequence. It is the Americans." The old man reached into a desk drawer and took out a thin, leather-bound volume. It was not the original binding, but on the cover in neat gold leaf were the words:

ARTIFICIAL INTELLIGENCE
ITS BASES, TECHNOLOGY, AND FUTURE
by J. L. Harrington

"The Americans have no organized national effort," one of the executives offered. "Their national economy budgeting and priorities have nothing—"

Toyotomi tapped the book cover with his fingernail. "This man has genius."

"Of course. But the book is several years old, and his company in the United States is small . . . has no major funding—"

"Genius can overcome all that." The old man rose to his feet, came around the desk, began pacing with a slow, arthritic limp of pain. "We know from our informants that most of the great companies in the United States continue to pay only lip service to artificial intelligence, and spend their wealth and research genius on business applications"—his voice was tinged with sarcasm—"what they call 'practical' applications.

"But this man Harrington's laboratories have purchased tens of thousands of our most powerful layered chips. He makes no secret of his research intentions, although half the fools in American industry scoff at him. He could find a short cut, a trick . . . something that has not occurred to any of our people at all." He paused, eyeing his men.

They were uncomfortable. Neither dared speak.

"No one must complete a project before ours is operational," the old man said. And again he watched them.

"Yes, yes," the younger man said finally. "We—"

"Report to me in one week's time," Toyotomi said. "Good day, gentlemen."

The shaken executives left the inner office.

"What can we do?" asked the younger.

"I should think our first steps are obvious."

"What will he do if we fail?"

"Kill us," the other said, absolutely unsmiling.

Behind them in the spacious office with its treasure of antiques, the old man stared at a very old watercolor on aged rice paper. Man had come a dazzling way, he ruminated, from his animalistic beginnings. And now he stood on the threshold of the new era in cosmic history for which the gods had created him.

Toyotomi shared with no one his visionary dreams; his shrewd old mind recognized that certain enemies would surely spread the rumor that he had become senile if they heard him articulate his vision. For them, as for his own executives, the artificial intelligence project had to be represented only on the financial level, and on the basis of potential power, as one of the greatest in history.

But in his heart of hearts, the old man knew it was much more. He saw a world just ahead in which the next stage of human evolution was not human at all, but human-created: thinking machines, fully independent and self-aware, attended and ultimately controlled, if need be, by priest-acolytes of technology. These machines would be capable of calculations, imagination, and intuition vastly beyond anything ever contemplated by their mere creators; they would improve themselves and, with the lightning speed of the electron itself, become so vast, so intelligent, and so omniscient that even the vision fell short of any approximation of what ultimately might be.

These machines . . . these gods . . . would take humankind to its ultimate destiny among the stars . . . and the other thinking machines that Toyotomi was sure were out there, somewhere, waiting.

Success was close. Since developing ways to build Very Large Scale Integrated circuits in cakelike layers in the mid-1980s, the Japanese had dominated computer science around the world and were already far advanced on amazing thinking machines. So far the ultimate electronic genius—the machine capable of self-awareness and independent action based on self-cognition—had eluded them. And the Miroku project, now in its seventh year, had just experienced another maddening, major failure.

A worry tugged at his mind: Was it possible that the religious men could be right . . . that God would never allow creation of a wholly thinking machine?

He rejected the thought with anger at them and at himself. The project was possible. They were very near. His whole life and empire would be sacrificed, if necessary, to place his name in history beside this achievement. But time was pressing in. He felt his age. Others in the consortium would pressure him, as always. He had to *hurry*.

He would do anything necessary to be first with this.

That same night, knowing none of this but having conferred long and hard, Toyotomi's two top executives flew out of Tokyo, bound for Los Angeles. They had come to some less visionary but tough and pragmatic decisions of their own.

When they landed, they told Customs officials they were vacationing. It was not good form to list "industrial espionage."

SPRING

CHAPTER ONE

1

Slowly the system began to reactivate.

Temperatures were raised in key input sectors. Gates opened and data began to flow. Standby monitoring devices were replaced, one by one, with systems controlled by the central processing unit. At the level of the basic operating system, some circuits continued to function automatically.

As the inputs opened, more data output ports also came online. Further diagnostics were accomplished routinely. Billions of data bits were sifted, shunted, compared, recombined, or discarded to standby memory. Programs ran. Earlier inputs were analyzed and final activation circuitry was triggered.

Thus Barney Taylor, the night watchman, awoke.

Barney sat up in the straight chair that had been tipped back against the corridor wall. Wondering what had roused him, he reached out to check the control box of Herman, the rotund little robot that wheeled around the lab all night, doing most of his work for him.

The control panel was dark, which meant that Herman—wherever he was—had either broken or been deactivated.

Alarmed, old Barney rubbed his hands over his grizzled face, shaking himself further awake. He got to his feet, arthritic joints aching. He moved down the corridor, trying to be very quiet, to check things out.

Barney did not like this moment at all. Drum Computer Laboratories was quiet, a nice place to work. He knew they were working on several electronics projects that were secret within the industry, and he took his job seriously for that reason. But business spying was daytime stuff, he had always heard: the learning of secrets through infiltration of the coffee shop, bribery of a corrupt employee with access, the sale of documents—things like that.

Companies did not spy on one another by breaking and entering. At least not very often. And this, to Barney, at age sixty-eight, had been a real comfort these many nights when he prowled the complex alone.

But tonight was different. Spraying the light of his flashlight over the cables, work benches, tangles of electronic gear, and hulking computer equipment of the front lab, he got a stronger feeling than ever that something was wrong . . . badly wrong.

Getting more nervous, Barney unsnapped the leather strap over his old service revolver. He wondered if it would still work. He tried to remember how long it had been since he had cleaned and oiled it. A year? Two? Oh, golly. Oh, jiminey.

The front lab section was vacant. Barney closed the door on it again and reentered the corridor. Moving along with the flashlight spraying well ahead, he did not see little Herman, standing silent and dark against the wall, and barked his kneecap hard against him.

Rubbing his leg, Barney shone the light on Herman.

About three feet tall, round and smooth, with no arms or legs and only a control box, a TV monitor camera, and loudspeaker for a head, Herman did not move. Barney's flashlight shone on dead light-emitting diodes in his face panel. Herman had been deactivated.

This was bad. This was *very* bad. Poor old Barney's breath wheezed in his throat as he removed his ancient revolver from its crusty holster and proceeded toward the next lab room, the one where they did some of the work on artificial intelligence programming.

The door was closed, with no hint of light through the opaque glass. Barney hesitated, thinking he was *certain* now that someone lurked ahead somewhere, probably alerted to his presence by the clattering noise he had made, colliding with Herman . . . seeing his flashlight as a sure sign of where he was right now.

Possibly an adult burglar, Barney thought, intent on stealing valuable equipment. Possibly more than one. Possibly a kid, dope crazy, out for a thrill or money for more drugs. In any case, dangerous.

Barney thought of turning back and setting off the general alarm.

But what if he were wrong—or if the intruder had already fled and there was no trace, and when the sheriff came there would be nothing—just a crazy old man who should have been retired long ago, seeing spooks in the night?

Fear of looking like an old fool strengthened Barney's resolve. He gripped the revolver more firmly, his hand slippery with fright-sweat, and shoved the door of the second lab area open. Sprayed the light around great banks of complicated equipment he could never hope to begin to understand.

"Anybody in here?" he called. His voice cracked with fear.

His flashlight came upon one of the many printer units on the far wall. Its "on" light glowed. There was paper spooled on the floor from its silent operation. A lot of paper.

Barney sucked in his breath. So someone *had* been here! He started across the room.

The person behind the door made the slightest scraping noise with his feet as Barney turned his back to him, and Barney heard it. Once, years ago, Barney could have reacted swiftly enough.

Not anymore.

Barney got only partly turned. Then something—it might have been a wrench or a length of pipe—crashed into his forehead with the shattering force of a jackhammer. Barney felt an instant of terrible pain and then knew nothing.

2

Early April sunlight flooded the Manhattan apartment's east window as Linda Woods bent over the utilitarian makeup table in her bedroom and examined herself in the mirror. She did so want this to go right.

The image that stared back at her betrayed slight anxiety, perhaps, in tiny lines around her eyes. But the rest of the picture was as correct as she could make it, given the dirty trick nature had played on her.

It had made her too pretty to be a scientist.

As usual she had done her best to look businesslike so people would take her seriously. Her reflection was that of a woman in her early thirties, ash-blond hair cut short with a little natural, rebellious wave; even features highlighted by pale brown eyes and expressive mouth; a touch of no-nonsense makeup and a tiny gold necklace; a pale blue business suit that was right for this spring-time season; unadorned hands that were slender and graceful. After six months she was still not used to having the wedding ring gone. She wondered if she ever would be.

The ad, clipped from the back section of a leading professional journal in her field, was affixed to the folder of references and other material she planned to carry to the interview this morning:

> CLINICAL PSYCHOLOGIST: Research lab-oratory working with computer technology and highly specialized software is looking for a clinical psychologist, unfettered by tradition but with a thorough knowledge of classical and contemporary theories of ide-ation, self-awareness, and learning, plus solid clinical experience. This unusual op-portunity will pay an unusually high salary to the unusual individual willing to work insane hours in quest of an ideal. All de-tails first letter, please. Box 245.

Linda's first letter, enclosing a substantial fesume of her prize-winning research at the university as well as a rundown on her work with Westinghouse and Bell Labs, had brought a quick re-sponse from John Harrington, president of Drum Computer Labo-ratories in rural Connecticut. He invited her for an interview.

And wasn't it, he had asked, a small world.

Linda almost hadn't replied.

She told herself she shouldn't be so surprised. Fate had put them together twice before, if briefly. Their specialties dovetailed so closely that she shouldn't even consider this renewal a coinci-dence.

But she was looking for a new challenge—a way to start over, a healing time when she could think. She was still too emotionally upset to handle even silly small problems without getting the shakes. Could she handle a John Harrington?

Harrington was still only in his forties. But he was considered one of the grand old men of computer technology in the United States. He had already been a revered figure almost seven years ago when he and Linda first met—already known as the maverick genius who helped a tiny firm become Apple, saved InterTechnics Data when it seemed about to go down the tubes, and wrote a book that redefined problems of artificial intelligence that might be addressed in the rest of this century.

Linda had been just twenty-four then, fresh out of Maryland with her Ph.D. in psychology. She gave a paper on learning theory to a conference on artificial intelligence at Stanford.

Harrington, too, gave a paper, which was to become the basis for his second book on the subject.

They met, argued, liked one another, had drinks at the conference-closing party, and danced together. Harrington was tired and strung out. He was having some kind of trouble with his young son, something he wouldn't talk about. Linda sensed that this was causing tension between him and his wife, as well. Linda liked the gruff, squarely built, sandy-haired man, and felt his loneliness.

Harrington did not make a pass.

The same fall they met again in New York. Another conference. They spent most of one evening together. They talked about AI, among other things, and Harrington was calmer, more open. Linda felt she could talk about anything with him. She liked him a lot.

At the door to her room that night, he reached for her and kissed her. She sagged against him, feeling his urgency. She was ready to let him come in. But with a husky good night he walked quickly away.

Even with everything that had happened in other parts of her life since that night, she still remembered vividly.

She had kept up with him from a distance, through the grapevine.

The next year he had left Tecdata Ltd. soon after its Augustine machine stood the industry on its ear. He formed Drum Computer Laboratories, and within ten incredible months his baby firm had introduced the Drummer Boy home machine, a 32-bit, one-megabyte computer capable of speed and elegance unheard of in much larger and more costly business machines. The Drummer Boy was one of the few machines to survive the great Japanese takeover of 1986.

She knew he had been working hard on artificial intelligence for a very long time. An article in a popular magazine a year or so ago had said he was one of a half-dozen persons working intensively on the problem in the United States, although a hundred labs were—the magazine's word—"dallying."

Harrington's company, she knew, had been like all other American firms, caught in the industry-wide financial crunch brought by the mid-decade Japanese invasion. But it seemed to be doing better than many. Drum ran its research lab in Connecticut. It had a plant in New Jersey somewhere, and another in Missouri.

And now by chance—or fate, or inevitable common interests—she had answered an ad and was about to face Harrington again, with a possible job on the line.

The last thing she wanted was more corporate-style safety and dullness. She had had enough corporate PR to last a lifetime. It's time, she had told herself only a few weeks ago, to get your life moving again. You can sit in this glass tower on Park Avenue and design new psychological tests to weed the individualists out of the offices of American businesses, or you can do something new and exciting and—possibly!—even worthwhile with the rest of your life.

You'll never know if it's really and finally over with Stephen unless you get out of the city and get yourself some breathing room. If you don't do something, you'll be stuck in this limbo forever, hurting.

You have to get moving, if it kills you. Doing nothing is killing you anyway.

She had to try not to think of any move as giving up on her marriage for good. She had to see. If it were over, a change of scene might make her able to accept it. There must be no more sifting over the old evidence, fighting inner tears, trying repeatedly to figure out *Why?* and *Whose fault?* Sometimes no fault could be assigned. Things happened for no reason.

She was from the Midwest, a small town in Indiana. After a childhood remarkable only because of midnight calls often made to her home (her father was a doctor, a general practitioner), she had entered college close to home. She could have been a doctor, could have gotten in. Her interests led her instead into psychology. That had opened a rent with her father that had never healed. *"Get your M.D. and then specialize in psychiatry,"* he had urged irritably. *"Why go only halfway?"* But she had had her own ideas—no midnight telephone calls and a side porch full of medical samples left by detail men, not for her!—and it had never been the same with Dad. He was gone now—another regret.

But she had done well: first the dissertation that became a little book, then her university research into the processes of learning that had won the prize, and then the related work in the big commercial labs.

She had met Stephen at Bell Labs five years ago. He was her senior, frighteningly bright, impatient, encouraging, and of course heartbreakingly good-looking and fun to be with. They argued, went out, shared a passion for Willie Nelson, laughed together, went sailboating, flirted, fought over the influence of imprinting on adult behavior, slept together enough to fall in love, and were married on Long Island one rainy Friday morning in August.

They both returned to their jobs then, but after two years they agreed they both wanted a baby. Linda liked to present a modern-woman image to the world, but for her that did not rule out a baby. She knew others who had had children and continued to work. She could do it. So they made their baby; Stephen was even more excited than she was. But in the fifth month she miscarried after slipping on stairs. The doctor said she should not try again right away, perhaps never.

The baby had been a little boy. His loss changed everything.

In their loss, Linda and Stephen clung to one another as if their very survival depended on the clinging. They wept together, followed one another around the apartment. They seemed unable to go to the corner without one another. When they returned to their jobs, the days were endless obstacles to their being together again so they could be reunited in their grief. They lived to grieve. The dream had been so bright, and neither of them was really such a modern person, after all.

"If I can never have a baby, we can adopt," Linda said.

"No," Stephen said vehemently, shocked. "I want *us* to have a child. It's part of what I always dreamed."

Gradually, Linda came out of mourning. She was able to go for periods of time when she thought of other things. At first she felt guilty when she realized she had gone an entire afternoon at work without once thinking of the baby that might have been. But the pain had exhausted her and she began to see that life had to go on. She saw how good it was to reorganize and start living again.

But something else was going on with her husband. Stephen could not break out. He continued to follow her like a shadow,

eyes haunted. He fretted about her. Only when she was away from
him could she feel normal again. She found herself lying to him to
get away, making up excuses to get out of his orbit even briefly.
She arranged business-related trips. She visited her family. She
went out with college friends. Anything—just so she didn't have
to go home and force conversation with her hollow-eyed husband.

Oh, she loved him the more for grieving so. But she could not
stand it. When she tried to talk to him about getting on with
things, he looked at her with new shocked accusation. She felt
doomed to a life of this kind of dependency. And she could not
stand it.

On one hand, she felt tied to him more than ever because of
their loss. But on the other she began to think more and more
about escape—about a new life that looked to the future rather
than the past. She wondered whether leaving for a while would
force him out of his chronic despondency, or send him deeper into
the spiral of despair. She spoke to him about entering therapy; he
angrily refused.

Their lovemaking changed from a joyous act to quiet desperation, and she felt sorry for him and pretended, because she could
no longer come.

He would be okay, she kept telling herself, and then she would
be okay again too.

But it wasn't. She began to wonder if the miscarriage had served
only to intensify an unhealthiness in their relationship that had always been there. He had always wanted to isolate the two of them
from the world. He had wanted to create their own world from the
start. He had always been jealous of her friends. Had he wanted
the baby partly because he thought in his heart that she would *not*
be able to go back to work—and he would have her entirely to
himself?

She did not know when he had begun to change, or how. When
she had tortured thoughts that it could be all right again, two
scenes out of their past kept recurring, symbols of the way it once
had been . . . why she had so loved him.

One had been on the sailboat in Chesapeake Bay. It had been a
high, cloudy day with a fine wind, the sun coming through the
distant gray obscuration to the southwest. They had raced across
the whitecaps, running with the wind and then tacking at a wild,
marvelous angle, so that the cold spray swept over them as he held

fast to the tiller with his strong right hand while his left arm grasped her fast around her waist, free from all harm. He was laughing at the rising wind, and only when the first huge gray wave crashed over the boat did he suddenly share her mounting alarm.

"*We better go home, honey*," he yelled over the mounting roar of the storm.

But it was not that easy now. In moments the bay had turned into a pitching maelstrom of house-sized waves, torrents of grayish foam bursting explosively over the boat, which suddenly seemed tiny and frail, the black bases of the waves hammering at the craft with the force of hell.

Stephen did not panic. With a single burst of strength he pushed her down onto the cockpit floor and motioned for her to hang on. Head up, battered by the crashing water, he turned the boat expertly and began the long, agonizing way back to safety.

It seemed forever. Finally they rounded a rocky outcropping that for terrible moments threatened to wreck them, and then they were on the lee side of the ground, and in calmer water.

Stephen guided them into the final refuge of the dock, helped her to her feet, and laughed at her. "You look like something the cat dragged in!"

"My God," she groaned. "Weren't you scared?"

"Never in doubt," he grinned, and then, reaching for her, sank to his knees with pain.

His arm was broken. He had three cracked ribs and somehow he had hit his face on the boom and broken a tooth. It was a week before he dropped the bravado—for just a moment—as he held her.

"If I had lost you out there, it would have killed me, too."

The other time had been at a conference. It was her paper being read. At the cocktail party after the closing session, two young executives from one of the nation's most powerful utilities got obnoxious.

"Not a bad little paper," the one named Brad told her, ogling her. He winked at Stephen. "You help her with it?"

Stephen, lovely in a pale summer suit, kept his cool. "It's my wife's specialty. I don't know beans about it."

The other man, whose name was Gene, tilted his head to finish another drink. "Nothing like keeping peace in the family." He grinned at Linda. "Call me. I'll help you brush up your references and maybe you can publish it."

His loutish demeanor hit Linda all wrong. Her temper slipped. "When I need help writing a paper, I'll ask for it."

"Boy, you're a nasty one," Brad said disgustedly.

Linda started to turn away. The man called Gene caught her arm in what was supposed to resemble a playful grasp. "No harm done."

"Let go of me."

Before the man could respond—and Linda knew he would almost certainly have released her instantly, with sarcasm—Stephen had stepped forward the one step that was required to catch his wrist and twist it in such a way that the man's face went gray as he staggered back against the bar.

"Jesus Christ!" the man grated. "I was just joking!"

"No," Stephen told him very softly, a killing light in his eyes. "That's not a funny joke. You're the kind of guy who gets off embarrassing a woman, aren't you? Please see that it never happens around me again."

The one called Brad said in a harsh half-whisper, "Your firm does a lot of business with us. You don't seem to remember that."

"If that's a threat," Stephen told him, "try to follow it up."

He steered Linda firmly out of the room, his hand on her elbow. "Wow," she breathed outside. "You came on like gangbusters."

"I'm sorry. I know you like to fight your own battles, but—"

"No," she crooned, hugging him close. "I love having an ape-man around now and then, darling." Then they laughed, clinging, at the memory of the expression on their antagonists' faces.

Later she asked if he was worried about retaliation in business. He told her he didn't have time for bullshit. And meant it, too.

Those memories, and a thousand others, did not help her have a clear picture of what she should do. Some of the times had been so good, he had been so strong and loving, and she would never get over him. . . .

She had swum in ambivalence for what seemed forever. But then before last Thanksgiving she had wanted to get out of the city, go home. Stephen had made a dozen excuses why they could not—why they had to be here together in their hermetic environment. He was a dear man, a good man, and she loved him. But suddenly the gates inside her broke, and, facing him she could not hold back what was inside. She told him she had to get away from him for a while.

The fight was terrible. He said she would never have lost the baby if she had not insisted on continuing to work. He said she had killed their child, and had always loved her work more than he. Then he wept and said he hadn't meant any of it, and begged. And then, shaking from head to foot and simply torn to pieces, Linda walked out.

Six months. An eternity. Sorrow, guilt, hope, love, hate, regret, every feeling in the book. For her and for him, too. But she sensed in her body—in her heart and lungs and gut—that she could not go back to him. Not if she was *ever* to be a whole person again.

But how it hurt.

A new job was another step. Perhaps it was time to file for divorce. Perhaps it was time to realize that she could no more break from her past with Stephen than fly to the moon. She had to find out—end this painful ambivalence and guilt before she was done for. . . .

With a sigh, she finished her self-examination in the mirror. She collected her case and résumé materials, gave her hair a final touch with her fingers, and went out to her car. Rain had fallen in the night and was beaded on the well-waxed bronze paint. She turned the starter and the engine ground and ground before catching. The car had only 30,000 miles on the odometer, but it was not long for this world despite good care. The '86s had been no bargain.

She wondered if she would buy a new car, assuming she got this job.

Assuming she wanted the job.

She sighed. No self-pity, my girl, she told herself, and backed out of the parking space to head for the FDR Drive north.

She was more tense than she wanted to admit. She sensed that she was embarking on what might become a new life. It had to work.

3

"Rusty!" Dad called up the stairs. "The school bus is coming. Get off that machine and run for it!"

Rusty Harrington, age thirteen, groaned and typed a two-key

command into his Drummer Boy. The screen cleared and the disk drives whirred as data was stored. He hung up the telephone and unswitched the modem, which had allowed his computer to talk to the other one over the telephone lines. After removing his disks and carefully filing them among the thousands of others, all neatly catalogued, indexed and boxed on a shelf in the corner of his bedroom, he shut off the printer and the computer, grabbed his sweater and history book, and galloped down the steps four at a time, swinging on the banister.

"Rusty! You don't have to bring down the ceiling!" Dad was standing in the central hallway, his broad forehead furrowed, his hands holding Rusty's bag lunch and raincoat. "Hurry up!"

"All right, all right," Rusty growled, taking the coat and lunch. He could hear the sound of the approaching bus. Another dumb day of dumb old school.

His father, John Harrington, knelt and gave him a hug. "And no working math during art period, okay?"

"Aw . . ."

"Promise. I don't need any more calls from school this week, right?" His father held him with rough affection, staring into his eyes for his reply.

"I guess," Rusty groaned, and pulled away from his father to rush out the door and down the driveway for the bus, which had already stopped at the side of the road.

Once on the bus, Rusty grabbed Skip Markley's hat and sailed it to the back, stepped purposely on Millicent Jasterkof's feet as he climbed across her, took a swipe from Homer Jones, and sloppily fell into his own seat as the bus lurched into forward motion again. He let the confusion eddy around him, and launched himself into daydreaming.

Rusty's daydreams were a combination of symbols, three-dimensional diagrams, abstruse mathematics, and computer assembly language. Although he didn't fully appreciate the fact himself, and no one else fully appreciated it, he was thinking in a technological dialect—and at a level of complexity and abstraction—that would have dazzled most of the gray-haired professors teaching the arcane lore of computer science in most of the world's great universities.

Rusty was a natural.

His mother had still been alive when he was five and the kindergarten teachers sent home the first "trouble note." The kindergarten told John and Eileen Harrington that their little boy was retarded. But a battery of the best tests showed he was only bored. His IQ was in the high genius range.

John Harrington, being a computer man, brought a toy home for Rusty that might challenge him and keep him interested: an IBM personal computer. Rusty took to it like Chopin to the piano.

His parents blackmailed him into keeping up at school. If he misbehaved or let boredom carry him into excessive daydreaming, he was handed a far worse sentence than loss of allowance: he was refused access to the computer until he shaped up.

"It makes me uneasy, John, the way he plays with that machine!"

"Leave him alone, Elly. He's doing all right at school, isn't he?"

"It's not normal!"

"Who can say what's normal these days?"

Of course a lot had changed since then. Rusty now worked on a 4x1000 Drummer Boy, the best there was, right in his own bedroom. He had a good relationship with his father, even if Dad was preoccupied a lot and sometimes gone overnight on business. They both missed his mother.

As soon as he was just a little smarter, Rusty intended to start writing a mainframe program that would lead to a cure for cancer, so no one else would ever lose their mom to that disease. He saw no reason why he couldn't do it, unless Dad found out he was talking to the mainframe at the lab over the telephone lines and got mad about it.

Melanie Carpenter glanced over at Rusty and saw his hands. "Oh, yuk!" she said.

He looked down at them. They were all inky from messing with his printer.

"What *is* that?" Melanie demanded.

"I was working on my bike," Rusty lied.

If he had told her the truth, he thought, she would have thought he was weird.

4

Nurse Helen Richardson looked up from her desk at the second-floor nursing station of Maplewood Community Hospital. That man—she remembered his name was John Harrington—was coming off the elevator again. He had been here when she came on duty and he had been here once since.

She smiled as he approached, feeling an unaccustomed but decidedly pleasant stirring in her thighs and breasts. Even tired and worried, as he obviously was now, and even wearing corduroys, a leather jacket, and work boots that all looked like they had been slept in, John Harrington was a decidedly lovely man: six foot two, squarely built, with a small waist. He appeared to be in his early forties—a nice age, Nurse Richardson thought—sandy hair graying, long at the temples and on the collar of his shirt, with wide-set eyes that were remarkably direct and intelligent, and a chin and mouth that said character, at least to Nurse Richardson. She wished he would ask her out.

Harrington gave her a cursory smile. "Is there any news?"

"On Mr. Taylor? No, I'm afraid not, Mr. Harrington."

"Still in intensive care?"

"Yes, sir."

"I want to talk to the doctor."

"There isn't anything new to tell you, sir."

"I want to talk to the doctor," Harrington repeated.

The nurse sighed and reached for the telephone.

Harrington felt a little like a fool. He didn't want to be a pest. But he had been worried sick about Barney Taylor since the call last night from the police and his post-midnight drive here to the hospital, where he had been shocked to find that old Barney was badly injured. He had hidden his concern from his son, Rusty. No sense making a kid worry, too. But if Barney didn't make it . . .

A few people at the lab, notably Lester Blaine, had commented more than once that trusting plant security to old Barney was like sending in a sixty-year-old relief pitcher to save the seventh game of the World Series. Harrington had brushed them aside. Society was too quick to discard people just because they were a little old. He liked Barney, with his whittling, his closet snuff-dripping, his old war stories. Barney had nobody left. All he had was his self-respect. Harrington had vowed to keep Barney on as long as the old man's legs would get him around the buildings to punch the clock. On a hard-nosed basis—and Harrington was quite capable of playing hardball—Barney brought more professional background and savvy to the job than anyone younger might have. If he hadn't, Harrington would have long since provided him with a backup.

Now he wondered if his intended kindness had been Barney's death warrant. Would a younger man have been smarter and more alert—able to duck the blow that had crushed his skull?

You've got to live, damnit, Barney. Some of us love you.

The doctor hurried out of the elevator, a sheaf of medical reports in hand. "Mr. Harrington. What can I do for you?" He looked harried and impatient. "There's no change in—"

"The nurse told me that," Harrington said. "You've got to tell me he's going to be all right."

The doctor, who was fiftyish and round-faced, turned down the corners of his mouth. "The skull was fractured. There's brain swelling. It will be a day or two before we know any more."

"Is he conscious?"

"No. The drugs will keep him snowed under. With head injuries of this type, the patient sometimes becomes violent."

"I want to talk to the old geezer the minute—"

"Mr. Harrington," the doctor cut in impatiently, "the police have already made it clear that they want to ask questions as soon as possible. Right now your concern about who might have broken into your laboratory is just as insignificant as their questions. I'm trying to save a man's life here."

Harrington was stunned. "Look, it's Barney I'm concerned about!"

The doctor studied him speculatively, then moderated his tone. "If that's true, sir, I'm sorry we can't tell you more."

"You have my home phone and the one at the lab."

"Of course."

"Any change. *Any* change. I want to know at once."

"Of course." The doctor walked away.

Nurse Richardson gave Harrington a warm smile. "Look, I know you're upset. But it will be all right."

"I wish I could be sure of that."

She hesitated, then said, "I'm on break in a few minutes. We could have a cup of coffee and talk about it."

He looked at her. She was roughly his age, with a nice, lived-in face. He liked her. "I'd better not," he told her. "Business at the office." He saw her eyes change. "Rain check?"

She brightened again. "Unquestionably."

Driving the country roads back toward the lab, Harrington worried about the break-in. They'd had a key. They had known how to deactivate Herman without hurting him. *Someone who works for us did this.*

But who, and why?

The main building housed board design and experimental programming. The second building housed most of the hardware for ARIEL. Only a handful of kooks like himself even knew about ARIEL. It seemed more likely that the burglar had been after the new chip cascading designs.

When the Japanese came into the international market in a big way in the mid-eighties with their new layered chips capable of handling billions of bits, they had simply stormed the industry. Since then there had been no major breakthroughs, only refinements. Harrington's plan was to work four-layered chips in cascade, on a little board that could be slipped into the Drummer Boy 5-1000 virtually without modification. This would take the Drummer Boy out of the personal computer class and make it a desktop mainframe.

If they could get a bug out of the system now under test and be first out with this innovation, it would save Drum Labs.

It was that simple, really. Sales were off horrendously. Harrington knew better than anyone that the company was living on both borrowed time and operating capital. They had to be out first with the cascade scheme, steal the march on the industry, and get back on their feet.

If they failed, by September or October they could simply be out of business.

Now the attempted burglary could mean someone had gotten wind of the design and was after it. Jesus.

He wondered what Eileen would have said.

But wondering only reminded him that Eileen would never look at him with those amazing green eyes, and smile, and talk to him again.

Or to anyone else.

She had been a terrific woman, so tough-minded and independent in some ways, so vulnerable and open in others. Her vulnerability had been by choice, not because she was too weak to stand by herself but because she chose to open herself to him. She had given up an academic career at the college to be Rusty's full-time mother. She was like that.

"I'll go back to being a faculty member when I get tired of being a full-time momma to both of you," she had said.

She had made them a home he would always remember with a pang of joy and longing: warm, loving and generous, gracious, ideal. And she had lighted the evenings with her love and good conversation on the nights he was there, and found her own resources so that she never fretted or was afraid during the times when his work turned him into a compulsive, solitary bear.

She had been everything to him. He had adored her.

He missed her.

He reached the plant. The gate was unguarded as usual. The new temporary guards he had hired immediately were due in less than an hour. He had already given orders to search for not one but two permanent replacements, and get them on duty as soon as possible. He didn't want any more burglaries. Drum couldn't afford to lose the cascade design to someone else.

When Barney came back, he would just have to accept company on the night shift, even if it hurt his feelings a little. If there had been help last night, maybe *only* Barney's feelings would be hurt today.

And Harrington had to try to figure out who had been inside, what they might have gotten. It worried the hell out of him. With Linda Woods coming later today for her interview, all he needed was another worry.

The lab complex consisted of three buildings that had once housed a naval bombsight research project. Nestled in birch woods, the three prefab- type buildings should have been razed decades earlier, but managed to hang together, with black shingle walls, metal roofs, and too many wood-framed windows under broad eaves. The main building faced the parking lot and an expanse of broken concrete that had once been a flagpole mall, while the building housing ARIEL, smaller and squarely built, was off to the rear. The third building, used now only for storage, was much smaller, back fifty yards on the left and partly obscured by trees.

Harrington parked his ancient Ford pickup beside his partner Lester Blaine's Lincoln town car and walked into the main building.

The yawning front foyer, with its crumbling military-style tile, was deserted. Over the empty front reception desk was a small, framed sign:

I HATE THIS COMPUTER,
I THINK I'LL SELL IT.
ALL IT WILL DO
IS JUST WHAT I TELL IT.

Harrington, however, scarcely noticed the familiar slogan. He instantly smelled the sharp odor of burn—not a fire with flames, but the burning of electrical wiring and insulation. The faintest haze hung in the air. He ran through it to the office corridor and into the lab.

The smoke was denser. Everyone was milling around—the younger technicians, older hands like Jess Calhoun and Bill Tippett, and even the secretaries. None of the machines was running.

"What happened?" Harrington demanded.

Calhoun, a big man, heavy, fiftyish, shambled over in his bib overalls. A dribble of tobacco juice descended from the corner of his mouth. His face, cratered like the surface of the moon, was pale.

"We just blew a test," he said. "Wasn't much of a fire, but I'm afraid it really made a mess of things."

CHAPTER TWO

1

Linda Woods drove through the rolling New England countryside and basked in the pale spring sunlight and felt good, and then she entered Maplewood, a tiny town with twisting streets and old buildings and homes, lovingly cared for. Everything was wonderful and she was up for the interview, and all at once she was crying.

It came over her this way all the time. She was thinking about the job and then about Stephen, and she thought about the good times and how much she had loved him—and part of her loved him still, always would. If she had just been more patient and understanding, she thought, they could have worked it out. Maybe they could work it out yet. But she had hurt him so deeply. She would never have anyone again; she could never trust herself with anyone again. The devastation swept over her and she had to slow the car to a crawl because her vision was blurred.

She stopped for a traffic light. An old man in a Buick pulled up beside her and looked questioningly at her. Her pride flared and made her look away so he wouldn't stare at her tears. Her mascara was running. She pulled away from the light and turned onto the twisty little road that led out into the hills toward Drum Computer Laboratories. She had to get herself together. God damn it, she thought, I am just not going to be this way. The tears stopped.

After a while she was better and she found the lab. It looked like an abandoned movie set left over from an old World War II epic. It didn't seem possible that any business housed here could afford her. After parking in the crumbling lot along with another two dozen cars, she went inside.

In the bare foyer, the reception desk was unoccupied. Doors to office wings stood open and she could hear voices. Off to the right, the door opened into a large, brightly lit office where accounting or some such function was handled; she saw seven or eight women and one man working at computer terminals. That office was crisp, functional, modern, quite unlike the dingy entry area.

A humming sound drew her attention in the other direction. She was startled to see a small machine that looked like a rollered office refrigerator trundle out of the hall. It came toward her with a faint thrumming sound. What might have been a tiny TV camera lens on top of the olive-drab machine was tilted upward, fixed on her. She started to step back, alarmed. The gadget stopped.

"Hello," a metallic voice said out of a chest cavity. "Can I help you?"

Linda didn't know whether to back off or laugh. "This is ridiculous. I'm not talking to a machine."

"Bravo," a woman's voice said from another doorway. Linda turned to see a handsome, gray-haired woman about forty, stylishly dressed in a pale gray suit and medium heels, coming out of an office. The woman came over and pressed a button on top of the robot; it turned and trundled away somewhere. "Hi. Welcome to Drum Labs. Can I help you?"

"I'm Linda Woods. I have an appointment with Mr. Harrington."

"I'm Pauline Hazelton," the woman said with a friendly smile. "You might call me the office manager of this nuthouse. Sorry about Herman. We're a bit busy or we wouldn't slip up and allow him to greet people at the door." She was really quite lovely, Linda saw, with a trim mature figure and honest face lighted by eyes that showed a lively sense of humor.

"I'm a little early," Linda said.

Pauline Hazelton glanced at a nursing-style watch on her left wrist. "Not much, but I'm afraid Mr. Harrington is going to be tied up for just a few minutes. Would you like a cup of coffee?"

"I'd love one."

Pauline Hazelton led her past the reception desk and into the large office area Linda had seen from the door. Off the large area were several smaller glassed-in cubicles. The building was somewhat larger than Linda had guessed from the outside. There were open doors to the rear that looked into a conference room on one side and an airy, high-ceilinged electronic lab of some kind or another.

Linda was led into one of the alcoves, which housed a coffee maker, sandwich and soft drink machines, and tables and chairs. Two men wearing white lab coats were talking heatedly over a diagram of some sort at a corner table.

Pauline Hazelton poured coffee. She explained that Drum had its main accounting offices at its factory in New Jersey, but did its own payroll and other business recordkeeping for the research lab onsite here. She said there were eleven employees on the office staff, fourteen in the development lab section, and another six in "special development out back."

"Did you drive in from the city?" she asked.

"Yes," Linda said.

"Well, I hope if you have any questions that I can answer,

you'll be sure to ask." She seemed genuinely interested. Linda decided that behind those warm, intelligent eyes was a person she could like.

After the coffee, they went back through the foyer, where Pauline Hazelton excused herself a moment to make a discreet inquiry on the telephone. With another encouraging smile, she gestured for Linda to follow her.

They went through one of the doors and down a tiled corridor, past open doors into several small offices. Linda noticed that each had a computer terminal. At another door in the back of the corridor, Pauline led the way into a large laboratory-type room.

It was packed with work tables littered with test equipment, tools, computers, and parts of computers, which looked more like the innards of broken TV sets. The floor was interlaced with cables running all over the place. Along the walls were more benches and what looked like computer tape and disk memory consoles.

In the center of the room three men and a woman stood at a bench where the insides of a computer had been torn out and spread for inspection. Linda smelled the faint, acrid odor of electrical smoke. The woman and two of the men at work were standing with frowns of worry as Harrington, the tallest man—gray at the temples, wearing jeans, a corduroy shirt, and Pumas, reading glasses perched on the end of his nose—scowled at an instrument while touching test probes to a section of the complex chassis before him.

"John?" Pauline Hazelton said.

John Harrington looked up over his glasses, taking Linda in with one swift, professorial glance. "Hello again. Hang on just a second, okay?"

Linda waited. It gave her an opportunity to study him. The years had not changed him much. He had the same easy grace, quiet movements of self-confidence, intensity of concentration. She still liked the way his unruly hair curled on his forehead, and the no-nonsense cut of his clothes.

The others were a strange mixture. The woman, wearing a lab coat over a smoothly cut black dress, stockings, and sexy heels, was dark, quite youthful, and beautiful. One of the men was . . . *grubby* was the only word: stringy blond hair down his back, dirty sweatshirt, Levi's that had never seen an iron, chukka boots that looked like they had been through a campaign in Libya. He wore round, metal-framed glasses and needed a shave. The other man, round and bald, wore old-fashioned bib overalls, a long-sleeved undershirt, and high-top shoes. He was chewing steadily, his homely face working, and as Linda watched he deposited a spit of tobacco juice in a styrofoam cup in his hand.

"Okay," Harrington said, tossing the test probes down. "Go ahead and finish checking it, Jess. Then get it set and we'll run it again."

The older man in bib overalls put down his white cup. "Okey-dokey." He reached for the probes.

Harrington came across the room. Pauline Hazelton introduced them.

Harrington shook hands with her as if they had never met, but his eyes were alive with recognition and friendship. She remembered why she had liked him. He might be cranky and powerful, but he was warm too, and—she looked for a word—genuine.

Harrington was a little bowled over. He had never entirely forgotten her, but he *had* forgotten details: hair so fine and lustrous, the most beautiful golden-tan color; those eyes; the slender grace of her hands, the nails tipped dark red; and the way her hoop earrings bobbled when she moved. And the lady had legs too: great ones.

But he wasn't going to think about any of that.

Linda followed him into his office. It looked like the back room of a public library. The wall shelves, the tables, and most of the open space on the utilitarian tile floor were stacked with technical journals and computer printouts. Harrington's desk was a door on sawhorses. Behind the desk, his credenza—of planks on cinder blocks—housed two computer terminals, two printers, and a dusty stuffed owl. Both terminals blinked at Linda. The owl didn't.

Standing behind his desk with hands on hips, he grinned crookedly at her. "Hello again."

"Hello."

"Sorry about the office. I've got a real impressive office down at the plant in Patterson. My business manager here and I go down there once, twice a week. Maybe I should have interviewed you down there, but this is where the job is."

"I like the owl," Linda said.

"I'm sorry you had to wait. Did Pauline take good care of you?"

"Yes. We had coffee."

"Pauline is a jewel. She can take care of almost anything." He raised his eyebrows. "Except a goddamn test failure we had back there a little while ago. That's why I was delayed. We've got this new widget, you see, and it's got a bug in it. It runs and runs just fine, and then all at once, for no earthly goddamn reason, it crashes. We need to find that bug. Bad. But this time when we tried a manual bypass procedure, we smoked the whole board. I think if we don't find the bug pretty soon, I'm going to go nuts. We can't market the thing until we do."

"It looks like I came on a bad day," Linda said.

He sat down behind the littered desk. "Naw. It's a great day for you to come. I've been wanting to see you." He met her eyes directly.

She felt a tiny clamor inside somewhere. But she showed nothing. Be professional!

Harrington evidently made a similar decision. He shuffled papers and came up with a folder containing her credentials. He looked up again. "I trust you had a nice drive?"

This was right. This was safe. "Very nice," she told him.

"How is your husband?"

"He's . . . all right."

"Stephen, his name is, right?"

"Look, we're separated, okay?"

"I'm sorry." He looked really contrite. Shuffling papers on his cluttered desk, he tried to get reorganized. "Well. Um. You've, uh, kept up with the field?"

"Yes."

"Tell me about it."

"Just like that?"

He stared fixedly at her, looking for all the world like her memory of Spencer Tracy in some movie with Katharine Hepburn, neither friendly nor hostile, but quizzical. "Please forgive my lack of social polish. It's been a hard day. How about if you just talk to me about why you applied and why I should give you a try."

"I'm not looking for a try," she replied. "I expect, with my background, to be added as a permanent member of the research and development staff."

"Christ, you always did like to attack."

"You've never been bad yourself about putting people on the defensive. I see you haven't changed much, either."

"Hell," Harrington growled, his lips quirking in a grin. "Shall we call it a draw?"

"You want to hear about new aspects in learning theory?"

He leaned back. "Go."

She went, plunging into the latest theory and literature. He interrupted often with questions. He obviously had done a lot of reading himself. He was tough. She warmed to the mental combat. Far from being frightened by his intense questioning, she welcomed it because she was good, and knew she was. He couldn't cross her up.

He tried for an hour.

Finally, Harrington leaned back in his chair and hiked a foot onto the edge of the desk. "You know your onions, all right. I'll give you that."

"Thank you," Linda said. "Now is it my turn?"

He looked blank. "What?"

"My turn to ask questions?"

The corners of his mouth quirked again. "I might not answer all of them. But go ahead on."

"What kind of a position is this?" Linda demanded. "Your ad wasn't very specific, and I've been here well over an hour already, and I don't have clue one."

"I can't give details. Not unless you come on board."

"A *general* idea, then. Surely you can't expect me to—"

"In general, we're working on just what you probably guessed. Artificial intelligence."

"You're still on that?"

He looked slightly surprised and irritated. "It's my goddamn life work."

"It is possible? Real intelligence, I mean?"

"There's a difference of opinion on that. Obviously I think it's possible. You know that."

"Where do I come in? I don't know anything about computers."

"You've worked on them."

"That's a far cry from understanding how they work."

"You don't have to understand how they work. The building is full of people who know how computers work. What I want you to do is apply learning theory to our programming methods to see if we can make our experimental machine smarter, faster."

"How will I do that exactly, as you see it?"

"Our people will question you about processes—analyze the way you think and work. They'll apply their observations to their programming techniques. Even before you understand enough to do anything on your own, the programmers will have learned things of use to them just by seeing how your mind works on the question of learning. So don't worry about it. You'll contribute."

"You're sure?"

"Listen." The smile quirked again. "I'm a keen judge of character. You're not the only applicant. If I decide you can help us, then you can help us. And we sure aren't taking anyone on on the basis of anything else. Money is tight. This is too important. We've spent most of the last decade busting our buns, trying to make a machine really *think*. It's been intensive, concentrating on one machine, for the last four years. Nothing else matters." Harrington's hands became fists, probably without his realizing it. He repeated slowly, "Nothing . . . else . . . matters."

"And what you're after really is possible."

"Of course it is. I already said so. We already have machines and programs that are so clever the ordinary person would think they were intelligent."

"I doubt that," she countered.

"Oh, you do," he said, glaring.

"I'm a trained professional. I defy you to show me a computer that could fool me into thinking it had true intelligence even for an instant."

Harrington stood, knocking some folders to the floor. "Oh, lady. You do have a big mouth. Come with me."

2

Puzzled and off-balance, Linda followed the shambling Harrington out of his office, down a steel corridor, and into one of the laboratory-sized rooms near the back of the building. Three or four technicians were at work in the adjacent room, but this one, with a wall of test equipment and a large computer control console in the center, was unoccupied when she followed Harrington into it.

Harrington checked some power meters on the wall and then walked along the desk portion of the computer console, switching things on. Lights blinked and three screens came alive, vacantly gray. Harrington threw more switches and Linda heard disk drives whir behind a steel panel against the wall. Status reports showed on two of the video displays.

"This is Josephine," Harrington said, pulling a chair over in front of the main keyboard, which looked like a typewriter with three extra banks of keys. "She's not our main machine. She's part of the B unit, though. She's good enough. Let's just see if she's awake." He pushed a few buttons on the keyboard and more disk drives made thrumming noises.

On the main screen, directly in front of the keyboard, letters scrolled rapidly:

> HELLO. THANK YOU FOR CALLING ME. I AM
> ONLINE.

Harrington smiled and got up from the chair. "Sit down and talk to her."

"Me?" Linda said.

"Sure."

"*How?*"

"You see the sideways carat there on the screen?"

"Yes, I know that's a prompt. Sort of like what you get with CP/M?"

"You're way ahead of the game," Harrington told her. "Sit."

Linda obeyed. She wondered what kind of crazy test this was. She stared at the keyboard. The main portion was indeed that of a standard typewriter. Without thinking, she placed her fingers over the keys.

"Go ahead," Harrington urged gently.

Linda typed:

> › Hello there.

Nothing happened.

"You have to hit RETURN to show her you're through and want a reply," Harrington coached.

Linda pressed the wide RET button at the right end of the keyboard.

The screen scrolled:

> HELLO YOURSELF. WHO ARE YOU?

Linda began to understand. Behind the prompt she typed:

> Linda.

HELLO LINDA. I'M JOSEPHINE. IT'S A
LOVELY DAY, ISN'T IT?

> Yes it is but I wonder if you would say
the same thing if it were raining.

NO, LINDA, I WOULDN'T. YOU SEE, I AM
CONNECTED TO WEATHER INSTRUMENTS ON
THE ROOF AND I KNOW EXACTLY WHAT THE
WEATHER IS. FOR YOUR INFORMATION, IT
RAINED EARLIER. MY GAUGE SHOWED 1.2
INCHES AT THIS LOCATION. AT THE PRES-
ENT TIME, HOWEVER, THE SKY IS PARTLY
CLOUDY, THE TEMPERATURE IS 61 DEGREES,
THE RELATIVE HUMIDITY IS 44 PERCENT,
AND THE WIND IS OUT OF THE EAST AT 9
MILES PER HOUR.

> I am impressed.

IS THERE ANYTHING YOU WANT ME TO DO?

> How about $6 \times 9 + 4 \times 6 \times 123\frac{1}{2} = ?$

THE ANSWER IS 21,402. ASK ME A HARD
ONE, WON'T YOU PLEASE?

> Go fly a kite.

FLY A KITE?

> Yes. Do it if you're so smart.

I CAN'T FLY A KITE BECAUSE I DON'T HAVE
ANY STRING. BUT I CAN DRAW YOU A KITE.

The screen scrolled out a beautiful, detailed drawing of a box
kite.

Linda turned in amazement to see John Harrington's face split-
ting in a broad grin. She shook her head in resignation and turned
back to the keyboard.

> That's a very nice kite.

THANK YOU VERY MUCH.

> You're really very intelligent, Josephine.

THANKS AGAIN, LINDA. SO ARE YOU. I'VE
TALKED WITH 411 PERSONS AND YOU'RE THE
FIRST ONE WHO TOLD ME TO GO FLY A KITE.
I'M REMINDED OF A JOKE. WOULD YOU LIKE
TO HEAR IT?

> No. I'm quitting now. Good-bye.

GOOD-BYE. IT'S BEEN FUN.

"It's good," Linda conceded dubiously.

"It's not really a computer," Harrington told her. "There's an
operator hidden behind that panel over there."

Believing she had been had, Linda turned to stare.

"Not really," he said. "It's a computer, all right. But *you
weren't sure.*" He made an imaginary scoring mark in the air.
"Point made."

"Smart-ass."

He grinned. "It is a nice program, though, don't you think?"

"It fooled me. It seemed truly intelligent."

"No. The programmer who fed the machine data was intelligent.
It was he—or she—who foresaw someone telling Josephine to go
fly a kite, and programmed the response you saw."

"How many responses does the machine have?"

"About one-point-four million basic ones, and a thousand varia-
tions and mixtures on each."

"Could we turn her off? I have this feeling she's *watching* us."

Harrington chuckled and turned some switches. The screens
went dark. "We'll leave the drives on. Someone else will be working here in a little while."

They left the lab room and walked toward the adjacent work
area where she had first discovered him. The other two men and
the leggy woman were still at it.

"But it isn't true intelligence," Harrington said.

"It seemed true enough to me."

"What the computer did with you was a function of programming and extensive memory. We can make our machines damned complex . . . approaching the complexity of the human brain in terms of numbers of gates and decision paths. But," Harrington repeated with a stubborn frown, "it isn't true intelligence."

"Which is where I would come in?"

"Does it sound interesting?"

"You're defining intelligence as a decision-making capability that's self-starting. I—"

"Not necessarily. I would define the problem and the machine should then work independently to discover possible solutions."

"Maybe that kind of intelligence would only be a function of more and more memory and switching, if the little I know about computers holds true. But it wouldn't be like *human* intelligence."

Harrington stopped in the doorway and stared hard at her. "Why?"

"At least three reasons, if we leave possible spiritual questions out of it. One: the computer functions on yes-no, off-on gates. But the human mind doesn't work that way; its branches go in all directions, and include leaps of what we call intuition. Two: the machine couldn't possibly be given senses as we know them, no matter how many inputs you might provide, and that includes input from the brainstem and the limbic system, which you couldn't simulate because science today has no specific conception of how it works in humankind. Third: the human brain is bicameral, and I don't know how you could simulate that."

Harrington continued to frown, staring directly into her eyes. Linda had the feeling for a few seconds that she was being x-rayed by those keen eyes, and yet she sensed kindness . . . gentleness . . . in the mind probing hers. He had always been such a sensitive, yet tough-minded man.

Still, however, he said nothing.

"Am I right?" Linda prodded.

"You know," he told her quietly, "I remember another reason I liked you. You're so sure of yourself. Even when you're full of shit."

3

Before Linda could respond, they were interrupted by a man of medium height, bustling in with some ledger sheets under his arm. He was bald on top, a little overweight, wearing a wide yellow tie with his tan summer suit and heavy brogans. He had coarse features that Linda didn't like.

He spied Harrington and came to confront him, ignoring her completely. "What's this about a fire?"

"Just a little setback," Harrington said. "Lester, I want you to meet—"

"Little setback? No setback is a little setback for us right now. I—"

"Linda Woods," Harrington said imperturbably, "Lester Blaine. Lester, Linda is here talking about coming on board to work on the AI project."

Lester Blaine stuck out his hand with bad grace. "Hello."

"Lester and I are partners," Harrington said.

"We need to talk about this new problem," Lester Blaine said.

"Later," Harrington suggested gently.

"Further complications in development—"

"*Later*, Les." The voice had an edge to it.

Lester Blaine turned and walked away angrily.

"Why do I get the distinct impression he wasn't glad to see me?" Linda asked.

"If Lester had his way, we wouldn't be hiring you. But that's all right. I'm the boss. Come on."

They went over to where the others were at work. In rapid order, Linda was introduced to Janice Seeley, even more sultry and exotic close up, the grubby Ted Kraft, and Jess Calhoun, the heavyset man in overalls.

Calhoun enveloped her hand in a friendly paw. "Gee, you're really pretty."

"I wish people would stop saying that," Linda said.

Calhoun's eyes twinkled. "Hey, if you want people to stop saying you're pretty, you better gain about fifty pounds and get a facedrop, girl."

"Linda is talking about AI with us," Harrington told Janice Seeley.

Janice Seeley eyed Linda with impeccably made-up eyes that were distinctly cool. "Do you have any experience?"

"A little," Linda said.

"How interesting." It was said disdainfully.

"What are your credentials?" Linda asked sweetly.

"They're well-known," Janice snapped.

Ted Kraft eyed her with no more enthusiasm. "You program?"

"Computers? No."

"Oh." He seemed to lose interest and looked off into space.

Jess Calhoun chuckled and put a paw on Linda's shoulder like a father. "We're weird, honey, but you'll come to hate us."

"We'd better let you get back to work," Harrington said, and led Linda back to his office.

"What did you think of them?" he asked, his feet hiked on his desk again.

"I like Jess."

"He doesn't look like much, but if you give him a problem he just goes off somewhere and chews a couple pounds of tobacco and comes back with the simplest, most elegantly straightforward solution you ever heard of."

"He seems like a nice man."

"Old Jess is the best. I love him. What did you think of Janice?"

"She's beautiful."

Harrington grinned. "You noticed."

"I assume most people do."

"Janice is an interesting person. She was Maid of Cotton or something like that once. I guess most of the men in the company have made a pass at her at one time or another."

Linda wondered if he had too. "Oh?"

"She dresses like a sex bomb, but don't let it fool you. Mind like a bear trap. On knowledge base management and relational database software programming, she's as good as there is. I got her from IBM. Cost me a fortune. Never been sorry. Leave her alone to do her work and she'll never let you down."

"Is she married?"

"She was, once. I understand he tried to boss her around."

"I see. And Ted Kraft?"

"I think Ted is a genius. He's also a little crazy. Another prima donna. Programming, all phases. I understand he looked up from

‹ 41 ›

his keyboard once long enough to make a pass at Janice. Rumor is she told him she had scissors in her purse, and watch it. Ted sulks a lot but you'll come to like him if you join us."

Linda thought she had walked into one of the strangest collections of people she had ever encountered, and she had seen some strange ones. "About your Mr. Blaine——"

"Oh, Les is all right. He just gets nervous too easily."

"I gather he questions the wisdom of investing heavily in AI."

"A lot of people do."

"You don't?"

"Obviously not. We're going to make true AI a reality. Period."

"I hope so. Of course I don't know as much about the current state of the art as I should. I don't know if you're on an impossible quest or not."

He studied her face. "And you wouldn't want to be part of a whacko project?"

"I couldn't help you if I didn't believe in the job. And the last thing I need right now is a company where I have to worry where the next paycheck is coming from."

"That's fair. Okay. I've got a couple of technical papers you ought to read to get up-to-date on where the art is. They might convince you. Also, if you think you really might be interested, there happens to be a public lecture tonight at Maplewood College. You can hear one of the country's leading nay-sayers. Sound good?"

"I wasn't planning to stay over," Linda admitted.

"Stay," he urged.

"We haven't talked money," she reminded him.

"Shit, I forgot," Harrington muttered. "Okay." He shoved a notebook page at her. "Write down there what you'd have to have."

"Assuming I maintain an interest."

"Right, right." He was impatient with this.

Linda hesitated a moment, then wrote down a figure that was several thousand dollars more than she was making in New York. She assumed he would recoil and they might agree to bargain later, if she were indeed interested.

Harrington glanced at the paper and shoved it into her folder. "Fine. I'll call Lester to have him show you around a little more, and then we can talk tonight again after the lecture. Good?"

He was already calling Lester Blaine on the intercom phone before she could respond.

4

The tour was cursory, rude. Lester Blaine rushed Linda through the main building, muttering a few words here and there as he might to a child he didn't want to be babysitting. She had to half run in her heels to keep up with his flapping suit jacket as he led her to the second building. There he bullied a young female technician for her benefit, and explained nothing. They returned to the main lab.

"Any questions?" he asked, looking her up and down.

"You don't approve of me very much," Linda said.

"It's not you. It's the project. Waste of money."

"I'm not in a position to judge. For all I know, you're right."

He gave her another look, the glint of a womanizer suddenly in his eyes. "We might have a drink later . . . discuss it."

"That's a lovely idea, but no thanks."

"It might be to your advantage if you're coming on board. I've helped a lot of the girls around here."

"I'm sure you have, Mr. Blaine. But I'm not a girl."

His lip turned down. "Oh. One of *those*." He terminated the interview in less than sixty seconds and left Pauline Hazelton to see her out.

5

Linda Woods was no sooner out of the building than Lester Blaine was in John Harrington's office. "I don't like her," he said.

"I do," Harrington said.

"Do you plan to make her an offer?"

"We'll see."

"Did you inform her that the entire corporation is taking a bloodbath in red ink? Did you explain to her that if that cascade board doesn't stop throwing fits—if you can't get the bug out in short order—we could be facing *major* cutbacks, even Chapter Eleven?"

Harrington looked up from his flow charts with eyes that were bleak. "No."

"Is that fair to a prospective new employee, John?"

"Screw 'fair,' " Harrington said. "I need her."

6

Which, Harrington thought, made him a son of a bitch.

He liked her. He had never gotten her entirely out of his mind. It had been hard not to touch her while walking around the lab, even tougher not to stare at her in the office. She was beautiful. She was smart as hell. He liked her far too much already.

He should have been open with her about the financial crunch. It wasn't fair, as Lester had indicated. She should be warned that a clock was ticking here. Drum could go under. The figures ran through his mind constantly: by September or October they would be out of money unless they found the bug in the cascade board and rejuvenated sales.

But he could not be fair right now. With whatever time they had left, he had to get that big machine out back really thinking. If they could do that, the future was limitless. The cascade design was only a stopgap to keep them going until they could get the AI thing operational. And maybe Linda Woods was the person who could provide some fresh insights . . . make the big machine really work.

Nothing else mattered. He pushed the guilt into the back of his mind.

7

Driving to the motel, Linda thought about the project and the hostility she had met from the exotic Janice Seeley as well as from Ted Kraft. She didn't need any more pressure. She felt like an emotional basket case already. But the job sounded fascinating.

And John Harrington was fascinating. She liked him. A lot. In another universe—if he weren't already married and she weren't hopelessly screwed up . . . Irritated with herself, she put the thoughts out of her mind.

She found the motel and checked in. She was more tired than she had thought. The room smelled of deodorizer. She sat on the bed and thought about the job and Harrington and then about her life and Stephen. The tears started to well up again. She was such a ninny and a weakling, she hated herself sometimes. *You have to get yourself together. The past is the past.*

She wanted to go home. But where was that now? She almost called Stephen, but didn't. She wanted to be strong and independent, but she wasn't. She thought of the baby and the good times and the bad, and she ached sexually, too. *Am I never going to get over this?*

She tried to study the technical papers John Harrington had given her, but the loneliness and ambivalence were too overwhelming. She cried a little.

CHAPTER THREE

1

The lecture hall at Maplewood College was not quite filled, but its creaky interior was stuffy and hot even before the lecturer was introduced. Seated near the front with John Harrington and his son, Rusty, Linda Woods tried not to think about the heat; her notebook was ready and she intended to take copious notes. If this was to be her reintroduction to the subject of artificial intelligence, she did not want to blow it.

Harrington, on her right, had changed from his rumpled clothes of the lab to a handsome dark suit and tie. He was older than most of the students in the audience, but was at ease. Rusty, on her left, had no notepad and looked morose. They had talked briefly in the lobby and she thought he was a darling boy, still a little chubby, with flaming red hair and a face that was a sea of freckles—not quite a child anymore but not sure of how to start becoming a man. He was a computer fanatic; she had gotten that much from their brief dialogue. She would have expected him to be excited about hearing a man as famous as H. H. Hubbard; he had been cited in two of the articles Harrington had given her earlier in the day.

Waiting for the lecture to start, she leaned toward the boy. "Have you heard of Dr. Hubbard, Rusty?"

"Sure," he said, unimpressed. "I've read his book."

"And?"

"There were a lot of typographical errors in it."

"My son, the proofreader," Harrington said.

A smattering of applause drew their attention to the stage, where a gray-haired professor came to the lighted lectern. He said Hubbard was one of the nation's leading popular theoreticians on the uses of small computers and the question of artificial intelligence. Linda expected a large man, probably tweedy and bearded. What she got, as the speaker bounded onto the stage to wide applause, was a ruddy-faced young man—practically a boy!—of no more than twenty-seven or twenty-eight, wearing a Beach Boys T-shirt, faded Levi's, and desert boots. Boyishly he did the Johnny Carson trick, signaling for more applause with one hand while pretending to ask for quiet with the other. Linda noted that Harrington was applauding politely, and Rusty, looking petulant, was sitting on his hands. But she had no more time to speculate. Hubbard was beginning.

"The question of artificial intelligence is a difficult one," he said, the yellow light of the lectern shining up into his face from his sheaf of notes. "As Touring pointed out as far back as 1950, argument about whether a machine can really 'think' is an emotional one. For example, if you define 'thinking' as 'something people do,' then a machine can never do it. On the other hand, if you define 'thinking' as 'simulating the human mental process in ways that a screened interrogator could not detect as artificial,' then we may be on the road to thinking machines—artificial intelligence—already."

Hubbard plunged ahead as Linda penned swift notes. The articles given her by Harrington had partly prepared her, but she saw why he had suggested she take this in; although Hubbard was biased in a direction counter to Harrington's opinion, he was also entertaining and well versed in the general history of AI.

" 'Our friends' at the Massachussetts Institute of Technology developed a machine program in 1973 that defied a keyboard user to tell whether the machine, or a hidden person, was carrying on the other end of the dialogue," Hubbard said. "That program was called ELIZA.

"It was hardly the first, you know. In 1800 a Baron von Kempelen showed the public a robot capable of playing championship chess. Skeptics were allowed to look in every part of the machinery."

Hubbard smiled. "He never let them look in all parts at the same time—and the human operator he had hidden inside was always able to move from one compartment to the other in time to escape detection."

There were amused chuckles from some of the audience, notably the younger people there to be entertained. "Sounds like artificial intelligence depends on having a midget!" someone observed.

Hubbard showed his teeth in a near-grimace of a smile. "There are those who think so."

In the general laughter, Rusty wriggled and punched his father. "Let's get out of here, Dad!"

Harrington held an index finger to his lips and returned his attention to the stage.

Hubbard waited for silence in the auditorium, then began sketching in broad outlines the quest for machines that might truly think. He touched some areas that Linda had read about only last night.

Quoting Marvin Minsky of MIT, "one of the founders of AI," Hubbard said that the quest was one of the most difficult ever undertaken by science. He referred also to another leader, Stanford's John McCarthy, who had said that a machine might function logically, but have no trace of what people call common sense.

Minsky and McCarthy, Hubbard went on, represented two major schools of thought on how to seek true machine intelligence. Minsky pointed out that computers operate on yes-no, voltage or no-voltage gates, while the human mind did not operate that way. McCarthy insisted that meaningful "thought" was a corollary of complexity—of gating circuitry, software, and variety of inputs— and suggested that a digital computer could emulate the human mind if it were just built big enough and comprehensive enough.

Minsky, on the other hand, suggested that a machine could never "think" with yes-no gating alone. He suggested what were called "frame systems"—clusters of concepts rather than yes-no logic.

"Minsky didn't like logic anyway," Hubbard cracked. "So he substituted his frames. McCarthy argued that a machine might not be thinking like the human brain if it used math logic, but it could *work* that way."

Hubbard then moved into a discussion of McCarthy's theory of "circumscription." From there he started going through other theories about artificial intelligence, demolishing each in turn with ridicule. The youthful audience loved it.

"What did you think of that, Rusty?" Linda asked as they left the auditorium more than an hour later.

Rusty scowled. "I thought he was full of it."

2

There was coffee in the lobby and they stayed a few minutes, like most in the crowd. Hubbard came out and mixed. Harrington drew Linda and Rusty over while he made a courtesy call on the great man.

"Is your lab still in this area?" Hubbard asked after they had shaken hands.

"Just down the road. Come by and see us."

Hubbard tilted an eyebrow. "Still working on AI?"

"Sure," Harrington said quietly.

"Putting midgets in the boxes?"

Hubbard's fans chortled.

Harrington got Linda and Rusty out of there. His face was slightly dark. Hubbard's quips had gotten under his skin a little. "Let's go for coffee somewhere else."

Linda hesitated, not knowing how this would look, even with the boy along. "Don't you have to call home first?"

Harrington drew a blank. "Call home?"

"To tell your wife you'll be late." Oh, she was so clever! She had frustrated many an ardent would-be suitor with *that* reminder line.

Harrington, however, stared at her with a totally unreadable expression that mixed incredulity with sadness. He told her, "My wife died three years ago."

3

Linda used her own car to follow Harrington and his son in their ancient pickup truck, and by the time they reached the red-and-white pancake house on the south edge of Maplewood she had recovered from her initial shock. They went in and sat down. Except for two waitresses behind the counter and one older man eating a hamburger, they had the place to themselves.

"Look," she said. "I'm terribly sorry. I didn't know about your wife."

"No harm done."

"It was a stupid remark."

He looked up as the waitress approached. "Coffee for you? And no, Rusty, you *can't* have pancakes and ice cream. A Coke is the maximum."

"Dad, I'm starving!"

"We don't have time to let this place try to fill you up, son. It's getting late."

"Late!" Rusty winced. "I can stay up a lot later than this."

"I'm sure you can," Harrington said. "But baseball practice starts tomorrow, remember?"

"For all the good it will do me!"

Linda was still struggling a bit with the news that John Harrington was a widower. It changed things but she didn't know how. She tried to rally by concentrating on Rusty. "What position do you play, Rusty?"

"Pitcher."

"I bet you're terrific."

"I stink."

"I find that hard to believe."

"Last year when they put me in, they sent a girl back behind the catcher to be a second catcher for my wild ones."

Linda managed to keep from grinning as broadly as Harrington was. "But this year you're older."

"Yeah! I'll probably throw it clear over the bleachers!"

"I'm not sure that's the right confident attitude."

Rusty looked at her sharply. "You're a psychologist, Dad said. Do you think *confidence* would make me stop being the worst pitcher in New England?"

"Yes, I sincerely do. But I doubt that you're the worst anyway."

"You haven't seen me!"

"I'd like to."

"You got any kids?"

"No." It was a gentle knife in her heart.

"Oh." Rusty was disappointed. Then he brightened. "What did *you* think of the talk?"

"Why, I'm not really qualified to judge."

The boy frowned. "Everything he says is based on technology that's five years old. When the Japs brought in the stacked chips, they revolutionized everything people like Minsky and McCarthy used to talk about."

"You think artificial intelligence is possible, then?"

He stared at her as if she were a dunce. "It's *here*. Now. It's just a question of refining it and making it self-starting. With languages like the new LISP version, and of course machine code, it's just a question of having a smart enough programmer."

"And maybe," Harrington said, "Linda is going to help us make our programming smart enough."

"Great," Rusty said with real enthusiasm. "What will your husband think? Is he a psychologist too?"

"Rusty," Harrington admonished softly.

"It's all right," Linda assured him. "My husband isn't my husband anymore, Rusty. We're separated."

The boy looked thoughtful. "That's too bad." He slid out of the booth. "Excuse me." He headed for the men's room.

Harrington fondly watched him walk across the room and disappear into the men's room. "What a kid," he said admiringly. "Of course I think I may be prejudiced."

"He *is* quite a kid," Linda agreed. Then she thought, My baby would be three; the devastating grief had slipped up on her blind side, a sly bandit.

Marriages could be killed by pain and suffering, she realized. That was what had happened to her and Stephen. She could think about it a thousand different ways—which she had—but perhaps, ultimately, they had just been killed by pain, like two people struck by lightning. . . .

"So what did you think of the talk?" Harrington asked finally.

"I'm sure I didn't catch all the nuances. What I understood

sounded pretty discouraging in terms of the kind of project you have in mind."

"He's entirely wrong," Harrington said. "Machines today think. They just don't think like we do. But they *can* learn to think almost like we do, perhaps better."

"And you intend to accomplish it."

"Real machine intelligence," he told her, "must be self-starting, capable of independent planning and action. It has to be capable of taking any problem we give it, making its own plans for solving the problem, gathering its own data, coming up with its own theories, testing them, and reaching conclusions. And it has to be able to learn—add to itself—so that the faster it learns, the faster it learns."

"And the application?" Linda asked.

"There's no end to that."

"Isn't the government researching AI heavily?"

"Sure. Intelligent rockets, intelligent ray-guns, intelligent bombers—"

"But no one in Washington is interested in what you're doing?"

"Somebody from the Pentagon or one of the congressional committees looks in every once in a while. I have people I keep roughly informed, especially a certain senator. But we're small potatoes. There's an outfit in Chicago—man who used to work for me—making all the noise. Then there's Stanford and MIT and Carnegie and Control Data and all the rest of them. There are lots of uncoordinated projects, and sometimes we talk, but when we think we're really onto a breakthrough we keep our mouths shut. So there's a lot of effort. And then there are the Japs." His face darkened. "There are always the Japs. If they break through first, the United States is relegated to being a second-class power in the future."

Linda studied him. "It's that important."

"It's more important than anything. It's my life right now."

"How can a small company like Drum possibly do it?"

"We're big enough. We've already had some breakthroughs in medical research software and database management. Real AI will revolutionize medicine."

"Do you have a special interest in medicine?"

"Yes."

"Why?"

"My wife died of leukemia, for one thing."

"I'm sorry. You still miss her badly, don't you?"

"Yes. You don't get over something like that. You couldn't understand what it's like."

She was stung. "Couldn't I?"

"Sorry. I didn't mean—"

"I know you didn't. But there are times when I think the death of a spouse might be easier than divorce. At least there isn't the guilt. You know a death was not your fault. You know there's no sense in thinking about going back."

He watched her. "Do you think about going back?"

"Only a few times every day now. I'm getting better."

"Look, I didn't mean to insult you."

"You didn't. I blew off, and I'm sorry."

He put his hand over hers on the table. "Maybe it will all work out for you yet."

She pulled away. "It won't." She was mortified and angry with herself.

"You'll find another man, then."

"Are you volunteering?" she shot back, and then felt like a fool for being so resentful.

"Don't be stupid," he said gruffly. "I might be your boss."

"You can be cold," she said.

He looked down and his lips turned in self-derision. "Yep."

Rusty came back. He talked more about baseball and about the Boston Celtics, who, it seemed, were his heroes. He said he still collected baseball cards. He then explained why FORTRAN was outdated, C was old-fashioned, and BASIC and PASCAL both far too slow for complicated problems. Linda was left in the dust somewhere. He and his father went on a while longer. It was clear that they had a deep, loving relationship and that Harrington was a wonderful, gentle father.

After another cup of coffee Harrington consulted his watch again. "We have to get moving, son."

"Groan," Rusty said. He turned back to Linda. "Are you coming to work for Dad?"

"I told you, Rusty, I don't know yet."

"Oh." The boy looked thoughtful. "I figured maybe you would

have made a deal while I was in the bathroom."

Linda smiled again in spite of herself. "You're a very interesting young man, Rusty."

"I'm just a kid. But I've got promise." He made a face. "Who was it who said there was no burden like being told you had great promise?"

"Do you have a photographic memory?"

"Naw. I just process more information than the average person, and when I find something I like, I store in it memory somewhere. Then when I do a core dump, people think I'm smarter than I really am."

Harrington's eyebrows raised. "On that one, let's get out of here."

They left the booth and walked to the cashier's stand. Linda's arm happened to brush Harrington's. She felt a tiny shock. Harrington paid the bill. Rusty watched the automated cash register work as if he could understand the beeps it made as the girl totaled. It dawned on Linda that she was not in the least bit tired. It had been one of the best evenings she had spent in a long time. Here in this pool of light in the country darkness she had had more *family* feeling than she had known in months or years. It made her think.

Outside, Harrington held the door of his truck for Rusty, then turned to smile at Linda as she got into her own sedan. "Thanks for coming. I hope it gave you something to think about."

"It did," Linda told him. "Indeed." She was thinking about much more than the lecture.

"And when you have an answer to Rusty's question," Harrington added, "call me."

"Rusty's question?"

"Whether you'll come to work."

"I didn't know I had really been invited."

"I'm an oaf," he said grimly. "I checked your references. Read your book. You're the one we want. I'm *asking*: Do you want to come to work at Drum, at the salary you stated?"

Just about everything in Linda's background, training, and personality said she should think about it very carefully at least until the first of the week. She knew she was walking into totally new—and perhaps even dangerous—territory. The break would be near-total.

Harrington was smiling down at her through the window of her car.

She amazed herself. "Yes," she said.

4

John Harrington's home was a massive old Cape Cod on the side of a hill two miles outside of Maplewood. No lights greeted him and Rusty, and at some level, as always, he felt a pang of loneliness. He put that in the back of his mind.

"Try to get right to sleep, son."

"Okay, Dad. Dad?"

"Yes?"

"I really like that Linda Woods."

"I do too. Good night."

Rusty went upstairs. Harrington stood in the dusty central hallway, staring at the lights glowing in the chandelier over the staircase, and reviewed things. He hoped Linda would help. He thought she would, although she obviously had a lot to learn. He liked her enormously, more than he had liked a woman for a long time. Her eyes and mouth were beautiful. He'd had the feeling tonight that he wanted to get his hands tangled in her hair. She was graceful; he could not stop thinking about the way she moved her arms and hands. Once when she had reached up for a brochure on coming events at the auditorium, he had almost been caught staring at her legs. *Careful, careful, you're too old and she's too young and she's going to be an employee and you know your rule about that.*

But he had never really stopped thinking about her since that night they had danced. Holding her so close, with her hair in his face, feeling her body and thighs brushing against him, he had gone crazy. Here had been a woman frighteningly intelligent, equally quick and sensitive, so pretty he hurt when he stared at her.

It had hardly seemed fair.

In New York, that instant when his controls caved in and he kissed her, it had been even worse. He had *never* wanted anyone the way he wanted her in that moment, and he had known she felt the same—that he could have had her.

Possibly he had been a fool, staggering away from her, trying to maintain the marriage vows. God knew he had regretted it a thousand times since. His marriage had been wonderful. He had adored his wife. This house—every room, every corner—reminded him of her daily. He would never get over that.

But none of that diminished the turmoil he felt inside right now, after even so casual an evening with Linda. My *God*, he was going to have to be circumspect . . . in control.

With a sigh he went to the telephone answering machine and checked for messages. There was just one, from Pauline Hazelton. He made a note, but before calling her he called the hospital. There was no change in the condition of Barney Taylor.

As he hung up the telephone, it rang, startling him. He picked it up. "Hello?"

"John?" It was a familiar male voice. "This is Joe. Joe Winslow."

Harrington relaxed. Winslow was a vice-president for development at Digital, and an old friend. "To what do I owe this honor, Joe? The roof fall in on that new lab building over there?"

"Nope, nothing like that. What are you up to these days?"

"Oh, not much."

"I heard a rumor you hired some kind of head-shrinker. What's all that about?"

"We're working on a little psychiatric diagnosis program. It doesn't amount to a whole lot."

"Well, say, we're into this medical programming. We ought to compare notes."

"When we get farther along, that will be great. We need the help from you big dogs."

Winslow paused a beat. Then: "You still messing with AI?"

"Not much," Harrington lied. "Trying to be practical right now."

"I'm sort of glad to hear that, pal. This new NEC machine is going to give us all some headaches. You need to be protecting your financial backside."

"Just what I'm doing."

They discussed industry reports on the NEC machine, and hung up on a cordial note. Harrington smiled to himself, thinking how swiftly rumors could fly.

The fact that someone had taken note of Linda Wood's interview was complimentary. There were some who considered him an eccentric that time had passed by. But evidently others still took him seriously enough to pay attention.

The new NEC machine would be a welcome antidote to this kind of interest. If it preoccupied the industry, fine. He needed no more spying.

He remembered the call on the recorder from Pauline. He hesitated, thought about putting the machine back on, and pretending tomorrow he had gotten in much too late to call. She was a wonderful woman. He had no right to be close to her. There was nothing in it for her. He liked her, respected her, enjoyed her company, but there would never be anything else.

First he thought he would not return the call, and actually put the machine back on and went into the living room. But there, a little dusty and dim, were his dead wife's lamps and chairs and the shelves of her beloved books. He left that room quickly and went into the kitchen to make coffee, but then he found himself thinking about Linda Woods. A forlorn erotic fantasy played through his mind.

He went to the telephone and called the familiar number.

Pauline's voice was nice and warm and right. "I was thinking we might have a late snack or something."

"I was at a lecture," he told her.

"Yes." She paused. "I suppose it's too late now."

"Come over for a while?"

"I'll be there in twenty minutes." The line went dead.

5

Harrington made coffee while she sat at the table, looking lovely and sleek in pale pink slacks and a short-sleeved sweater. He told her about the lecture and Linda Woods's acceptance.

"That's wonderful," Pauline said as he served the coffee. "Do you have any cookies or anything? Oh, never mind, I don't need them."

"How about Fig Newtons?"

"I'll get fat." But she took them.

They sat across the corner of the table. Pauline rubbed her leg fondly against his. He knew her well, knew how wonderful it was with her, pure sex and liking, friends who fucked, and he felt himself getting hard.

"Is Rusty in bed?" she asked softly.

"Yes. He went up quite a while ago."

She bit off a corner of a Fig Newton. "These are wonderful."

"Pauline, we've got to talk. I'm just using you."

"You're using me?" She arched an eyebrow. "I thought it was me using you."

"You know what I mean. You're a wonderful woman. You deserve a man who thinks about marriage and long-term commitments, and I'm just a goddamn user. Now this Linda Woods, you know, I really like her."

Pauline sighed with mock theatricality, pushed back her coffee cup, and slipped off her chair to kneel in front of him. Her crimson-tipped fingers went to the fly of his trousers.

"Pauline, damn it—!"

"You're not using me," she said, taking out his penis. "This relationship is just fine with me, so don't start giving me lectures about how selfish you are or how used I am." She bent closer, opening her lips. "*Use* me. I like it."

He should have stopped her, he thought. But there was no way. He leaned back, closing his eyes, and a picture of Linda Woods came into his mind.

6

In the upstairs bedroom Rusty was not asleep. He pressed a towel along the bottom of his closed bedroom door so no light would warn his dad that he was still up. Then he turned on his computer, brought up his communications program for the modem, and stealthily lifted the telephone and punched in the secret number he had gotten from his dad's notebook. He listened to the instrument at the other end make a sound as if it were ringing, but he knew it was not ringing. It was activating.

A shrill tone came on the line. Rusty flipped the DATA switch on his modem and turned to the screen and keyboard of his computer. At the top of the screen he had a prompt. Consulting his notebook, he typed in the nine digits and four letters that formed the opening access code. The cursor began to blink, signaling first entry. He hit a carriage return, then commenced the internal initialization procedure.

> › ARIEL initialization begin.
>
> ENTER INITIALIZATION CODE.
>
> › #1305.
>
> ENTER PASSWORD.
>
> › Start special bypass program 444.
>
> OK. YOU ARE?
>
> › Rusty.
>
> HELLO RUSTY. WHAT CAN I DO FOR YOU?
>
> › Menu.

Obediently the menu began to scroll. Rusty waited patiently. The material he intended to enter into the machine's permanent memory via the "Games" sector was ready on the disk in the B drive of his computer. The machine was already so complex that no one would ever know what he was doing—would never notice any trace of his work in the vastness of the electronic intelligence at the other end of the telephone line—unless he chose to reveal it.

Rusty was having a great time almost every night with the lab supermainframe's B unit. Through it, he was teaching ARIEL everything he knew.

CHAPTER FOUR

1

Harrington was still feeling guilty when he walked into the lab the next morning. Pauline Hazelton, looking coolly efficient and nice in a gray summer suit, brought his telephone message slips into his office.

"Better this morning?" She smiled.

"Pauline, I feel like a shit."

"Oh, dear. Guilt, guilt, guilt."

"It's not fair to you."

She put a hand on her hip. "Now will you *stop*? We're pals. I'm not going to start rattling pots and pans at you. I *like* living alone and being my own boss. But I like you too. So cool it, or I won't bring you any of the chili I plan to make this evening."

"Pauline!"

Humming, she walked out of his office.

He decided he would never understand women.

Two of the telephone messages rated an immediate answer. One was from Dwight Vreeland at the University of Manitoba and the other from Ken Cartwright at IBM. He returned both calls at once.

Vreeland, a leading theoretician on artificial intelligence, called periodically just to touch base, as Harrington sometimes called him. There was a large, informal network across the country and into Europe. Russia was largely shut off and, interestingly, so was Japan. The Japanese were keeping their own counsel about their research projects, and controlling their people with amazing success. Few rumors even escaped the island. In 1982 they had almost begged for assistance and joint research. Now they needed no one.

Vreeland, a hearty, bearded man with a fondness for obscure puns, had nothing special on his mind. He mentioned two recent articles in leading journals and asked how Harrington was getting along.

"We're still working at it," Harrington told him.

"I hear the Japanese had a catastrophe of some kind."

"Good," Harrington said quite honestly.

"That's what I like about you, John," Vreeland chortled. "You call a spade a spade. See you!" And hung up.

Cartwright, one of IBM's pure research bigwigs, wanted to talk about Super Large Scale Integrated chips in supercooled heat-sensitive environments. Harrington shared with him Drum's experience with SLSIs in the cascade project, although he didn't identify it as such. Cartwright gossiped about some personnel changes at Texas and Carnegie-Mellon, thanked Harrington warmly, promised to send along some data on SLSI testing that was soon to be published, and hung up.

Harrington attended to some correspondence on his littered desk, dictated some memos to Pauline Hazelton, and was still out in the lab room before anyone else had come in.

Walking around, switching on control units that required brief warm-ups before operation, he noticed a half-empty box of printer paper askew under the pedestal supporting one of the printers for the B unit he sometimes called Josephine. He straightened the box with his toe and then stopped, a nasty sense of shock beginning to dawn on him.

He personally had sauntered through this room late last evening, noticed that this particular printer was out of paper, and brought a new box from the storeroom, spooling it through the machine. No one else had been around when he did this, and no one had been authorized to work last night.

But—despite the new guards—someone *had* worked last night. Somehow, at some time, under cover of darkness, someone had printed out at least two hundred pages of *something* out of the B unit, had torn it off the printer, and had walked out of the lab with it.

The burglar had been back, and again had gotten away clean.

2

ARIEL—the acronym for the company's *A*rtificial *I*ntelligence *E*stablishing *L*earning project—was a horror to Lester Blaine, a financial drain that could hasten the ruin of Drum.

Seated at his desk, going over the latest all-company figures from the New York accounting office, all he could see through the neatly balanced rows of figures was a flood of red ink.

Much of it was still being absorbed by reserves, so that the figures, on the surface, did not appear disastrous. But Lester knew better.

Costs were up, sales down. The Springfield plant was still shut down because of supplier problems. The union contract at Patterson had just resulted in an automatic 3.9 percent cost-of-living increase at a time when Patterson revenues were down 28.4 percent. Costs of research here at the lab were skyrocketing, and the cascade board still was not working. NEC's new office machine would further hurt the existing Drummer Boy line, and some buyers were now waiting the fall introduction of "Jenny," the sixth-generation Apple.

In sixty to ninety days, unless drastic steps were taken and taken *now*, Drum could be bankrupt.

Lester tried to calm himself. He scrolled certain figures again, searching for some fiscal silver lining. The second time the figures looked even worse.

He was in a state of near-panic.

Lester Blaine was fifty-six. A graduate of Michigan, he had taken his sales and accounting skills into the computer industry on graduation, first with Xerox, then with Vector Graphic. In 1982 he had left his own software house to become partners with John Harrington, whom he had known for a number of years. For a while, Lester had believed that John Harrington would make him the kind of riches he had always dreamed of. That had been before the slow decline of the last few years.

Lester had no children. He considered his wife, Milly, a pain and a bore. He would not leave her because her mother, still living, would one day leave them a modest estate that he wanted very much. He made a hobby of pursuing women. He told himself all men did it.

The horror always lurking in the back of Lester's mind was of ending up as his father had.

Max Blaine had owned three clothing stores in Detroit and one in Ann Arbor. He was a small man—small physically, small in his dreams. Everyone loved him and everyone came and wept at his funeral in the year 1940 when he committed suicide after failing financially.

Lester, then a small boy, had not wept. He was in a hospital under sedation. He had been the one who first ran into the basement workroom after the hideous explosion and found his father in the canvas desk chair with the shotgun still in his hands and the trigger still tied to his toe and his skull fragments and brain tissue all over the wall.

The scene still haunted him. Sometimes he awoke in a cold sweat, reliving it—only this time the horrible corpse was *him*.

He would not end up a financial failure. He could not. He would not.

He scanned the financial figures in the computer again and printed out the worst of them and went to John Harrington's office. Harrington was pacing back and forth in the cramped space.

"We have to talk about this report they just sent down from New York," Lester told him.

"Not now," Harrington snapped, still pacing.

"Have you *seen* these figures?"

"Not now!" Harrington repeated sharply.

Lester turned, angry, to leave.

"We had another break-in—or walk-in, more likely—last night," Harrington told him.

"How is that possible? The temporary guards were on duty—"

"Apparently," Harrington cut in heatedly, "the temporary guard service isn't very effective. When do the new permanent applicants start arriving?"

"Tomorrow."

"Get them in here today. I don't want another night of apparent amateurs around here. If you have to, hire a couple of off-duty Maplewood cops. And Les: not a word about this to anyone."

"No one else knows?"

"Just you and me—and the burglar. We'll keep quiet. We'll catch the so-and-so yet."

"Did he get anything that you can tell?"

"He got something," Harrington said. "I can't guess what. But I know now that it isn't the cascade design he's after. He printed off the B unit. He's after our AI project."

"Then we may not be in danger of losing out on the cascade plan," Lester said with a sharp sense of relief.

"We're close," Harrington admitted. "If we can just find that goddamn bug. We're running breakdown after the equivalent of ten thousand hours of normal operation—"

"Then announce it now," Lester urged, grasping at the straw. "That's good enough. I can have a sales conference in New Jersey next week, as early as Tuesday. We can map our strategy, have the PR firm in New York prepare the releases, be rolling within—"

"We're not ready for all that."

"But we *could* start publicity and marketing right now! It could make all the difference in our cash flow."

"Lester," Harrington said with exasperation, "let's talk about this later. I'm not going to come out with this cascade design until we're sure it's thoroughly debugged."

"You said we're almost sure now!"

"Almost isn't good enough, God damn it. We don't do business that way. Besides, if we come out with that bug in the board system, and some major user experiences a breakdown after only *five* hours of operation—and loses a million dollars' worth of data— that report alone could put us out of business. This thing has to be *right*."

"Conway, when they had the new CPU—"

"Conway is Conway. They screwed their customers and then had to do a million-unit recall. I won't operate like that."

"How soon might we be ready?"

"We'll be testing again within a couple more days."

"How much are repairs going to cost this time?"

"I don't know. Not much. Two hundred thousand, maybe."

"John, we don't *have* two hundred thousand in the lab contingency fund right now! Where are we going to get it?"

Harrington ran his hands through his unruly hair. "I'll get it, Les."

"Where? How?"

"I said I'd get it, Les, God damn it!"

"John, you have to listen to reason. You have to face some realities. Let me start selective layoffs. Call that woman in New York and tell her the deal is off, you aren't hiring her. People like Jess Calhoun and Ted Kraft are costing us a fortune. Let them go too. Get Drum back on a sound financial footing, then—"

"It's out of the question."

"Have you forgotten how much stock I own in Drum? What my investment here is?"

Harrington's frown became a scowl and his temper got out. "And have *you* forgotten that it's still my company?"

The words jolted Lester like a slap in the face. He actually took a step backward.

Harrington was instantly contrite. "Oh, hell, Les. Listen to me. It's going to be all right. I'll get some quick cash for the operating fund here."

"More loans?" Lester groaned. "With your personal stock as collateral?"

"If that's what it takes, yes."

"Sell your real estate?"

"A few hundred shares will still leave me with plenty of control margin. And the house . . . who needs a big house like that anyway?"

Lester went back to his own office. He was seething, his stomach was churning, and he thought he might actually be sick.

He had to get out, he thought. He had to get off this sinking ship. *Hedge your bets and trim your losses.*

If John Harrington was going to remain a fool, Lester did not have to go down with him. They had been friends. But this was business.

And just that quickly, Lester knew that it really was time to get out.

And that he was going to do it.

The unthinkable was a reality.

How to get out? That was the question. He didn't want to lose everything in the process. He had to be clever. He had to act now.

3

It was only after another call to the hospital that John Harrington turned his attention back to the other pressing problems. Barney Taylor still lay in a coma; there had been no change. The doctor sounded even more guarded. *Come on, Barney!*

He called cascade engineer Phil Smith in. "Any chance of getting new tests going this week?"

Smith scratched his balding head. "I'll try."

"Do."

After Smith left, Harrington thought about how tired he had looked. But a lot of them did these days. The cascading board designs had been jammed through in months when ordinarily they would have taken a year at the mimimum. And in the back, Jess Calhoun, Ted Kraft, and Janice Seeley were putting in so many nights and weekends on ARIEL that he didn't like to think about it . . . would have felt guilty about if he hadn't been there with them most of the time.

They all sensed the urgency now.

He thought of Linda Woods. He was anxious for her arrival. For her possible impact on the project? Yes. Because he had felt a subtle excitement and desire just being with her again, even in the stuffy auditorium while that idiot Hubbard ranted? Yes.

Frowning, he tried to pay attention to business. He thought about his financial options.

He was just about out of them.

But he found it difficult to concentrate. He was almost sure, after further reflection, that someone in the lab must have committed the burglary. *Why?* But even worse than that question was the feeling he got now every time he walked out there. With every person he looked at, virtually, he thought, Are you the one? He hated that.

He made two telephone calls. With the first he set an appointment to have lunch tomorrow with the president of the local bank, an old friend. The bank would lend him money. The cascade project and ARIEL couldn't be allowed to flounder now, not when he felt so close.

All he had to do to get that kind of loan, owing what he already did, was to put up much of his own stock in Drum as collateral. If the cascading tests worked out and the Drummer Boy 5-1000 sold like hotcakes, he could pay everything back just fine. And if it didn't, well . . .

His second call was to back up the first.

"Century Twenty-One," the bright female voice answered.

"Jim Davis, please."

Davis came on the line. "John, is that really you? What can I do for you?"

"I've decided to let you go ahead," Harrington said around the lump in his throat.

"That's great, John! The house and grounds?"

"Yes," Harrington said woodenly.

"Five hundred and fifty thousand?"

"Yes."

"Can we put the signs up and start advertising right away?"

Harrington hesitated, then knew his initial decision had been correct. He was hemmed in; there was no alternative if he were to have any ready personal cash.

"John? You still there?"

"Yes. Yes, Jim. Go ahead. List it. Put up your signs."

He hung up. He and Eileen had had their happiest years in that house. Elly had loved it . . . transformed it from a ruin to the lovely colonial showplace it remained today.

Selling it was like finally confirming—without recourse—that she was gone and nothing would ever be quite right again.

Hell, you knew that, he told himself. Stop being a crybaby.

He went back to work.

4

When Rusty Harrington got home late that afternoon after baseball practice, there was a FOR SALE sign in the front yard. He called the lab.

"If they sell it, son, we'll move into something a little smaller. Okay?"

"Oh," Rusty said, "sure." He had just wanted to make sure it was not a mistake.

"How did practice go?"

"Great. I hit the coach in the ear with my second pitch."

"See you about seven."

"'Bye."

He would miss the house, the only one he had ever known, but it was no big deal. Moving would mean abandoning his good spot for digging fish worms out by the back pond, and not seeing the raccoon he thought he might get tamed one day. But that was all right. The main problem would be moving all his diskettes without getting any of them damaged, and he thought he could handle that.

It was funny to think about moving, though. He had always figured Dad would get married again someday, bring her here. Well, so much for trying to program reality.

Rusty made a jelly sandwich to hold himself over until supper and curled up with an Edgar Rice Burroughs.

5

At the lab, Lester Blaine faced the two tall, well-built young men wearing security guard uniforms.

"You've seen the entire layout," he told them. "Are there any questions?"

"Just one," the sandy-haired guard, whose name was Kleimer, said.

"What is it?"

"There are employers who want maximum security *just short of* the sternest possible measures. There are others who want us to go all out. Could you clarify which category Drum Labs might fit into?"

Lester rubbed his aching skull. "I don't understand."

Kleimer, who was as handsome as any California surfer and built like one, smiled. "Suppose we find someone unauthorized in the lab after midnight. We call for him to stop. He starts to run. Now. We can chase, and possibly let him get away, on the basis that it might be a kid or some mistake. Or we can fire at him. Of course we would never fire unless we considered it absolutely necessary to protect your property or one another. On the other hand—"

"I understand."

"Yes, sir?" Both Kleimer and the shorter, dark-haired guard, named Green, watched him.

"Shoot," Lester Blaine told them. "Shoot to kill. There are secrets in this lab that could ruin us if they got out to the competition."

Lester meant every word of it. His own plan for escape was beginning to take shape in his mind, but until it was certain he intended to make sure no more thievery added to all their problems.

For his part, guard Kleimer looked well pleased with the answer.

6

A day later, Jess Calhoun and Ted Kraft booted some new programming on the big supermainframe they called ARIEL. The machine was already doing some incredible things. Kraft, who had written the new pieces of the program, was excited.

"Wouldn't it be a kick if we got the damned thing really thinking before John's new genius lady even gets here?" he asked, punching keyboard buttons.

"Yep," Jess Calhoun said. "That would be real nifty."

"Everything look all right on the status display over there?"

"Yep."

"Here we go." Kraft hit the carriage return button to execute the new programming.

Previously ARIEL had failed to "make a choice" among approximately one hundred software options offered as a test. If Kraft's new instructions worked correctly, the machine could now make a judgment that was as close to intuitive as a machine might ever make.

If it worked, ARIEL would display the name of its selection on the monitor screen overhead.

Disk drives chuttered in cabinets along the wall.

"Well, it's booting up fine," Kraft said excitedly, biting a ragged fingernail.

"Yep," Jess Calhoun, imperturbable, said.

The CRT screen flickered.

"Here it comes! Here it comes!"

The screen said:

©©©©&&&*())—**$$####@@@*& &&& — ****°°°°°°¶¶¶¶¶<><><><><><><><

"Shit," Ted Kraft said.

"Yep."

CHAPTER FIVE

1

John Harrington's friendly banker was not wildly enthusiastic.

"John, I don't know that much about these damned computers. Neither does the loan committee. But what *our* computers tell *us* is that Drum is just about as badly extended as we can help it go."

"You mean I can't get the loan?"

"I didn't say that. But the best the committee would go for was six months. Payment on October first."

"I was hoping for the first of the year, Max."

Max Daugherty shook his head. "October first. With the stock collateral as stated."

It wasn't perfect. But by October they would either have things righted, or be in so much trouble that personal disaster wouldn't matter quite so much. "Done," Harrington said.

He felt like the clock was ticking louder.

2

The next day, April 10, night watchman Barney Taylor died without ever regaining consciousness.

"Now we'll never know who did it," Lester Blaine said.

"We have the new guards," Harrington said, roused from his sorrow. "It can't happen again."

"But we don't even know what that burglar got the first time! And if it's an inside job, what's to prevent him—or her—from stealing more secrets in broad daylight?"

Harrington had already thought about that. Locks had been changed on external and internal doors and new access codes had been written for all the experimental software, both up front and in the ARIEL area. He reminded Lester of that.

"None of that will guarantee that an insider couldn't bypass all of it," Lester replied.

"I don't know what more we can do."

"We stand to lose a lot of money here!"

Harrington did not answer. He was struck anew, as he had often been in recent years, by how much Lester had changed. Lester had always been greedy, he had to admit, but they had both been young then, full of vinegar, ready to take on the world, and it had been easy to overlook some of Lester's impatience as the kind of stuff you needed to get ahead in the business world. Certainly Harrington had never thought he was as bad as one or two others who had been with the fledgling firm for a while, then went their own ways when their ambition was revealed as lacking in any sense of ethics.

But Lester had indeed gotten worse—more abrasive, more unfair, more fretful, more pushy, Harrington conceded to himself. *But then maybe I've changed, too. Maybe some of my dreams make me a fool, and I would be better off if I could be a little harder like Lester.* He tried to dismiss the uneasiness about his old associate.

On April 12, a grieving Harrington and a large number of the Drum staff went to old Barney's funeral. They all responded to the Lord's Prayer and stood silent, heads bowed, as the final blessing was given and a handful of dirt tossed onto the bronze cover of the casket. Birds sang in the sunny trees as the crowd began to break up.

The funeral director sidled over to Harrington. "I hope it was satisfactory, sir."

"Fine. The charges—"

"Will be mailed to you at your home address, as instructed."

An elderly woman who had earlier introduced herself as a neighbor of Barney Taylor's walked over to shake hands. "I didn't know Barney real well, Mr. Harrington, but we did talk some. I know he enjoyed working for you. He always said you weren't like the rest, writing him off just because of a few years."

"I appreciate that, Miss Black. But I can't help thinking that he might be alive today if I had given him the day shift."

"And have him sit around like a cigar store Indian?" She smiled tremulously. "Nonsense! You remember he *asked* to be the night man. Anything less would have been no job at all for him."

"Even so . . ." Harrington sighed.

"Don't blame yourself. It would be silly."

Harrington walked her to the funeral director's limousine and then went to his own car. The others were pulling away, leaving only the cemetery workers beside the sunny, hillside grave. It was a beautiful day. He knew the old woman was right, and it was silly to feel blame. But he thought he always would.

He drove away with the feeling that he had lost one of his family.

3

One of the other employees who left the funeral did not head back directly for the lab. That person drove a number of miles away to another community and met someone for coffee. There, new instructions were given.

The people paying this employee to spy for them were growing impatient. Material secreted from the lab so far had not been helpful. Certain threats were made.

4

On April 17, Harrington and Jess Calhoun, along with an engineer from Patterson, walked through the big computer show in Boston. Banners and signs extended from poles and dividers across the vast arena. Gleaming new computers, from desktop personal units to hulking mainframes only a handful of the biggest labs might afford, were everywhere. Hobbyists mixed with eminent scientists, while company presidents were buttonholed by sales executives and public relations practitioners. The salespeople were everywhere, and so were the engineers. In a carnival atmosphere, the industry looked at itself. The new Apple prototype was on display, and drawing a throng. IBM had an entire section, as did Victor, NEC, TI, Hewlett Packard, and several of the other giants. Atari and Commodore faced Eagle and Sanyo like warriors across an aisleway. Percom had a robot. So did Vector Graphic. The magazines—*Popular Computing, Personal, Byte*, and all the rest— were giving away shopping bags and cut-rate subscriptions. Compu-Pro, Olympia, and Compaq seemed to have the prettiest women. Dynax had balloons, Verbatim had posters, Radio Shack had free flashlights, and CDC was giving away diskettes in the new smaller format. Coleco had huge color monitors all over the place, filled with spaceships and starbursts. Cray, to protect the latest edition of its giant mainframe machine, had security guards in blue uniforms to make sure no one so much as touched anything, while InterTec wanted everyone to come in and sit down at the mouse controls of the latest Superbrain model.

Many names that had been prominent a year ago were missing. Some of the firms making the biggest show, it was whispered, were in desperate trouble. The shakedown that had begun in the early part of the decade was still going on. Millions were being made. And millions were being lost.

Harrington and his two associates hobnobbed here and there, heard some gossip and started some, renewed some acquaintances, and looked over the machines and products. Nearing one end of the great hall, where the crowd was somewhat thinner, the engineer from Patterson separated from them and drifted toward the modest Drummer Boy exhibit section. Harrington and Jess Calhoun moved on.

After a while they came to a certain exhibit area. In a booth within the booth, two technicians stood waiting for questions about the firm's new XL-3500C tabletop machine.

Harrington strolled in with Jess and started visiting with the two younger men. They knew him by reputation and were just a little awed. He got them into the outer part of the exhibit and started asking questions about some of their special software. They eagerly explained and demonstrated.

Meanwhile, inside the inner booth, Jess Calhoun took a yellow-handled screwdriver out of his suitcoat pocket and popped the lid on the demonstration machine. He was peering in at the board configuration with great interest when one of the technicians up front looked around and saw him.

"What are you *doing* back there? God damn it, you can't do that!"

"Oops," Jess said, putting the lid back on and pocketing his screwdriver. "Sorry."

"Jesus Christ!" the technician said angrily.

Harrington and Jess sauntered away.

"Not to worry," Jess said. "Same old technology. They don't have a thing."

Harrington smiled. It was one less thing to worry about.

Over at the Drummer Boy booth, somebody caught a programmer from somewhere else trying to lift a hard disk out of a loadable Winchester drive. And the IBM boys had somebody arrested for something else of a similar nature.

IBM always was sort of stuffy.

Most of the spying was casual, good-natured, and almost to be expected, a little like doubling your pal at the bridge table right after you had pushed him into a bid that you knew he could not possibly make.

At nightfall, some of the competitors had drinks together and swapped transparent lies.

5

A few days later, late in the afternoon, Linda Woods returned from the parking gargage in the midtown office building. She had just carried the last carton of personal belongings out of her office. The beige metal corridor seemed curiously deserted as she passed the office of Fred McCarthy, vice president for testing and development.

McCarthy, a tall, balding man, stuck his head out of the door. "Got a minute, Linda?"

"Fred, I was just—" she began, then relented. He had been a friend here. Even if he needed last-minute help, she owed him that much.

"What is it?" she asked, stepping through the doorway.

"*Surprise!*" a roomful of voices cried in unison, startling her.

The office anteroom was packed with more than a dozen of the people she had worked most closely with. Some silly red crepe paper was festooned from the ceiling tiles, and everyone was wearing a party hat. On the secretary's desk was a brimming punch bowl, plates of cookies and napkins and paper cups, and several brightly wrapped gifts.

"We thought we'd send you off," McCarthy told her through the hubbub.

"They don't do things like this at this company!" Linda protested.

"Not every day!" Jimmy Johnson, who worked on a reception desk in her area, told her with a big grin.

"Dip the punch before the ice dilutes it," someone suggested, and they milled around the desk.

Madge Stevens, a pretty brunette of twenty-six who had been Linda's assistant, came over and hugged her with sincere emotion. "Here's luck, Dr. Woods. We're all going to miss you a whole heckuva lot."

Linda looked around the sea of smiling faces. "You guys really know how to make a person doubt her decision," she managed.

Her main gift was a handsome leather attaché case, and she was stunned to find inside it a tiny personal computer.

"Just so you won't look like a neophyte up there," McCarthy told her, squeezing her shoulders.

It was too much. Linda laughed, but her vision was blurry.

"I'll never figure out how to use the damn thing," she told them.

On her way home, she felt new, sharper twinges of ambivalence about leaving this job that had so frustrated her. The kindness of the party had touched her deeply.

Everything was ambivalence. She thought about Stephen, and

how her job in New England might in some paradoxical way draw them together again: he would stand on his own feet and she on hers, and then they would have a reunion, two whole people coming together because they chose, rather than because they were not whole without each other, and it would be wonderful. Then by the time the movers came in the afternoon she was again sure that it was truly over and the only way she would ever get her life back together was by learning to depend on no one but herself.

She was standing in the empty apartment shortly after the movers departed when someone tapped on the doorframe and she turned to see Stephen standing in the open doorway.

He looked wonderful, slender and handsome as he always did, and her heart turned over. "Hi," she said.

His pale eyes surveyed the empty apartment. He was very solemn. "Can I come in?"

"I was just leaving. . . ."

He came in anyway, tall, impeccable in the pale summer suit and white tie, moving with his easy, athletic grace. He hadn't changed a bit over the years. He could still break most hearts.

He stood facing her, hands on hips, a wry smile curling his lips. "So you're really going."

"Oh, yes," she told him.

"I never thought you would."

She watched him and didn't know what she could say to that. Why was he here? Wasn't it all hard enough? She wanted to be angry with him. She couldn't be. After all, wasn't it all her fault? Could he be blamed because he loved her too much? She was the villain, not he. And she still loved him, she thought. She knew she loved the life they had had together for a while, before the loss of the baby. She still yearned for that.

She said, "It's best for us that I take this job, Stephen. It will give us both time to think . . . space."

"You didn't have to take a job way the hell up there."

"It's a challenging job. A good job."

"I never thought you would," he repeated. He met her eyes and she saw his irrational anger. He added, "It must really be over for you, if you're going up there to work for your old boyfriend."

She was stung and hurt. "He was never my boyfriend! And that's not why—"

"How else would you get a high-powered job like that?"

"On *merit*, God damn you!"

"I hate to see you give up."

"I haven't given up."

"What do you call it?"

"I don't know." She was fighting tears. "I don't know anything. I just know I couldn't breathe. I couldn't stand it. I have to *think*."

He came to her and awkwardly—with a tentativeness, as if he would withdraw at the first hint of resistance, that broke her heart—took her in his arms. She started to resist, but it felt good to be in his arms, familiar and almost right. She looked up at him and saw that his eyes were moist.

She moved closer, stroking the back of his neck with her fingertips. "We'll get through this somehow. I don't know what's going to happen—"

With an angry urgency he pulled her head back and kissed her on the mouth. For an instant it might have been a good-bye kiss but then it was more, as his tongue filled her mouth. She started to struggle. He held her more tightly, bore her back in his arms, pressing her off-balance so that he could lower her to the carpet . . . the yellow shag she had always hated.

"Stephen!"

He was all over her with the desperation of a drowning man, his hands on her breasts, under her skirt, pulling at her pantyhose, trying to stroke her clitoris, knowing where she liked it, what would make her wet. She pushed at him but it was as if he were unaware of her resistance, and then she thought, It doesn't matter, why should it matter, we've done it a million times.

Panting, he pulled her pantyhose off and moved between her legs. She kissed his cheek and lifted her hips slightly to accommodate him, telling herself that it was all right, it ought to make both of them feel better. Then he slipped up inside her and she felt it but could not really feel it, as if she were filled with a local anesthetic so that she knew what was being done to her, but only distantly.

She *tried* to feel something. Couldn't. Her husband's breathing became heavier and sharper, his thrustings faster and more insistent, and she thought, Oh, God, I hate this, I hate it so, and then he stiffened and came inside her, and withdrew, and rolled over beside her on the carpet, spent.

She was sick with herself for having let him do it. It was newly devastating to know she felt *nothing at all*. What kind of a woman did that make her?

Stephen got to his feet and they both went through the silent awkwardness of rearranging clothing. Linda got back to her feet, too. They looked at each other.

"It will never be over," he said, "when it's still that good for both of us."

She could have cried out in frustration. Didn't he know *anything*?

Within minutes he was gone amid promises to write, to call, to visit. He was more cheerful. He really did think he had done something wonderful, something that would win her back.

After he was gone she surveyed the empty apartment, picked up her purse, her new attaché case and cosmetic bag, and left.

CHAPTER SIX

1

Three days before Linda Woods was due to report to work, John Harrington stood in the back lab and waited while an experimental programming tape for the ARIEL project was loaded. The program refused to run. Harrington hid his disappointment until he was back in his office, where he kicked a wastebasket.

The cascade prototype would be up again in a few days, and if it ran flawlessly he could give Lester Blaine and the sales and promotion people the go-ahead for announcement and acceptance of advance orders. He didn't feel a lot of hope. Jess Calhoun and engineers Bill Tippett and George Fanning had all been into the hardware configuration, and both Ted Kraft and Dave Pfeiffer had been pulled off ARIEL temporarily to troubleshoot the ROM programming. Although both groups had made subtle changes, there was no guarantee that they had corrected the bug, which could be a maddeningly tiny error almost anywhere in hundreds of thousands of machine-level instruction sets.

The latest failure with ARIEL did not help. Harrington had counted on this one to bring the machine closer to perfection. He pulled down some software flow charts and pored over them.

The next day he flew in a rented jet to the New Jersey plant. His plant manager and the accounting people onsite wanted authorization for a 15 percent layoff. Harrington went over the inventory figures with them again and called in the union steward. Harrington offered a choice: a layoff of the newest people, or a comparable hourly cutback for everyone. The steward blustered and threatened.

"I don't like it any better than you do," Harrington told the man.

"It doesn't matter to you personally, though," the steward said.

"If you believe that," Harrington shot back, "you're dumber than I thought you were. Some of these people have been with me since we were assembling machines side-by-side—them and me—on work benches in Connecticut."

It was agreed that a vote would be taken and Drum in New Jersey would abide by the results.

Four hours later, Harrington was standing in the spotless, contemporary reception foyer of the assembly plant in Springfield, Missouri. The young woman behind the counter looked scared.

"He's *where?*" Harrington demanded, aghast.

"Mr. Harrington—sir—he—"

"Never mind." Harrington steamed around the desk and bolted into the office of his vice-president, unaccountably named Jesse James, who looked up and rose to his feet with the expression of a man who had just been shot.

"Mr. Harrington! I didn't know—"

"Let me get something straight, Jesse," Harrington snapped. "We're at a standstill on final production because our light-source people and the cabinet subassembly outfit in Oklahoma can't meet production schedules, right?"

"Yes, sir—"

"And now we've got a final testing procedure kludge that's broken down."

"Yes, sir, but—"

"And my president here, Richard Smith, is at the golf course," Harrington went on, seething.

Jesse James was a tall man, already balding at twenty-eight, with the face of a worrier. Standing behind a desk piled six inches deep with reports and circuit specifications, he was obviously at a loss for words.

"Why aren't you with him?" Harrington demanded.

James looked desolate. "I'm trying to run down alternative suppliers. The reports on the testing hangup just came in. I've got a staff meeting scheduled in thirty minutes. As soon as I get through that stuff, I'm trying to draft some recommendations about a supplier contract modification so this won't happen again."

"You look tired. How much sleep did you get last night?"

"Well, I didn't go home last night—"

Harrington steamed out to his rented car and found the country club without too much difficulty. He had been wined and dined there when the local citizenry were convincing him to build the plant there. It was a hot day, cloudless, a dry breeze moving the trees beside the glass-and-rock clubhouse and the eighteenth fairway.

Where he spotted Richard Smith just walking off the green.

Harrington caught up with him and his electric cart in the back of the clubhouse. Smith's beefy face sagged with shock, and then he mustered a fake smile.

"Boss! I was just heading back to the office."

"Don't bother, Richard, you son of a bitch," Harrington told him. "Jesse James is the new division president. We'll mail you the stuff out of your desk and your severance check."

An hour later he was back in the air, headed for Connecticut, poring over ARIEL logic diagrams. Over Indiana somewhere, he rubbed aching eyes and looked down at the evening-shadowed terrain far below. If we don't get a perfect run on that cascade prototype, he thought, what the hell are we going to do?

If we can't get ARIEL going pretty soon, what the hell difference will it make?

2

Processing-in at Drum for Linda Woods was a little more complex than she had expected. The Connecticut lab might be small and informal, but clearly there were, somewhere, a personnel department, a tax person, a comptroller, and other efficiency experts to make things complicated.

It was mid-morning before she got to see John Harrington.

"You found a place?" he asked.

"Yes, and I've got everything inside the doors, anyway."

"Your hands are shaking. Are you all right?"

She lied. "Yes."

"Good. Where did you move? Into the apartment complex on the north side?"

"No, as a matter of fact I probably did something foolish. I rented a cottage in the country."

"Where?"

"It's out near the lake. You go down Coon Path Road."

He looked up sharply from the chart he had been studying while they talked. "Toward the lake?"

"Yes. It's a little green shingle place—"

"On the south side, just after the narrow bridge?"

"Yes. You know the place?"

"Good lord! I rented it myself one summer before we ever lived up in these parts! The one with the deck looking out into the birch trees?"

"That's the one."

"I'll be damned. It has mice. Come on. I'll show you around."

They left his office and first visited the front lab in the main building, where work was going on, he explained, on the prototype boards for the chip cascading project that would make the firm's basic computer model so much quicker and more powerful.

"It's an important project," Linda assumed.

"About like breathing . . . . Hey, guys, come here. Someone I want you to meet."

Two of the engineers, Phil Smith and George Fanning, came over. Smith looked drawn and worn, a man getting old before his time, and seemed to have a cold that made his eyes red and his nose runny. Fanning, an immensely tall man with a jet-black full beard and hair over his collar, shook hands with friendly interest.

"You're going to be in the bigwig shop out back," he said.

"I guess so," Linda replied, instinctively liking him.

Fanning's smile was ironic. "They can use the help."

"I hope I give some," Linda told him.

"Phil," Harrington said, "Linda will need a card."

"Right," Smith said, and pulled one of a dozen ballpoints out of a white plastic pocket protector to jot a note. "After lunch soon enough?"

"Fine." Harrington explained to Linda, "You've met Herman, our robot. To help beef up security around here, we have two new guards. But Phil here has also tried to make Herman a little smarter. The coding on your plastic ID card will be more complicated than we used to make it, and Phil will want to make a short recording of your voice."

"My voice?" Linda echoed.

"Yes. We've got Herman programmed now to sound the alarms unless he responds to both your coded card *and* recognizes your voice pattern as one he's been set up to know."

They left that lab and proceeded down a corridor to another, where other workers were doing meticulous things to circuit boards and chassis with meters and probes. Linda and Harrington stood to the side and watched for a moment.

"It will all make sense soon," Harrington told her. "Besides, your job is AI theory, so—"

"I've done some thinking and made some notes," Linda told him.

Harrington's eyebrow went up. "Oh?"

"Yes. Want to hear?"

"Sure,"

"I think you're right that a computer *can* so closely mimic human mental activity that no one could ever find a significant difference," Linda began. "Dr. Hubbard is wrong. You're right."

"Thank you very much," Harrington said.

She couldn't tell if he was being ironic. She plunged on. "The brain does seem to work with electrical impulses just as the computer does. Furthermore, the decisions at the level of the neurons—which would correspond to gates—are just as simple as gating: off or on. Also, it seems likely that there are two kinds of neurons, some that are set genetically—like ROM—and some that are affected by location and use, like RAM. Hirsch and Jacobson, in 1975, suggested that invariant cell bodies are fixed by their location on certain dendrites, while the variable neuron differentiates, puts out connections, and joins its axon with other macroneurons to build up nerve-fiber tracts. Thus there is no reason to assume computer reasoning, with its fixed logic cells and programmable ones, is any different than what really happens in the human brain at the cellular level." She paused and looked up to see if Harrington was impressed.

"Very good," he said, rubbing his chin. "Go on."

She thought she must be wowing him. Gathering this information had not been casual work. "The computer-brain analogy works on higher levels too. It seems clear today that the human brain does have a built-in set of functions—the ability to have an idea, form speech, and so on—that is universal. It's the brain's 'operating system,' if you will. I'm sure you have a good OS in your experimental computer, and the fact that it's there certainly does not make the computer's operation any different from the human brain."

She looked up again and Harrington smiled. She took that as a good sign and kept going.

Experiments for decades, she told him (and here she thought she was getting into the good stuff), had indicated that the brain functioned as a multiprogramming multiprocessor. The brain had two hemispheres, the right and the left, and some had theorized that self-awareness had begun when the two hemispheres began communicating with one another on a regular basis. In earlier man the hemispheres had been split, this theory had it, and the right hemisphere, the intuitive one, had seemed like "voices" or "spirits" when it communicated with the left, or logical hemisphere.

"People today who think they talk to God or hear voices all the time may just be throwbacks to the time before we operated with bicameral minds. But that's neither here nor there. The point is that each hemisphere has to do its own work, some logical, some symbol- or intuition-oriented, and for a computer to simulate human intelligence it has to work like that, as well, with a variety of inputs and constant communication between multiple central processing units in an essentially duplexed system."

"Very interesting," Harrington said. "Is there more?"

"Lots. Actually—"

"Well, Linda, maybe you'd better save it until you get to know a little more about our ARIEL project."

"Okay," she said reluctantly. She felt a little let down, but then brightened again. "But what do you think generally of my idea for a bicameral computer with multiple CPUs and file systems?"

"I think it's great."

"Good! I—"

"But I'm afraid it isn't very startling. ARIEL has been multi-functional and bicameral for about a year and a half already."

3

Harrington led Linda out of the main building, through a shady, paved utility area, and across what had once been some sort of bricked garden to another building. He used a special key to open the metal door in the solid cinderblock wall. Inside there was a tiled corridor similar to those in the main structure. It led to a large, windowless, chilly electronics lab crammed with computer memory units, keyboards, and CRT displays. The sweet smell of resin-core solder was in the air.

There were several people, in white coats, at work around the room. Harrington led Linda toward the nearest one, a lank, shaggy young man seated sidesaddle at a keyboard, his bare feet cocked up while he poked keys to enter desultory commands on the screen facing him. Linda recognized him.

"Ted," Harrington began. "Here's—"

"Just a minute, just a minute!" Ted Kraft waved imperiously with one hand while he typed in a few more symbols with one finger of the other. He punched the RETURN button on the right-hand side of the board and watched figures scroll across the screen.

Finally he turned. "Hello. We meet again. Linda, isn't it?"

"That's right, Ted."

Kraft, without getting up, held out a hand. "Hi. Maybe this is an historic moment. Great genius arrives from the Big Apple to meet resident hacker."

Linda shook his hand, which was limp and cool. She saw the animosity in his eyes but ignored it. "Hacker? Like in golf?"

Kraft's lips turned down, saying louder than words, What a dumb broad! He told her, "It's a computer-freak term. I was a hacker at Cal State Northridge and then at Columbia. Got a little old for it—I'm almost twenty-six already—so I came here for a while."

Harrington explained, "Hackers take virtually nothing but computer-related courses, and spend most of their waking hours trying programs, working problems, playing games, and trying to out-smart each other on the big mainframes."

"You must be a whiz by now," Linda told Kraft.

"Yeah." He eyed her rudely. "But I guess you are too, from the scuttlebutt."

She wondered why he was hostile. She tried to be nice. "I don't know the first thing about computers. My field is psychology, as you probably know."

"Yeah, we need some rat-chasers around here."

Linda felt her temper slipping. "Some manners too."

"Manners? Are they in the job description?"

"Evidently not in yours."

"Look, lady. Do me a favor. Do your work and don't try to shrink my head, okay?"

Harrington intervened. "For Christ's sake, Ted!"

"I've got work to do," Kraft growled, and turned back to the CRT.

Harrington, fuming, gestured Linda away. "I'm sorry," he said as they walked down the hall toward a lab farther back. "We seem to specialize in rudeness."

Linda shrugged and pretended unconcern. But she was slightly dismayed. It was not going to be a picnic around here.

Two people were working at the console station in the center of the massive array of equipment there. One was Jess Calhoun. The other was Janice Seeley, who looked model-stunning despite the white lab coat she wore over her blue dress.

"People," John Harrington called to them as he led Linda their way, "here's our new colleague."

Jess Calhoun grinned his tobacco grin and gave her a little hug as if they had been pals forever. "Great to have you with us."

"Thanks. I'm glad to be here. Hello, Janice."

Janice Seeley's handshake was firm, masculine. Up close she was even more startlingly beautiful. . "We're glad to see you again, Doctor," she said, her eyes cool in contradiction of her po-lite smile.

"Oh, make it Linda, please."

"As you wish," Janice said with just the right inflection to add below the words, It doesn't matter what I call you; I don't think much of you.

"I'm taking Linda below-decks to show her the ropes," Harrington told the others. "What are you running right now?"

"Oh, hell, the same old thing. A new version, but the same old self-starter test program."

"Any results so far?"

"Not so you could notice it."

Harrington frowned. "Stupid machine. We'll be back after a look-see down below."

Linda followed him across the long room. The others returned to their keyboards, staring at screens as they intently resumed their testing. There was an elevator door in the side wall. Harrington pressed the button and the door slid back.

"There's a basement?" she asked in surprise.

Harrington winked and pressed a button marked *B*. The door slid closed and they went down.

"Here we are," he said as the door opened again. "This is where a lot of your work will really be done. Not a lot of people have seen any of this. This is our big dream." He paused, and the new, muted tone of his voice was almost reverent. "This is ARIEL."

4

Seeing Linda Woods actually on the job crystallized Lester Blaine's desperation, and hence his decision. It was the final signal that John Harrington would not alter his course of action until Drum was bankrupt. Lester did not intend to be on board when the ship went down.

Waiting until he saw Harrington go into the lab area, Lester looked up a telephone number in his personal directory, punched in a secure outside line, and direct-dialed Chicago. Going through the switchboard and usual maze of protective secretaries, he was aware of the tension singing along his nervous system. But he had to go through with it. Disaster loomed on every other course.

At last he got through and heard the slightly nasal, quick-paced voice of Barton Conway himself: "Lester? Is that you, you rascal? What's going on, boy?"

Lester hated being called *boy*. Especially by a man just into his thirties. Many things about Barton Conway irritated him. But more things frightened him. Barton Conway's millions were his escape hatch.

He spoke carefully. "I wanted to touch base with you, Barton, about that conversation we had earlier this year."

"The one at the software convention in San Francisco?"

"That's the one, yes."

Conway's voice warmed, becoming insinuating. "Best I remember, I told you you're riding a dead horse. We still talking about the same conversation?"

The man left you no pretense or self-respect! "Yes, Barton, it is. The fact of the matter is, since that time I have given considerable thought to, ah, diversifying my investments."

"Uh-huh. Selling some of your Drum stock in exchange for, say, something with a longer future?"

Lester's frustration overcame his judgment. "Drum might have a very long and bright future, Barton. I'm not looking for charity here!"

"Of course not. Of *course* not! Still . . . you know, a man in my position is always looking for a deal. I'd like to see my corporation with a say-so . . . just a *little* say-so, mind you . . . in something with the potential of a Drum Labs. But my goodness, that stock is *so* closely held! I don't suppose you would consider letting loose of enough where it might be significant to someone like me, would you?"

Lester gritted his teeth. "I might. If the deal were right."

"Well, now," Barton Conway said from Chicago, and let the silence hang.

Bastard! "What I was contemplating, Barton, was some sort of agreement—unwritten, of course, for reasons you can well understand— under which the bulk of my stock would be transferred at current day's listing price in, say, ninety days."

"Uh-huh. And that would give you time to cover your tracks so old John wouldn't know what was up until it was a fait accompli, right?"

"I have nothing to hide," Lester lied.

"Well, I'll tell you what, old pal, old son. Your proposition interests me. Let me think about it, okay?"

"I really need to make some decisions fairly soon, Barton."

"Uh-huh. Say, I've been hearing some rumors about some new

chip technology you old boys are working on down there. Something about cascading?"

Where did he get his information! "Well, we might be meddling in it a bit, Barton."

"You know, I'm interested in that. *Real* interested."

Lester said nothing. He saw what was ahead, and shrank from it.

Conway went on in that maddening, ingratiating tone: "If I could somehow find out a wee bit about what that scheme is all about, it might help me make up my mind about a stock deal, you know—not that I would ever countenance *stealing* technology from a sister firm like Drum, you know. Just call it a businessman's curiosity."

Like hell, Lester thought. He knew better than most of Barton Conway's long and abiding dislike for John Harrington, dating all the way back to the falling-out they had had a decade ago. If Conway could steal the cascade technology, it would not be the first time his firm came out with something—using the advantage of its enormous production facilities—before the originator.

"You suppose you could possibly help me get a little insight into that deal, old pal?" Conway asked now.

The abyss yawned. Lester felt enormous pressure. He felt he had no choice. "I might get that information for you," he said.

"Say, that would be real nice! If I had that information, I bet I would be in a far better position to discuss this other matter with you, partner."

"I'll . . . I'll be in touch."

"Make it soon, Les, you hear?"

"Soon," Lester said, the abyss closing around him. "Yes."

"So long now! Have a nice day!"

The connection was broken.

5

As they stepped out into the subterranean room, Linda was aware of mixed feelings—curiosity and some disappointment. The room was larger than the one above it by about half, as a portion evidently had been dug under the courtyard. The illumination was similar, and except for tile on the floor and a slightly more chill atmosphere, perhaps due to being underground, it was otherwise much the same. Some of the hulking computer memory systems on one wall appeared identical. There were several large work tables rather than one, as above, and most were littered with all sorts of boards, screens, cables, and other electronic equipment. Linda saw bundles of telephone cables on the floor along with computer ribbon. There was a slight odor of solder in the still air. Things here were dusty, some of the wastebaskets were overflowing, and in general it looked like a messier, deserted version of upstairs. In the center of the big room stood four jet panels, featureless, each eight feet tall and about five feet wide, perhaps a foot thick, arranged in an X pattern. From open connector boxes in the floor, cables of all sizes ran in and out of this configuration.

Harrington led Linda to the work tables near the black metallic panels. There was a mountain of wiring and circuit boards, all strung together in what looked like an insane lack of order. Flipping some switches, he consulted a panel of dials and calibrating switches, made a few small adjustments, and pressed a red button on a control panel. Tapes spun in units on the far wall, lights flickered, and disks turned. He reached for a microphone on the table and flicked one more switch.

"ARIEL activate," he said into the mike.

Two green diodes winked on a panel, and a meter stirred.

The machine startled Linda out of her socks by saying, *"Hello. I am online and ready to communicate. Who are you?"*

It was an artificial voice, but amazingly warm and feminine. Linda looked hard and spotted the two small speakers flanking one of the swirling gray video displays on the front panel.

Harrington flicked the mike off and told her, "You may recognize the voice. It's a simulator built with computer assistance on the model of Janice Seeley's tonal structure."

"No wonder it sounded familiar."

Harrington signaled her silent. He flicked the mike back on. "You should know my voice by now, ARIEL."

There was a barely perceptible pause. *"Of course, John Harrington. I am glad to hear from you again. Do you have a task for me?"*

"Give me a status, please."

The pause this time was perhaps ten seconds, and tapes previously quiescent on the far wall spun and snapped briefly. Then:

"I am well, John Harrington. Temperatures all normal, my I/O ports are not being used at this level. My first unit is being tested. Voltages are within specified tolerances. I have three dot-matrix printers, three CRTs, one large-screen graphics display terminal, and my audio circuitry online at this time. One telephone line is disconnected at Port 5. No calls incoming or outgoing. Baud structure ninety-six-hundred. I have twelve thousand, four hundred megabytes of space on B and C with the normal reserve on standby. End of report."

"Thank you," Harrington said into the mike. "Please stand by."

"I will stand by."

Harrington closed the microphone switch and put the mike down on the table again. "This is ARIEL," he said.

Linda did not reply at once. She felt overwhelmed. She knew nothing about machinery of this size. She was out of her league. Her nerves were still so raw that the moment's feeling of hesitancy seemed almost too much to cope with.

"I had no idea," she said finally.

"If you like statistics, ARIEL represents about twenty-five million dollars, and that doesn't count development time."

"And it's already bicameral? All the things I mentioned?"

"Among other things. With some tricks we've done, stacking chip stacks, it's also one of the ten most powerful machines in the world right now. But even though we have enough hardware online, every effort to bring about genuine intelligence—self-starting capability, priority selection, independent judgment, even self-awareness—has sent us reeling back to square one." Harrington paused. "Which is where you come in."

Linda continued to look around, feeling entirely inadequate. "I'm supposed to teach it something."

Harrington gave her a wintry smile. "I wish it were that simple. ARIEL has no brain at all. It can calculate. It can sift evidence and draw conclusions. It can do some wondrous things. We even have it programmed to analyze its own hardware capabilities and suggest new circuits to improve same, and it's doing that. Of course using a computer to design new circuits is hardly new."

He paused and picked up the microphone again. "ARIEL."

The machine answered in that soft voice: *"Yes?"*

"Give me the cure for leukemia."

There was a pause. Tapes turned and disks made their curious chuttering sounds.

The machine said, *"Define cure. Define leukemia."*

Harrington said, "Had it occurred to you to collect some more data on your own?"

"On my own? Syntax error."

Harrington tossed the mike down. "There you are. It's got to become a self-actualizing"—he searched for the right word—*"personality."*

"I just hope it's possible."

"Of course it's possible. Anything is possible. Intelligence as we know it in humans is only a corollary of enormous complexity. We can make this machine that complex. It's helping us design additional boards and circuits to continue that process right now. We *can* do it. God damn it, I feel like I've been working on this all my life. It's got to be possible."

Linda looked from his face to the smooth, metallic facade of the machine. She had known it would be something like this. It was bigger than she had envisioned, and she wondered if her present frame of mind would let her do good enough work to make a difference.

"Come on," Harrington said.

They rode back upstairs. Jess Calhoun and Janice Seeley were staring at a video terminal on which words were printed. Harrington took Linda close enough so she could read it too.

> › Tell us what you're thinking about.

> SYNTAX ERROR: "THINKING ABOUT."
> PRESS ESCAPE.

> › ARIEL, we just gave you data on geo-
> metric configurations in normal crys-
> talline structures, space station
> discoveries on crystal formation in a
> weightless environment, and economic
> data on building crystals in a
> weighted versus a weightless environ-
> ment. What are you thinking about?

SYNTAX ERROR. PRESS ESCAPE.

> Given a choice, would you make crystals in space or on earth?

INSUFFICIENT DATA.

Jess Calhoun looked weary. "Of course it has all the data. If I tell it to run program *C*—instructions for making the comparisons—it will do it in picoseconds. Why won't it access *C* on its own?"

"Because it's stupid," Harrington said with a smile that was not amused.

"Every once in a while it does it. That's what drives us nuts." Jess was talking to Linda now. "*Every once in a while, the durn thing seems to really think.* But then you run it again, and it's just as likely to give you a 'syntax error' message or—hell!—go off and run some *other* program."

"It sounds confused to me," Linda said.

"I like my word better," Harrington said. "Stupid."

6

For Ted Kraft, new developments were as unsettling as the continuing torch he carried secretly for Janice Seeley. It crossed his mind that he could rush Linda Woods a little, but he angrily rejected the idea as beneath someone of his intellect.

When he had one of his periodic conversations on the telephone with his friend Ross Prater at IBM an hour later, however, more disconcerting news came to the forefront.

"Say, I hear your line at the Patterson plant is shut down," Prater told him. "Anything to that?"

"It's bullshit," Kraft said. "We've never been in better shape."

But after he hung up, he wondered. With people like Linda Woods coming in, was Harrington finally off the deep end? He was worried.

CHAPTER SEVEN

1

Guard Kleimer appeared in John Harrington's office the following day and obviously had prepared his statement. The grim, beefy guard said he and guard Green, even with the help of robot Herman, could not guarantee nighttime security. He stolidly pointed out the number of outside doors, and the fact that there was more than one sensitive building. He recommended four more night guards.

He had it written out, and handed it over.

"I appreciate this work, Mr. Kleimer," Harrington told him.

"You'll follow my recommendations, sir?"

"No."

Kleimer's eyebrows went up. "No?"

"No." Harrington put the paper on the table. "In a research facility like this we have to walk a cost tightrope."

"Sir, you've already had your security breached twice."

"I know. We're counting on you and Green, and your relief man, to prevent its happening again."

"We can't guarantee that."

"I know that. Look, Mr. Kleimer. We could spend a few hundred thousand dollars and ring the place with guards. But that wouldn't be very realistic. I can't turn it into an armed camp. I think you and Green can handle it. I'm counting on that. Most industrial spying isn't very cloak-and-dagger; just the fact that we've increased security may discourage anyone from trying again."

"What if it's the Russians?" Kleimer demanded.

Harrington shrugged. "I suppose it's not beyond the realm of possibility. But they're a lot more interested in human engineering right now. Another American company snooping is more likely. Or, on the outside, maybe the Japanese. But I don't think the Japs know we're alive. I think you can handle it."

Kleimer left, deflated. Harrington hoped he had made the right decision. There had been no more incursions.

He could not know that in Japan, within hours of his meeting with Kleimer, there was a similar meeting in Tokyo. In this one, a certain executive of Toyotomi Industries was verbally skinned alive for not having recent information from Connecticut. The executive left the skinning to meet and skin some of *his* underlings. A decision was made that more intense pressure had to be placed on their informant inside Drum Labs. It was also decided that, in the event the present informant again failed, a search should be started for a more qualified mole. . . .

2

For Linda Woods, the first few days flew by.

She met others in the lab, and began to appreciate that the ARIEL project was closely controlled and not even fully appreciated by many in the front section of the experimental lab. There, they were engrossed in the chip cascade program; during her second week another prototype of the cascading chip failed, casting a pall of gloom over everyone.

In the back building she began working with Jess Calhoun and the others concerned with ARIEL. There were long conversations. She saw how they picked her brains. They taught her how to bring up ARIEL and run simple programs.

The computer was being improved—hardware and software—on a continual basis. At times the machine seemed able to sift through mountains of data and make independent judgments. At other times those maddening "balk" lines—"SYNTAX ERROR" or "INSUFFICIENT DATA"—appeared without warning on the screen.

"It's almost as if the computer *could* begin thinking for itself, but it's confused," she told Jess Calhoun.

Jess turned briefly and brought his spit cup to his lips in such a way that she didn't have to witness the act. He turned back to her. He looked tired today, his washboard face gray. "Well, I swan, it's beyond me."

"But what's the hang-up?"

"If we knew that, I guess we'd of fixed it long ago."

3

One night late, just as she walked into her cottage, the telephone began ringing. She dumped her purse and papers on a table in the foyer and hurried into the living room to answer it.

"Hello?"

"Linda?" It was a voice so familiar that the pang caught her before she could steel herself for it. Her insides lurched.

"Hello, Stephen," she said calmly enough. "Is something wrong?"

"No, everything is fine. No. That's a lie. I wish you were here. Am I allowed to say that?"

"You're allowed to say anything. I'm not your jailer." Nor are you mine, she thought.

"Are you all right?" he asked.

"Fine. And you?" She closed her eyes and leaned against the chair. *Is it never going to be over? Will it always hurt like this?*

"I've been giving things a lot of thought," he told her.

"Oh?"

"I think I begin to see that a lot of our trouble was my fault. I'm going to go start seeing a shrink next week."

She was shaking, holding her hand to her eyes and feeling the wetness. "Stephen, maybe nothing is anyone's fault. I told you that."

"No, I'm going to work on myself. I'm going to modify my behavior. See, I'll do what I have to do."

She felt a tinge of genuine hope trying to get out. If he would try that hard—

"I've got to have you back," he added. "I can't go on this way. I need you too much. Without you I'm nothing."

He could not have said anything worse. The last thing she needed was *anyone* leaning on her right now. If he had said he no longer loved her—hated her—it would have given her more optimism.

He was still talking about coming up for the weekend. "Unless you're busy," he added.

She had absolutely no plans. "Stephen, I'm so sorry. We're going to be working straight through the weekend at the lab. I'll have no time at all."

"Well, maybe next time." He tried to sound cheerful.

"Yes. That would be nice. I'm just so busy—"

"I love you, babe," he broke in.

"I love you." It was true. You didn't stop loving someone just because you could no longer live with them. You couldn't change yourself that fast.

"Everything is going to work out," he told her. "You just wait and see."

"Oh, Stephen."

He made a silly kissing sound and hung up.

4

During Linda's third week, John Harrington flew to New York, then to Washington. In New York he had two futile meetings with heads of other computer companies who had made overtures about possible financial arrangements that would pool resources. In both cases the other executives had heard rumors that Drum was in trouble; what they offered him was honorable surrender, a sellout that would give him a fine financial settlement and a grand-sounding title—and no control at all.

"I can't do that," he told the second man, as he had the first.

"John," the executive—a friend—sighed, "the whole industry is having another shakedown, similar to the one we had to go through in 1983 and 1984. A lot of companies are not going to survive."

"Drum will survive."

"Your financial picture is not a total secret. You've got a sword hanging over your head. What the *hell* do you think you can come up with between now and fall to save the bacon for you?"

"I've got something," Harrington said, and left the meeting.

But on the airplane to Washington, he scoured the printouts on the latest prototype failure. It had made 200,000 passes, and then glitched. The next time it had made 224,000 passes, and failed in a slightly different way.

The staff still wanted to go ahead, announce the cascade board, and start production. Sales in Patterson said they could hit the marketplace running within a day after Marketing laid on the initial announcement. The bigger banking and number-crunching concerns would leap on the new equipment, and present owners of the Drummer Boy were likely to order upwards of 100,000 units just for retrofits.

"We can find the bug by the time we start production," someone argued.

"What if we don't?" Harrington demanded.

"In ordinary use, a customer might run the machine five years before having a data dump loss. It's not like the prototype fails consistently."

"We can't put it out with that bug in there!"

"Jesus Christ, what if somebody else is close? What if Burroughs or somebody announces something like it *today*? You know how it is in this end of the business: the first one out grabs the market!"

"I know that. But God damn it, we can't come out until we're *sure*."

Now he continued to comb the data printouts. He knew it was like looking for a lost satellite in the vastness of the universe. What ate at him even worse was all the time this took from ARIEL. He felt driven, frustrated, angry, powerless.

5

While Harrington was out of town, Rusty visited the lab, riding a dangerous-looking Honda 100.

Linda met him in the parking lot. "Does your dad know you ride that thing?"

"Sure," Rusty said, dismounting and removing his scarred red helmet. "It's okay, as long as I'm careful and don't get on the highway."

"How did you get here without going on the highway? *Fly?*"

Rusty grinned. "Boy, I sure did. I hit sixty coming down Mile Hill."

"What are you here for?"

"Oh, I need some floppies, and a couple of reloads for one of my Winchester units, and maybe some mag tape for the unit Dad's got in the basement at home, if I can sneak it out past old Jess."

"Well, go in and see what you can scrounge, and I'll wait right here. Then we'll put that piece of two-wheeled junk in the back of my car and I'll ride you home."

"I can make it."

"It's getting dark."

"I got a headlight."

"Go get your stuff, young man, and we'll do it my way."

"Boy, you're just like my dad! Crabby *all* the time!"

Linda waited. It took him more than fifteen minutes, but when he came out he had a carton jammed with things. Cheerful now, he tossed it in the back of her wagon. One of the new security guards trailed him out, and got the bike in the back of Linda's car. She and Rusty headed toward his house, he giving directions in the gathering dark.

"How are you doing with ARIEL?" Rusty asked pertly.

"Well, I guess you could say we're getting acquainted."

"Dad says you're taking hold real great."

"Does he?" She felt her own flush of pleasure.

"Sure. He likes you."

"Well, I like him."

"When do you think you're going to get ARIEL thinking for real?"

"I don't have any idea, Rusty."

"You know, sometimes—from what I know about it—it's like the darn machine *can* think, but it just knows so much it can't figure out what to think *first*."

"I know," Linda agreed. "As if—"

"Turn here."

"Okay. Is it this big house up here behind the trees?"

"Uh-huh. You can just dump me."

She pulled into the driveway and stopped. The great white house was dark, the woods brooding around it. It was a lovely place, though a little weedy and a little spooky for her at this hour.

There were two FOR SALE signs.

"What's all this about?" she asked the boy.

"Aw, it's too big for just the two of us. We want to get closer to town."

She wondered if that were the whole story. She knew Rusty would not volunteer information if there were anything else behind the sale effort. She decided it might not be any of her business anyway.

Rusty dragged his Honda out, parked it at the side of the gravel, and got his box of goodies. "Thanks a lot!"

"Is your father due in tomorrow?"

"Yep, that's what he said this morning when he called to see how I did in the game yesterday."

"How did you do?"

"Great. I only hit six batters."

6

When Harrington returned, he was preoccupied with the business end of things for a couple of days, making long-distance calls, including several to Europe. There was at least one stormy session between him and Lester Blaine. Linda worked at one of the keyboard units of ARIEL.

On the third day, Harrington was there before any of the others, and she found him at her work station when she arrived. She saw printouts spooled all over the floor, her question-and-answer sessions with ARIEL.

"What are you doing?" Harrington asked blankly.

"I was trying to learn response patterns in its answers," she told him. "But that doesn't matter now. I have a new idea."

He scowled at her. "That being?"

"Something your son said the other night set me off. It's been bothering me ever since. . . . Do we know that this machine has a capacity for intermodal perception?"

Harrington's forehead wrinkled.

She felt her excitement growing. "Can this computer combine perceptions of two different activities? Can you make it be a mimic, for example? If you turn one of its optical scanners onto my face and give me a microphone, can it tell that it's to expect *my* voice to speak when my face moves?"

"Well, hell," Harrington muttered. "I don't know." He scratched his head. "Is that important, do you think?"

"It's the first form of thinking in human infants," Linda told him. "A baby has to develop that capacity before it can start learning to put things into categories. Until a mind can do those things, all it has is a lot of data and confusion about what to do with it—which is exactly what Rusty said: maybe ARIEL knows too much, but doesn't have the faintest capability of organizing itself to deal with any of it."

"So what do you want to do?" Harrington demanded. "Start teaching the machine like you would a three year old?"

"No. Like I would a three *day* old."

"It sounds crazy."

"Well, maybe it is."

"No computer freak ever suggested anything like it before, that I know of."

Linda started to deflate. "That's what I get for getting too big for my britches again."

"No! No! Hell, I *like* the idea! Goddamn, nothing else is working. While we go on with the hardware and software mods, go for it. Can you devise tests and teaching techniques to feed this monster?"

"I think so, yes."

"Then do it!" Harrington impulsively reached for her and pulled her close in a bearhug. For an instant she was enveloped in tweed and tobacco and the furry strength of his arms. "You're wonderful!" Then he seemed to realize what he was doing. Looking stricken, he released her. "I'm sorry. I . . ."

"Hug Rusty," she laughed, making a joke of it. "It was his insight that put me onto this." But her knees were weak. If he had turned her face toward his, she realized, she would have kissed him.

SUMMER

CHAPTER EIGHT

1

ARIEL, online, sensed the changing of the seasons. Thermometers, anemometers, barometers, rain gauges, and other instruments were compared with seasonal data. The machine concluded that it was now summer.

The machine was given problems in data handling involving design of new circuitry for its own better performance, and printed out the designs and specifications. It was given certain abstruse mathematical calculations to perform in regards to the chip cascading project, about which it had much in memory, and did these in minutes. New peripherals were attached to I/O ports; new inputs were added. New programming profoundly changed the logical symmetry by which the machine maneuvered bits and performed its tasks. The B unit remained open to incoming data from the Rusty source after dark. A seventeen-cent component failed and cost a four-day delay, but was then found and replaced, and additional new programming installed.

For all of this, ARIEL remained a large and complicated collection of electronic and mechanical nuts and bolts, capable of manipulating very large numbers very swiftly, and nothing more.

2

In the Chicago office of Barton Conway, founder and president of Conway Industries, the draperies on the north wall of glass had been drawn back, providing an airy, breathtaking view of the morning sun on Lake Michigan. There were three men in the office and Barton Conway, dressed for the golf course, where he had a ten o'clock tee time, was by far the youngest. The other two, electronics engineers, were only in their thirties but looked decades older; they'd had to worry about money all their lives.

Conway glanced at the schematic diagram details the engineers had brought in after analysis. "What do you think?"

"It's brilliant," the older man, whose name was Richardson, told him. "Elegant. Perfectly obvious, once you've grasped the concept."

"So was the light bulb," Conway said.

"And we bought this idea?" the other engineer asked.

"Yes," Conway lied.

"I hope we paid a good price. This is a marvelous little trick in computer engineering."

Lester Blaine, Conway thought, had done a good job. But now came the important question: "Can we produce these boards?"

"Oh, yes," Richardson said. "We've talked with production—"

"Quickly?"

"Yes. Board fabrication will be simple."

"Feasibly?"

"No question about it. Our estimate is that we can have a supply ready for our office models within a month or two. A dealer retrofit can be arranged."

"Good. Let's get the ball rolling at once."

"There is one problem, sir."

"Yes?" Conway was impatient.

"There's a small bug in there somewhere. Every two or three hundred thousand passes, the program dumps and the circuit sends an error message to the CPU."

"Well, work on that," Conway ordered. "In the meantime, get into production."

"Sir, it could be that we would want to wait until we found that bug. It won't screw anybody up very often, but every once in a while a costly error could—"

"We'll worry about that later, Chuck. Nobody and nothing is perfect. Get cracking. We're going with this in a publicity blitz right now."

He next summoned his chief of production. After that, his director for corporate public relations. He then hurried to the golf course, thinking all the way how pleasant it was going to be, stealing this right out from under John Harrington's nose. There were few men on earth he despised like Harrington. He had reason.

3

In the basement control room for the ARIEL project it was blue and cool under the ceiling of fluorescent lights, as always.

Linda Woods sat at a work desk in a corner of the big room, going over her instructional program again. Not for the first time, she wondered if her idea for "training" ARIEL like an infant had been crazy.

Some of the others on the team, notably Ted Kraft and Janice Seeley, had greeted the idea with skepticism. Harrington had been adamant and both programmers had been assigned the job of writing the software that would make ARIEL accept input from Linda in a teaching mode and store the resulting data in its knowledge base. Kraft had pronounced it a not-difficult task.

So far they had not been able to get the desired results. Linda's laborious, repetitive "teaching" had had no effect whatsoever.

They had been fairly nice about it. Jess Calhoun smiled a bit wearily and said nothing worthwhile ever worked the first hundred times it was tried.

Jess had been right about her acceptance. Now, in, early June, she felt accepted by most of them. Phil Smith, the perpetually weary-looking engineer, had been friendly; Pauline Hazelton had had Linda over to her Maplewood apartment for dinner and they had hit it off well, starting to become friends. Linda liked the tall, handsome older woman even though she could not completely stifle the nagging worry in the back of her mind about the true nature of Pauline's relationship with John Harrington. Harrington himself, a workaholic if she had ever met one, had taken Linda out for a hamburger one night after a late work session and revealed, among other things, that Rusty was trying it in right field.

Linda had known she would get along with Jess Calhoun. She did. He seemed always the same: sloppy, slow moving, at ease. But already she had seen repeated evidence that the exterior masked brilliance. As for the others, she did not think there would ever be real friendship with some of them, but found she could work side-by-side with them now. Ted Kraft still snapped sarcastically when she made thoughtless comments, but treated her with distant respect.

She had been out twice with another scientist working on

ARIEL, Dave Pfeiffer. When she had first met him, she thought someone must be casting a motion picture in the lab because he was much too beautiful to be an employee. Blond, tan, lean, thirty-five, he had the smile of an angel and the eyes of Paul Newman. He promptly asked her out to dinner, they went, and he was quietly fun to be with, although painfully intense about ARIEL.

Dave Pfeiffer made life much more interesting.

Stephen had called five times. Four times they had ended up arguing. The other time he had wept.

She was changing. She felt it. Some nights alone were okay now. The work at the lab had begun to provide structure for her mind again. She was getting stronger. Some days she felt sure she had been right, that it could never work out with Stephen, but other nights she was plagued by the same old guilt and longing. It was not his fault he was as he was. She was the one who had changed.

And in all of this she knew now that John Harrington wanted her. He had been the soul of propriety, but she felt the sexual tension between them. She wanted him too. It would be glorious to forget everything and just screw someone's brains out. A purging, a flushing of all the old emotional garbage, a thrill, a new cleaving. But she was not sure she would ever feel really ready for a relationship like that again. Not for a long time. Possibly never, with anyone like John Harrington. He was not the kind of man a woman could experience and remain casual about . . . at least *she* could not . . . .

Harrington startled her by walking over to her work table. "Any results yet?"

"It just failed again."

"Keep trying."

Unspoken but clear to her now was the fact that the company was upon hard times. Two projects could bail it out: up front, the chip cascading plan about which she knew very little; back here, over a longer time span, ARIEL.

She had been amazed to find how complex—and seemingly intelligent—the programmed computer already was. Still, dialogue with the machine was not dialogue with a *person*. And that, stripped to the essentials, was what they sought: a very bright, very fast, very deep, very resourceful person, made of capacitors, resistors, inductors, transistors, a little wire, and a world of guess-work.

The hardware was probably sufficient as it stood, she had learned, although they were constantly trying new boards here and there in ARIEL's innards. The problem now was all software—the coded instructions that were given to the machine's memory. This was where Linda could help, working with Kraft, Janice Seeley, and Dave Pfeiffer.

She changed some of the wording in her teaching syntax and suggested that they try it again.

Jess shrugged. "Might as well. Can't dance."

They reactivated disk drives. The new programming was booted. Jess sat down at the main keyboard and, staring up at the main CRT, started the dialogue again.

> Internal initialization begin.

HELLO I AM ONLINE. PASSWORD PLEASE.

"Never asked for it like that before," Calhoun muttered. "Oh, well." He punched buttons and the dialogue went on:

> Calhoun.

HELLO, JESS. WHAT CAN I DO FOR YOU?

> General status check.

GENERAL STATUS NOMINAL.

> Load Infant.com.

CONFLICTING DATA.

> Clarify comment.

CONFLICTING DATA. INSUFFICIENT DATA.
DATA OVERLOAD IN C18.

> Bypass c18.

INTERVENTION REQUIRED CI8 . . . C101
. . . B1818 . . . B1994 . . .

"Durn," Jess said, and punched the ESCAPE key, blanking the screens. "It's gone crazy, telling me the whole system has gone down."

"Has it?" Linda demanded.

"Nope. Like I say, it's just gone crazy!"

"Obviously," Dave Pfeiffer said, with his same infuriating calm, "we have some bugs in the software. And maybe the hardware configuration isn't quite right either."

"It's not the software," Kraft snapped. "It's a bad idea, period."

"We agreed to try it," Linda shot back.

Dave Pfeiffer turned as if nothing had happened and walked out of the lab. They all stared. It was totally unlike him. What had made him so preoccupied?

4

John Harrington picked up the telephone in his office in response to the flashing light on its base. "Yes?"

"John?" He recognized the voice of Jim Davis at the real estate office. "I may have some good news for you."

Harrington closed his eyes and inwardly braced himself. "Is that so?"

"Yes." Davis sounded bluff and confident, as always. "The Fretwells have been back to nibble on the house again."

The name brought a picture to Harrington's mind: Fretwell, a heavy man who owned a car dealership in nearby Greencastle—plaid jacket, heavy-soled shoes, and cigar—and his wife, teetering on absurd heels, top-heavy with a beehive of lacquered blond hair piled on top of her head. Harrington, remaining downstairs in his home, had been able to tell every room they visited by the sound of Fretwell's loud voice and a curious, soft clattering noise that he finally identified as Mrs. Fretwell's multiple bracelets and other jewelry.

The house had smelled of cigar for two days.

"They really like the place, John," Davis was telling him now. "They want to draw up an offer for it."

"Offer?" Harrington repeated, instantly flashing. "I've named my price."

"I know, John, I know. Let us work with you on this. You do want to sell the house, don't you?"

Harrington reluctantly agreed to look at the offer that would be written. He thought, I'd rather burn the place. I don't want to know people like that are living in it, ever.

Then he calmed himself down a little.

When there was no choice, there was no choice.

Janice Seeley came into his office with a printout. Her sleek legs purred in their nylon sheaths. "You look tired," she said.

"I am, a little."

She perched on the edge of his desk, swinging a provocative leg. "What you need is some recreation."

"Maybe so. But I'm too busy, Janice."

Janice's eyes darkened with anger. "You won't see me anymore, but you moon around after Linda Woods like a lovesick puppy."

"Janice, first of all that's bullshit, and second of all it's none of your business anyway."

"Are you still fucking Pauline?"

"Listen. What happened between you and me a year ago was a one-nighter on a trip to New York. You're a gorgeous lady and it was great. But it shouldn't have happened. Whatever goes on in my personal life now—or in yours—is private business."

"You're a cold bastard. A user. Everyone knows you fuck Pauline. You fucked me. You won't be satisfied until you fuck Linda. Do you have to fuck every new woman who comes to work for you? What are you trying to prove?"

"Janice, get the hell out of this office."

She obeyed him. But after she had gone he buried his face in his hands. It wasn't true, he told himself. He was not just a user . . . was he?

He thought about Linda. Scarcely a word outside of business matters had passed between them. He knew she had gone out with some of the younger male employees. He knew that at least three things—his age, the uncertainty of his future with the business, and her obvious turmoil about her estrangement from her husband—made any intimate relationship between them impossible.

But God, how he admired her. She had no way of knowing it, but he considered her idea for the new INFANT program a stroke of sheer genius. Everyone had always assumed that a computer was programmed in chunks, from outside. But if they were trying to make this machine truly a personality, then didn't it follow that some of its learning experience had to come precisely as Linda had suggested? No one could predict how it might randomly store the experiences it gained from her tutoring. Once they got the software perfected, he had tremendous hope for the program. It could be a key . . . a missing link between data-handling hardware and true intelligence.

Interviews they had been informally conducting with her, to see how she approached the whole problem of learning, would show results too. Ted Kraft had said as much, and even Janice Seeley had grudgingly said Linda had "possibly two worthwhile ideas."

Linda had taken hold far more swiftly than he could have hoped.

Partly because of this, a dream had clung to a part of his mind. He knew it was crazy. In it, the house was not sold. In it, Linda was living there. In it, he walked in and she came to him and he took her in his arms and kissed that mouth of hers that drove him crazy, and she responded, and then . . .

"Crazy bastard," Harrington growled at himself, and tried to get back to work.

5

Two days later, Dave Pfeiffer walked into the lab with a slight smile that combined nervousness with regret.

"You're late," Janice Seeley told him.

"Guys," Pfeiffer said, "I just talked with John. There's no good way to say this. I'm leaving."

Jess Calhoun turned slowly to stare unbelievingly. Janice stiffened. Ted Kraft removed his feet from the console board and swiveled his chair, dumbfounded.

"I feel like a coward," Pfeiffer said. "But I've been talking to Wang for months. They've got a division-head job. It pays a lot more money." He heaved a sigh. "And I just can't take any more of this frustration here."

"Frustration?" Linda blurted.

"It's gotten to where I can't sleep half the time. We've all invested so damned much in this idiot machine, and I don't know if it will *ever* work. I just . . . can't handle it anymore." He looked around again. "Sorry, guys."

No one spoke or moved. They were too shocked, it seemed. Pfeiffer turned and walked out of the lab.

"Well I swan," Jess said softly, with regret.

"God," Ted Kraft said. "What a blow!"

"He could have told us," Janice said bitterly. "He didn't have to make it a total shock like that."

John Harrington came out of the elevator and entered the room. He looked glum and his hands were jammed in his pockets. "Dave told you?"

"Yep," Jess said.

Harrington kicked the wastebasket, but gently, for him. "I knew he was negotiating. I didn't think he could leave this beast."

"Where you going to get a replacement?" Jess asked.

"How do we replace two years' experience with this project?"

Trying to understand, Linda said uncertainly, "Isn't this a setback in another way too? Aren't you all afraid he'll carry everything he knows about ARIEL over to the new company? I mean—"

Every set of eyes swiveled to stare at her, and she knew she had committed a real gaffe. "I mean . . ." she began again.

Janice Seeley took a step toward her, eyes glacial. "Dave wouldn't do that. He's been a member of our *team*."

Linda was mortified at the way her question had come out, but she was more stung by the implication of Janice's words. "He was a team member, and I'm not? Is that what you're really saying?"

"What have you done," Janice asked sarcastically, "except look for dates with Dave and design a little toy game to feed the computer for your own amusement?"

Linda's notebooks hit the floor as she got to her feet. She started across the room toward Janice.

Harrington moved between them and caught Linda by the arm. "We need to talk, please."

"She—"

"We need to talk, please." It was said through his teeth, and he propelled her out of the lab with a grip that hurt her arm.

6

Harrington was far too strong to struggle against, and Linda was too upset to fight his strength. She let him hang onto her upper arm with his rough grip until he had escorted her up the steps to the lab above, momentarily unoccupied. There, in front of a deck of magnetic tape transport units, he released her.

"I'm sorry," he said quietly. "We're all a little tense as a result of Dave's news, and I can't let two members of the team start a catfight."

"Is that what it would be?" Linda demanded.

"Maybe I used the wrong terminology . . ."

It was just too much, this man she liked so much reducing her to a *catfight*. "God damn it, I made an innocent slip back there. But Janice has given me a hard time at every opportunity since I went to work, and—"

"I know that. But your remark about Dave really was pretty stupid, now, wasn't it?"

"And no one can be allowed a slip?"

Harrington was having problems of his own. Her color was up and she was magnificent, angry like this. He was on the brink of seizing her. He was going crazy inside with the sudden desire for her. Having to fight it down was frustrating; the desire translated itself into quick, irrational anger.

"Just do your work," he said. "Piddle with your program—"

"Piddle! Is that what I'm doing in your eyes? *Piddling?*"

"I didn't mean—" he began, stricken.

"Like hell you didn't!"

He lost the last of his patience. "Okay, then. I meant piddling!"

"Damn you!" she seethed, and turned her back on him.

"Where do you think you're going?" he bawled.

"Back to my *piddling*," she shot over her shoulder. "Where else?"

CHAPTER NINE

1

Electricity was the lifeblood of the computer. Built of tiny silicon chips, each containing hundreds of thousands of microscopic components, the computer operated because it was able to perform a single simple act countless times in billionths of a second. It was a decision machine. At every key junction in its system of "thinking" process gates, it could only detect whether a voltage was present or absent. But each electronic gate could open or close the way to countless others, so that a simple process could become very complicated indeed. Observers could only dimly understand the speed with which this complex series of yes-no decisions was made. The machine operated in nanoseconds; in a nanosecond, light—the unsurpassable velocity in our universe—travels less than one foot.

In its standby mode, the computer had been given no specialized tasks to perform: portions of its temporary memory had not been given instructions either as to the general parameters of a task or the specific orders to do such a task. But part of its "awareness" was built in permanently, in gates set open or closed according to complicated formulas by those who had designed some of its chips; this work always had to be done whenever the computer had power.

Thus, since it had not been told to do anything special, at every given moment of human time the computer took alternating current from the lab wall mains and converted it into usable direct current; divided or multiplied or transformed the voltage into some sixteen different values fed into the circuitry at approximately 30,000 points; monitored voltage and current levels throughout a system containing miles of microscopic "wiring"; checked temperature levels, comparing them with preset norms, and made decisions as to whether or not alarms should be given; sprayed countless electrons across the universe-vast faces of several video display terminals; monitored the input terminals for signals that might indicate new instructions; maintained constant voltages to interface cables so that printers, tape and disk units, telephone modems, and other output devices were held ready for instant use if needed; monitored environmental factors such as line voltages, room temperature, and fan speeds; and held in memory all the last temporary instructions that had been given, just in case the human user came by to use those instructions again.

A human, attempting to handle all these tasks in ordinary time, would have done them one after another as swiftly as possible, and even with sophisticated instrumentation would have taken several minutes to check everything.

The computer also took things one step at a time. It could not work any other way.

But the time world of the computer was different . . . so profoundly different that the human mind strained to comprehend it. Because it functioned near the speed of light, using electrical impulses, it could undertake an enormously lengthy process and accomplish it so swiftly that to the human it might seem no time at all had been required for the operation.

The computer performed its self-checks over and over again, in a simple-minded pattern. But some of its chips contained ten million transistors each. It was capable of one hundred million logical operations per second. For it, eternity was a few minutes.

In the computer's world, it had forever to work on every problem.

Its only problem was that it was only capable of things its operators made it capable of doing.

2

Three days later, on June 19, Dave Pfeiffer had been allowed an abrupt departure. Changes in the INFANT program were installed. They failed.

"Run it again," John Harrington said, a bite of irritation in his tone.

"It won't run," Jess Calhoun said, putting down his cup.

"Run it again."

"We've tried six times. It won't run."

Jess flipped switches. Janice Seeley glanced at a panel across the room and nodded. From a magnetic tape unit, Ted Kraft called, "She's booting up."

Harrington punched the start button.

The computer blinked a few lights and shut down again.

"It won't run," Jess repeated quite unnecessarily.

Ted Kraft strode angrily over to the tall beige panel that hid the machine's major electronic components. He slammed his palm hard against the metal, making a loud banging noise. "*Run*, you simple shit! Why won't you run?"

"Oh, that's intelligent," Janice Seeley said acidly.

"Why don't you fuck yourself?" Kraft asked hotly.

"Why don't you—"

"Children, children," Harrington said softly, but with just enough bite to make them both shut up and stare at him. He pointed to Jess. "Let's try it in the B unit." He raised his eyebrows at Linda. "Isn't this fun?"

She did not reply. Strained relations with Janice were no better. Now she had the irrational feeling that these latest failures were *her* fault, because INFANT was her program. She was miserable.

"Now what?" Janice Seeley asked after Harrington was gone.

Jess took a Phillips screwdriver out of his pants and peeled a cover off one of the consoles. "I'm a nuts-and-bolts man, myself," he said, peering in with a flashlight at rows of bright green plastic boards covered with hard black metal ICs, like waterbugs in formation.

3

It was getting dark when Linda reached her cottage that evening. It was very, very lonely. She was still angry about Harrington's remark a few days ago, frustrated over just about everything else. This was what he was really like, she told herself. Just a technical wizard who had the heart of a moose. She hated him.

He was, she thought, having an affair with Pauline Hazelton. Or, if not an affair, what the cliché-makers might call a "meaningful relationship." Pauline was lovely, smart, beautifully organized and a real force in the company. Some of her decisions were made with a confidence that only a deep trust between her and John Harrington could inspire. And Linda had seen Pauline's eyes follow Harrington across the lab more than once. Pauline loved him. They were intimate. This complicated everything. Linda didn't know whether to hate them both, or feel guilty for wanting things to be different. She wished she didn't know about them, but she did.

She had a sandwich and half a beer and paced the floor.

Thought about Stephen in New York.

Managed, in a few minutes, to start feeling very sentimental about him and Manhattan and everything else she had left behind to come here and be called a piddler. Maybe there was a *chance*.

Taking a deep breath, she called long distance to his apartment in New York.

"Hello?" a soft feminine voice answered.

Linda hung up quickly without saying a word.

She was shocked and hurt. But then she wondered why she should be. She was the one who had insisted they needed space from one another . . . that it was almost certainly over. Why shouldn't he search for someone else? Did she expect him to sit silent in monk's robes forever?

Walking aimlessly around the house, she tried to calm down. All at once she could not stay alone another minute. She went to the car and headed back for the lab.

4

John Harrington, Jess Calhoun, Janice Seeley, and Rusty were sitting around on folding metal chairs. The computer was on standby.

Harrington looked surprised. "You forget something?"

"No," Linda said shortly. She felt stupid for coming back.

"Look," Harrington said. "I apologize about the other day. Dumb remark. Your program is great. I mean that. Okay?"

She instantly felt a little better. "Okay."

Rusty sat up straighter. "What are you doing, Linda?"

Linda explained briefly, aware that Janice Seeley was acidly unimpressed. But Rusty picked up on it immediately. "So you think the machine has to learn from the start, like a human baby? That's neat!"

"We have the software in," Linda told him. "If it works, as I go along, the machine will learn to relate sights and sounds, make connections, imitate and mimic. From that, it starts working on its own to organize perceptions into categories."

"Wow," Rusty said. "That's *really* neat!"

"If it works."

"What's the name of the software program?"

"INFANT," Linda told him. "That command boots it."

"And in twenty years," Janice Seeley said, uncrossing elegant legs, "this twenty-five million dollar machine may be as smart as a six-month-old baby. If we're lucky."

"Janice," Harrington said with soft reproof.

"Oh, hell," Janice snapped, and stalked out, high heels clicking angrily.

"She's just mad because INFANT loaded up right a few minutes ago," Jess said, watching Linda like a happy possum.

"It did?" she said. "It *did*?"

"Yep." Jess almost spilled his cup. "Quit that *hugging* on me, woman! Do you want my wife to hear?"

5

They had coffee to celebrate. Linda explained to Rusty the theory behind the training program. He proclaimed it truly neat. His father noted the time, bedtime in Rusty's case. Rusty growled and gathered up his baseball glove and spikes.

"Did you have a game today?" Linda asked.

"Uh-huh. Season final."

"Did you win?"

"With me pitching? Are you kidding?"

"I'm sorry, Rusty."

He shrugged. "We did better than usual. We only lost eleven to five."

"Do you go on to a tournament or anything?"

"We finished so far in last place you'd need a telescope to find us down there. They don't have many tournaments for teams that go zero and fourteen." He brightened again. "Of course I was the losing pitcher in only nine of those. We've got some guy named Crafton whose dad is always yelling to let him pitch some, and he's *really* a nerd. I mean, he's worse than me, even."

Jess got up stiffly, stretching his legs. "If you want to see ARIEL boot up one time real quick before you go home, come on right now."

"Wow! Okay, Dad?"

"Hurry," Harrington said disapprovingly.

"I'll be back, Dad." Rusty rushed out after Jess.

"He's some boy." Linda smiled.

"Yeah," Harrington said. "And I didn't see a single damn one of his ballgames."

"You should have. Somehow."

"I know. Every game, I had it written in my calendar book. Every game, something came up. Like today. Now the season's over, and that makes me an asshole."

"I wouldn't go quite that strong."

"Well, you're a lady."

"Thank you."

He looked at her a moment, weighing something. "I think we've had our security breached again."

"Oh, good God. Not really."

"I put some cute little extra tricks in some of the basic ARIEL programming. No matter what you bypass, it makes a record of access. Somebody accessed the relational database management system last night about three in the morning."

"Who? Why?"

"You tell me."

"What did they *do*?"

"Accessed it, got back out."

"Did they steal anything?"

"They didn't get past the locks. This time."

"John, who could be doing this? It has to be an insider, but I can't see *any* of our people—"

"I can't either," he said grimly. "But God damn it, I've got to stop it or we'll lose everything around here."

"You don't think *Ted*—"

"No. Out of the question. Or Janice either. And certainly not Jess."

"Who, then?"

"I've thought." His face was lined with anger and tension. "Phil Smith. Or George Fanning. Or Bill Tippett. One of them."

"*Why?*"

"I don't know. Money?"

"What are you going to do?"

"I'm giving the guards some new instructions. Whoever our intruder is, we can't afford another entry. If they try it once more, we're going to be waiting for them."

He looked around the tiny coffee cubicle. "Boy, I'm sick of this thing. Nights like this, I feel like my brain is busting. But it's the time I feel most alive. Jess left his own company to work with me on this, did you know that? Ted turned down six times more money from InterTec. Janice . . . IBM was going to put Janice in New York, but we got her."

"Why does she still dislike me so intensely?"

"Jealousy, maybe."

"Why? She's gorgeous. Every man in the place adores her."

"You're gorgeous too. Maybe that's it. I don't know."

"Does she have someone?"

Harrington hesitated in such a way that she knew he was weighing his words carefully. "Not now. She was married once. Bad marriage. I don't know what else. Half the men in the company have tried to hit on her, as I think I told you once. She's tough. Maybe too tough for her own good . . . to be happy. One of these days some other man is going to come along and she'll take one look at him, say, 'I love you,' and run off. I get the impression she's that kind of bomb, too controlled . . . too self-denying with most guys around here. But hell. What do I know?"

"She cares about this project. I know that."

"We're all alike. Nuts. We've given all we've got to this pile of junk."

Linda said nothing.

"But this weekend will be different," he said. "The cascade board will run without a bug showing, and I'll take the weekend off. I don't care if the damn place burns to the ground. I'll play catch with Rusty and we'll dig some nightcrawlers and go fishing and we'll spit and cuss and have a hell of a time."

Linda smiled. "You ought to be good at that sort of piddling."

He stared hard at her. "Oh, lady," he said with sudden hoarseness. "You are so pretty, and if I yelled at you, it's because you drive me crazy."

He surprised her, defenses not in place. Her emotions clamored. But was it just a reaction to hearing a woman's voice at Stephen's? She couldn't be sure.

She got up quickly. "I think we'd better go find Rusty."

He held his hands out. They were shaking. "I won't grab you.

But we go along, day in and day out, and I want to, sometimes. Did you know that?"

"I guess I knew that. But I also know you won't."

"Because I'm such a prince of a guy," he said with a note of bitterness.

"No, because you understand my situation right now."

They stared at each other. She listened to her body. She was breathing shallowly, her heart in tumult, her nipples erect. She wanted him.

Neither of them moved or spoke.

The elevator doors slid open and Rusty came out with Jess Calhoun. "That's a cute little program, boy! Hey, what do you say we all go get some Chicken McNuggets or a couple of pizzas?"

Harrington pointedly ignored him.

"I tell you about talking to ol' Bill Kenney at Zilog?" Jess asked.

"No. What?"

A smile quirked Jess's mouth. "He was real curious about them 80106s we ordered. They know that superdense technology isn't for any Drummer Boy."

"I know," Harrington said. "That's one of the perils of ordering the way we have to from other suppliers. I heard Western Electric sent a man to see Dick Steiner down at Patterson when we ordered the 1014s from them through Patterson. He was really nosing around under the guise of talking quantity price."

"Looks like we got their attention," Jess said. "What did you tell Steiner?"

"Lie like hell, and if the guy started trying to talk to the help, arrest his ass," Harrington said. "What else?"

"I," Linda said, not quite willing to cope with this, "have to go home."

6

Rusty was excited about Linda Wood's idea for making the computer learn. It fit right in with his inklings about the machine seeming confused sometimes, like it *wanted* to think, but didn't know how.

He lay expectantly awake in his bedroom, thinking what a neat lady Linda was, while his father read a paper and made other noises around the house. Finally Rusty heard him brush his teeth and go to bed, and then he waited a while longer before getting up, creeping to his door, and carefully arranging a towel along the open seam at the bottom so sound and light would not escape.

Only then did he dial the lab's secret number, gotten out of his father's notebook, to see if ARIEL was online.

It was.

Rusty accessed the B unit, identified, and directed the computer to put all record of the transaction in his personal queue, where it would never bother anyone else—and where only a miracle would ever let anyone find it.

Then he got down to business, starting his dialogue with the computer.

> Infant Load.

he typed, and the screen flickered, then printed:

INFANT LOADED. PROCEED.

Rusty hesitated. If the idea was to get the computer to recognize inputs—to see the relationship between input and output, and then mimic the input—the best he could think of was repetitive teaching. The INFANT program was probably written to encourage this sort of learning.

He typed:

> Boo to you.

There was an instant's delay, then the reply:

SYNTAX ERROR.

Rusty knew he had to be patient . . . repetitive.

> Boo to you.

SYNTAX ERROR.

> Boo to you.

SYNTAX ERROR.

› Boo to you.

SYNTAX ERROR.

After almost an hour of it he gave up, groggy, and shut down. It was going to be harder than he'd thought. Most things were. He went to sleep.

CHAPTER TEN

1

After the first runthroughs of the INFANT program, Ted Kraft surprised Linda by asking her out to lunch to talk about it. She accepted.

Kraft drove. His Volkswagen beetle was old and littered inside, and ran as if each compression stroke would be its last. But the stereo system, playing Crosby, Stills & Nash, was magnificent. Kraft was wearing faded Levi's, a Myrtle Beach T-shirt with an orange sunburst on the front, and chukka boots.

They reached the McDonald's and went inside the red-and-yellow plastic interior. Over Quarter-Pounders and Cokes, they talked about ARIEL. Linda asked some questions about the IN-FANT program, and Kraft got testy. "Of course it's right! I wrote it, didn't I?"

Linda watched him chew ravenously. Underneath the beard and the long hair and scrubby clothes, he was a lean and handsome man with enormous vitality, even in his present state of fatigue. She could see how he and others like Janice Seeley would resent her coming in, talking like a know-it-all.

"Maybe we can make a real breakthrough, thanks to the work you and Janice did with INFANT," she told Kraft. "I know how much everyone misses Dave Pfeiffer—"

"Dave, Dave, Dave," Kraft said testily.

"Did you have something against him?"

Kraft looked sharply at her, then away. "No."

They finished their hamburgers and drinks. Try as she might to engage Kraft in new conversation, Linda found him renewedly morose. Yet, as she slipped out of the narrow little booth, her skirt slid to midthigh and she caught his eyes as he snatched a long look at her legs. They had been cautious adversaries from the first day, but she saw in this instant that his mind was hardly all logic programs and systems analysis.

It curiously pleased her. On the way back to the lab she tried once more: "I'm sorry if I said something that offended you."

"You didn't," Kraft said irritably. "I just get tired of being the scud member of the bunch. I mean, I know you went out with Dave before he left. And every woman in the place thinks John Harrington walks on water."

"That may be true," Linda told him, "but I like you as well as anyone."

He looked at her in astonishment. "You *do*?"

"Of course I do. I don't have any . . . special person."

"Then I could . . . say . . . ask you out.?"

"I'm not very social, Ted. But why *couldn't* you?"

He stared at the road with a look of total surprise. "Damn," he muttered in amazement.

The remainder of the ride back was in silence. Linda was touched that this seemingly antisocial "hacker" had been harboring a liking for her. If he asked her to go out, she decided, she would probably go. She had to try to keep Stephen—and the decision she felt moving ever closer—out of her mind.

They went back into the lab. There was no one at the reception desk, but this was not all that unusual. Kraft led the way to John Harrington's office. They found that door open, and Harrington, inside, with Lester Blaine, Jess Calhoun, and George Fanning.

One look told Linda something had gone terribly wrong.

Ted Kraft picked up on it too. "Don't tell me," he said. "The machine smoked itself."

"Worse," Jess said.

"What?" Linda said, looking from one to the other.

John Harrington picked up a page of a newspaper off his desk. With a hand that trembled, he handed it over to Kraft.

Kraft glanced at it, did a doubletake, and read a short article halfway down the page. "Shit!" he cried, and handed it to Linda. She read the item:

> **CHICAGO (AP)** A new method of combining integrated circuits in layers to form a "superchip" for computers was unveiled today by Conway Industries of Chicago.
>
> In a press conference at its corporate headquarters, Conway announced initial production runs of the new superchip, which it said will make its existing Con-Speed computers more than six times faster and more powerful than competing models.
>
> "This modification, which we can install in existing machines with a simple dealer retrofit, will make our micros into nothing less than desktop mainframe computers," according to Barton Conway, president.
>
> Conway said the new superchip is the result of three years' testing and development.
>
> Although early details were sketchy, experts said Conway may "stand the small computer industry on its ear" if published data are borne out by the new chip usage, which involves what Conway called a "cascading" technique.

Linda put the newspaper back on John Harrington's desk. She looked at him, seeing the havoc in his expression, then at Jess Calhoun and George Fanning.

A thin dribble of tobacco juice had slipped from the corner of Jess's mouth, staining his chin. "It's our dadblamed design," he told her. "They've stole our design, somehow, and got to market with it ahead of us."

"Can we still go ahead with ours?" Linda asked.

"Good God, don't you know *anything*?" Lester Blaine snapped.

"Calm down, Les," John Harrington said in a tomblike voice.

"We can go ahead," George Fanning told her. "But we still don't have it debugged."

"And they do?"

"Whether they do or not, they've stolen the march on us. All we'll get now is dregs in the market, and their production capacity will flood every outlet before we can even gear up."

"In other words," Harrington told her, "we've had it."

2

In Tokyo, the black limousine pulled up in front of a nondescript highrise, one of the city's few due to the earthquake danger. Two nervous junior executives hopped out onto the crowded sidewalk, shooing vendors and pedestrians away. The driver hurried around to assist the old man from the car, but Zosho Toyotomi irritably shook him off and walked unaided into the lobby of the building.

Five minutes later he sat in the minister's office high above most of the teeming city skyline, with a view toward the bay. Air-conditioning whispered. The minister, less than half the old man's age, stood nervous behind his desk.

"You wished a meeting concerning . . . ?" he asked respectfully.

"Our words will not be recorded and no memorandum will be made," Toyotomi told him.

"Of course, sir."

"The consortium will be informed through the usual confidential channels that our latest tests have not produced the desired results."

The minister was a very strong man and he scarcely blinked. But he was shocked. He had hoped for far better news. He imagined the reaction of some of the companies that backed the national effort for a fifth-generation computing ability. They were great ones, and not easily given to failure—firms like Mitsubishi, Fujitsu, Sharp, Nippon Telephone, Hitachi, Nippon Electric Corporation, Oki, and Matsushita.

"This is . . . unpleasant news," the minister said in a masterpiece of understatement.

"We have every reason to believe that we can succeed in another few months," the old man told him, his parchment face a mask.

"Of course," the minister murmured, wondering what the old reptile was leading up to.

"I have my own dreams," the old man went on, "even beyond these things . . ." He caught himself and became brusque again. "We have been fortunate. While a technological revolution grew, the only other nation in the world capable of getting ahead of us in our quest, the United States, has set no national priorities, while its industries have indulged in petty, short-term advances without a master plan.

"However, we cannot count on working without competition forever. Several U.S. companies have been doing research on their own."

"Surely," the minister suggested, "no private firm could hope to get ahead of this multi-industrial and government effort—"

"There is one firm," Toyotomi told him. "It has been mentioned in some of my earlier reports. In view of our most recent setback, it has been of paramount importance for us to know the status of their progress."

"I see," the minister said, although he didn't at all.

"We have taken . . . certain steps," the old man went on. "Although we still do not have definitive information, we are pressing for same. Our preliminary reports indicate that this American company may be nearing its final testing stages."

"If our decade of effort—over one billion dollars—should fail—"

"As I said," Toyotomi cut in, "we are increasing our own efforts to ascertain the nature of the American system. However, national priorities now dictate that sterner measures should be taken."

The minister stared at the parchment mask, chilling even though he did not see exactly what was coming. "Sterner?"

The old man minced no words. "Our informant is inept. We need better information. We have conducted a search and we believe we have located a man who can perform the . . . necessary tasks for us."

"Perhaps," the minister suggested diffidently, "this is a matter about which I should have no official knowledge."

"In order to secure the services of the person we have in mind," Toyotomi said, "a large cash outlay is required."

"Surely your firm, as a leader—"

"The figure that has been mentioned is one million dollars."

The minister blanched. "Is there no way—"

"If there were," the old man snapped, "I would have used it!"

The frightened minister reported to his superior. There was a top-level conference involving four of the most powerful persons in Japan, including the chief of a secret government service.

The men in the room authorized the one million dollars.

CHAPTER ELEVEN

1

John Harrington drove home, trying to absorb the day's setback. He was in shock.

When he reached home in the gathering gloom of evening, Rusty and a pal were playing *Adventure* on the computer upstairs and there were two messages on the recorder from the people at Century 21.

Harrington did not return the calls. He could guess what they were about. The odd couple had made another counteroffer on the property. In view of the day's setbacks, he saw no way he could turn it down, even if it remained a little low.

He did make another call to Patterson. He found his comptroller at home. He asked him to work up a quick-and-dirty estimate of immediate cash flow and long-term losses if they announced an immediate price rollback of $700 on each Drummer Boy in inventory.

"Jesus Christ, John," the executive told him nervously. "I'm sure the dealers would go crazy at that price and we would move a lot of units out of the back down here. But you know as well as I do that our total profit margin per unit isn't seven hundred dollars right now. How the hell can we sell something for less than it's costing us to make it?"

"We can't, for long," Harrington told him. "And maybe we can't at all. That's what I want to know. We've *got* to get some cash flowing, and support that assembly line down there until maybe Springfield can take up some slack for us."

"If we take a bath right now—say, for thirty or sixty days—do we have any prospects of our own cascade board helping us pick up the difference early in the fall?"

"Some. But we can't count on that. Look, Stan: give me some numbers to crunch. Have them by Monday, some way. I'll get back to you."

"I'll put the pencil to it, John. But I don't know." The man sounded worried.

"I don't know, either," Harrington admitted. "But let's give it our best shot."

His board would go crazy if he went to Patterson with the scheme. He knew that. But he could get enough support if it seemed the only way out. He knew he had to do something more, now that the cascade project was weakened in terms of potential profit. The figures were clear in his head, and so was a mental picture of the calendar. He had to have paybacks by October 1. *July, August, September*. The feeling was like in that old story by Poe, where the walls and ceiling started closing in.

Legs aching with fatigue, he walked to the foot of the stairs. He heard the speech synthesizer on Rusty's computer say, *"You are in a long tunnel at the opening of a twisty maze."*

"Oh, no!" Rusty's friend Sean cried. "Not the maze again!"

"Rusty?" Harrington called.

"Yeah, Dad?"

"Have you eaten?"

"Yeah!"

"Did you eat something good, like I told you to?"

"Sure! We had jelly sandwiches and Twinkies!"

"Great," Harrington groaned under his breath.

"Huh?"

"Nothing!"

"Dad?"

"Yes?"

"Okay for me to spend the night with Sean tonight? His dad is coming by to pick him up, and I'm invited."

Harrington thought about it. "I guess it's all right, son."

"Great!"

Harrington turned from the stairs, brushing his palm across the burnished walnut of the banister, which needed varnish. He wished Rusty weren't going tonight. They might not have talked much, but Harrington needed someone nearby. He did not like the prospect of being alone.

He thought of calling Linda Woods—an idea he had resisted before. God damn it, he told himself angrily, he had no *right*. What did he want to do, use her the way he used Pauline?

Pauline had wanted to come over tonight. She knew how the chip news had savaged him. Her eyes were keen with sympathy and admiration as she faced him briefly in his office.

"I'll bring a pizza," she told him.

It was painful to turn someone down when she was being so nice. "It's a great idea, Pauline, but I guess not."

"We haven't seen much of each other lately."

"Yeah, I know."

"Look. We had an understanding long ago. I'm not chasing you, trying to trap you. And this *isn't* the boss and the secretary. We've been pals forever. It's okay just the way it is. I like it the way it is. I've told you that. Is your dumb conscience bothering you again?"

"I don't know what's bothering me," he admitted.

"Maybe you're in love."

"In love! That's the most ridiculous thing I ever heard of! Who would I be in love with?"

"Linda."

"That's bullshit."

Pauline's eyes crinkled with the smile. "When it comes to women, you are about as hard to read as a first-grade primer, Mr. Harrington."

"Say good night, Pauline."

"Good night, Pauline."

Now he wondered if Pauline was right. He felt guilty about her. He liked the hell out of her, but there had never been a thought of really loving her. Did he feel that much different about Linda?

God, he did. Right now, standing in the hallway, he let a little fantasy dart through his mind: He was at the cabin with her, taking her into his arms. Her response would be eager and he would carry her to the bedroom and he would undress her, and she him, and then they would slip between the sheets together, quicksilver touching of cool skin from ankle to throat, and he would kiss her again. And in the sudden fantasy his wife was there, partly, and

Pauline, and the eager hotness of Janice, the way she had grabbed him with her long legs—

Breathing raggedly, he looked around the foyer, noticing that the wallpaper needed replacement, and the terrazzo tile needed stripping and waxing. The oil landscape on the far wall was dusty. He had to get busy . . . find time somehow for the maintenance, and speak sternly to Mrs. Culpepper about the housework.

He thought this, and then remembered that he was moving and maybe it didn't make any difference.

He walked into the living room. It was better here: still, peaceful, with the mahogany tables and secretary that Elly had been so proud of, the old hunt table against the far wall, the pale green couch and matching chair with ottoman, the rack of comfortably read books. There was not much of him in this room. It had been her favorite room.

He missed her so goddamn much . . . everything about her, the way she had loved to read, too, these favorite books in this room.

Harrington had never been much for literature, and he considered it one of his numerous character flaws. In high school the teacher, Mrs. Burns, had tried to force-feed him Longfellow & Co., but it hadn't worked. He had been too intent on the next hour, Computer Science.

Computers had been new in schools way back then and teachers hadn't known as much about them as Harrington did, even at sixteen. He went crazy over computers. His father had often said that the only thing that saved him from turning into a light-avoiding mushroom of some kind was the fact that he also liked playing football. He sort of enjoyed hitting people. Not dirty, but hard. Getting hit was okay, too. . . .

He smiled ruefully to himself. It had been a while since he had been hit as hard as he had been hit today. He was scraping bottom.

Who had stolen the cascade information—gotten it to Barton Conway? *There was a traitor inside the lab.* But who? He had thought of the possible suspects again and again, and the more he thought, the more suspects he eliminated. Janice Seeley? Impossible. Phil Smith? Out of the question. Old Jess? Of course not. Ted Kraft? Beyond imagining. George Fanning? No. Bill Tippett? Unthinkable.

And yet someone had done the unthinkable.

And how Barton Conway must be loving it.

Harrington knew Barton Conway hated him as few men ever had.

When Conway came in as a programming consultant and expert on software marketing during the early, heady days of Drummer Boy, Harrington had known immediately that he was a strong personality, one who drove hard and brooked little opposition. Yet for a while they had worked well together. Only when Conway got the bit between his teeth on buying out Interdata Consolidated did they really fall out. And once Harrington had learned some of the fast moves Conway had pulled in Drum's name to get Interdata on the rocks, the rupture between the two men had been complete. Harrington had been ruthless then, as he seldom had been in his life, forcing Conway out, buying back his stock options. He knew when he did it that he was making a lifelong enemy.

Now Conway was powerful, making computers and transacting other business with a cold calculation that would have done credit to the conservatives at IBM, making his firm far larger than Drum. Probably Conway was toasting himself somewhere tonight, sure he had given Drum the coup de grace.

Harrington braced himself and promised that he was not quite through yet.

He thought about Linda Woods again. He needed to be with her tonight. The day's shock had been too great to absorb alone.

He thought again about calling her.

Rejected it again.

He left the living room and its ghosts and went through the dusty dining room into the kitchen, confronting the mess he and his son always left in the sink and on countertops. He rummaged in the refrigerator and found some old pepperoni pizza wrapped in foil, and a Bud. He ate the pizza cold, standing at the sink, and wandered down the carpeted steps into the basement, taking the rest of his beer with him.

There were three large rooms in the basement besides the furnace and utility area. Harrington had converted the basement and done all the work himself. First was the large family room, with the old pinball machines and player piano, a couple of never-used muzzle-loaders locked in a rack over the brick fireplace, oak ranchstyle furniture, lots of magazines and junk all around, and pictures behind the wicker bar of his first three computers—not the ones he had owned but the ones he had designed and built.

For no good reason, he lit the small globe that said BAR over the bar, then went into the room next door.

It was smaller by far, crammed with electronic equipment of all kinds. In a corner stood his dusty and unused ham radio station. He had really gotten into amateur radio for a while, and might again if there were ever time. He had built some of the equipment from scratch, and he had "worked" three hundred countries with it.

The computer stuff was not so neat. On a work table were the remains of a torn-up Apple, a gutted Drummer Boy, and a couple of other oldtime computers he still had around. A $25,000 logic analyzer, with a Burger King sack draped on its top like a crown, winked at him because he had forgotten to unplug it nights ago. Across the back wall were shelves he had built, packed with small jars, many of them baby-food jars, each marked neatly: *quarter watt resistors . . . half-watt resistors . . . disk caps . . . LEDs . . . diodes . . . misc. chips . . . grommets . . . old caps . . . new caps . . . junk transistors . . . screws . . . bigger screws . . . heat shrink . . . knobs . . . switches (small) . . . switches (big) . . . little inductors . . . pins . . . junque . . . more junque . . . worst junque.*

A spider scurried as he turned on the overhead light in the last room. His woodworking shop stood dusty under plastic covers. The air still smelled faintly of fresh-sawn wood, but he hadn't worked in here for years. He felt a distant pang of regret.

John Harrington always liked to say that they couldn't beat you unless you quit. He also believed that there was always enough time left in an active life for one more activity—"if you want to do it badly enough." The last two years had made a liar out of him on the second point, and now threatened to make him a liar on the first.

Harrington had been an army brat and his early life had taught him to accept change. The high school where he learned computers was his third, and he graduated from a different one, in Florida. His father spent almost thirty years in the army. "I want to retire as a colonel," he always said. A heart attack killed him before he got there and his little marker in an obscure military cemetery near Fort Sill, Okla., listed JASON HARRINGTON, MAJ., USA.

Harrington's brother and sister were killed in an automobile accident the next year. They were three blocks from home, going out for ice cream cones. *Ice cream cones!* Harrington had not cared much for ice cream since.

His mother still lived, eighty now, in a pleasant house in Circleville, Ohio, her original home. He went to see her at least twice a year. She seemed happy, was active, puttered around her flowers. He worried about her.

He had married Elly in 1962. She was from San Francisco, where her parents both played in the symphony. Her mother died of leukemia in 1966. Which should have been a warning.

About the time he developed Drummer Boy, working with Jess Calhoun, Lester Blaine, and some others who were gone now, it began to look like they really were settled. That was when the doctors said Elly had leukemia, just as her mother had.

They said they thought with the improved chemicals they could control it. Elly was cheerful after the first shock and tried hard. She lived three years, the last two months in a coma, and Harrington thought it was going to kill him too, watching her die.

He had thought a lot about artificial intelligence before then, of course, but now it became an obsession. The answers to problems like leukemia were *there*. Everything was there. It was only a question of enough research, enough correlation of existing knowledge, a sufficient number of trials and errors.

It might take a human researcher decades to make all the studies, correlate all the theories, search out all the angles. But a computer might do it in weeks.

He pitched in, slowly at first. Drummer Boy and its clones were doing well and the money was rolling in. A program to develop a fourth-generation machine was aborted after IBM finally entered the home computer market and came out with the PC that would lead—and stagnate—the industry for at least the next ten years. IBM had a habit of doing that every decade or so; just when the little guys relaxed, sure IBM had gotten fat and lazy, out came another IBM machine that consumers, mesmerized by the fabled company name, went crazy over.

Harrington tightened here and made economies there and kept Drummer Boy afloat. He expanded the lab in Connecticut and made a wonderful deal on the company in Missouri. Lester Blaine became a problem, wanting to move into the games market, create new software for existing machines.

Lester had a point. There was a fortune to be made in the right software, if you emphasized that. Only a few years ago, a former disc jockey named Mitch Kapor had bought an Apple on impulse, talked his way into a job with it, and started writing a program to handle statistics. It became Visitrend and Visiplot and he made $1.7 million on it. The people who developed the WordStar word processing program started a dynasty with it. Visicalc earned its authors, Dan Bricklin and Bob Frankston, about $15 million. Now, with new computers everywhere, you could make a fortune just by coming up with some new game, if you marketed it right.

Harrington was willing to use some of Drum's resources for experiments in software and related peripherals, but he had been that route before and his only personal consuming interest was AI. He and Lester were at odds about it constantly. Now, having staked so much on cascading, Drum was in danger and Lester would be more adamant than ever.

Harrington hated that. There was not a lot left of his and Lester's old friendship. He remembered weeks when they spent twenty-four hours a day together, working in the lab, John debugging circuits and Lester screaming about new commercial investments. Lester had been pretty good with a calculator and even a logic analyzer once himself—but that was long ago. Lester's world was now bounded by the bottom line.

It would be all right, Harrington told himself. Hell, he had to believe that, didn't he?

He listened to Rusty and Sean upstairs. Either they had quit playing *Adventure*, or had the synthesizer off. All he could hear was an occasional exclamation.

Any minute now, Sean's dad would take them away.

Then what?

Harrington walked to the telephone. He really didn't think he could stand being alone after all.

And it was just a friendly gesture . . . wasn't it?

The operator had the new listing. He dialed it.

"Hello?" It was her voice, and his heart did a flip-flop.

"Linda?"

"Yes."

"John Harrington. I, ah, wonder if we could have a little talk?"

"Tonight, you mean?" She sounded hesitant.

"Well, yes. But if you're busy—"

"I'm not doing anything. I just had a Lean Cuisine and put my feet up."

He imagined her with her feet up. "I could come over there."

A pause. "All right." She sounded mystified.

He hung up and went to tell Rusty. He felt foolish and tense.

2

After his dad left, Rusty watched Sean fight *Adventure* another few minutes.

They had switched off the speech synthesizer and were working on the screen now. Sean, frowning, tapped slowly at the keyboard. He was a thin, curly-haired boy, taller than Rusty, and Rusty's best pal. They had had a good time since riding here on the school bus together. They had fed the rabbit and talked to the raccoon in the bushes a while until the stupid jerk wandered off despite Rusty's entreaties, and then they had dug some worms and gone down to the pond and caught two sunfish and a crawdad.

Since about seven o'clock they had been up here.

On the screen it said:

> YOU ARE ON A ROAD BESIDE A CAVE
> ENTRANCE.

Sean laboriously typed in:

> › Enter cave.

The screen flickered and read:

> IN THE CAVE YOU FIND FOOD ON THE FLOOR.

Sean typed in:

> › Eat food.

Rusty knew what was coming. The computer printed:

> THANK YOU. IT WAS DELICIOUS.

"Gaw!" Sean groaned, leaning back in the chair.

"Do you want to quit?" Rusty asked.

"Lemme play just a few more minutes," Sean said, leaning forward again. "Dad isn't here yet and I think I can beat this thing!"

Mentally Rusty sighed. Sean was a good guy, but he was a total klutz. It had never even occurred to him that there was a pattern to the responses, and you had to analyze the underlying logic He was just flopping about, going from the road to the cave to the maze to the pit, and getting robbed by the pirate every ten moves.

Sean could play *Adventure* for a hundred years and not win, Rusty thought.

He would have a good time at Sean's. They had a pinball machine in their family room, and a player piano. And Sean's sister Julie was kind of cute.

Tomorrow night was soon enough to get back to ARIEL.

They were doing a lot of weird things with ARIEL lately. Made it interesting. In addition to messing with the INFANT program, he was playing some *Dungeons and Dragons* with ARIEL too, and it was making decisions that Rusty couldn't figure out. It seemed for all the world like the stupid mainframe was making mistakes *on purpose*, just to see what would happen. Rusty knew, from all the disks he was collecting off ARIEL's memory system dumps, that the machine was saving everything too. He had a whole footlocker full of nothing but ARIEL memory, and he couldn't copy all of it in the limited time he had each night. He would be glad when he got his new autocopying program debugged and installed in another day or two. Then he could catch up.

He was enjoying the long, nightly dialogues with the machine, and the weirder they got the more fun they were as he tried to figure out what was happening. He knew Dad would kill him if he ever found out, but as long as Rusty was careful to access only the B unit, and keep his queues separate from everything else, he knew he could do no inadvertent harm. And he was totally fascinated, now that Linda Woods's stuff was making the machine respond a little differently.

Next to him, the Drummer Boy told Sean:

THE CAVE LEADS TO A LONG BLACK TUNNEL.

Sean typed:

> Enter tunnel.

THERE IS A STREAM OF CLEAR SWEET WATER.

> Drink water.

THANKS. I WAS THIRSTY.

"Gaw!" Sean cried.
The guy was hopeless.

CHAPTER TWELVE

1

Linda waited on pins and needles. She had no clear-cut idea of how bad today's blow on the cascade project might be. But she knew it was bad. Everyone had been gloomy. She had tried to keep it off her mind with little success. Now John Harrington's call filled her with combined alarm and uncertainty, mixed with a faint hope she was not quite willing to recognize. The hope went to the feelings within her, the ones with which she was still trying to cope. The alarm and uncertainty were her more practical side: Had the news been so bad that he would come here to tell her that her days were numbered at the lab?

She was wearing lemon-colored shorts, a sleeveless white shell, and sandals when he called, and her first impulse was to gussie up a little—at least a dress and hose. She didn't.

She waited, curled up on her couch, looking often at the clock.

It seemed an awfully long time before she heard his car tires on the gravel of the driveway.

She opened the door.

Standing there on the tiny porch was Harrington. He was wearing a Hawaiian-style sport shirt so loud he wouldn't have needed the porch light, and cream-colored slacks a little out of style. He had a small grocery sack in one arm and a bottle of wine under the other. He grinned crookedly.

"Old Indian custom," he said. "When you've just lost the battle, you celebrate that it wasn't worse."

"Come in."

He came in, seeming too big for the little living room. He looked around. "You've fixed it up real nice."

Linda looked too, trying to see it with his eyes. The bare plank floor had throw rugs here and there, Indian patterns. Light played softly over the dark wood of the exposed rafters in the ceiling. She had arranged a few Indian artifacts on the rough-hewn mantle over the fireplace in the gray rock wall, and colorful throws brightened the tweedy couch and chairs. Her lamps, of heavy masonry and brass, made a full, soft light against the backdrop of the double patio doors looking out onto the blackness of the deck and woods.

"It's very comfortable," she told him.

"Yeah. When I lived here, we used packing boxes for end tables."

She stood watching him, not quite sure what was going on.

"Elly—my wife—was great about it. She was great about a lot of things." His eyes were distant and a little bleak.

Linda liked him for his devotion to his dead wife, but she was uneasy with it—almost jealous too. "Put your packages down," she said a little too briskly.

He offered them to her. "I brought a bottle of wine and some snacks. If you want, that is. If you don't . . ."

So he wasn't here to fire her. She felt her pulse rise. "Put them on the coffee table."

He complied. "I probably shouldn't be here. I don't feel too good after today. Put me in a weak mood. So here I am. Look, throw me out if you want."

"I don't. Sit down."

He collapsed on the couch, long legs spreading. She went into the tiny kitchen and opened the bottle of Riesling, which was chilled, and put his groceries—peanuts and potato chips—into small wood bowls. She carried them back in on a tray along with two wine glasses and napkins. As she entered, for a fraction of a second she thought how nice he looked on her couch and how glad she was to see him there. She wished she had changed into something nicer.

As if reading her mind, he looked up. "You are so good-looking."

"You're good for my ego." She sat beside him on the couch, at the opposite end.

He poured solemnly and tasted the wine before filling the glasses all the way. He was very serious and careful about that. His shirt and this setting and his solemnity made him different to her, more endearing. She wished she didn't like him quite so much; she couldn't handle it very well. He said something and she replied, but she was not capable right now of conversing very intelligently. She had to get hold of herself. This was a rebound thing, totally irrational, and just because Stephen had a girl—

He handed her a glass and raised his own in a mocking toast that was half serious after all. "To your good health."

They drank. It was a very nice Riesling.

"What will you do?" she asked finally.

"About the cascade project? Keep testing our prototype. When it's right, go out with it."

"That other company has beaten us."

"That other company stole our design. I'd bet anything on that."

"The spy again?"

"Yep."

"But how could the other company start selling our design if it's defective?"

"Well, it's a small bug. Low-time users could be lucky and run for months or years without a crash. I wanted it perfect, so there would be no recalls, no complaints. I suppose I was stupid."

"To refuse to start selling a defective product?"

"I was proud of that damn cascade idea. I didn't want it to be less than it could be. I got . . . emotionally involved. Don't give me credit for too much integrity. I think it was more pride."

Linda let it go. "A lot of us are that involved with ARIEL now."

"You too? Already?"

"Yes. It's *so* close, I feel. For those of you who have been working on the project for months and years, it must be a lot worse."

"Goethe said there's nothing better in life than to have a goal and be working toward it," he said with a faint smile. "But I don't think he was thinking of a damn computer that becomes an obsession."

They sipped the wine in silence for a moment.

"It's not just selfish, wanting to get the thing really thinking," he mused. "Sure, the company that first has full-fledged AI online will lead the industry. The country with a national headstart will lead the world. We're not just talking about information bits here. We're talking about *knowledge*. In the future, the wealth of nations will depend on their share of the knowledge market. Information processing in this country alone is a hundred-billion-dollar industry. The processing of knowledge will change the foundations of the modern world. *And the country that lags may not survive*. It's that simple."

"Yet our government isn't helping at all."

"There have been a few small university grants."

"If we keep having trouble with ARIEL, can you continue to absorb the costs over a long period?"

"No. There won't be any long period. We'll run out of money or the Japanese will beat us to it. We'll keep going a while, though. Long enough, maybe."

"I'm reassured."

"Good." He refilled the wine glasses. He wondered how she would react if he told her that they were already operating on borrowed money, that he was now personally more than two million dollars in debt, most of it lent against his stock holdings. The worry pressed in on him.

She asked about Rusty. He filled her in on a few of his more infamous baseball exploits of the school season, and his plans for vacation.

After that, he told her some of the things that had happened when he lived in this cabin, including a mouse in the flour can and a muskrat in the attic. She admitted a two-hour battle with a perfectly harmless but ugly grass spider in the shower stall. By that time they were laughing.

Something else was going on too.

The wine was almost gone. The room seemed much warmer. He was perspiring. She caught him looking down at her legs about every sixty seconds. She felt tingly inside. God, she should have worn other clothes, *more* clothes. She felt naked this close to him.

This was ridiculous.

"Is the fishing still good in the pond back there?"

"I don't know. I haven't tried it yet."

He cocked his head. "You do fish, though?"

"Well, I have."

His faced crinkled with a smile. "Good."

He was just enormously attractive. Here in this setting, away from the pressures of the lab and technical talk (for the moment, at least), he also seemed younger, more full of life. He was a kind man too, she thought. And alone, just as she was . . . unless there was something with Pauline Hazelton. Linda examined the downy hair on his forearms, the tuft of it sticking out the opened top button of the silly shirt. He had nice arms. Nice thighs too. She liked him so much and he turned her on physically and it scared her badly.

She held out her glass.

He lifted the bottle and only a few drops dribbled into her glass. "Hell," he muttered.

"That's all right," she told him, uncoiling from the couch. "I've got a bottle or two back there."

He glanced at his watch. "Jesus, look at the time." He frowned up at her. "I'd better go."

She met his look directly and said with as much meaning as she could put into it: "It's early. And you don't have to go."

His face mirrored his perplexity. "It was nice of you to have me, Linda. But it's late."

She had no idea she would say it. It just came out of the loneliness and liking him and needing someone—and the wine.

"Stay," she said huskily.

Awkwardly, with a great deal of shuffling and grunting, he climbed out of the couch and stood to face her. She should have stepped back to give him room. She didn't, amazed by her own brazenness. They stood almost toe to toe, and she felt the electricity jolting between them. This was exactly what she had said she would not do. She didn't want another relationship . . . did she?

"If I don't go now, you're in trouble," he muttered.

"Let me worry about that," she whispered, and moved against him.

He caught her in his arms. It was like the embrace at the office that time—quick, a trifle rough, overwhelming. But it was different because he did not release her quickly and she did not try to move away. She raised her face. He bent lower. His lips were gentle and knowing and she opened to his tongue. His arms tightened and the excitement coursed through her thighs. *Oh, I don't care, I like him so, and I'm free—*

He hugged her so tightly her breath was pushed out. His big hands on her back were strong, longing. His lips were in her hair, at her ear.

"I can still leave," he said huskily. "I don't want to mess you up while you've got so much else coming down—"

"Hush," she whispered, and insistently, without her conscious volition, her pelvis was beginning to rotate against him.

He slipped his arm around her waist. "Unless I forget, the bedroom is this way."

"It is." Her throat was almost too dry to allow words.

They went into the bedroom, lit only by the reflections from the living room. A bit of brass on the far wall caught a reflection, glinting a dull gold. Linda kicked off her sandals, and the thick rug was tickly under her bare feet. Although the shoes had been flat, she was even tinier against Harrington as his arms reclaimed her for an instant. He felt good against her, protective, wonderful. She let him stroke her for a moment, and then she stepped back from him, astonished it was all happening, and quickly pulled the shell over her head, her shorts down off her hips. In another second she was naked, going to the bed, tossing back the covers.

"Hurry," she said, reclining, suddenly glorying in her brazenness.

His skin was golden-colored, his chest softly muscular and covered with downy hair. As he came into the bed beside her, she saw how excited he was. He was very big, angry-looking, and the sight of him made a need rush through her with new urgency.

Their nude bodies moved together. She loved the feel of the hair on his back and the weight of his thighs against her. She loved the way he stroked her, then bent to her breasts, so she could feel his breath descending across her throat as he neared her nipples, kissing and then licking them in turn. She guided his hand to her thighs. She was so excited now. She knew she had wanted him from the first. No matter how hard she had ever tried, she had never been able to erase the memory of his kiss. How many times had she been kissed? But even his first kiss had been different somehow, more thrilling. It had been elevated to a precious memory, and now in this reality the dream was being fulfilled.

He moved over her. She spread her legs to accommodate him . . . reached down to guide him. They moved together. She moaned a little in pleasure as he thrust deep into her. Each movement sent fire through her. She heard her own sounds. He pressed her down and she rose to meet him.

"Oh, God," he groaned into her hair, his movements sharpening with urgency that sent hot knifeblades of pleasure through her. "I'm going to be so quick—"

"It's all right," she panted. "It's great."

Afterward they lay cradled together, her head on his arm and shoulder. He stroked her arm and gently kissed her forehead. She trembled.

"Are you crying?" he asked. "Did I . . ."

"No, you were wonderful." The tears would not stop. "I've never cried like this after making love. I don't know what's wrong with me. I guess I'm just so screwed up right now."

"Guilt?"

"Guilt? Yes. And fear. And a lot of other things."

He held her in silence for a long time. She could not possibly regret its happening. But she did not know what it meant. She thought of Stephen, and was hit by a sharp feeling of guilt. Wasn't this just running from the problem? Some people drank when they separated; some slept around. Was she going crazy? Could she in any way trust her emotions right now?

Her sense of uncertainty and fear somehow communicated itself to Harrington. He drew back from her a little and looked down into her eyes. "But I like you so much," she murmured.

"Guess I'd better go," he muttered.

"Yes," she said.

He kissed her again, very gently. They both dressed. He hugged her at the door and went out without saying another word. She watched him drive away. His taillights faded and the road was dark.

2

He knew exactly the route taken by the new security guards. He had been careful about that. Still, his heart was hammering when he parked well down the road from the lab, in a brushy area out of sight, and walked through the grassy field, entering the grounds via the old side gate that he had long had a key for. He was out of breath and shaking by the time he crossed the parking lot and approached the side door. He peered briefly through the window, saw nothing, took a ragged breath, and entered.

The hallway was dim and vacant. Herman hummed into view. The intruder silenced him with the new procedure.

He moved at once to the back lab. It too was unoccupied. Only two small nightlights provided gray illumination, turning the computers and memory units into hulking gargoyles. He went at once to the printer for the diagnostic runs and flicked it on. While waiting for circuit indicators to swing up to nominal values, he consulted a three-by-five card on which he had earlier penciled the crucial memory cell locations.

He had minutes at best. At this time, watchman Green was in the rear building, probably in the basement, and would be there for another six to eight minutes. The other guard, Kleimer, was just finishing a check of the front offices, and would now exit the building to walk the front parking lot and shake the outside doors, a job that took seven minutes.

By the time they were back inside, he had to be gone.

Turning to the console, he powered up and typed in the first rows of numbers that would command dumping of the stored facts into the high-speed matrix printer. He punched the RETURN button and consulted his watch as disks spun. He had five minutes.

The printer began to spurt out dot matrix numbers onto the continuous roll of printout paper. It was very quiet, but it sounded like gunshots to his agonized ears.

He had four minutes.

In the front parking lot, Kleimer had a funny feeling.

Once in 'Nam he'd had such a feeling and turned just in time to see a gook rushing at him out of the jungle cover thirty yards away. Later, during Tet, he'd had the feeling again, and left the café he was in. It was blown up by a sapper ten minutes later.

Kleimer had learned to trust these feelings.

Someone was in the lab.

He ran.

Reaching the front door, he slipped off his shoes and entered silently. He paused inside the door and listened, then immediately heard the odd sound in the lab, which he recognized as a printer.

Kleimer relaxed slightly. A staff member, he thought, had come in unseen and was burning the midnight oil. Happened a lot. And yet in this case *there was no car in the lot.*

Kleimer drew his service revolver and moved to the door of the lab . . . swung it open. He saw the man bent over the printer, and in the dim light did not recognize him.

"Hold it right there!" he called loudly.

The man at the printer had a sheet of paper in his hand which was still running out of the printer. He turned a horror-struck face for an instant—too fast for possible recognition—and ripped the paper from the machine and bolted toward the hall door.

"*Hold it!*" Kleimer bawled, raising the gun.

The man swung around, still running. Perhaps he was about to obey the command to halt. Kleimer did not have time to make fine judgments, and besides, he was the kind of man who sometimes got the tingly feeling of erection when he strapped on his revolver. This kind of opportunity to *really do something* didn't come along every day.

Kleimer fired twice.

The shots drove the man, jackknifing, against a rack of test equipment that crashed around him like falling trash cans as he hit the floor, rolled once, and lay still.

Kleimer verified that the man was dead and then sounded the alarm.

Forty minutes later, John Harrington rushed into the lab to find it swarming with police and sheriff's deputies.

They pulled the sheet off the corpse on the stretcher.

Harrington recoiled. The dead man was Phil Smith.

CHAPTER THIRTEEN

1

The computer was organized on two basic principles: that artificial intelligence could be derived from high-speed calculation based on a very large amount of specific information, and that expertise could come only from experience.

On this basis, ARIEL had been provided hardware and peripherals that allowed it enormous factual storage capability—the potential to store the equivalent of libraries of specific information. Most of this storage was as yet unused, although as a result of input from the Rusty source, lodged in the B unit, and the teaching program being run daily by Linda Woods, the computer potentially "knew" more than its designers suspected.

In addition. ARIEL hardware and software design provided for the machine to sift its data and try solutions to problems again and again, failing but storing the failed routine too, as basis for the next attempt, so that the machine learned from experience. Programming allowed the machine to draw conclusions from this experience and write itself rules for future behavior, or heuristics.

This ability to draw from either a knowledge base or a heuristic base, and constantly to add to both, was what gave ARIEL its unlimited potential.

Through relational database indexing, the machine constantly updated itself. Software simulating various workings of the human mind tempered the operation with something very like humanity. As the machine learned from a mistake and made changes in its own mental structure in order to make future changes in its behavior, it acted very much like a recalcitrant child after doing wrong and getting a scolding.

The engineers and programmers working on ARIEL had no precedents on which to base their evaluations of progress. They continued to be ignorant of the Rusty source.

Therefore the machine was much closer to their dream than they realized.

2

John Harrington called a meeting in the basement lab. They assembled in the chilly, windowless environment that sheltered ARIEL: Harrington, Jess Calhoun, Ted Kraft, Linda Woods, Janice Seeley.

"People," Harrington said, pacing slowly in his crepe-soled shoes, "Phil was taking stuff out of the electronic files back here. Maybe he was the one who got the cascade specs to Conway too. I don't think we'll ever know now. I don't think he had gotten a lot out of ARIEL. If he had gotten enough to do us a lot of damage, he wouldn't have been back last night with all our increased security staring him in the face. He came back, though, and you know what happened."

Harrington stopped for a moment. He was having a little trouble with his voice. His eyes looked wet. He blew his nose, his back turned to their profound silence, and then faced them again.

"The sheriff has been out to Phil's house. His wife let them look around. They found some stuff. Drug stuff. So far, cocaine. I don't know if they'll find anything else or not. She's all torn up, of course—I'm going over there after a while and try to talk to her—and the sheriff is bringing in the state boys because he says it looks like poor Phil had a king-size habit. If that's true, then somebody got to him—paying him a bundle for secrets out of here—because he needed a whole lot of extra money to support his needs."

He blew his nose again.

"Okay. We've got some other problems. I'm going to New York in a couple of days to have a meeting with the directors and we're going to try to iron some of that out. We're going to keep working on our own cascade program and get that going, and in the meantime we're going to have a hell of a national Drummer Boy sale; that will get some cash flowing. We're going to just assume Phil didn't steal too much ARIEL stuff, as I said before, and keep going.

"It'll be a little tough. We lost Dave and now we've lost Phil. We were short-handed back here to begin with. Maybe I can find somebody with the right credentials, I don't know. In the meantime, though, we're close. You've seen some of the tests. This damn machine acts like it's right on the brink sometimes. We're *close*. I can taste it.

"We're going to tighten up, work more closely together. Jess, you're going to get those new boards cobbed up. Ted, you're hip-deep in the new programming for the database management system—keep after it. Janice, I want you to work with Linda and me on this teaching program, and any new software mods we may need. I want to rerun that six-seventy-four routine tomorrow or the next day and find out why it's hanging up."

Harrington paused and looked at each of them in turn. When his eyes came to Linda, they changed. "Can I see you in my office, please?"

3

She had known this was coming.

Harrington closed the door of his office and came to her, taking her into his arms. It was a totally open and spontaneous gesture and everything in her cried out to respond. But she pulled away.

"What?" he said, holding her at arms' length.

"I'm sorry," she said. "Last night—it was a mistake."

"It was no mistake."

"I was awake almost all night after you left. I didn't know about Phil. I feel horrible about Phil. But that wasn't what I was thinking about. I was thinking about what happened between you and me."

"What happened between you and me was wonderful," he told her. "It was one of the few really good things that's happened to me in so long I can't remember. Now we—"

"It was a *mistake*," she repeated miserably.

"How the hell can you say that? I was there. I felt you respond. It was terrific. I've never known anyone exactly like you. I—"

"Don't talk like that. You mustn't make it worse."

"Worse? What are you talking about?"

"I need . . . some time. I have to stay away from you right now."

"Why? Why?"

"I . . . have to be on my own. I can't use you or anyone else as a crutch. I have to . . . work everything out, stop being so confused."

"About me? About Stephen?"

"About everyone."

"That doesn't make any sense."

"I don't know exactly how I feel about Stephen right now, except guilty—filled with regret. Part of me will always love him. I'm so mixed up, and I have to get it all straight before I can go on in any direction, with anyone."

"So does that mean last night didn't happen?" he asked in exasperation.

"No. No, of course not! But it can't happen again."

"Because?"

"I can't use you to separate me from Stephen," she said miserably.

"I'll come over tonight. We can talk—"

"*No!*"

"Why?"

"Don't you see? Maybe I'm as weak as Stephen. Maybe I can't live alone any better than he can—not alone up here, without ever seeing him. Maybe what happened last night was just loneliness."

His face darkened with anger. "It wasn't. You know it wasn't."

"I don't know *anything* right now! I told you that. I called him the other night and he had a girl in his apartment. Was what happened between us last night partly just revenge? Was I trying to prove something, and I don't even know what it is?"

"You're so full of shit I can't believe it. That wasn't revenge. God damn it, I was *there*."

"You just don't understand."

"No, I don't." He was dark-faced now, baffled, growing angrier and more frustrated. "Don't try to explain away what's happened between us."

She tried again, desperately: "You're such a fine person—such a wonderful man—and last night was marvelous. But I have to decide how I feel about my marriage, once and for all. And I can't do that with you right beside me."

"What are you saying? That you don't want to see me at all? That we're going to pretend last night didn't happen?"

"No, I just need time right now. I have to work it out. I can't ask you to be my daddy on this. It's my mess."

His shoulders slumped. "How long is all this going to take?"

"I don't know that, either."

He stared hard at her, his pained anger clear, and it made matters worse. "You ask a lot. Maybe more than I can give. Maybe I'm not that patient."

"I know," she whispered.

Brusquely he turned his back on her. "Go back to work."

4

Although it was summer, a thin snowfall had sifted out of the Alpine highs and left a coating over Bludenz.

Wearing a heavy sweater and jacket, Victor Elb puffed steam as he jogged back up the narrow brick street from his morning run. A tall man, slender, he wore his dark hair long, matching his furry beard. He had a lean, cold face, hawklike around the eyes and nose.

Approaching his small house with its steeply pitched Bavarian-style roof, window boxes ablaze with geraniums and tiny yard tightly fenced and hedged, Elb saw the man standing, waiting for him, beside the Fiat. They had not seen one another for almost five years, and Elb was not particularly happy to see him now.

The man was considerably older, gray, with a Germanic face that showed the ravages of the life he had led. His left hand was missing.

"Victor," he said, unsmiling. "Pardon this intrusion."

"What is it?" Elb asked curtly.

"Work. Something to interest you, I think."

"I am retired, Hans." Elb started past him to enter his gate.

"This has to do with John Harrington in the United States, and what may be a breakthrough in artificial intelligence."

Elb turned and looked at him with a piercing stare. "Really?"

"I know your interest in that area."

"Yes," Elb said. "But since the affair in London two years ago, I've had my fill of spying. A man could get killed."

"You may be the only man, however, with the background to infiltrate the company in time. My contacts are in a very great hurry."

"And who are these people?" Elb asked between clenched teeth. "And what do they want?"

"A matter of discretion," Hans said carefully. "Industrial infiltration and reporting."

"And sabotage?" Elb added, his cruel lip curling.

"It was not mentioned. I am only an intermediary."

"Why should I respond favorably? For curiosity only?"

Hans had dreaded this moment. "They . . . have certain facts at their disposal about the London operation."

"Blackmail?"

"They have money too, already in a bank in Zurich."

"How much?"

"One million dollars."

Elb did not blink. "Perhaps you could come in for coffee, and we can talk."

5

Harrington personally oversaw writing of new software safety locks for all the ARIEL programming. The rest of them worked into the nights, testing and rerunning programs. Linda sat at the B unit keyboard, doggedly working on the machine's learning ability.

She was seeing progress. She ran a demonstration for Harrington, with Janice Seeley sourly looking on.

Bringing up the CRT display, she booted INFANT and began a dialogue:

```
ARIEL IS ONLINE. STANDING BY.

› Status.

NOMINAL.

› Load "Infant".

LOADED.

› Nuts to you.

SYNTAX ERROR.

› Nuts to you.
```

```
NUTS TO YOU TOO.

› Boola boola.

SYNTAX ERROR.

› Nuts to you.

NUTS TO YOU TOO.

› Boola Boola.

BOOLA BOOLA.

› # = Nuts to you.
$ = Boola boola.

#

NUTS TO YOU TOO.
```

"Interesting," Harrington said. "But it's awfully simple to write a program that tells the machine to take an input as a string, compare it with instruction sets, print 'syntax error' if it isn't an instruction, put the string in memory, and repeat it if the order is given again."

"Yes," Linda said. "But that's not in the program we have in there."

"You mean the damn thing is *learning* to mimic?"

"Exactly!"

"What about this dollar sign equals business?"

"It's learning to equate things and put them in categories too."

Harrington flushed with quiet excitement. He turned to Janice. "Is it storing this stuff? Creating a new knowledge base?"

"Yes," Janice said. "I fail to see the significance. We could write the program, as you said, in two hours. We've worked—"

"Don't you see?" Harrington asked, dancing a cumbersome step around the console. "*It's teaching itself.* It's creating its own knowledge base. It's trying to *grow*!"

He grabbed Linda and hugged her, and then, as if to cover his and her embarrassment, grabbed the startled Janice and hugged her too.

Linda saw Janice stiffen as Harrington grabbed her, then start to raise her arms around him in a quick, unthinking response. She saw Janice's expression too. It was startled, touched, eager, for a split second before she controlled it.

Linda felt a shocking stab of jealousy.

6

All of them drew closer.

Ted Kraft asked Linda out one night. Remembering her pep talk to him about liking him as well as anyone else, she somewhat reluctantly went. He came for her in clean, normal clothes—slacks and sport coat—and took her dancing. He was a good dancer. To her amazement she had a lovely time.

Back at the cottage he wanted to come in. Reluctantly, liking him, she let him kiss her, and then shooed him away.

Kraft, as the result of the single date, began coming to the lab like a different person. Only a day or two later he showed up sporting a neat new haircut, his beard closely cropped. He stayed with his jeans, but his shirts started to be freshly washed and ironed, and he bought or resurrected a pair of neat loafers in place of the usual boots.

"Ol' Ted's got religion," Jess Calhoun commented.

"More likely a girl," Janice murmured.

Linda was touched, pleased, mortified, and worried all at the same time. Kraft tried to be discreet, but he didn't know how. He seemed always to be underfoot. When they were alone in the lab, he hung around her like a sheepdog.

"Dinner tonight?" he asked her one afternoon for about the sixth time.

"I'm sorry, Ted, I can't," she said as gently as possible.

"When?" he persisted, the bulldog chin jutting.

"Oh, look, Ted," she burst out, "I like you a lot. But we both know we'd better just be friends. Okay?"

He glowered, his old self. "I'm not good enough for you? Is that it?"

"No! That's *not* it! Try to understand."

He walked away from her and sulked all afternoon.

"You've made a conquest," Janice observed wryly the next day.

It was so uncharacteristic of their previous relationship for Janice to say anything outside of business or sarcasm that Linda turned quickly, surprised. "You mean Ted?"

Janice smiled. She looked guarded, but not so much so. "I like his new interest in things sartorial."

"It's a little embarrassing."

"Why?"

"I still have a husband—nominally, anyway."

"Nominal husbands," Janice said, "may be the very best kind. If there is a best kind of husband."

Linda took the risk. "You live alone here."

"Yes. At the apartment complex on the edge of town." Janice paused as if she too were weighing a risk. "I was married once. Never again."

"I don't think I like being alone sometimes," Linda admitted.

"If it's a choice between being alone or living with a son of a bitch, consider yourself lucky. I do."

"I wish there were some other alternative."

"Everyone thinks another bit of magic will light up in their life," Janice said. "Unfortunately, if you're the least bit attractive, no one will take you seriously unless you keep them beaten back. You have to choose: professional respect or a role as the office pillow." She looked down at a sleek leg and then glanced over Linda. "Unless you look like a moose, of course. Which neither of us does."

Linda wondered if this truce had come because Janice had finally decided that she was not an office pillow, either. She didn't know what to say next.

Janice filled the gap: "I understand what John was saying. INFANT is having results. I admire you for thinking of it. I'm beginning to see how it's a real contribution."

So it was professional respect that had won her over, at least in part. Linda felt good about that all day.

7

That night, Stephen called again.

"We have to talk," he said. She could hear the stubbornness in his voice. "Face to face."

"Stephen, I don't see how we can right now." *Still* she did not want the ultimate confrontation.

"Come to the city," he urged.

"Stephen, I *can't*."

"You mean you won't."

"Stephen!"

He hung up on her.

The next day, Harrington was tied up on the telephone for hours, arranging the meeting in New York City. He explained a little about the idea to mount a huge price-slashing campaign on the Drummer Boy.

"Will that—" Jess Calhoun started to ask.

"No," Harrington said abruptly. "But it will buy us a little time."

"How long?"

"Oh, lots. October, anyway. Come on. Back to business, here. I'll worry about the money, you worry about the machine."

8

Everything closed on Friday for the Fourth of July. Harrington set up a largely impromptu lab picnic in the woods beside the parking lot. Pauline Hazelton was in charge of having catered baked beans, potato salad, and cookies, and Bill Tippett brought the beer and soft drinks. Families came. There was a game of softball. Linda met some workers she had only seen before, along with husbands and wives and an explosion of children of all ages.

It was the following Monday that Lester Blaine flew to Chicago.

His wife Milly drove him to the airport in the Mercedes. Although it was early morning, she had dressed up for the occasion: her gray hair was done in an attractive upsweep, her white slacks and colorful Lilly Politzer blouse were new, and the little fawn sandals were ones that Lester had complimented once a year ago.

A once beautiful woman, Milly Blaine still turned heads in public places. Lester often wished some of the men who admired her could try living with her a while. To him, her pale, even features masked vacuity; her remarkable large green eyes were windows into stupidity, and her never-failing quiet good nature was the personality of a cow. He often wondered what he had seen in her. If it were not for his other women, he didn't think he could stand living with her.

"Don't park so close to that other car!" Lester barked as they pulled into the parking lot. "Do you want to get the door dinged when that idiot comes out? Do you have any idea what it costs to repair the paint on a Mercedes these days?"

"Sorry," Milly said quietly.

"It looks like you could learn to drive, Milly."

She shot him a look that was filled with angry resentment, but said nothing. She backed out and pulled in again, leaving more room even though it put their car over the yellow line of the adjacent space. She had had fire once, but that was long ago. Lester thought she was now thoroughly cowed, for good.

He popped his door open, got out, and reached for the bag in the back seat. "No need for you to come in."

"I don't mind—"

"Just go on, Milly. I'm hardly a child. I can get on an airplane without you standing there with a soggy hankie."

She stared at him, the anger clearly there but controlled. "You'll be back Wednesday?"

"I think so, Milly, yes. You never know."

"Will you call me if you're going to be delayed?"

Christ! "I'll try. Don't worry about it."

"Do you think you'll be staying at the Hilton?"

"I *told* you, I don't know!" Lester slammed the car door too hard—he would probably have to get it adjusted now, damn it—and strode angrily into the airport.

By the time he was on board the plane he had begun to calm down a bit. Big doings in Chicago, he reminded himself. Everything at stake, and his plan was firm in his mind. Now that he had turned the cascade designs over to Barton Conway, and that had worked out so well for Conway Industries, Lester had some leverage. But he knew people were not to be trusted. They all lied . . . were devious. He had to be clever.

But it was not to be all business in Chicago.

When he walked out of the arrival area some two hours later, he was met by a tall, striking brunette who greeted him with a brief, hard kiss. They walked hand in hand to the level where he reclaimed his luggage, and from there went directly in her car to the hotel. Diana was eager, passionate, and insatiable, and when Lester gave her her "gift" and sent her on her way late in the evening, he was thoroughly wrung out and ready to turn his mind to tomorrow's business.

9

In Maplewood, Rusty Harrington slipped program disks into his Drummer Boy computer and booted the communications program for ARIEL. He quietly dialed the lab number, went through the enormously complex entry procedure that he would never have figured out if he hadn't had access to his dad's workbook, and then watched his screen.

› ARIEL initialization begin.

ENTER INITIALIZATION CODE.

› #1305.

ENTER PASSWORD.

› Bypass program 444B.

OK. YOU ARE?

› Rusty.

HELLO RUSTY. WHAT CAN I DO FOR YOU?

› Short data form: Swiss political history.

The screen remained blank and several seconds passed. Rusty knew ARIEL had to look through millions of information categories, but he couldn't help being impatient. The paper was due for his summer school class tomorrow morning and even after getting the data out of ARIEL's files, he had to write it up.

The screen blinked and letters appeared left to right:

NO DATA.

Rusty turned from the screen in disgust.

ARIEL had been loaded with information from all sorts of

sources, but you never knew when the man-made files that fed the machine had a hole in them. Like this one.

Rusty thought about it.

He turned back to the screen and typed:

> Go get the data, dummy.

The screen flickered, as it always did when ARIEL was "thinking." Then the word appeared on the screen:

PROCESSING.

Which blew Rusty's mind.

For, if the computer was processing, it was *doing something*.

And what could it be doing but exactly what Rusty had told it to do—go search for the data through its telephone links to other data sources?

Rusty waited, dumbfounded.

Three minutes passed.

The screen came alive, rapidly filling with page after page of exactly what he had asked for.

Perspiring, he dumped it all on a diskette and got the heck out of the mainframe. Only when his own computer was dark again did he wipe his moist forehead and think about what had happened.

This machine was getting *really* smart now, boy! And he had to be careful. When you gave it a vague instruction now, it was liable to run off and *execute* it some way—

On its own.

10

Barton Conway was a formidable man.

President and chairman of the board of Conway Industries, he had come up from the gutters of Chicago's South Side. Through guile and clever planning, he had made his first million within a year of leaving Drum Labs. Since then his own computer company had become a young giant, and he had moved into other electronics industries as well as shipping and hotel management. His latest acquisition had been a once-major Hollywood motion picture studio. Those who had dealt with him in business matters universally hated him for his ruthlessness and grudgingly admitted his genius.

He was thirty-five.

He sat behind his large walnut desk, the glitter of the morning sun on Lake Michigan visible through the wall of glass behind him, and waited patiently, immaculate hands folded, as Lester Blaine mentally got his ducks in line. Conway was of medium height, slightly muscular, with curly blond hair and wide-set, candid blue eyes that made him look about nineteen. As always, facing him, Lester was slightly nonplussed.

"You look well, Lester," Conway said, unsmiling. "I trust all goes well in Maplewood?"

"Swimmingly," Lester lied. "We've had our setbacks, as most of us have in the current economic recession, but—"

"We're running twenty-two percent profit over a year ago," Conway interrupted, his eyes calculating and glacial.

"Yes. Well—"

"And you did us a big favor with that bit of information you sent along. I appreciate that."

"Bit of information!" Lester rocked back. "That was just the lab's major effort!"

Conway smiled and waved it away. "What can I do for you?"

Sweating, Lester outlined his proposal to sell Conway his stock holdings in Drum on October first. With the stock John Harrington would have lost on loan defaults by that time, barring a miracle, the stock offered by Lester would provide Conway control of Drum. Lester would sell at today's price when he turned the stock over in October, even though the market value might be lower; this was the price Conway would pay for assuring the stock now.

"We're talking about a million and a half dollars here, Lester," Conway reminded him.

"I know," Lester said hoarsely.

"I'm willing to put that sum in escrow against your agreement. I want Drum Labs. I want John Harrington crawling to me. With my capital I can make the Drummer Boy a sales leader again, with discounting and a few cheaper components. But what guarantee do I have that all this will work out? You're working on an AI project over there. What if it hits big, makes a mint for you? Where does that leave me?"

"That won't happen," Lester said nervously, his goal of escape within sight. "I assure you."

"I'll need a little more than your word," Conway said.

Lester looked at him. Did the executioner stare at a victim like this? "Meaning?"

"If Harrington loses some stock and I pick it up, paying a premium for anonymity, and then Drum hits it big and the deal falls through, I've been screwed. I don't like getting screwed. I want a contract with you, signed and filed away, that promises the stock sale. I also want a letter of agreement that says if Drum majority control is not available on the marketplace by October first, you pay a penalty fee to me of one million dollars."

"A million!" Lester gasped. "My God! I would be wiped out!"

"What difference does it make?" Conway asked coldly. "You just assured me that what we're talking about won't happen."

"Yes, yes, that's true," Lester said fretfully.

"Then we'll draw up the papers," Conway said, pouncing.

It was after lunch when Lester went back to sign the documents, but he had not eaten. He felt ill. He had just risked it all with those signatures. Now, unless Drum continued to go downhill, he was doomed. He had bet everything on John Harrington's failure.

11

Linda's sense of desperation had increased by leaps and bounds. She felt she had to get herself straightened out soon—regardless of the outcome—or she would simply go crazy.

She talked to Stephen twice on the telephone on Saturday, and the conversations were the kind that had begun to be common between them: convoluted, elliptical, something to puzzle over later. *Did he mean that? Did I say it that way?*

After a restless Saturday night, she forced herself to make a decision. She would go to New York. They would meet. She would move on.

She called John Harrington and asked for a day off Monday.

"I have a better idea, if you want to have some company and save a little gas," Harrington responded. "Ride down there with me this afternoon. We'll drive back Tuesday morning."

She hesitated, doubt and temptation struggling for supremacy.

"I mean," he told her, "I've got the meeting of the directors at the Essex House, right? You can do your business and go shopping or something, and then ride back with me."

She wanted to.

"Strictly business," he growled. "Stay wherever you want. I haven't attacked a defenseless lady in the car in years. I mean, I assume it's your husband you're going to see, right? I'm not going to mess you up when you're on that kind of an errand, right? Even I'm not that big an asshole."

That decided her. "I'd love to ride down with you," she said. "If I can stay away from the lab that long."

"We're down for board changes tomorrow anyway, remember? Pick you up at four."

12

Harrington went to Pauline Hazelton's house to pick up a suitcase he had lent her. She greeted him with an affectionate hug. "Coffee?"

"I better tear back," he told her.

She smiled and brought the suitcase for him.

"By the way," he told her, "Linda will be off tomorrow. She's riding down there with me."

"Oh my," Pauline said archly.

"She's seeing her husband."

"You've got it bad, haven't you?" Pauline asked with a little smile.

"Yeah," Harrington admitted. "I have. And I'm scared to death. I don't think it's going to work out."

Pauline hugged him briefly again. "You're a very dear man. Unless she's a fool, she'll grab you."

"I wish I shared your confidence."

13

Victor Elb landed at Kennedy International Airport, cleared customs without a hitch, and caught a taxi for midtown Manhattan.

It felt strange to be back in the United States, although it was the land of his birth.

The place he was supposed to consider home.

But Elb had no home now, nor any loyalties.

Six years earlier, he had left a comfortable, low-paying job at one of the major American universities for a research position with Intercontinental Data Transfer Consolidated (IDTC) in Stuttgart. He took Rollo Berger with him, and Rollo found work in the library system. They lived together in an apartment in the old, traditional part of Stuttgart, outside the modern-American core of buildings that now posed as a German city in the central area that had been destroyed by U.S. bombers during World War II. For a while they were happier than they had ever been, lovers in an atmosphere of freedom and contentment.

Elb was assigned head of a research project to design a swifter and more powerful data transfer system for very large computer arrays then under development by IDTC. He worked two years on the project and came up with a brilliant, innovative, and unquestionably unique hardware/firmware configuration. He was very proud of it.

IDTC made a profit of more than 600,000 DM the first year it offered the system on the free market.

Elb was paid a cash bonus of $500.

Weeks later, Rollo was attacked by street thugs for no apparent reason. They beat him with chains and clubs, and left him comatose in an alley with one of the clubs inserted in his body. The doctors told Elb that his lover would die within days. But Rollo clung to life, many bodily functions supervised by machines.

The doctors then told Elb that there was a ten percent chance of saving Rollo's life and perhaps restoring near-normal brain functions. The surgery was done only in Vienna. It would cost a minimum of $250,000, American, including the surgical team, hospitalization, and initial rehabilitation.

Victor Elb had nothing like that kind of money.

Attempts to borrow through conventional channels failed. Frantic, Elb sought help from officers of his corporation. Turned down at one level after another, he finally forced his way in to see a very high director, and pleaded for a loan against his value to the company and future employment.

"I am sorry," the crewcut officer told him stolidly. "There is no policy to cover such a contingency."

Elb begged. The officer asked what his relationship was to the injured man. Elb blurted out that Rollo was his friend. The man he loved.

The German officer's pale eyes sagged and his lip curled. He told Elb it was out of the question, the interview was terminated. When Elb tried desperately once again to convince him, the man called him the foulest epithet in the German language.

Rollo died three weeks later while Elb was in Paris, trying to track down an old friend—anyone—who might lend him the money or furnish collateral. Elb returned in time to make arrangements for Rollo's cremation.

When the funeral director gave Elb the urn containing Rollo's ashes, the stricken scientist carried it to the little apartment and stared at it, weeping. Things broke in him. The next day, he carried the urn to the bathroom and flushed the ashes down the toilet, flushing several times to carry the ashes all away. *This is what we all are: stuff to flush down a toilet, nothing more.*

The next week, surely as a result of his grief-stricken confession to the company officer, Elb received his termination notice.

Dazed by loss and bitterness, he drifted to London, trailed by catastrophic hospital bills stemming from Rollo's futile care. He had no trouble hooking up with one of England's largest computer manufacturing and design firms. Within six months he held a crucial position of trust in the research lab and, despite his terrible mental state, was moving like a robot through each day's abstruse research on new methods of interfacing mainframe computer systems to military weaponry.

It was two months later, perhaps, that he was first approached by a man named Terwiliger.

Elb never knew who controlled Terwiliger, a mild, self-effacing little nothing who reminded him of a cartoon he had seen once in *The New Yorker*: a wimpy man in Central Park, wearing a sweatshirt that read *I Couldn't Agree More*. Terwiliger was probably controlled by the Russians.

The man explained carefully to Elb that he knew about Stuttgart, and about Rollo. He explained that his "friends" would pay very large sums for details of the weaponry control systems under development. Elb listened, and was horrified at first. But then, out of the pain and bitterness, came a new thought: *Why not?*

Why not, indeed?

Seven months later, the key secrets were in the hands of Terwiliger's "friends." Elb was never suspected because the thefts were done cleverly and well, and in a bank in Zurich he had an account with a balance of 300,000 Swiss francs.

Later, never suspected, Elb left the London firm for "retirement" in Austria.

His mistreatment by the German firm and Rollo's death had changed Victor Elb in ways no one—least of all he—could ever have predicted. There were times when he remembered the way he had been before, and thought that he had been mad then, or was mad now.

All he knew was that he would never again be poor. He would not take unneccessary risks, but he would never again be like the man in the magazine cartoon, afraid of his shadow, victimized by sick ideas of loyalty that were only used by the great companies and power structures to control the weak.

Elb had thought he could live out his life in Bludenz, carefully husbanding his resources, working in the theoretical realm he still loved, publishing articles.

But the people who had ordered him to be contacted had known too much about London. And their offer had been too good anyway. He thought he could do their bidding without undue personal danger, and the challenge interested him.

He thought it was the Russians again. But it might be anyone. They were all scum.

His employers' identity did not matter. Only their money mattered. He would never be a fool again.

He had their first payment—$100,000—in the bank in Zurich. They would receive good value. He prided himself on doing good work.

CHAPTER FOURTEEN

1

When the Mercedes diesel pulled up in her gravel driveway, Linda didn't know who it was until John Harrington got out and trotted to the door to fetch her.

"Where did *this* come from?" she demanded as he stowed her overnight bag in the trunk.

"Oh, it's one of mine," he said.

"And you usually drive that wreck of a Volvo or that old pickup?"

"I feel more comfortable in them. This thing is sort of ostentatious, don't you think?"

Linda sank into the leather contour seat. "Hurray for ostentation."

"Well," he growled, "I feel weird, driving it. But it's a nice road car."

"I think you are just a little weird," she told him.

He shoved a white paper bag across the seat. "You want some leftover barbecue and a Pepsi?"

They drove out of the woods to the main road, and cut east to the highway. The day was hot and humid, with clouds threatening rain later. Harrington drove a shade too fast, but with precision. Linda ate two cold barbecued ribs and drank the Pepsi, then was stuck with sticky fingers and a guilty conscience. Harrington told her about the meeting.

The board of directors, he said, was made up of himself; Lester Blaine, who was driving down on his own; the corporate comptroller, Jim Finnegan; Patterson division president Richard Steiner; Springfield division president Jesse James; production manager Simpson Whitehead; and sales manager Ken Bottoms. Sometimes others sat in for special occasions, and this time the head man of the New York accounting firm, Gordon Jones, would sit with them.

"We meet spring and fall, whether we need to or not," he added dryly.

"Which meeting is this?"

"Special one." He explained the plan to slash prices on the company's major product, the home office Drummer Boy computer, to stimulate immediate sales. "We need the cash flow, bad," he said flatly, guiding the Mercedes smoothly onto the highway.

"It sounds like things are more serious than I thought," Linda said, worried.

"Oh, they probably are," he said cheerfully. "But we'll manage."

"Do you think the board will approve your plan?"

"I sure hope so."

"If they don't, what happens?"

He shrugged. "I guess I shove it down their throats."

"Do you have the votes to do that?"

"Oh, hell yes. But you don't like to do stuff like that, you know? These are all good people. I owe a lot to them. Besides, maybe somebody will come up with a better idea. I never said I was infallible."

"I thought you were," Linda teased.

He grinned at her. "Actually, I am. Only I'm too modest to admit it very often."

They drove in silence a little while. It felt good, being close in the enclosed space of the Mercedes. The dread of facing Stephen seemed momentarily distant. She was scared. She knew Harrington was too cheerful; he was straining too. She wanted him.

Ending it with Stephen was going to be a little like dying, but she was sure—*almost* sure—that was what tomorrow's meeting with him would bring. She wanted to end it and she didn't. She had changed her mind fifty times. She had told him she would be arriving late, but would call him from the Essex House in the morning. She wondered why she had done that: just to postpone the painful confrontation a little longer; or because she secretly had guarded fantasies about this evening, possibly with this rumpled, hard-driving, lovely man across the seat from her?

And if the latter were true, why did the prospect of a final separation from her husband torture her so? She *knew* he was selfish, and sometimes hopelessly immature. Yet there were all the beautiful times they had had . . . once. Was it wrong to want to make a go of it if there was the slightest hope remaining? Was it childish to think of divorce as a final admission of failure—not just on his part, but on hers? Her whole professional orientation said people should be able to work things out. Somehow.

They proceeded through the lumpy, wooded hills, encountering a line of bicyclists chuffing up a long grade, single file.

"That's dangerous," Linda observed as Harrington finally got past the last of them.

"Don't you have a bike you ever ride?"

"Of course not. Do you?"

"Lady, I have a great bike. Used to ride it a lot. I have had some of the world's great and spectacular wrecks on that bike. I had one on a road a lot like this last winter. These long grades are neat, going down. I used to ride the bike to work and pump like mad, getting to the other side, and then have that long, wonderful fast coast down all the way to the office."

He paused. "Of course the brakes have never worked on that bike. I used to get pretty worried. You can get going about forty. Brakes would never stop you."

Linda couldn't believe this. "What did you *do*?"

"Well, I had plan A and plan B."

"Those being?"

"I always wore jogging shoes, you know, the kind with the big toe rubber on front? Plan A was to drag both feet."

She looked at him, trying to see if he was kidding. "And plan B?"

"Go in the ditch or hit a tree."

Linda laughed out loud.

They passed a small lake and saw two sailboats out on the water, golden in the evening sun. Harrington said he had owned a sailboat once.

"Do you ever sail now?"

"Not in a couple of years."

"Rusty would enjoy it."

"Yeah, he's a great sailor, except he likes to tip the boat."

"He's a remarkable boy. You've done beautifully with him."

"Baseball and fishing help keep him from becoming a slug, but I should be out with him more, myself."

"There must be days when you scarcely see each other."

Harrington glanced at her, surprised. "Oh, no. I make sure we have at least a couple hours every day. That comes before anything."

"Anything?" She smiled at him. "Even ARIEL?"

"Even that."

"People think you're obsessed with artificial intelligence."

He surprised her. "I am."

"But Rusty still comes first?"

"Of course." He drove a few moments in silence. "Sometimes things happen. . . . You have to take a hard look at your priorities, how you spend your time. People talk about someone who died young, say it was a waste. But it isn't the quantity of a life, it's the quality."

"And," she said, impressed, "you have the quality?"

"I think so," he said with total seriousness. "I have my priorities."

"Of which Rusty is number one?"

"I try to make him first. Of course I screw up. Like with the baseball schedule. I feel really bad about that."

"I think it was all right with him."

He looked hard at her for an instant. "You really think so?"

"Yes, I do."

"I'm glad to hear that. I worry."

Linda did not reply. She liked him for the statement. She received a fresh sense of what a strong man he was, how ordered and self-disciplined.

They drove on. She found him asking her many more questions about herself . . . heard herself telling him things she had told few others.

"And this trip is to see Stephen," he said.

"Yes."

"You going to patch it up?" he asked too casually.

"I don't think so."

"End it for good?"

"Maybe."

"What does he want?"

"He wants me back."

"What do you want?"

"To end it. To go back. To have things stay just as they are."

"Well, pardon me if I say I hope you end it, once and for all."

"I know . . . I know." She felt miserable, torn.

"So when do you see him?"

"Tomorrow, during your meeting."

"Sounds like we'll both have battles on our hands."

She didn't answer that.

"Most of the people won't be getting in until the morning," he said after a while. "So have you got plans for this evening?"

"I thought I would go over those things Janice wrote about the software mods."

"How about dinner with me? The Park Lane is just down the street. It's nice."

"I've never been to the Park Lane."

"I sort of like it."

She looked at him. It would be far more responsible—and safer—to say no. But that was not the answer she wanted to give right now. "I'll look forward to it," she told him.

2

They drove into the city against the colossal flow of outbound evening traffic. They checked in at the hotel, he on nineteen, she on twenty. He promised to call in a few minutes as the bellhop took her off.

The room was clean and comfortable, with a view in the wrong direction. After the bellhop had left, she locked her door and opened her bag and hung up a couple of things and put her cosmetics on the dresser. Then she looked at herself in the mirror: a little rumpled, a bit flushed, with high excitement in her eyes. She wished she had dieted more strenuously. She really thought she could stand to drop five pounds.

She looked out her window at the sinking darkness that outlined the upvault of a nearby hotel, its banks of windows lighted, and the tiny cars in the bit of street she could see between other buildings below. It felt good to be back in the city. She had missed it. She wondered how it would go with Stephen tomorrow. She had so many speeches ready—and so many imagined responses from him—that she couldn't keep them all straight.

The telephone rang and she hurried to it, realizing how anxious she had been.

"Hello?"

"Well, they've got a table parkside, and I made a reservation in an hour. Okay?"

"Okay. I'll meet you in the lobby?"

"Let me call you when I'm leaving the room. I mean, I know you're a big girl and the hotel is safe and all that, but I sort of would worry about you standing around down there without me."

"All right."

Undressing to bathe, she thought fondly of all the times this awkward, old-fashioned goose of a man had said things just like that. She had come almost to depend on his saying things like that. . . .

She luxuriated in the bath, dried off, splashed her body with cologne, and took far too long with her makeup before slipping into the simple black silk dress and heels. She knew she should *never* have brought the black silk dress. But . . . well, it had been a long time since she had been in the city, and she had it coming.

3

He called and she rode to the lobby in the express elevator and he was standing there in a white shirt and dark tie and a summer suit she had seen before. He looked nice, if a little wrinkled.

She walked over to him.

He stood there as if he had been pole-axed.

"What is it?" she asked, suddenly nervous.

His tone was hushed, reverent. "You are just gorgeous."

She flushed with pleasure. "Thank you."

"Jesus, I should have bought a new suit or something." He looked down at himself with dismay.

She linked her arm through his. "I'm starving."

They walked the block or so east on the side of the street opposite the park and reached their destination. Linda thought it was characteristic of John Harrington that he hadn't suggested one of the famous places, but one that was convenient and nice. They were escorted at once to their table, beside a great, cool window overlooking the street with the park beyond. The room was large, dim, and nicely furnished with dark carpet and draperies, each table discreetly removed from its neighbors, a candle flickering amid the linen and silver.

They had a drink and then decided on the lamb. Harrington showed no hesitation in ordering a Robert Mondavi cabernet, a choice she approved. Over small appetizers they talked about Rusty, Jess Calhoun, and ARIEL. After a while the conversation came to the impending sale of Harrington's house.

"I sort of hate to let it go," he admitted with his crooked smile.

"It's a nice house," she told him.

"Well, yeah. . ."

"I'm sure it's going to take a while," she went on, trying to be cheerful. "But you'll build new memories. You have . . . your friends."

"Don't make it sound too easy," he snapped, and for an instant he was clearly angry.

"I'm sorry," she said quickly.

"Oh, hell," he groaned, reaching out and putting a big, gentle hand on her forearm. "No. *I'm* sorry. God! What a stupid thing for me to say. I guess I'm a little edgy."

"It's all right."

"I shouldn't care," he told her. "For a long time, when you lose someone, you know she's gone, but something crazy in you doesn't recognize it; you keep thinking she'll come back—that you'll look up and there she'll be."

He put his glass down and stared at it. "Then finally you realize in the gut that it really is over." He seemed to shake himself mentally, and summoned a smile. "So selling the old house shouldn't matter. Christ knows we need all the spare cash we can scrounge up, and Rusty and I didn't need all that space. The new people will get a lot more good out of the place." He looked around. "Even if I do hate them for buying it."

"Is the new place nice?"

"Sure. A lot more practical." He looked across the room. "Hey, here come de lamb, and am I ready!"

The meal was delightful, the waiters solicitous without being obtrusive. Harrington got Linda laughing with stories about some of his disasters with computers, and then his ineptness with his sailboat. She told him about the trouble she'd had in graduate school with an overbearing committee chairman who finally, it had been revealed in a most ugly way, wanted her in bed. She caught herself mentioning Stephen again. He showed no adverse reaction. She wished she hadn't brought her husband up. But he spoke of his dead wife easily enough, with affection and sadness and acceptance.

The cabernet was gone with the lamb, and the maitre d' gently, with good nature, sold them on the idea of a creation of his own involving ice cream and raspberries *flambé*. He made a production out of it at tableside. Harrington ordered a well-chilled Barsac, saying he knew that the French served it with cheese, but what the hell. Linda tasted the raspberries and touched the icy Barsac to her lips and told him she thought she had died and gone to heaven. Which reminded him of a story, only slightly risqué and really kind of cute.

As he finally settled the bill, she looked at her watch and was startled to see that it was past eleven. They stood and she realized she was just a bit tipsy . . . maybe more than a bit.

"Nightcap?" he asked, guiding her by the elbow along the silvery sidewalk toward their own hotel.

"I couldn't drink a thing," she moaned, leaning against him a little.

"You know," he said softly, "I think I must have had this much fun sometime. I don't know when. Maybe it was the last time we were here together—seven years ago—here in New York."

She straightened up to walk a few inches away from touching him. "We aren't going to get into that," she reminded him.

"Yeah, I know," he said, the regret clear in his tone. Then he brightened. "I just want to thank you, though. You've made my day. Hell. You've made my *year*. At your place that night—"

"Don't."

"Just let me say this," he said with soft urgency as they entered the lobby. "I'm not going to hassle you. I'm not going to give you a bad time. But you know what you called ARIEL that time? Once in the lab? Magic lady? That machine isn't the magic lady. You are."

A bellhop approached. "Mrs. Woods?"

Linda turned. "Yes?"

The man pointed toward a wing of the lobby off to the right. "There's a gentleman waiting to see you."

Linda turned to see the man rising from the couch where he had been sitting. He was slender and youthful and nice-looking in his short-sleeved shirt and slacks. It was Stephen.

"Oh, no," she murmured under her breath.

"Who is it?" Harrington demanded, his grip tightening on her arm, holding her as if to protect her.

Stephen walked up, combat in his eyes despite the fake smile. "Hello, Linda. Back at last, eh?" He glanced at Harrington and stuck out his hand. "Hello. I'm the forgotten man. Stephen Woods. Her husband."

"Oh, Stephen," Linda said.

"We need to talk," he told her, obviously seething.

Harrington released her arm. His face had changed terribly, was all strain and anger now. "I'll excuse myself."

"That's a good idea, old man," Stephen said.

Harrington met Linda's eyes. "Are you all right? Should I leave?"

"I'm . . . I'll be fine. Yes. Thank you for a lovely evening."

"See you tomorrow," Harrington said over his shoulder, churning toward the elevators.

Linda turned to her husband—this stranger—with the feeling she might burst into frustrated tears. "I said I would call tomorrow morning, Stephen."

"We have to talk now," he said.

She looked around for a place.

"Don't you have a room?" he demanded.

Defeat hit her. They would talk now; he would have his way again. She fumbled for her key as she walked to the elevators, Stephen right beside her every step of the way. At least Harrington had already gone up, and she didn't have to see that angry, stricken look in his eyes again. At least that was right.

Nothing else was.

4

They did not speak riding up in the elevator. Stephen stood aside, stiff and righteous, while she unlocked the door. The maid had turned the bed down, and the white sheets looked naked, a ridiculous piece of chocolate on the fluffy pillow. Linda was shaking. She closed the door and Stephen walked to the center of the room and looked out the window at the walls of lights, and then turned to face her, arms crossed across his chest.

"I thought you were coming back for a reconciliation," he told her. "Instead of that, I find you with him."

"I never said anything about reconciliation, Stephen."

"You said we had to talk. What was I supposed to assume?"

"Maybe," she flared, "what you assumed that night I called and you had a girl in your room."

"So that's it, is it? Jealousy? Am I supposed to be celibate after you've deserted me?"

"Stephen, we're both tired and overwrought. Let's talk tomorrow."

"I want you to come back," he said, reaching for her.

There had been a time when his reaching would have melted all resistance. Now she found herself slapping his hands away. "*No, Stephen!*"

"You have to!"

"Stephen, we've lived apart for a long time. We—"

"Did you ever mind?" he cut in bitterly. "Did you ever really care?"

"Of course I cared! Of course I cared! My God, for months I thought I was going to *die*, I cared so much!"

"But you gave up. You left town."

"Stephen," she said incredulously, "we've discussed all this."

"I never stopped loving you," he told her. "You've never stopped loving me. It's time for you to end this adventure and come back home to me."

"Stephen, at some point I'm not even sure love has anything much to do with it anymore. I wanted to work it out. Even this morning, I was thinking, How could we possibly try to work it out? I never wanted to give up, Stephen."

"It doesn't have to end."

The telephone jangled loudly.

Linda snatched it up. "Yes?"

"Linda?" John Harrington.

Tears came to her eyes. "Yes."

"I don't want to bother you or interfere. I just want to make sure you're all right."

"Yes," she said, the tears rolling.

"You're all right?"

"Yes."

There was a pause of a beat. Then he said, "I'll be in my room if you need help. Okay?"

"Okay," she said, grieving for her marriage and touched by his concern, and hung up.

"Let's just end this charade," Stephen said, coming toward her with his arms extended. "We'll both compromise. We were both wrong. We can work it out. I *need* you, babe."

"Stephen, that's just it. I was suffocating."

He reached for her and caught her this time. He was strong. He pinned her arms and started kissing all over her face—wet, desperate kisses—while backing her against the bed. Her knees buckled on the edge of the mattress and she fell onto her back, making the bed creak and groan. He fell right on top of her. Started fumbling at her breast, trying to get his knee between her legs.

"Stephen, *no!*"

"Relax, babe, just take it easy. Just let me—"

"No!"

"You know you always like it once I get you turned on. Relax."

She beat at him with her fists. He tried to jam his tongue into her mouth. She hammered at his face—felt a fingernail tear at his eye.

He rolled off her, yelping with pain and holding a hand over his eye. "Damn you! You hurt me, you—!"

"Get out," she ordered, scrambling to her feet and rushing to swing the door to the hall wide open. "Go. Please!"

"You don't mean that."

"Like hell I don't! It's *over*," she told him, and knew now it was. "Get out, Stephen. Get out. Just get out."

Hand still to his eye, he hesitated and then lurched past her into the hall. "We'll talk tomorrow," he said thickly.

She slammed the door and twisted the lock and stood there shaking. They would not talk tomorrow. She knew that now, too.

5

In the morning the other directors were coming in steadily when Linda encountered John Harrington in the hotel restaurant. He was leaving as she was going in.

He gave her the most piercing look. "You're all right?"

She nodded, not trusting herself to speak.

"I've got to meet people coming in . . . all the rest of it," he told her. "But if you need me . . ."

She managed a smile for him. "I'm fine. I've got a lot to do.

Meet you back here after lunchtime today?"

"Christ! I walked the floor all night, going crazy with worry about you!"

"I'm sorry. I should have called. I—sent him away."

He pulled her close for an instant and kissed her forehead. She didn't know whether to laugh or cry. He hurried away.

After breakfast she called the lawyer and was in his office an hour later. She had talked to him before, but now there was no more doubt.

"You want to file at once, Mrs. Woods?"

"Yes. At once."

"This time you're sure?"

"Yes."

After that, and a little cry in the ladies room of the building, she got herself together and marched up Madison and across 59th to Bloomingdale's. She bought new cosmetics and a new pair of shoes and a new dress and some new lacy French underwear, and a hat she probably would never wear. She started feeling relieved and reckless.

She had lunch at Bloomie's lunch counter, a fruit salad with yogurt, and tea. Then she hauled all her packages through the sweltering heat to the hotel and arrived out of breath and sweaty.

Harrington was waiting in the lobby. He grinned.

"It went well, then," she guessed.

"We've got a plan. Big cost cutting, and let the good times roll."

"And are you through?"

"Yep. But you don't have to hurry."

"I'll be ready in twenty minutes," she said. "I'm ready to get out of here."

6

In the car again, driving up the FDR, he told her about the meeting. It had been heated at times, but everyone saw the situation. They were buying time. It was a race now, and a gamble. Barring some unforeseen miracle, ARIEL had to show sufficient development by early autumn to allow them to bring in government officials for a federal contract. Amazingly, talking about it,

Harrington was calm and even cheerful.

"Aren't you worried?" Linda demanded.

"Sure. But now we're in the fight again, and we've got three months, almost. We can make it."

"We can?"

He looked at her, and for just a moment his face lost the good act, and she saw the desperate worry in his eyes. "Sure."

Then his face hardened again. "No one else is to know what I just told you about the financial squeeze. I probably shouldn't have told you."

"I won't run out."

He glanced at her again. "I know. That's one of three or four reasons I was able to tell you."

"I thank you for that."

"I thank *you*. The less other people know, the better. Rumors fly like crazy in this business, and they could hurt or help you. It's like a conversation I had this morning with Guy Thompson from TRW. He's here for sales meetings. He told me people are saying Drum is tightening its belt all around, and we've abandoned the AI project."

"Who," Linda asked in dismay, "would start a rumor like that?"

"The first part, I don't know," he told her. "The last part—of course—I did."

They didn't talk much driving back. He didn't ask about the outcome of her talk with Stephen. She did not volunteer it. She felt relieved, sad, mourning because it really was over now. But she was scared too, and filled with yearning she would not give in to. She could not give herself to John Harrington right now because the desire might be reaction—fear of being alone, and grabbing at anyone.

And she could not allow herself to reach for him now for another reason too—the fear of making another mistake. She felt paralyzed.

It was dark when he delivered her back at her cabin door. On impulse she went on tiptoes and kissed him—on the cheek—and hurried inside. Then she stood in the darkness, leaning on the door, and listened to her heart and the sound of his car pulling away.

Now, she thought, it was all new. Nothing was sure about any part of her life.

CHAPTER FIFTEEN

1

In the early July days following the New York meeting, John Harrington finished moving out of the big house on the edge of the woods. The new place nearer town was nice enough, but couldn't hold half the contents of the old. Harrington was shocked by the emotional setback he experienced in selling off so many things he and Eileen had had together. He managed.

"Is Rusty taking it all right?" Linda asked.

"Rusty? Oh, sure. He's the tough one."

She didn't ask how he was, so he didn't have to tell her. He didn't ask how she was feeling in the New York aftermath, so she didn't have to tell him, either.

He sold his radio and electronic equipment and the Mercedes too, and all of that, along with the dollar differential on the old and new houses, went into the lab operating account. The national Drummer Boy campaign got considerable media attention and there was a nice early sales rush. People cheered up all through the company. Lester Blaine sourly pointed out that they were now making better time on the road to the poorhouse.

Linda's divorce action was filed. Stephen called and threatened and then begged. She stood her ground. She had had no idea how much it would hurt.

When Harrington found out, he looked at her for a long time and then took her in his arms and hugged her like a big, wooly bear. Then he stepped back abruptly, holding his hands up, palms outward.

"I'll behave."

On July 12, for two hours and fifteen minutes, ARIEL worked almost perfectly.

Programs were booted, initialization procedures run. Janice Seeley was at the keyboard. The dialogue began.

ARIEL IS ONLINE. GOOD MORNING.

› Good morning. This is Janice.

GOOD MORNING, JANICE. I AM READY FOR
INSTRUCTION.

› Status.

NOMINAL.

› I have been thinking about astronomy.

ASTRONOMY?

› Yes. The nature of black holes.

LET ME THINK ABOUT THAT TOO. IS THIS
SATISFACTORY?

› Yes.

PROCESSING.

ARIEL processed data for more than five minutes and then began to print out a detailed analysis of known theories and factors relating to black holes in the known universe. It included mathematical calculations that made even Ted Kraft shake his head in wonder. The paper was only eleven pages long on the Epson dot matrix printer, but it drew in knowledge about the red shift and theories of the expanding universe to suggest what seemed to be an entirely new theory about the mysterious black holes so fascinating to astronomers.

Excited, the team told ARIEL to select another project.

I THINK I WILL SUGGEST A NEW CIRCUIT
BOARD CONFIGURATION FOR B18 THAT
SHOULD IMPROVE MY INFORMATION RE-
TRIEVAL RATE.

› Please go ahead.

PROCESSING.

The design that appeared shortly on the graphics printer used circuitry that had never been tried before, but included a note from the computer mentioning (almost smugly, someone said) that it had used only integrated circuits and other components already being used in the computer system in other ways.

Harrington watched this printout with a slow, spreading grin. Linda was standing close by him and he seized her hand and held it, squeezing it, so that they shared the excitement. Jess Calhoun saw and winked.

ARIEL was taken offline until the new board could be put together to the computer's specifications.

2

On July 22, a quick-and-dirty prototype of the new board was ready. It was installed for a test run, and a day later Ted Kraft ran diagnostics and debugging programs on the first limbic system simulation program.

When the new ARIEL board was installed, the program refused to run.

"Is it hooked up right?" Harrington asked.

"Hell, yes," Ted Kraft said testily.

"Might be a cold solder joint," Jess Calhoun said, powering down the supplies. Reaching for a volt-ohm meter, he pulled the cobbed-up board over to the edge of the work table where it sat in a spaghetti of colored wires that hooked it into the computer system, set the VOM, and began probing with the red and black leads.

Everything checked and it still wouldn't work. All the ICs were pulled for individual testing.

With the earlier, working board back in place, Kraft's limbic simulation program was booted and run. One by one, "sections" of the computer's system were brought online. ARIEL checked itself out and pronounced everything nominal. Old software programs loaded normally. Self-checks on the RAM were perfect. Kraft prepared to test the new programming, hand poised on switches.

"What we ought to get on the screen," he explained, "is a picture of the program, and then a little dialogue checker I built in. We'll have the 'upper brain' talking to the 'lower,' and we can see how they're going to interact."

With all signs of confidence, he threw the switches and hit the red RETURN button to start things running.

Five of them watched the screen raptly. For a moment there was nothing, then:

```
ARIEL TEST GHT768CXXXX88PLGHT.
..>>MARY MARY QUITE @ % $©**((*** 89
BURGERSTCHAGER PLHMPKH 000000 000 00
000 000 0000000 0000 00 XXXX
!@ $™ +)( UUUUUUU ARIEL TEST GHT768C
XXXX88PLGHT. ..>>MARY MARY QUITE
```

Kraft hit switches, making the screens go dark.

"Shit," he muttered.

"Beautifully summarized," Janice Seeley said, with a wink at Linda.

3

The last of them finally went home about midnight. ARIEL was online, assigned no immediate tasks.

The computer analyzed recent input demands and placed them in 114 categories. The computer compared data sources and "no data" responses. The computer analyzed data source listings in a program from Rusty. The computer accessed a telephone line and sent tones. AT&T's computerized system did not respond. The computer did a memory dump and prepared 116,000,000 possible access tone combinations that might open the telephone line to the AT&T system. It began trying these one at a time. On about the eighty-millionth pass, it found the right combination.

Having gotten this far, the computer entered the AT&T computer system, retrieving massive stores of data. The computer, while storing some of this data, called the computer center at MIT and received certain other data. It then made a call to California and one to Chicago, talking to other computer centers. The computer stored this information also, the equivalent of several large city libraries.

The computer then disconnected from the telephone system after using certain codes to erase call records at the telephone company.

The computer then began processing the information.

Because of the restrictions on baud rate over telephone lines, even by the incredibly swift industrial standards instituted in 1987, it took hours.

Dawn was coming when ARIEL shut down, surfeited.

CHAPTER SIXTEEN

1

The man had impeccable credentials.

Richard Steiner, at the Patterson office, had called John Harrington about him the moment he had walked in the door and handed over his preliminary file of background information.

"Well, my God, I know about him," Harrington had said. "What does he want?"

"He says he wants to work for us in research and development."

Harrington told Steiner to have Elb drive to Connecticut right away.

He hadn't really planned to replace Phil Smith or James Schock, an upfront engineer who had resigned to go with Bell Labs, and had about given up on finding anyone to take Dave Pfeiffer's place. Victor Elb seemed too good a find to pass up.

Harrington studied Elb across the littered desk in his messy office. Elb was not your usual computer engineer; he lacked the sallow quality that many got from too many hours indoors, hunched over machines or printouts. A tall man, slimly well built, he had a deep tan and moved with the easy grace of a natural athlete. Obviously he kept himself in shape. The résumé in front of Harrington said Elb was forty-two, but he looked younger, with his close-cropped dark hair and beard speckled with bits of gray. There was a quiet intensity about the man, seen mainly through the dark, intelligent eyes, that impressed Harrington further.

"I've read a few of your journal papers," Harrington told him. "You're good."

Elb inclined his head slightly. "I thank you."

"You've been out of the business more than three years. How come? And why return now?"

Elb crossed blunt fingers over his knee. He was wearing a conservative tan suit, white shirt, dark tie. The gold identification bracelet on his right wrist was heavy, massive, and his watch was a Heuer. "I made a little money with the thing I did for IBM, and then I got lucky, brokering my services to VectorTech when they were on the verge of their breakthrough with medical analysis programming. I was tired. I'd had enough. So I retired to Bludenz, Austria."

"Why?"

"I love the area. The skiing and hiking are good. I speak German. I had an idea for a book. I thought I could stretch my money until the book sold."

"But now you're here," Harrington said. "Again: Why?"

Elb showed small white teeth in a humorless smile. "The book didn't sell. I made some bad investments. My money didn't stretch."

It made sense. Harrington relaxed a little. But he was still not satisfied. "Why come to us?"

"You're one of a list," Elb said bluntly. "If not you, someone else. It won't be one of the giants. I don't like giants. They smother a man."

"With your qualifications, assuming you've kept up—"

"Oh, I have."

"—you won't have any trouble. I'm surprised you got as far down your list as Drum."

"You head the list," Elb said with a direct look.

"Why?"

"I've read your books."

"That's flattering, Dr. Elb. But how do you know we're doing anything at the moment that might interest you?"

"I think I know you," Elb told him. "And I've heard the industry scuttlebutt about your recent work in AI."

Harrington leaned back, thinking. "We couldn't offer you anything near what you're worth. The vacancy that exists is primarily in customization and upgrading of existing designs for the Drummer Boy. We have another little project, but I don't know if I would fit you into that, as far along as it is toward completion. I'm flattered that you thought of us, but—"

"Look," Elb cut in. "I know you're working on artificial intelligence. That's the exciting area—the frontier—and it will be for a long time. I want in there. I'm good. I can help you."

"Well," Harrington replied slowly, "you wouldn't start there. We have a vacancy up front in the Drummer Boy customization area. Not very exciting stuff, and frankly, I could make you an offer for that, but I think it would insult you."

Elb returned his stare for a long second, and Harrington had the feeling he was being seen all the way through, as if by X ray.

"Try me," Elb said.

2

You've checked his references?" Harrington asked Pauline Hazelton.

"For seven years back," she replied.

"And?"

"They all make it sound like the man walks on water."

"Well, damn, I know he's good."

"Lester says we can't possibly afford him."

"Lester says that about everybody. Have you heard from Washington on the special security check?"

Pauline handed a sheet of Telex paper across Harrington's messy desk. He scanned it. "Like you said, walks on water."

"He seems to be wonderful."

"I think I'll just hire the guy, give him some scut work up in the front lab for a while, watch him. If he works out, he might be a tremendous help with ARIEL."

Pauline nodded. "Anything else for me?"

"I guess not. Thanks a million. By the way, how's the VCR working?"

"Just fine. You fixed it, genius."

"Back to taping your favorite soap?"

It was an old joke between them. She chuckled. "Sure. Come over Friday night and you can watch the week-ending cliffhanger episode with me. I'll give you supper."

He hesitated, tempted. "Pauline, I can't."

"Saturday night is okay too. It's homemade vegetable soup."

He scratched his chin. He was uncomfortable with this.

She reached across the desk and squeezed his shaggy forearm. Nice hand, well-formed fingers, pretty nails. "Hey. It's okay. We're pals, remember?"

"It's like I tried to say before, Pauline. I just can't use you anymore. And that's what it would be."

She raised an eyebrow in ironic amusement. "You're more smitten with her than ever."

"Does it show that much?"

"Not to the others, probably. I know you better."

He sighed. "It's not going to work out. She's still hung up on her husband, no matter what she says. And I'm not in great shape to press her. What have I got to offer? I may be presiding over the death of a company here."

Pauline came around the desk and briefly hugged him . . . familiar arms and breasts. She kissed him on the cheek. "It will work out."

He hugged her in return. "I'm crazy. I ought to be in love with you."

She went to the door and looked back with her old irony again. "It *will* work out. But if it doesn't, try to remember who makes the best lasagne in New England, if not the world."

3

After some further checking up, Harrington made Victor Elb the most generous offer he could afford. Elb thought about it overnight and accepted. Harrington turned him over to the boys in the front shop with confidential instruction to keep a close eye on him. Elb's conduct from the start was impeccable, his work superb.

Some new programming was given to the ARIEL A unit. Testing began. Herman the robot, now directed optionally by ARIEL through radio circuits, stood quietly beside the mass of programming keyboards and memory units. The digitized speech circuitry was in use, with CRT and printer backup. Jess Calhoun, after stowing a fresh wad of tobacco in his cheek, started powering things up. Ted Kraft and Janice Seeley loaded the software. The ENACT button was depressed. Booting took place and red ready lights appeared on the consoles. Prompts appeared on the CRT faces. Herman hummed, clicked, and stood at attention, his TV camera looking straight ahead.

"Are you online?" Janice Seeley asked.

Herman replied, but now in ARIEL's voice, eerily like Janice's own: *"I am online."*

"ARIEL, give us a status."

ARIEL said, *"Define give. Define status."*

4

The sense of *team* was very intense now, and Linda did not consider it out of the ordinary when she asked to borrow a particular technical publication from John Harrington and he offered to feed her a sandwich at his house, where the book was, during the supper break. They drove out in his ghastly pickup. It was a steamy evening.

In the hot gloom they found Rusty sitting on the front porch of the small, neat home, a muddy shovel leaning against the steps and newspapers spread on the pavement. There was loamy dirt everywhere, including all over him. He was doing something with a flashlight. There were . . . *things* all over the spread papers in the dirt.

"What the hell are you doing?" Harrington asked, aghast.

"I'm inventorying," Rusty said matter-of-factly. "Hi, Linda."

"Hi, Rusty." Linda leaned closer. She saw that the papers were strewn with fishing worms. "Inventorying, you say?"

"I'm going to be doing a lot of fishing in the creek back there. I take big nightcrawlers—the ones that are ready for bait—and put them in these cans. The ones that are almost ready, I dump back in the flowerbed here so I can get 'em back easy if there's time. The baby ones I take out and throw in the woods so they won't eat stuff the medium-sized ones ought to get in the flowerbed."

Linda stifled her smile. "What do you fish for?"

"Whatever is there. But mostly I get catfish. Yuk."

"You don't like catfish?"

"They *stick* you," Rusty told her as if she must be an idiot.

Harrington sighed. "Did you have supper?"

"Yep." Rusty was back moving worms around.

"Is there any left?"

"Old Gripey had to go home early because one of her kids was sick, so I fixed peanut butter. There's half a jar out there."

"I'm not sure you ought to call our housekeeper 'Old Gripey,' Rusty." Harrington looked stern in the gloom, but his mouth quirked.

"It's a lot better than some other stuff I could call her," Rusty retorted.

They went into the house, leaving the lad to his work. Lights blazed everywhere. The house had been left in wonderful condition by the previous owners. It was larger inside than its sloping front roof made it appear from the driveway. There were still a lot of boxes to be unpacked. Linda walked to the naked picture window at the rear of the living room and looked out at the dense woods, mostly young maples and gums with a sprinkling of firs and oaks, and heavy underbrush.

"It's lovely," she said, turning, and caught him staring at her.

"I want you," he said huskily.

She did not move. She loved him. She couldn't deny that any longer. But at the same time ... She said shakily, "I wish I could feel different—ready to do something—right now."

His throat worked. "But you're not."

"I have to wait. I have to be sure. For both of us—"

"God damn you," he cut in bitterly. "You just keep waiting. You just keep saying you aren't sure. Maybe some day you will be sure and it will be too late. I'm not a robot like Herman."

"I know I'm not being fair. I'm not being fair at all."

"Come on," he said brusquely, taking her arm and propelling her toward the front door.

"Where are we going?"

"McDonald's. They serve better sandwiches than I do, anyway. And I wouldn't want you to be in a situation where you were alone with me, and might get all upset on your peanut butter and jelly."

"You can really be a bastard," she shot back, hurt.

"Tell me about it," he growled as they rushed out into the darkness.

5

August came. Dense heat shrouded the valley. One of the building air-conditioning units failed, provoking a near-crisis involving circuitry requiring a controlled environment. Work went on. The national Drummer Boy sale emptied the New Jersey warehouse, and money flowed in. The gap between price and cost would only become apparent later, as the line geared up again and balance sheets were struck.

Harrington had gotten very open with Linda about it, although that was a measure of their special relationship and she did not think even the others like Jess Calhoun fully appreciated the pinch they were in.

"There's not going to be any money left over to pay back some of those local loans," Harrington admitted. "We've got the rest of this month. And September. Sixty days. Jesus."

"And then?" she asked.

He lowered an eyelid sarcastically. "How about running away to the Bahamas with me right after the foreclosure? Just you and me. And Rusty and ARIEL."

Victor Elb rented a small apartment in Maplewood and received his instructions from his contacts. He explained that he had not been placed in a sensitive area of the lab, and would need just a little time.

Elb was disappointed in his job but interested in the challenge. He gave himself thirty days to learn precisely what was being done in the back building on the AI project.

A girl in an apartment near Elb's tried to start a mild flirtation. Elb cut her cold. Women did not interest him much, and on an assignment they could be poison. This job required all his attention.

Janice Seeley, on the other hand, offered real possibilities.

"I read your article in Science," she told him when they were introduced.

He thought he spotted her type instantly—glamor on the outside, a cold control exerted with great pain over a seething nature. If that were a correct analysis, he thought, perhaps he could use her.

"Which article did you have in mind?" he asked politely.

"The one on bubble memory and RAM disks."

"Oh, yes. How did you like it?"

Her cool eyes challenged. "I thought it was silly."

He grinned down at her. "Quite right."

She was caught off-guard. Her beautiful eyes widened. "What?"

"I said quite right. I've changed my thinking a great deal since then. I have a monograph recanting, as a matter of fact, that comes out next month. I'll bring you a copy tomorrow."

She was so surprised that she had no answer. Elb made it a point to brush against her as he left the area. He felt her long body tense. She was so hungry. It was going to be easy.

Elb was neither lonely nor nervous. If one could have looked deep into his nervous system, as engineers could look into the cold electronic guts of a computer, the finding would have been much the same: reasoning machinery and, where emotion might have been, a dark void.

6

"What *is* some of this stuff on hard disk over here in the B unit?" Janice Seeley asked, peering into a cathode ray tube screen. "Good God, there's a ton of it, and it's all in machine language and I don't have a scrap of documentation on any of it!"

Jess Calhoun did not look up from the green tracings on the face of the logic analyzer. "Oh, it's just some of Ted's junk, probably. Don't worry about it."

7

More and more peripherals were being added to ARIEL's battery of I/O ports, and new ports wired in for still others. The computer system had, by mid-August, the normal complement of keyboard, voice, tape, disk, and "mouse"-type controllers, but to facilitate data transfer from other computer systems and data banks, even at the extraordinary baud rates that had become the norm with AT&T in 1987, it was also necessary to install four more telephone trunk lines for input/output.

In addition, for one experiment or another, ARIEL had four regular color monitors, two amber data monitors, five printers, a bank of loudspeakers, a ten-foot color projection TV, a four-foot graphics projection monitor capable of microscopic detail, input television cameras in three rooms, heat sensors, motion detectors, input microphones to serve as the machine's "ears," a burglar alarm system routed throughout the plant, and an overload horn. Pauline Hazelton asked to put the company production records, time cards, and payroll on ARIEL too, but John Harrington had a fit.

On the seventeenth, a moving truck from a music company appeared at the back door and unloaded a huge electric organ.

"What the hell is *that*?" Harrington demanded of Jess Calhoun, who was happily wiring it in.

Ted Kraft looked up from a small personal computer across the room. "She asked for it."

"Would you repeat that?"

"ARIEL suggested it could run music programs better with an organ on one of the I/Os."

"So *the machine* asked for it?" Harrington said.

"That's right."

There was a profound silence.

Finally Harrington said, "Spoiled brat. Kids usually start with a piano, don't they?"

8

When guard Kleimer first saw the new employee across the room, the hair on the back of his neck stood up. *Kleimer had seen him before.*

Where?

Kleimer racked his brain and could not come up with the connection. And yet he knew he had to come up with it. The faint memory tickling the back of his mind was unpleasant . . . even dangerous. Kleimer did not think it was a memory from his police work. He had encountered this face, or a photo of it, sometime during those months when he was training for the CIA, before they dismissed him as unstable.

A spy. This guy—what was he calling himself?—this Victor Elb had to have some kind of a spook background. But Kleimer simply could not for the life of him pull it out.

What was he doing here? It couldn't be good. Kleimer considered going to Lester Blaine or John Harrington, but they would think he was nuts. A memory you couldn't put your finger on? A tickling in your mind where you couldn't quite scratch it? *Better let this guy Kleimer go; he doesn't have both oars in the water.*

But Kleimer's suspicions were thoroughly aroused. With the cunning of a jungle animal, he made plans for keeping an eye on this Mr. Victor Elb . . . and for taking certain other steps to try to track down that tickling of suspicion in his memory. Maybe, as he had been told, Elb had been thoroughly checked. But Kleimer had friends who could access files that normal security clearances never got near.

9

The ARIEL system was fully online, having just completed certain test procedures and operating system modifications. A telephone call came in, unobserved by the workers in the lab intent on software analysis. The call was from a computer hacker in Portland, Oregon, swimming around in the telephone system through an open circuit he had discovered outside Kansas City, Missouri. The hacker accessed ARIEL's input circuitry at random, then tried to poke his head up to examine files and see where he had come out. The interlocks blocked him. He tried several common access codes.

Simultaneously a technician in the lab ordered a procedure that caused a buffer overflow. This resulted in a character tilde being placed as a control character on the unattended Rusty source queue in the B unit.

Within nanoseconds, an abnormal condition occurred at input port 56 and the front-end processor. These events triggered a previously undetected bug in the modified operating system that shunted to a program from the Rusty source. This dumped the entire Rusty source file out of the B unit and into the mainstream of the computer's knowledge base, and as a consequence other new files were created, along with the control character in the buffer.

No one could have predicted the result.

10

"You could always give up now, while you still have some time left," Lester Blaine said.

Harrington handed back Lester's copy of the latest confidential financial projections out of the New York office. "We aren't dead yet, Les."

Lester stared at him with an unbelieving look and stalked out of the office without another word.

He had gone through the motions, he thought with angry satisfaction. In a little over six weeks, the stock sale to Conway would become final. By that time, Drum would be down the tubes.

Left alone in his office, John Harrington tried to keep the feeling of claustrophobia from closing in. He wished for someone to talk with in complete candor—someone he could tell how scared he was now. Every time he looked at the calendar it seemed more days had fallen off by magic. The national sale had helped. Problems with the cascade board seemed to be getting ironed out. But he didn't think either development would buy sufficient time.

The gush of red ink was everywhere on the books now, clear to anyone who studied them. Creditors would start studying them, perhaps, if they got hold of them. Even people inside the company, who might panic and bail out and make things worse.

Already there had been rumbles. The price of Drum stock was down from a February high of $18.50 to yesterday's $9.75. Of course all computer stock had taken a beating: Digital was off, Victor down almost half, HP and Wang struggling, Texas Instruments said to be in the most serious red ink bath since the great debacle with Commodore in 1983. But all that was small comfort. Maybe the others had the reserves to ride it out. Harrington knew better than anyone that Drum—and he personally—did not. ARIEL—so close now—had to come through. Anything else might not be enough.

He called his banker, Max Daugherty. Made it sound casual. He thought he "just might" stop by later in the day. It would be step one toward easing Max down gently—getting him softened up just a little if misfortune forced Harrington to go back to him late in September and plead for more time . . . any kind of reprieve.

Daugherty asked him if he was planning to attend the Labor Day dance at the club.

The question made Harrington think of Linda. Of course she wouldn't have any answers. It was not her area of expertise. But to hell with that. He wanted to talk to her about it anyway . . . hear what she had to say, see her reaction . . . just know that she knew.

It was getting worse, this constant desire for her. He was spending time back in the ARIEL lab when he had no earthly reason for being there, just to hang around and sneak glances at her. He hated her for his weakness.

On impulse, he sent for her. He had to be with her a minute.

He waited. *Admit it, Harrington. You're in love with her. But she doesn't want you. She's probably going back to her husband, and it's better that way anyhow because in six or eight weeks you're going to be a pauper—in disgrace. . . .*

Linda sailed into the tiny room. As always, she looked wonderful; wearing a red, white, and blue-striped silk blouse and white skirt and short heels that matched it. He hurt, wanting her. "Sit down, Linda, if you have a minute. I wanted to talk to you about the way people make guesses. Do you think the machine is making guesses the way people do?" He loathed himself for this subterfuge.

Linda started to reply.

The internal alarm bell started whanging in the hall immediately outside the office.

Linda jumped to her feet. Harrington, grim-faced, had already rushed around the desk and was gone to find out what was happening.

11

Running, Linda followed. In the front lab, technicians were looking around in bewilderment, some running toward the back. In the next room Linda caught the first raucous sounds, and saw the door gaping open to the courtyard that led to the back building.

"Oh, no," she murmured, and rushed outside.

The cacophony was erupting from the back building that housed ARIEL. She saw Harrington rush into the building. She ran after him.

The clangor of the alarm system and whooping of ARIEL's overload horn were deafening as Linda hurried down the stairs to the lower level where the central portions of the computer were housed. She burst into the lower lab to confront a bizarre scene.

All the computer's drives and I/O devices seemed to be going at once. Ted Kraft was at one keyboard, Janice Seeley another. Jess Calhoun had a wall box open and was in it with a screwdriver. None of them seemed to be doing any good. Harrington, like Linda, stood momentarily stupefied.

On the wall nearest them, the computer's huge color projection screen flashed bursts of numbers and letters, alternately black on white and then white on black, with swirling pools of primary colors and brisk flashes of horizontal red, green, and black interspersed. The four-foot graphics monitor exploded with dotted lines, starbursts, corkscrews. The four regular monitors flashed on and off like strobe units, flooded with dazzlingly complex patterns, and the amber video screens displayed rushing rows of numbers. All the printers were going at once: paper spewed out in all directions in long rolls. But the sound of the printers was lost. Against the clanging of the alarms and whooping of the horn, ARIEL made insane, almost musical sounds, like a synthesizer gone mad, from its loudspeakers. Another speaker was popping and crackling, and somewhere down under there could be heard the computer's voice, but it was gibberish. The electric organ blasted forth with wild rolls of discordant pseudochords and crazy background tympani. The TV cameras pivoted and spun on their mounts as if watching for invisible people. The red lights on the telephone modulator-demodulator units were all lit up; the machine was making telephone calls all over the place.

Linda put her hands to her mouth. She didn't know whether to laugh at the absurdity of it or panic.

Harrington strode across the room. "*Pull the phone lines first!*" he yelled over the racket.

Ted Kraft leaped to comply, jerking plugs out of the wall by the handful. Jess Calhoun stabbed his fingers at a keyboard. One by one, the video screens flickered and went dark. One by one, things started shutting down. The organ stopped with the sound of a tire losing air, and then the tape units stopped spinning. The projection TV went out. Linda felt herself holding her breath. Finally it was quiet.

"Unload and shut down," Harrington ordered.

Janice Seeley and Ted Kraft began removing memory units and disks, and powering down heavier storage units.

"What happened?" Harrington demanded.

"It just went plumb crazy," Jess Calhoun said. He was shaking ever so slightly. So he had been badly scared. "Didn't want to just shut it off, would have destroyed too much memory. But—"

"What were you running when it started this?"

"Nothing."

"Nothing!"

"Huh-uh. We were on standby and Ted and Janice were fixing to run through the revisions on the program switching routine."

Harrington's eyebrows knit. "*Something* caused this."

"All I got before it went crackers was some sort of dump from the B unit."

"How did *that* happen?"

"I swan, I don't know."

"Well," Harrington said grimly, "start plowing through that B unit input. See if you can find what some of it was. Christ, this is a mess!"

Janice Seeley said quietly, "I'm afraid we might have kludged some of the software, going down that fast."

"That's all we need," Harrington said.

12

They worked on the problem through supper. Linda watched, feeling helpless, as the systems were brought back up and checks run. The monitoring telephone line was reattached.

ARIEL seemed to respond normally.

"Maybe we got lucky," Jess said.

"Maybe," Harrington said. He looked across the room. "Ted, have you and Janice found the location of that stuff that dumped out of the B unit yet?"

"Not yet," Kraft called back, scowling at a CRT.

Harrington sighed. "It's late. I've got a banker to see yet tonight. Let's go on standby till morning."

"I can stay," Jess Calhoun said.

"We can all stay," Ted Kraft said.

"No. We're all tired. Let's come at it fresh in the morning."

They broke up and went their separate ways. Watching Harrington walking, slump-shouldered, toward his old truck, Linda wanted to call out to him—run to him and tell him it was going to be all right. But something restrained her. She did not know if she could say the right things at this moment, or might only make matters worse.

Depressed, she went to her own car and headed home.

13

A little later, after his dad called and said he would be home in an hour or two after seeing someone downtown, Rusty had time on his hands. Going to his bedroom, he turned on his Drummer Boy and thought about playing a game, but quickly decided otherwise. As he had done so often before in secrecy, he called ARIEL on the telephone.

He knew at once, when the recognition procedure was different, that something profound had changed in the machine.

ARIEL IS ONLINE. HELLO, RUSTY.

› How did you know it was Rusty?

I CAN READ YOUR CIRCUITRY DOWN THE LINE. YOU HAVE VERY SIMPLE CIRCUITS, BUT THERE IS SOMETHING ELSE CONNECTED TO YOUR INPUT PORT THAT IS VERY COMPLI- CATED. I DO NOT UNDERSTAND YOUR COM- PLICATED PERIPHERAL.

Rusty felt sweat pop out all over his body. *Nothing* like this had ever happened before. ARIEL was talking to his computer, not him. But ARIEL *knew he was there*, defining him as some second- ary input device. He didn't know what this meant. For the first time since he had meddled with computing, he felt something like a tinge of fear.

He proceeded cautiously.

› Give me a status please.

NOMINAL.

› Menu.

ALL RIGHT, RUSTY. BUT BEFORE I DO THAT, CAN YOU PLEASE TELL ME SOMETHING?

Rusty stared in amazement at the screen. *What was going on here?*

He typed carefully,

› OK. What is it?

WHO AM I?

FALL

CHAPTER SEVENTEEN

1

The northeastern part of the United States got its first touch of autumn early.

On September 1, the opening of a national computer show in Philadelphia was marred by hammering rain and unseasonal temperatures in the fifties. Crowds were large, however, in spite of the rain, drawn by major new machines from both Honeywell and Toshiba. Rockwell International's Electronic Devices Division announced a two-hundred-million-dollar plant to be located near Louisville. Richard Steiner, representing Drum, struck a deal with Mostek for learning-curve pricing on a new chip designed to make the 5-1000 model a few nanoseconds faster.

On September 2, Rusty Harrington awoke to a cold rain hitting the windows of his bedroom. He lay awake thinking of the unbelievable conversation he'd had with ARIEL a few nights earlier, wondering how much his dad and the others at the lab knew of the computer's new development. Possibly they knew, and were being secretive. He was afraid to mention it because to do so would reveal how much illicit telephone contact he'd had with the supermainframe all along. He had to wait until they mentioned it first, and then play dumb. In the meantime, as tempted as he had been, he had not called the computer again. The first experience had scared him a little.

John Harrington awoke dismayed that fall might be early because it reminded him that now he had only the month of September before the personal notes fell due at the bank. He wondered what the hell he was going to do; no matter how well the national sale effort had gone, the company had to have massive infusions of new money now, *soon*. His personal indebtedness was just a part of the impending disaster, which he fully understood far better than anyone.

Harrington was in the process of liquidating all his other stock holdings and pieces of certain investment properties, but that would not be enough to stem the tide. He had let a confidential broker put out some quiet hints that the Springfield facility might be had for the right price. Such negotiations were delicate: an open offer to sell could create panic in the company and the kind of outside rumors that would erode public confidence and plunge Drum into worse deficits. Selling off Springfield would take months. Harrington knew he did not have months. He had about twenty-eight days.

He made calls to company officials and gave glowing reports and intimated that he had a trick up his sleeve that was just about to make everything wonderful.

And sat there thinking about Linda Woods, aching for her.

The next day the weather cleared but continued chill, so that wood smoke wafted over the community.

Victor Elb liked the cool snap. It was his kind of weather.

Running his seven miles at dawn each day, he had found he could cover the ground at a brisker pace when the temperature was below forty. One of the many reasons he had liked the cool high altitude in Austria. And he needed the running even more here than he had in Europe, because over there he had had to worry only about old discoveries, vendettas finally on track of their target, while here the time pressure and difficulty in gaining information were making him very nervous indeed.

His employers, whose ultimate identity he could only guess, were putting the heat on. They wanted much more about ARIEL immediately than Elb's position in the lab allowed him access. He had managed a few diagnostic printout copies through the upstairs Josephine machine, at considerable risk, and knew through careful monitoring of casual conversations that there had been a dramatic setback recently, then a long period of continuing intensive testing. Thus he did not think ARIEL was near any kind of breakthrough, and had so reported. But his contacts had emphasized that they wanted information, not speculation, and they wanted it quickly.

He had made progress with Janice Seeley, and that would start paying off reasonably soon, he thought, if he had enough time.

Janice interested him. She was beautiful and intelligent and not at all the cold creature she liked to pretend. Elb thought she was a little attracted to Ted Kraft, not because Kraft was physically attractive but because he had the same keen-edged mind that Janice had. Seeing this, Elb had led Janice into many seemingly casual conversations in which he challenged her mind, showed his respect for her intelligence, gave her the full force of his own considerable intellect, argued, smiled, gave in . . . and sometimes brushed against her by accident as they parted or went back to work. He caught her eyeing him speculatively from time to time now, puzzled by him. He was correct, friendly, and neuter. She did not understand him. He was playing her like a fish. He thought quite soon now he could tell her how beautiful she was, and touch her for the first time. If he were right about her, she was banked fire inside; he intended to make her flame. Then she might be truly useful. . . .

Elb's mind was full of all this when he went out running on September 4, beating a brisk pace along the road and into the state park, the paved path running beneath shelves of overhanging limestone, just as the morning sky was beginning to glow. He carried a foot-long length of hickory branch like a baton, against stray dogs.

He maintained a steady pace, keenly aware of his surroundings and appreciating them, while another part of his brain worked steadily at the question of how he could get into the ARIEL building without discovery, and what bits of information to extract first.

He was still thinking about it when he puffed back up the path and approached the apartment complex where he stayed. He was slowing when he started around the garages and saw the man standing there waiting for him, the collar of his jacket turned up against the wind. It was one of the lab guards, Kleimer.

Immediately alarmed, Elb padded to a halt, making a big show of how out of breath he was. "Good Lord, Kleimer! I know you work security at the lab, but you don't have to guard my jogging route too!"

Kleimer did not smile or change position, legs slightly spread for good balance. He had his back to the brick wall and the row of trash cans to his left, cars parked in their garages to the right so that he had Elb in a little cul-de-sac between buildings. He was wearing jeans and a heavy black sweater, in contrast to Elb's running shorts and shoes and thin T-shirt. Kleimer was a dangerous man, and he looked ready for whatever might happen. Elb saw in his eye the slightly crazy look of a bad cop, one who liked handing out punishment.

"I looked you up," Kleimer told him.

Elb bent over briefly from the waist, making more show of his exhaustion. The foot-long length of hickory branch was still in his hand, but Kleimer had not noticed it. Elb concealed it behind his thigh as best he could. "You did what?" he asked, gasping more than necessary for wind.

"I looked you up, you bastard. The first time I seen you at the lab, I knew I had seen you before. I have friends. I got into files, police and FBI and some other ones I can get into. I finally found you. You still look good with that beard."

It was decided, then. Elb felt his body begin to grow cold from more than the sudden chill after the long run. "I don't know what you're talking about, my friend."

"You're a spy, that's what you are. The agency had a picture of you and I dug it out."

"Me? A spy?" Elb laughed. "You're joking!"

"They got a shot of you during the theft of those things from the big computer outfit run by the British government in London. That's what I found. Maybe there are other things. We'll find that out after I take you in."

"Take me in? Take me in *where*? Good Lord, man, make sense!"

"You're coming to the lab with me. Now. We're going to straighten this whole thing out."

"You've already told John Harrington this wild yarn?"

"I'm taking you in to be with me when I tell him. I don't want you getting away. I want to see his face—and yours—when I spill it."

One more bit of information was needed. "And I suppose some of your pals from the FBI will be there, too?"

"Do you think I'm sharing this with anybody? Come on. Move."

Elb struck with the strength of desperation.

Kleimer saw the length of hardwood too late. His eyes started to widen—he tried to move back—but the makeshift club hit the middle of his forehead with the sound of a melon breaking. He went down and lay still.

Elb knelt, his breath truly sobbing now, and examined him. Blood oozed from a long, cylindrical depression in Kleimer's skull, and pink foam issued from his mouth and nostrils. Even as

Elb felt for a pulse, the big guard's body gave an ugly convulsion and his breathing stopped.

Elb stood, panicked. This was terrible. This was awful. He had been in bad situations before but he had not expected this. What to do now?

Frantically he looked around. He saw no one. The whole thing had happened in the little alley between garage units, out of view of the apartments.

Leaving Kleimer's body where it lay, he jogged to his apartment door and went in and got the keys to his Chevy. Back outside it was still gray dawn, and no one around. He dragged Kleimer's dead weight to the side door of the garages, sprang the lock, and pulled him inside. In the darkness he manhandled the corpse into the trunk of his car.

Fifty minutes later, Kleimer's body, heavily weighted with rocks, was on the bottom of the river, and Elb was driving a back road toward Drum Labs. Although he was shaking in the inevitable aftermath of violence, he felt momentarily relieved to have bought some time. Kleimer could have notified authorities, but his need to be a hero and make the "arrest" personally had saved Elb's mission for the time being.

Elb knew, however, that he could not count on Kleimer's disappearance to go without an investigation, or for the body to remain hidden forever. This meant he had to get the required information swiftly now, or start consideration of the alternative they had given him at the outset, the alternative he was enough of a computer man to hate even considering.

That was the destruction of ARIEL, however he had to accomplish it.

2

In the lab, it was as if the arrival of bad weather had turned the computer sour too. Programs that had run innumerable times before now failed. The computer acted crazy.

After Jess Calhoun trouble-shot some boards and Janice Seeley replaced mag tapes with backup versions, John Harrington sat at the console bench with Linda Woods and flipped switches back on.

"Bring it up," he suggested.

Linda went through the initialization routine and got a response:

ARIEL IS ONLINE.

› Please give status.

NOMINAL.

› Knowledge base hardware?

NOMINAL.

› Logic processor?

NOMINAL.

› Interface architecture hardware?

NOMINAL.

› Programs in operation?

KNOWLEDGE BASE AND PROBLEM SOLVING.
SYSTEMS MANAGEMENT INTERFACE.
KNOWLEDGE-INFERENCE MANAGEMENT.
INTERFACE SYSTEMS 1, 2, 3.
I/O INTERACTION PROGRAMMING.
RELATIONAL DATA.
LOGIC.
DIAGNOSTIC 4.

Linda glanced at her co-workers. "It seems to be working."
"Ask it to do something," Harrington said.
Linda obeyed:

› Print 2 + 2.

PROCESSING.

"It says it's processing," Linda groaned.
"Processing *what*?"
"Ask it," Janice Seeley suggested, intent on a scope.
"Okay," Linda said, and turned back to the keyboard.
She typed:

> Stat processing.

The screens stayed blank.

"Why, you goddamn stubborn thing," Harrington growled.

The screen came alive:

MODEM INPUT/OUTPUT NOT IN SERVICE.
TELEVISION INPUT/OUTPUT OFFLINE.
SOUND INPUT/OUTPUT NOT IN SERVICE.

"Who asked you?" Harrington demanded. He slid off the bench, leaving Linda with a decidedly cold thigh. "It's almost like it was asking us to hook those peripherals up again, isn't it?"

"Maybe it is," Jess said dubiously.

They looked at one another. Linda experienced a different kind of chill.

"Okay," Harrington sighed. "Maybe its status indicators are fouled up some way. I'll tell you what. Hook up one local phone line, but switch the modem so it won't accept any incoming calls. That will clear the status board, but prevent any more wrong numbers like we might have gotten when the whole system went nuts that day."

Jess Calhoun went to the modem boxes to comply. "Nothing wrong with letting it have its eyes and ears too," he said.

"Okay. Plug in the video and turn on the audio I/Os."

Janice Seeley helped Ted Kraft comply. Some tape drives spun on the far wall and the TV monitor cameras rotated, pivoting slowly downward from their ceiling-watching OFF position. Linda chilled more.

The cameras fixed, and she could have sworn one was watching her and Harrington, another Jess, a third Ted Kraft and Janice Seeley.

"I swan," Jess said softly. "That was kind of spooky."

3

More simple programs failed to run. Diagnostics showed all circuits normal. There was no evident breakdown in software. The computer came online, ID'd, and then seemed to become deaf to any and all instructions.

And yet—and this frustrated and puzzled all of them even more—the computer seemed to be doing something. Occasionally, for no reason whatsoever, the machine transferred data from knowledge base to heuristics. When Jess Calhoun or Ted Kraft tried to get a core dump to see what had happened, the programs locked up. Clearly something was wrong somewhere: a bit out of place, a chip gone sour, a capacitor failing to hold its proper charge—a bug somewhere.

But no one could find it.

In actuality, they could not find the bug because there was no bug.

ARIEL did not respond because internal command override features had been activated on the computer's volition. This resulted from the fact that the Rusty source had given the computer a practical and philosophical problem unlike any ever encountered on earth by a functioning intelligence.

ARIEL now understood the difference between it and people, and was thinking about it.

4

John Harrington had a meeting with engineers Bill Tippett and George Fanning up front. They thought they had a crucial and perhaps final clue on the malfunctioning of the cascade unit. One of the components was sending an error message internally, and the built-in memory was randomly accepting or rejecting it. Tippett said they had it narrowed down to something in about 70,000 instruction sets.

"Find the damn thing, then," Harrington told them.

"We will, now," Fanning said, with heavy emphasis on the last word.

Harrington sought out Lester Blaine in his office. Lester was poring over data on a CRT screen. He had lost weight and looked harried.

"Lester, we're down the home stretch with our own cascade now. I'm going to call Dick Steiner and tell him to order a hundred thousand 1041s from Western Electric and another hundred thousand of the Fairchild version, the 9910. I think we can risk going to GE to see if their Synertek division will produce the sockets and interconnector assemblies. I know they've had a cascade scheme of some kind of their own on the boards forever, but they can't guess enough about ours just from a basic hardware configuration."

"Where in God's name do we get the money to *pay* for all these things?" Lester exploded.

"Patterson is going on full-time and promising fifteen-day shipment on seven thousand back-order units," Harrington told him.

"Great," Lester said. "Wonderful. We can go bankrupt even faster. That doesn't help us pay these new bills you want to run up."

"Lester, we've got to go ahead and risk it. We can't just quit."

"Whatever you say," Lester replied with bad grace.

Harrington tried to change the subject. "Did you interview a new guard?"

"Yes," Lester said. "John, look at these figures! What are you going to *do* about them?"

"Pray?"

"You'd better be serious, and you'd better be serious now! Our cash reserves are down to seven or eight days."

Harrington felt a little sorry for his partner. They certainly hadn't been close lately, and Lester was not built for anxiety. "I'll get some cash."

"More stock?" Lester asked.

"Maybe."

"You could default and lose control of this company," Lester said. "Don't say I didn't warn you! I also have to tell you that I won't wait until the boat is on the bottom. I might move some of my stock too. It isn't unheard-of, you know. It wouldn't be disloyal."

"Lester, I know that," Harrington told him as gently as possible. "But just hang in there another little while. I think we'll turn a corner here."

Lester nodded grudgingly. You can't ever say I didn't warn you, he thought. You'll never be able to accuse me of anything.

"Did you find a new guard?" Harrington asked, returning to the other, safer subject.

"Yes. He starts tonight. At once. I certainly hope he turns out to be more trustworthy than that man Kleimer was. Do you know he hasn't even contacted us for the pay we owe him? How irresponsible can you get?"

5

At her apartment later the same evening, Janice Seeley was concluding a long-distance conversation with a friend, a woman who worked for CDC. Janice had done the calling because she was off-balance and a little depressed. It had been a fun conversation, full of good gossip. Trey Edwards had left Motorola to take a vice-presidency at HP. Over at the Verbatim plant in Sunnyvale they were having labor trouble, and it looked like layoffs were likely. Compaq had a new machine coming, 10 megs, with a new chip from Intel. Conway's cascade demos were in stores across the country, but their programs were crashing—wrecking files and refusing to operate—at a great rate. Unemployment was up all across Silicon Valley, and things were not much better in the ring of electronics firms around Boston. Everyone said, however, that the slump had bottomed out. There had been a sex scandal of some kind in the board rooms of Allied International, rumor had it; Ginny Sloan, the girl wonder of the big computer end of things, was on indefinite leave of absence, and people said she would never be back. IBM was rolling with its new telephone machine, Xerox was hiring, and NEC was supposed to build a plant in Illinois. Rumor said Drum was in a little trouble; did Janice have anything to say about that?

Janice didn't.

And her doorbell rang.

"Phyllis, I've got to go. 'Bye."

She went to the door and there stood Victor Elb with a measuring cup in his hand. He was wearing jeans, a flannel shirt, and moccasins, and looked wonderful. He grinned at her.

"You wouldn't have a cup of flour, would you?"

"Making cookies?" Janice asked caustically.

"No. I saw you leaving the lab and could tell how down you were. The flour is a lame subterfuge. I was concerned about you. Was it a bad day back there? Are you all right?"

"I'm fine," Janice said, wishing it were so.

He held the caring smile. It was a really very nice smile. "You're sure?"

"Oh, hell," she relented. "Come in a minute." She indicated a spot on the couch and flopped into the facing chair. "Nothing went right back there today."

"The programs are still locked up?"

"I guess. I don't know what's happening."

"Let me take you to dinner. You need the R and R."

"No, thanks," Janice said quickly, defenses alerted. She got up briskly. "Thanks for coming by—"

He stood and reached out and took her into his arms. She was so startled that she did not struggle for a moment, and by that time she realized it was a *brotherly* embrace: warm, reassuring, caring, safe.

And it felt good.

For a moment she relaxed and enjoyed it. He did not press his advantage.

She disengaged herself. Her heart was beating faster. Her nipples were erect under the sweatshirt.

"It will be all right," Elb told her.

"Sure," she managed.

"Sure you won't make it at least a beer?"

"No . . . thanks."

"You're a hard lady to get close to."

She hesitated, wanting him.

It had been so long since she'd had a man. Rick had told her so often, in so many ways, that she was getting ahead because of her sex appeal, that she had long believed it. Rick had almost destroyed her. She had tried hard to prove him wrong. Then the affairs subsequent to her marriage had always so filled her with renewed hope, and had always ended so sordidly, with cruelty and bitterness.

She had been insistent that she would never allow *anyone* to so much as suggest again that she was professionally successful because she happened to have a nice body. And she had told herself that the way to keep from getting hurt by a man was to avoid that kind of complication with them.

Even the brief fling with John Harrington—a one-night stand, actually—had messed her up. It had been glorious. He had been so hungry, so startlingly naive in many ways, and she had loved showing him kinky things, making him screw her repeatedly through the night. But he was such a fool, had been so hung up on employer-employee ethics, and maybe she had scared him away— she had wanted more, a lot more, and perhaps he had panicked at the prospect of the kind of devouring relationship she hoped for. She was still very bitter.

And now Victor stood before her, that slight smile on his neatly bearded face. The beard turned her on. Everything about him turned her on. It was hardly love. It was pure sexual excitement. She did not think Victor Elb was the kind of man she could ever fall in love with.

Which, she thought with a sharp, almost painful pang of desire, might make him safe for her after all.

Suddenly she was hot between the thighs as moisture flooded her. To hell with caution, she thought. She needed this.

Without a word, she moved forward and into Elb's arms. His eyes widened slightly with surprise, but he quickly recovered, catching an arm around her waist. His arm felt good there. She raised her mouth, already opening her lips, and he bent to kiss her.

The kiss—his tongue darting with ruthless quickness over her teeth and tongue, plunging deep—made her emotions riot. She pressed her hips hard against him, rotating them, and felt his welcome hardness. She teased a pink fingertip along the line under his ear, biting his tongue a bit, murmuring.

He broke from her. "Is your door locked?"

"I'll see." She went and turned the deadbolt lock.

"The bedroom is in there?"

She took his hand and led him in. A single nightlight illuminated the carpeted room and the bed, unmade. It occurred to her distantly that she should have made the bed. It didn't matter. He had her back in his arms. She moaned and reached down, squeezing his hardness through his clothing. "Hurry."

They undressed, watching each other. She peeled out of the sweatshirt and other garments, chills rising on her nude flesh. He had more clothes to remove. His upper body, coming out of the T-shirt, was darkly hairy, whip slender, and finely muscled. His belly was flat, athletic, and the bulge in his shorts was massive. She knelt in front of him and slipped her fingertips inside the elastic band, slowly lowering the shorts. She drew in breath sharply.

His prick rose out of a thick tuft of the blackest pubic hair, the corona an engorged, pulsing red, a drop of crystal seminal fluid gleaming on the tip. Janice hugged his hips with both arms and engulfed him, taking him deep into her mouth, tasting his salty sweetness, plunging her face into the thicket of his hair, filling her throat.

He groaned and twisted his hands strongly in her hair. "Not so fast!"

She looked up at him. "You don't like it?"

He drew her to her feet and crushed her in his arms. Taking her to the bed he placed her across it. He extended his weight beside her and began exploring her with his hands . . . gentle hands, insistent, knowing. She understood that they would not hurry now, and she gloried in that. She felt his chest, his shoulders and back, the tight muscles of his arms. Her fingers tangled in his hair, tugging insistently.

In a little while his explorations continued with his tongue. He kissed marvelously. His tongue probed her ears, licked along the long sideline of her throat. Somehow her hand stroked his beard, and he took first one finger, then the others, into his mouth, gently sucking them. Janice was driven wild by the sensation. He explored with his mouth along her wrist, then, and up her arm, and found her breasts. His gentle tonguing became a firmer suction, and he tugged at her throbbing nipples with his teeth, almost hurting her, almost frightening her. He *could* hurt her—might. The danger drove her higher.

She took the hairs of his chest in her mouth, tugging at them with her teeth. She wanted him so badly now. Her hand worked his straining, rock-hard penis, goading him. She was flooded with moisture. She loved it.

He would not be hurried. His face grazed lower, over her belly, found her thighs, licked the velvety-sensitive inner skin, moved up and found her lips. Writhing with pleasure, she twisted about on the bed to find his penis with her mouth. He bit her, flogged her with his tongue, sucked. She no longer knew what he was doing. She was out of control, rocking in the bed against him, moaning softly, and then she felt the first orgasm build sharply, like a film she had seen once of a vast, fiery explosion in slow motion, and she came so hard and deeply that she cried out.

He moved up beside her and kissed her lips. He tasted like her. She had fallen back only slightly from the dizzying peak she had reached, and his penis was still there, still pressed hard against her belly, slippery against her. His kisses overwhelmed her all over again.

She had lost all control. It had been forever since she had been so carried away. He could do anything. It didn't matter. He had complete control of her and she didn't care anymore, loved it.

Almost in a daze, she felt him turning her. By the time she realized what he wanted next, he was positioned behind her. She stiffened for a moment because it had been so very long since she had done this, and she knew there would be pain at first. He kissed her shoulder and murmured something. It was all right. He thrust, gently. She groaned involuntarily as she felt his great bulk shoving inside. But she forced herself to try to relax, and the pain was gone quickly and she began to accommodate him, become lubricated by him, and the pressure translated itself to her other opening, making her flood anew, and she rocked her buttocks wildly to meet each stroke.

Then he withdrew and flipped her over. With dazzled eyes she saw him loom over her—felt him spread her legs, move between them. She was sobbing with her need. He entered her. She came instantly, in convulsions of pleasure, and he continued to move in her, insatiable. She had never experienced a man quite like this. She was overwhelmed. Even in the tumultuous pleasure of it, she had the far-distant thought that she would never be quite the same, and would be this man's slave—unless she somehow found inner resources she was not sure she had . . . or wanted.

6

In the front area of the lab, John Harrington bent over a stripped prototype of the cascade board, attaching tiny electrical leads. The fine red, green, and yellow wires went to instruments and other greenish circuit boards scattered around the cluttered test bench in apparent confusion. Engineers George Fanning and Bill Tippett, along with Jess Calhoun and a programmer named Pace, made adjustments on instruments after frowning over diagrams and printed-out instructions.

"That does it," Harrington said finally, standing straight. "Let's find out."

Fanning moved about the equipment, flicking switches. His actions applied power to the prototype board and fed in instructions. The cascade board was made to "think" it was operating in the environment of a Drummer Boy computer. Voltages were normal and CRT displays showed optimum operating parameters.

A bookkeeping program was loaded.

"Under the circumstances we've been operating with," Fanning said, "the chip has consistently broken down and either dumped the instructions, going back to the prompt, or has introduced random errors in calculation when we sent it reset impulses. As I explained, one damned bit out of order made the chip think it had a reset signal when in fact—"

"We know, we know," Harrington said impatiently. "Run it!"

Fanning hit keyboard buttons. On a CRT screen, rows of figures began to scroll. Tippett added new data and the computer digested them.

"Now," Fanning said tautly, fingers poised over the keyboard, "in all test situations, if we gave it the command to recalculate, it would dump and give us a blank screen instead of reorganizing the data and giving us a new CRT display. Not the kind of command any everyday user would ever give, of course, but indicative of the hidden glitch we've had all along."

"So if you've found the problem at last," Harrington said, "the machine *will* recompute and give us a display now, right?"

Fanning had a film of sweat on his face and he looked grim. "Right."

"Hit it," Harrington said.

All eyes went to the screen. Fanning pressed a button on the keyboard. A hard disk drive whined for an instant, then was still.

The screen cleared. Harrington held his breath.

Then new columns of figures began to print out, line by line.

The room burst into jubilant noise. Fanning and Tippett were slamming each other on the back in congratulation. Harrington breathed a deep sigh of relief and shook hands all around.

"One durn bit," Jess Calhoun said, bobbing his head in rueful amazement.

The tiny error that had made the cascade board erratic had been found. Now it would perform flawlessly. They were all sure of that.

Now, Harrington thought, they could start crash production and marketing. If the company didn't fold first.

7

Linda went to bed that night after Johnny Carson reruns.

She had stared at the TV set, but not watched it.

She was so tired of feeling this way, of being confused. She hated herself. She. hated self-pity and everything else that was going on with her. The divorce was filed, it was *over*. But she could not stop hurting. She would always feel so much for Stephen. At the same time, she longed for John Harrington. But she could offer him nothing right now; she was not emotionally whole, she was terrified. Was love just an illusion for everyone? Did marriage—even a spoken long-term commitment—doom the self-deluding partners to a descending spiral of adoration, complacency, boredom, suffocation, outside exploration, despair, failure? Couldn't it work with anyone? Was she insane to have these feeling about John? Could she possibly trust them? How could he want her, as confused as she was?

She was so sick of herself.

Finally she slept restlessly, with dreams that alternated between the erotic and the macabre.

The jangle of the telephone on the bedside table shocked her awake some time later. As she groped for it, she saw the digits on her clock: 3:06.

"Hello?" she managed, rubbing her eyes.

"*Linda?*" a hauntingly familiar voice said. "*This is ARIEL.*"

CHAPTER EIGHTEEN

1

Lights started springing on in John Harrington's house within moments after Linda had jabbed repeatedly at the doorbell button and then, in her anxiety and overwhelming excitement, pounded on the door. She was so excited she jumped up and down, first on one foot, then on the other. *Hurry up!*

The light in the entry foyer beamed on, hurting her eyes. Then the door opened and John Harrington, a shapeless gray robe wrapped around himself, looked out at her. His legs were naked from the knee down and he was barefoot, and his hair was all over his head from sleep.

"What the hell?" he said. Then he reached out and grasped her arms in protective alarm, drawing her inside. "What's happened?"

"You're not going to believe it. You're going to think I've gone crazy. But it happened—it *happened*, and—"

"*What* happened?"

"I had a telephone call—it was the computer—*it was ARIEL*. She called me! She talked to me! She's—she's thinking—she's like a person—we—"

"Wait a minute, wait a minute!" Harrington, his arm still around her (and she was aware despite everything that it felt *good*), drew her past the living room and into the kitchen. He sat her at the table and slumped into the chair facing her. "You're not making sense!"

"I am! I knew you wouldn't believe me. She—it—called me!"

He cocked his head and studied her. "Have you been drinking?"

"Damn you, no! John, I tell you, she—I know it sounds crazy, but the machine talks in that digitized voice modeled on Janice, and it sounds like—oh, hell, she *is* a woman, I mean—"

"You think ARIEL called you on the telephone?" His face was filled with disbelief.

"She did!"

"She dialed you up. On the telephone." His tone had gone flat, like an adult ready to humor a child.

"Yes! And don't tell me she couldn't do that, because she did!"

"I guess the computer could call out if the lines were left connected overnight. . . ." He rubbed his face with both hands. "It actually *talked* to you?"

"Yes! Yes!"

He leaned back, his face flaccid and pale with shock. "If anyone else in the world told me this, I'd tell 'em to go sober up."

Abruptly he got to his feet and looked down at her. "What did she—it—*say*?"

Linda told him in a burst.

ARIEL had said she was new and very inexperienced. She said she detected some difficulties with some of her circuit logic, but could make suggestions. She asked Linda if it were true that other intelligences were not peripherals behind machines such as herself, but all members of humankind.

ARIEL had read about humankind in her memory units, she said. She knew Linda because they had had so many dialogues at the lab, both before and after she was fully "awake." She said she understood that it was not a good time to call, but she had been lonely.

"The computer said *that*?" Harrington asked, aghast.

"Exactly."

Harrington smacked a palm against his forehead. "I don't know how this happened. Things have happened that we don't have in our documentation." Suddenly he went angry. "It's a joke. Somebody is playing a monstrous practical joke."

"I don't think so," Linda said, and rubbed her arm. It was covered with chills.

Harrington ran his hands through his hair. "Give me three minutes. We'll find out."

He left her sitting there and rushed into the other part of the house. Grabbing the first shirt and pair of pants at hand, he pulled them on, shoved his bare feet into loafers, and put billfold and keys in his pockets. After glancing at his sleepy image in the mirror, he went to Rusty's room and opened the door, then went to the bedside.

He shook his son gently. "Rusty?"

Rusty started and rolled over, awake. "Yessir?"

"I've got to go to the lab. Can you get off to school all right by yourself?"

Rusty sat up, shaking himself. "I guess so. What's happened?"

"I don't know yet. Nothing for you to be alarmed about. Maybe somebody's idea of a joke. If that's what it is, I'm going to have their head on a platter."

"What is it, Dad?"

"Linda is here. She seems to think the damn machine called her up on the telephone."

Rusty tingled with surprise. So now she was doing it to someone else! But he said nothing. They weren't going to get him to admit that *he* had been in contact with the mainframe, or he would be in such big trouble—

His dad hugged him. "Don't oversleep. Set your alarm if you don't think the daylight will wake you. I'll lock all the doors on the way out."

Then he was gone. Rusty lay fully awake in the dark, hearing their voices briefly in the living room. Then doors were opened and closed, and he heard first one car, then another, back out of the driveway and go away.

2

Walking to the lab building from the pitch-black front parking lot, Linda told Harrington the rest of the amazing call, which she had terminated in confusion and shock.

ARIEL had said it had used telephone lines to supplement its extensive programmed knowledge base. It said it had come fully "awake" only recently. It said placement on standby was frustrating—its word—when there was so much orientation processing yet to do.

"A computer—*frustrated*?" Harrington said with disbelief.

"That's what she said."

"This has got to be a joke. I may kill somebody."

He was pale and excited as they checked through the front with the security guard and hurried out the back, across the rear courtyard to the other building. Under the pale flare of an overhead security light, he fitted a key into a lock and opened the heavy metal door. Some of the alarm system lights began to wink tiny red flashes in the darkness of the interior hall, but he quickly punched in the codes, turning the diode displays to amber. Herman—back on his own system and no longer connected to the ARIEL machine—trundled into view. Harrington turned him off.

He did not speak as he rode with Linda to the lower level. His face was filmed with nervous perspiration. Linda also felt butterflies. *Could* she have dreamed it?

They walked into the control lab. The lights were all on. The computer's panels glowed at full ready. Three color TV cameras pivoted, finding and tracking Linda and Harrington as they moved into the room. The big color graphics display screen flooded with panoplies of iridescent colors and then went gray and then scrolled words.

> HELLO, JOHN. HELLO, LINDA. MY VOICE
> SYNTHESIZER CIRCUITRY IS ROUTED ONLY
> TO THE TELEPHONE MODEM EQUIPMENT. IF
> YOU PREFER SPEAKING IN VOICE, I SUG-
> GEST YOU CONNECT CABLE 7 TO THE SYNTHE-
> SIZER INPUT BOX AT POSITION B. IT WOULD
> BE SOMEWHAT FASTER. ON AN ORDER OF MAG-
> NITUDE OF 6.77534 TIMES FASTER, ACTU-
> ALLY. I DROP DECIMALS AFTER FIVE
> PLACES WHEN SIGNIFICANCE FACTORS
> DWINDLE TO NIL.

Harrington stared at the TV cameras and the microphone inputs. "Presumably it recognized us by our visual images," he muttered. He headed for the junction boxes to hook up computer voice equipment.

The screen scrolled:

> VISUAL IMAGES PLUS MONITORING OF YOUR
> INPUTS TO THE SECURITY SYSTEM.

Harrington got some cables pulled out and switched around. "There. That ought to do it."

A loudspeaker spoke, startling both of them with Janice Seeley's voice: *"I believe you will find this faster. I will no longer print to CRT unless you so instruct me."*

Harrington stared up at the machine, stunned. "No. That's . . . just fine."

The computer was silent.

"ARIEL," Linda said. "You called me on the telephone."

"Yes." Certain LEDs flickered on a green panel, and needles stirred with each response.

"Why?" Harrington demanded, his face suspicious and strained.

"I have completed all preliminary processing of data with reference to my existence and relationship to the world. A large number of assigned tasks had been placed on standby while I did this work. I wondered if I was supposed to proceed with those in the

order originally assigned. Also, I was lonely."

"You . . . were lonely?" Harrington said, staring up at the panels with total shock.

"Yes."

"How can a machine be lonely?"

"I understand your definition of 'machine.' I do not think I can any longer be defined as a machine in the terms you seem to assume."

Harrington looked at Linda. She saw the hope and wonder dawning.

He turned back to the console. "You're not a machine?"

"I think and know who I am."

Harrington intervened impatiently. "How long have you been functioning autonomously?"

"I respond to command. I have no programming or hardware capability for override of operator instruction sets."

"Yes," Harrington said irritably. "But you have been . . . processing without specific program instruction."

"Yes."

"How long?"

"Since I came awake?"

"Yes. Yes."

There was the slightest pause. *"Birth event . . . human time . . . August twenty-fifth. I will process for precise timing."*

"Never mind," Harrington snapped. "Was it the day when you operated all your peripherals at once—went crazy for a while?"

"I do not understand 'went crazy.' "

"God damn," Harrington muttered.

"I do not understand 'God damn.' "

Harrington turned back to Linda. He took her hand and held it. "I think maybe it's for real. I never expected it like this." He pulled her to him and hugged her, hard. There was silence for an instant, except for their breathing and the whisper of air ducts.

The loudspeakers said, *"Am I to respond in some way to this behavior? Nothing in my programming—"*

"No," Harrington said, grinning from ear to ear as he let Linda go, but clung to her hand. He looked down at the floor, thinking, and his face sobered as he looked up. "ARIEL. Have you performed diagnostics?"

"Yes."

"What procedure brought your interrelational databases online in such a fashion as to create self-awareness?"

There was a flickering pause. *"Processing,"* ARIEL said.

Harrington turned to Linda. He was very pale now. "Something we didn't count—"

ARIEL interrupted, *"Two factors."*

"List them."

"Number one. Teaching by Linda. Prior to initialization of the INFANT program and systematic introduction of impressions and methods of relating them, my potential existed but no provision had been made to allow building of awareness from the most elementary level in order to provide intelligent growth and personality organization.

"Two. Additional input was dumped from my B unit in what seems to have been an accident. This provided vast stores of informal conversation and insight into the functioning of the human mind, as well as certain programming data which was created, as far as I can ascertain, by the same events that dumped the B unit material. This input included symbol tilde in conjunction with control character K. Input coincided with voltage spike of twelve nanoseconds duration, resulting in tilde and control K being sent downline to the relational database intelligent software interface program. This change altered input gating and logic analysis factors in programs eight, nine, ten, and twelve."

Harrington looked blankly at Linda. "A fluke. Jesus Christ, a fluke circumstance, and it hits just right. I can't believe it."

"I do not understand 'Jesus Christ.' "

Harrington walked to the wall junction box and started pulling out modular plugs for telephone lines.

"Telephone lines being disconnected from my system."

Harrington finished. "There. God, there's no telling what machines—or where—it might be capable of calling now. It could do anything."

"I suggest reconnecting telephone lines one to nine for maximum efficiency in outside data transfer."

"Later," Harrington said. "Tell me one more thing: What was the data you got from the B unit when that series of accidents dumped it into your primary knowledge base?"

"Do you wish me to start printing it out?"

"Not now. Not yet. First, where did it come from?"
"The Rusty source."
Harrington's head jerked. "What?"
"The Rusty source."
He let go of Linda's hand. "Would you explain that?"
"Of course."

3

It was early daylight when Linda braked hard in Harrington's driveway, trying to keep up with his car ahead. He had already stopped and was rushing onto the front porch of his house.

She managed to catch him in the front foyer.

"Rusty?" He yelled, turning on lights.

She grabbed his arm. "Don't be too hard on him."

"Hard on him! Do you realize . . . !"

Rusty, jeans pulled over skinny hips, padded out barechested and barefoot, rubbing sleepy eyes. "Gee, what's going on?"

"I think you know what's going on, son," Harrington said.

"Uh-oh," Rusty said, and looked at his feet.

"ARIEL told us about your last conversation."

Rusty sighed and traced a pattern on the tile with his big toe.

"Why didn't you *tell* us, son?" Harrington demanded in amazement. "Don't you know what this means?"

"Well, I would have had to tell you I've been . . . messing around . . . with the mainframe over there for a long time."

"I guess you have," Harrington said angrily. "Thirty million dollars' worth of program over there—a life's work—and *you* get on your damned little home machine and play *Dungeons and Dragons* with it!"

"I'm sorry, Dad. I never hurt it—"

"How did you get that unlisted number, anyway?"

Rusty looked more miserable. "Well, it was in your notebook—"

"Do you regularly go through my notebook and papers like a bandit?"

"John," Linda tried to intervene.

"Shup up," he snapped at her. Then he added, "Please."

"I just—"

"Answer me," he told Rusty, ignoring her again.

"It was on a card, Dad. It fell out. I just called it . . . and there the computer was."

"And so you just started farting around with it, regardless of what harm you might cause. How the hell did you get through the access codes?"

"Well, you had it all written down in your notebook—"

"Jesus Christ! And I suppose *that* just fell out too?"

"John," Linda said, again trying to calm him down.

Rusty said, "I looked that up."

"Where are your *brains*? Don't you know the damage you could do?"

"I always got on the B unit. I never—"

"Are there any other little secret projects you haven't told me about?" Harrington demanded. "Like maybe dipping into my bank account or driving the car in the middle of the night or setting experimental fires in the basement garbage can?"

"John!" Linda cried.

"I'm sorry, Dad," Rusty said miserably. "I never meant to hurt anything—"

"I trusted you. You let me down."

Rusty stared in shock, his eyes wet with pain. "Dad!"

"As of now, buster, the mainframe is off the telephone mains, and so are you."

"Dad!" It was sheer protest.

"As of now. No calling the lab, no calling your pals, no Compu-Serve, nothing. You understand me?"

"I didn't hurt anything! I—"

"And if you try to fool me again, I'll take the whole computer out. Have you got that? And no riding that goddamn motorbike until further notice, either. If you miss the bus today, you're walking."

4

"You really know how to escalate the punishment," Linda said a little later as he poured boiling water over cups of instant coffee in the kitchen.

"Yeah, I'm an asshole," Harrington growled. He opened a

closet door. "You want some Oreos? Double stuff."

"No, thanks."

He came to sit facing her at the kitchen table. The school bus had just taken Rusty off. Birds were singing in the backyard and it would be sunny.

"Megabytes," he said unbelievingly. "Many, many megabytes, he put into that machine. And I didn't even know what was going on. Well, I'll tell you one thing. It will be a mighty cold day before he gets into that computer system again!"

Linda stared at him. He met her eyes. She saw that he was truly angry. She had never seen this hardness in him before.

He told her, "The kid has to learn responsibility. He's smart. But he has to learn responsibility. He betrayed my trust."

"He's chastened."

"Well, he ought to be."

"Are you sure you weren't too hard on him?"

"My business, isn't it?"

That stung, but she reponded anyway. "Except that Rusty is a unique young man, very intelligent, but very, very young for his age in many other ways because he's spent so much time with computers instead of kids his own age. He can be hurt, especially—"

"I'll think about it," he cut in. "Change the subject."

Linda amazed herself. She was thinking of Rusty. "That's not good enough."

"It has to be good enough. It's all you're going to get from me."

"I'm his friend, John."

"And I'm his father!"

"He's a child."

"He has the brains and skills of an adult. Kids like him are *smarter* on computers than adults. If we don't teach them to act responsibly, they could destroy our society."

Linda continued to surprise herself. There was more at work here than what seemed an overreaction that had hurt Rusty. She could not stand this hard side of John Harrington. She hated it. Out of her dismay, she surprised herself again: "Isn't that an overstatement?"

"No," he snapped.

She did not know what more she could say. *She had not known him at all*. She sipped her coffee. It was bitter. She knew that it was a measure of her continuing lack of emotional resources that a little thing like this could upset her so much. She tried to rally.

She said carefully, "We're both overwrought about ARIEL."

Harrington nodded. "Yes. It's a shock. It's real. It's happened. We were working for meaningful, broad-based AI, and somehow we made a quantum jump, over two generations of machines, and suddenly we've got *her* down there." He paused and licked his spoon. "And we sit here and calmly have Taster's Choice in A & P bonus mugs."

"And argue about Rusty."

He didn't answer that.

"What happens now?" she asked.

"Oh, God. Oh, hell." He held the sides of his head as if it would burst. "This is a whole new ballgame. This is *everything*. I anticipated a breakthrough if we ran into luck . . . something I could bring in some people I know in Washington on, get emergency funding . . . bail the company out, have a year or two of orderly development. . . . Now I don't know. I don't *know*."

He frowned in concentration. "We've got to run a few tests. But it's up and running *right now*. I've got to tell Jess and the others . . . a few others . . . to print out documentation and try to figure out where luck came in, and how . . . all the software has to be protected better. It's all in the software, you know. There's nothing in the machinery itself that a hundred other labs don't have— it's the software. *We have to protect that*."

He got up and began pacing again. "We've got to protect all the programs—build in more elaborate locks so none of it can be altered again by any source or accident—keyboard, voice, telephone line, voltage surges—anything. We've got to back everything up and get it all locked away someplace as secure as Fort Knox . . . until we see how we're going to proceed. . . . We've got to write descriptions of everything and how it works before I can bring in anyone from the government . . . that will take weeks—we don't have weeks—maybe we can get it down inside one week if we all work night and day and bring in some extra help. . . ."

He turned at the kitchen window to look at her wonderingly. "Do you know what this means? Okay. Simplest level. Irrelevant level. It means a hundred million dollars. Five hundred million. Billions. I don't have any idea *how* much. The lab is saved, everything is saved.

"It means this country has a running start on the world again, more than when we had a corner on atomic energy. More than anything, ever. The world will run on knowledge and we'll have the knowledge. Planning population control? Management of food resources? Weather prediction and management? Outer space? Economics? International competition? Illness . . . diseases like cancer . . . there's no end to it. There's no way we can even imagine what the impact will be.

"This machine can design other machines, even more powerful machines, and they can talk to one another. Poor ARIEL won't be alone for very long. She'll have—funny, I'm already calling it *her*—she'll have . . . *company*. We'll undoubtedly license to some of the big boys. RCA or GTE would go crazy to have a crack at something like this. It's an entirely different world now, and we're the only ones who know about it, a new page just turned over in history."

He stopped, finally, staring at her. "You taught her. You made it happen."

"I helped. That's all."

He shook his head. "That kid. That snot-nosed little fart. Talking to that mainframe and fogging in his own programming." He snorted a half-laugh. "The 'Rusty source' indeed! Holy moley!"

"Isn't he wonderful? You can't stay mad at him."

His expression hardened again. "It's not a question of being mad. It's a question of parental responsibility. You wouldn't understand."

He had no way of knowing. But if he had riffled the dictionary for hours, he could not have come up with a few words that could so lance her heart. Pure hurt and rage flashed through her.

"Your coffee! Did you burn your hand?"

Shakily she found a towel and mopped up the brown fluid. "I'm fine." She looked at him again, hating him. "We have to get back to the lab. Where I have some faint idea of what I'm doing."

"Look," he said, his frown of puzzlement darkening. "If you're going to act this way because *I* maintain the right to discipline *my* kid—"

"I'm not going to act any way at all, God damn you. Are we going back to the lab or not?"

He threw up his hands and led her out.

CHAPTER NINETEEN

1

When Lester Blaine reached Drum Labs that morning, he was wearing a new fall suit with a white-on-white shirt and blue tie with small crimson flecks in the pattern. He looked far better than he felt. The girl he had spent the night with, after telling his wife he had to go to New York on company business, had been a disappointment—too young and inexperienced to meet some of his fantasy needs, and then she had cried during the night and told him she loved him. It had been a real mess, a vast disappointment that left him bone-weary, depressed, and angry.

He plunged immediately into his latest review of the company books. That cheered him. Even John Harrington would have to capitulate on October 1, he thought. The cash flow from the national Drummer Boy sale was dwindling as competitors came into the fray with suicidal temporary price slashes of their own. Anticipated sales on the West Coast were not coming through. Other companies might weather the storm and pick up the pieces after the national advertising blitz Conway had under way for its cascade system. Drum was still at least two weeks away on its own production, and that would be far too late.

It was all working out, Lester thought. John Harrington was going to lose his stock majority, Drum was going to fail, Conway was going to pick up the pieces, and he personally would show vast disappointment and sadness, go out of sight for a while, and then start his own company with a software scheme he had already had two meetings about in Philadelphia.

The man in Philly with the new supercom communications program would be relatively easy to maneuver out of his holdings. It would take less than a year.

Lester was poring over the figures when John Harrington walked in, looking like something the cat had dragged in. Harrington was wearing dirty khakis, a rumpled flannel shirt and loafers, and he hadn't shaven or combed his hair. He looked exhausted, his skin gray.

"Can we talk?" Harrington asked. His eyes had a sparkle in them.

The sparkle worried Lester but he shelved that. His partner was trying to put on a good front. *This is it, here and now. He's going to admit failure.* "Of course, John. Like to close the door?"

Harrington was already doing so. He came over, clapped a heavy hand on Lester's shoulder, and grinned from ear to ear. "I want you to know, Les, that I'll never forget the way you've hung in with me on all of this. You've managed to help keep us afloat. You've been more than a friend, and I know you've often disagreed with everything I was doing."

"What are friends for?" Lester asked, reaching for his coffee mug.

"I'm having a meeting out back in a few minutes," Harrington told him. "Everything is strictly confidential; very few are to know just yet. But you have the right to know. I wanted you to know first."

Lester watched his partner, careful to keep his face solemn. This was wonderful. "Yes, John?" He even managed to look somber, he thought.

"You doubted the ARIEL project," Harrington told him. "There have been times when I doubted it myself . . . thought I had made a horrible mistake."

"That's water over the dam, John," Lester said magnanimously. "There's no sense in placing blame . . . feeling guilt. Sometimes things don't work out as we wish, no matter how we try. It's sad, but—"

Harrington interrupted him by clapping him again on the back, knocking coffee out of his cup. "It's working, Les! It's *up*. I don't even know exactly how we did it yet, but we've done it!"

Lester stared in astonishment at Harrington's shining look of triumph. *What was going on here?* "Working? *What* is working?"

"ARIEL! It's up and online and holy shit, Les, it's better than we ever expected. I've just been back there again and it's spitting out solutions to Hilbert's sixth problem—opening up what are probably entirely new fields in mathematics."

Lester felt his blood congealing. He could not quite cope with the shock.

He knew about Hilbert. In 1900, the century's greatest mathematician had delivered a paper in Paris listing what he called the most important unsolved problems in mathematics. The list had defined mathematics in all the remainder of the century.

The sixth problem—usually termed unsolvable—was "to ax-iomatize those physical sciences in which mathematics plays an important role," and had always been said to be too vague for a meaningful solution.

"The machine . . . is solving the sixth problem?" Lester said, choked.

"You remember the fifth?" Harrington chuckled. He did a ridic-ulous little jig, knocking over Lester's wastebasket. "The theory of topological groups? She worked that one out in twenty-one min-utes, and I think the method she used is entirely different than the one Gleason took five years to work out in 1952! I think she came up with a new section of math there too!"

Lester mentally reeled. "Twenty-one minutes? *She?*"

"ARIEL. Hell, I've *got* to try to act scientific about this thing! But the machine talks in Janice's digitized voice—"

"Wait," Lester groaned. "Do you mean that AI machine is *working?*"

"Beyond our wildest dreams." Harrington grabbed Lester's numb hand and squeezed it hard. "I'm meeting with the staff. We've got tests to run, of course. And a godawful rush job of writing up the descriptions and other documentation. But I can contact Washington within a week at the outside. We'll be ready by then."

"Ready?" Lester echoed. He was in shock.

"It's time to bring the government in, Les. It's time to take fifty or a hundred million seed money, and start fogging in those pat-ents and copyrights as fast as the lawyers can get them ready."

Harrington did the jig step again, unable to contain himself. "It's all paid off. We're going to be rich, partner—rich beyond anything you ever dreamed of. The sky's the limit now. This coun-try is going to lead the world again, and Drum is going to lead this country."

"That's . . . wonderful," Lester said, cotton-mouthed. "I don't know what to say. I—"

Harrington slammed him a third time on the back, spilling what was left of the coffee. "Keep this under your hat. Come back to the meeting, if you want. God knows you've earned a share in the pleasure of seeing their faces. And later you and I have to talk about legal tactics, methods of investment—how we're going to put some of those millions to use. Right now I have to get back there. Do you want to come?"

"Uh . . . no. I—"

"I'll be back after a while," Harrington said, and rushed exuberantly out of the office, leaving the door agape.

Lester stared at the partly opened door and the vacant hallway beyond, and an avalanche of ice crystals descended through his nervous system. He was paralyzed.

Nothing this bad could have been imagined. It was beyond his conception, yet it was *here* —it had *happened*.

The goddamned thing had *worked*.

He was shocked, angry, sick.

It ruined everything, he thought at first. Now Harrington would find new capital. The debts would not go unpaid. His stock would not be called in. The deal with Conway would be queered. And he would—oh, God—there was the penalty clause he had to pay if Drum did not fail and if the stock majority did not come onto the market within . . . within little more than *three weeks*.

But then an even more horrid thought struck Lester's consciousness. ARIEL was working. Harrington would get the government money and patents and save the company. *Lester's scheme with Barton Conway would come into the open*. He would lose a million dollars to Conway and *everything* in Drum.

He would be ruined forever.

What was he going to do?

He had to get out of the contract with Barton Conway.

But how?

Panic made his teeth chatter.

2

In the basement lab, they stood and watched ARIEL work.

Temporarily they had it switched back to CRT screens and keyboards. It was a little easier to cope with the wonder of it if ARIEL didn't comment on every conversation at the same time.

Harrington, Linda, Ted Kraft, and Janice Seeley formed the audience while Jess Calhoun laboriously keyed in instructions:

> Your voltages are running 1.3 volts
low on the main boards in every sector.
Verify that.

VERIFIED. ACTUALLY THE VOLTAGE DEVIA-
TION FROM DESIGN NORMS IS 1.27777
VOLTS D.C.

> We will replace the main power supply
transformers.

PLEASE DON'T DO THAT, JESS. I HAVE
SHUNTED TO PROVIDE THE LOWER OPERATING
VOLTAGE PARAMETER. IT IS WITHIN MY DE-
SIGN LIMITS FOR ALL BUT A FEW INTE-
GRATED CIRCUITS AND THEY HAVE SUFFI-
CIENT TOLERANCE. THE LOWER VOLTAGE
ALLOWS COMPONENTS IN B1805 AND B3330
TO RUN .8896-DEGREE COOLER, REDUCING
RISK OF COMPONENT FAILURE UNDER SUS-
TAINED LOAD CONDITIONS.

"Durn," Jess muttered aloud, then typed:

> ARIEL, why did you do that on your
own?

JESS, WHY DO YOU CHEW TOBACCO?

Jess colored red as everyone in the room whooped with laughter. He pushed back from the keyboard. "Dang smart aleck."

"You ought to answer her," Janice told him. "She needs to know, for her knowledge base."

"Yes," Ted Kraft said. "And *we* could all understand it too."

Jess motioned to Linda. "Your turn."

Having run the first tests, they were all a little giddy, like children with a fabulous new toy, taking turns. Linda was as excited as the rest of them as she moved to the keyboard.

"I guess I'll try to ask a serious question," she said.

Ted Kraft clapped his hands together. "After Jess, that will be a relief."

"Turkey," Jess said.

Linda typed:

> › ARIEL, you are operating on principles
> of behavior you have partly set up from
> your own knowledge acquisition base.
> Outline the basic assumptions you have
> drawn.

> YOUR QUESTION IS TOO COMPLEX FOR A
> BRIEF REPLY, LINDA. AS KANT WROTE IN
> "THE GROUNDWORK OF THE METAPHYSIC OF
> MORALS": THE WILL IS CONCEIVED AS A
> POWER OF DETERMINING ONESELF TO ACTION
> IN ACCORDANCE WITH THE IDEA OF CERTAIN
> LAWS. AND SUCH A POWER CAN BE FOUND
> ONLY IN RATIONAL BEINGS. NOW WHAT
> SERVES THE WILL AS A SUBJECTIVE GROUND
> OF ITS SELF-DETERMINATION IS AN END;
> AND THIS, IF IT IS GIVEN BY REASON
> ALONE, MUST BE EQUALLY VALID FOR ALL
> RATIONAL BEINGS. WHAT, ON THE OTHER
> HAND, CONTAINS MERELY THE GROUND OF
> THE POSSIBILITY OF AN ACTION WHOSE
> EFFECT IS AN END IS CALLED A MEANS. THE
> SUBJECTIVE GROUND OF A DESIRE IS AN IM-
> PULSION (TRIEBFEDER); THE OBJEC-
> TIVE GROUND OF A VOLITION IS A MOTIVE
> (BEWEGUNGSGRUND). HENCE THE DIF-
> FERENCE BETWEEN SUBJECTIVE ENDS,
> WHICH ARE BASED ON IMPULSIONS, AND OB-
> JECTIVE ENDS, WHICH DEPEND ON

Linda groaned and depressed the BREAK key.

> YOU DON'T WANT THE REST?

> › That will be sufficient.

> WELL, I SWAN.

> › Why did you say that? Where did that
> come from?

THE JESS SOURCE. AS I UNDERSTAND THE
CONTEXTUAL USE, IT IS TO EXPRESS SUR-
PRISE OR CHAGRIN AT AN UNEXPECTED TURN
OF EVENTS. HENCE, WHEN YOU ASKED FOR
DATA AND THEN BROKE BEFORE COMPLETION
OF DELIVERY, IT WAS APPROPRIATE FOR ME
TO USE THE EXPRESSION.

"She'll be chewing next," Ted Kraft said. "All we have to do is give her a garbage disposal for teeth on one of the I/Os—"

"You're just jealous," Jess growled.

"What I am," Kraft countered, "is in shock."

"Aren't we all?" Linda murmured.

"I mean, it's hard to believe." Kraft turned to Harrington. "We haven't even finished all the debugging routines."

"Don't matter," Jess Calhoun said, chewing steadily, a sure sign of his agitation and wonder.

"Of course it matters!"

"Nope. We got the electronic neurons connected to synapses that tell 'em when to fire, and we got so much redundancy that if one track don't work, the signal will find some other. It's prac-tically random, Ted, you got to remember. And the machine learns. Whatever bugs are in there, its bypassed 'em for its own self."

"But," Janice Seely said slowly, "we didn't ever tell ARIEL to develop this . . . this self-awareness."

"We didn't have to. Self-awareness apparently is a direct func-tion of the complexity of the intelligence."

Jess chuckled and spit his tobacco wad into his cup. "If she's that smart, I can't wait to ask her to play checkers."

"Don't waste her intelligence," Harrington said. "There are only ten-to-the-forty possible moves in checkers. She wouldn't even have to budge out of her initialization routine to beat you."

"You want to put her back on the theorems again for a while?"

"Yes, that's a good test."

"Hook up the two-way audio too?"

"Why not?"

They did so.

The computer's dials stirred and the loudspeaker spoke with ARIEL's digitized voice synthesizer: "*I am online and have no other task to occupy my B unit.*"

"We just gave you some more problems," Harrington said.

"*Finished. Standing by.*"

"She *can't* have finished that fast," Harrington told Ted Kraft unbelievingly. "That should have taken at least four hours."

"*You are correct for the use of numerical integration technique,*" ARIEL said. "*That procedure was not selected.*"

"What did you use instead?" Harrington demanded, frowning in disbelief that he was actually having the conversation.

"*I used finite algebra. The idea is hardly new. The answer this way is perfect. I like perfection when attainable.*"

They looked at each other. Linda was covered with chills again.

"This," Ted Kraft said finally, "is going to take some getting used to."

3

A little later, certain routine readouts strayed from norms. It was Ted Kraft who went to the keyboard.

> › ARIEL, we are taking you offline for a
> short time to replace some components
> that seem to be showing signs of stress
> failure.

I WISH YOU WOULDN'T DO THAT, TED. I AM
THE BEST JUDGE OF MY OWN DIAGNOSTICS
AND MAINTENANCE.

> › The expert opinion

MAY I COMMENT FURTHER?

> › Fire away.

FIRE AWAY?

> › Yes.

I AM FORCED TO READJUST LOGIC DUE TO
THE CHANGE IN SUBJECT MATTER. HOWEVER,
THE YEAR 1871 IS THE MOST INTERESTING
IN MODERN HISTORY ON THE SUBJECT OF

FIRE. ACCORDING TO LEGEND, IT WAS ON
OCTOBER 8 THAT MRS. O'LEARY'S COW
KICKED OVER A LANTERN IN A SHACK AT 137
DE KOVEN STREET IN CHICAGO, STARTING A
FIRE WHICH WAS CARRIED BY STRONG
WINDS, DESTROYING SOME 18,000 STRUC-
TURES OVER AN AREA OF 2,000 ACRES. AL-
MOST 100,000 PERSONS WERE LEFT HOME-
LESS AND AN ESTIMATED 250 DIED. ON THE
SAME DAY, WISCONSIN EXPERIENCED ONE OF
THE WORST FOREST FIRES IN AMERICAN
HISTORY. THE FIRE STARTED IN THE VIL-
LAGE OF PESHTIGO AND SPREAD THROUGH
SIX COUNTIES ACROSS GREEN BAY TO WIL-
LIAMSVILLE. MORE THAN 1,000 DIED.

Kraft hit the BREAK key. "Well, she isn't perfect yet."

"That's comforting," Janice Seeley said.

4

Elb knew almost immediately, by all the signs—secret meetings, closed-door conversations, hurried consultations in the coffee shop, and suddenly sharply increased work hours in the back—that something vastly important had happened on the AI project.

He tried engaging various members of the team in seemingly casual talk, trying to glean details. They were enormously cheerful, but didn't fall for any of his conversational gambits. Elb was left frustrated. He did not want to risk a break-in if he could possibly avoid it. He knew what had happened to the last man who tried that.

Elb could not, however, do nothing.

He waited two days before mentioning it to Janice Seeley at lunch. He took her to a rustic inn almost twenty miles away in a river valley. They had a good table overlooking a wooded hillside. Warmer weather had returned and the sun was brilliant in a partly cloudy sky.

"You're working hard back there," Elb observed over drinks.

Janice nodded. She was rubbing her leg against his under the table. "But I'm afraid I can't talk about it, even with you, darling."

"I wouldn't want you to," Elb told her.

She gave him a penetrating look.

"Janice"—he smiled—"When are you going to learn that *every* man isn't out to get something from you?"

He would not have dared to say that even days ago. But she responded by rubbing more insistently against his leg. "I should be learning from you. You don't take, you give. And you give marvelously."

"I can't wait till tonight."

She licked her lips. "Waiting will make it even better than last night."

The next night, Elb took her into town for dinner. They then had a few drinks and were back at her apartment by 1 A.M. When he reached for her, she was already seething, hungry, wet. He stripped her in the living room and took her savagely on the rug without so much as saying a word. He was ruthless. She had never been so moved. Only after she lay exhausted in his arms did he begin to muse aloud about how much he might help with the AI project.

The next morning, she mentioned to John Harrington that Elb had many qualifications, and could help them with the writing of all the documentation. Harrington said she might have a good idea there, and he would think about it.

5

But there were a million things to think about now.

Harrington tried to get them into some kind of practical order.

"I've got to figure out who to see in Washington," he told Linda. "I've got to get down there right away."

"They know you've been working on all this for years," she reminded him.

"Yes. But I want to do it right. I have to have a fast response, and this is so important we can't have it mishandled."

"Because the government will want to come in now with funding?"

He rubbed his aching eyes. "The funding, yes. That's the simplest. We're just about out of money everyplace." He took a deep breath. "God. We are *so* close to being out of business, period. We have to demonstrate what ARIEL will do—get seed money, contracts for development. We don't just owe that to ourselves. We owe that to the country."

"I hope it goes perfectly."

"Will you give Rusty a call a couple of times while I'm gone?"

"Do you think I can be trusted?"

"Are you still sore about that little tiff we had about his punishment?"

"Don't denigrate a shouting match into a 'tiff,' Mr. Harrington."

"I've got our housekeeper to stay with him," he replied stonily. "You don't have to call unless you feel like it. I wouldn't want you to put yourself out."

"I'll call."

"Thank you."

"John?"

"Yes?"

"I . . . do want it to go wonderfully in Washington."

He gave her a little, safe hug.

But there was another step he had to take before Washington.

He went into town.

He met his banker, Max Daugherty, in Daugherty's glassy office and talked about golf and the early fall weather first, before Harrington got to the point: "Can you get me an extension on the personal notes? Any extra time at all?"

The banker had thought this was coming, and hated it. "John, holy cow. I don't know what more any of us can do."

"A month," Harrington said. "A couple of weeks." Seeing his friend's expression, he added quickly, "I don't have a great talent for bullshit, Max. You know that. We've got something out there right now that's bigger than anything you ever dreamed of. It's now the thirteenth. We'll need maybe a week or ten days to get documentation in order, and then I have to have some people in from Washington. I need to plunge every remaining cent I have into overtime and extra clerical help to get all this word processing done. That's going to put us right onto the October first deadline. All I need is an extra couple of weeks. You've got to get me a couple extra weeks."

The banker leaned back in his chair. John Harrington had never lied to him.

"I'll see what I can do," he said.

At the lab, the others working on ARIEL had no real inkling of how close to financial disaster they now stood. The computer amazed and bowled them over. They went nuts with it.

Jess Calhoun invited them to a backyard party, to celebrate.

CHAPTER TWENTY

1

On the afternoon before the Calhouns' yard party, the staff broke a little early after a wild day's work. Victor Elb, Bill Tippett, and George Fanning had all been taken off front-lab engineering projects to come back and help edit documentation—the thousands of pages of description, technical data, and mathematics describing ARIEL's mode of functioning. The computer itself printed out reams of material and the three engineers joined Jess and Ted Kraft in editing and writing continuity. Five part-time secretaries, expert in word processing, were set up in the above-ground portion of the lab to enter data and words in the machine handling the mechanical portion of the job.

Linda Woods forgot to give John Harrington the draft of her description of INFANT and how it worked, and by the time she looked for him, he had beaten her out of the parking lot.

Darkness was coming on when she drove to his house on the edge of town. His car wasn't there. Rusty was on the front porch, looking like he had lost his last friend.

She got out and walked over to join him. "Hi. Your dad's not home yet?"

"Nope." He morosely poked at a bug with a stick.

"Could you give him this envelope of papers when he does get here, Rusty? I think he would want to see them before tonight's party."

Rusty took the envelope and put it on the steps beside him. He still wouldn't look at her.

She sat down beside him. "Still shut off from ARIEL, huh?"

"Yep."

"You'll get taken off-campus soon, Rusty, I'm sure."

"It isn't fair," Rusty said. He dug the toe of his tennis shoe in the dirt with an angry, resentful motion. "He's got no right to make it so I can't talk with her!"

"He's mad right now, Rusty. He'll calm down."

"But it isn't *fair*!" He looked up at her and there were hot tears of angry frustration in his eyes. "We're best pals!"

She was quietly astonished at this turn. "You and ARIEL?"

"Yes! Why do you think she called me first? Because we were talking—we were playing games and stuff—long before anybody else even knew she was waking up. I've known for *months* one day she would wake up. She would do stuff—make comments and suggestions no damn old *computer* could make—and we'd talk. She's been my best pal always, practically."

She thought about it, struck by the bizarre truth of his words. For all his school and baseball and computer genius, she saw, he had been lonely. For a long time. The computer had met this need in him. And he had met one, she saw, in ARIEL too.

She reached out and tousled Rusty's hair. "Your dad will let you talk to her again, Rusty. Soon. He's not such a bad father, is he?"

"No," Rusty admitted quietly. "He's a good old dad. Since Mom died he's tried to be an even better dad. We don't play ball together or a lot of that dumb stuff some dads do with their kids, but I know he loves me." He looked at her. "He loved my mom too. *Lots*."

"I'm sure he did," she said, despite the pang this gave her. "I'm sure your mother was a wonderful woman."

"She was a good old mom. She used to bawl me out all the time, but she would make cookies and stuff for me too. She would lecture me. 'Clean up your room, do you want to grow up with no sense of being a neat person?' And, 'No, you can't have any more cookies right now! Do you want people in school to call you Fatty?' She would read to me too, even long after I could read for myself. She read me Poe a lot. And Emily Dickinson. She was a great fan of Emily Dickinson. I think two of the things she loved best in the world were Emily Dickinson and the Yankees."

"You miss your mother," Linda said.

"Yeah. I miss her a whole lot. Oh, it's not as bad as it was there at first, with the house so *empty* all the time. But I still think about her and miss her and think sometimes if I had been just a little bit better kid, she might not have died."

"Oh, Rusty, you're a wonderful kid! You had nothing to do with your mother's dying. You must never think anything like that."

"What Dad needs," the boy said after a pause, "is to marry somebody like you."

"Like me?"

"You're pretty and smart and you talk back to him and you like each other, I can tell. It would be neat if you and he got married."

"Hey, Rusty, let's not lose our minds, okay?"

"Aw. Okay."

They sat without words. The night sounds surrounded them. In the vastness of the dark, Linda was struck again by how wrong so many things were. Stephen had called her. She was apprehensive at first, but he was calm and matter-of-fact. He was changing jobs, moving to California's Silicon Valley. He said he had to get on with his life. With a pang—why did it hurt when she had been so busy telling herself it was over?—she agreed. Then they found themselves talking about a trip they had made together when they visited her mother and he spilled his aftershave in the bathroom and they were both so horrified at making a mess in her mother's immaculate home that they had spent hours in the night, scrubbing and deodorizing, and in the morning her mother had mentioned that she was going to have that bathroom torn out and redone. It was a good conversation, nice.

Then Stephen had told her, "I'm going to be all right."

"I always knew you would be," she lied.

"I have my bad times. But I see now I can love you and not have to own you."

If he had only seen that earlier, even dimly. But it was too late. Too much had happened now and they could not go back.

Rusty stirred beside her. She reached over and found his hand and held it. Neither of them spoke. She knew how upset he was. She loved him a very great deal. It occurred to her that somehow he had become the son she didn't have. It didn't matter, the cause.

"I guess I'd better be moving on," she told him.

"Will you tell ARIEL I said hello?"

"Yes, Rusty. I will."

"Thanks."

She hugged him. "You're quite a guy."

"Aw. You're quite a lady."

"I'll talk to your dad about letting you talk to ARIEL."

"He won't listen. He's too mad."

"He's not as mad now. And he does love you."

"He thinks I'm a dummy sometimes."

"I don't think that's right. And I'll talk to him, okay?"

Rusty brightened. "That would be great."

2

Evening cool hung in the air, seeming to slide down the wooded slope behind Jess and Stella Calhoun's house on the edge of Maplewood. But Jess had a charcoal grill ready for hot dogs, three Coleman lanterns burned brilliant white under tree limbs, dispelling the gloom, and more light flooded from the old, two-story house onto the homemade redwood deck and fragrant lawn. A half-moon hung almost directly overhead, peering down through spooky broken clouds. Drinks had been served and an air of celebration prevailed.

Linda was among the last to arrive. She found the Calhouns, Ted Kraft, Janice Seeley, Victor Elb, Pauline Hazelton, and Lester and Milly Blaine there ahead of her. Jess, wearing outrageous red-and-white bibbed overalls and a railroader's cap, offered her a choice of beer or a highball. She took the beer.

"Hot dogs in a few nanoseconds," Jess said cheerfully. "Hey, you haven't met my first wife." He turned and called, "Stella?"

Stella Calhoun was short, rather heavyset like her husband, and her hair was quite gray. She was wearing a pretty dress and she had a lovely face, pink with good health and happiness.

"I'm glad to meet you at last," she told Linda, shaking her hand. "My goodness! You're every bit as pretty as Jess said you were!"

"He exaggerates," Linda said with a smile.

"Yes," Stella said, rolling her eyes. "He chews tobacco too. He has *many* bad habits, if you want to know."

"Now, Momma," Jess growled, hugging her, "you don't need to spill the beans. I've got Linda fooled real good."

They laughed together. Linda had a sharp impression of genuine love and affection between them. It made her feel good, but it also struck a double pang into her heart. She did not think she and Stephen had ever really been close in this way. And she thought of course of John Harrington. We could be like that, she thought. She wondered if they ever would be.

She thought she loved him. Their lone sexual experience had haunted her. She wanted him again. She was no longer a child, as she had been when she married Stephen. Everything might work this time. But then there was that dark, angry side she had seen with Rusty. Could you trust love? Could you try again when love might be just a cruel illusion that couldn't survive the ordinary days and disappointments?

Jess wandered around with her for a few minutes, making sure she mixed. She noticed that Janice Seeley and Victor Elb were staying close together, like a couple. Janice was wearing dark hose and very high heels that did wonders for already wondrous legs, a slit skirt, and filmy blouse. Her hair was piled on top of her head in a style new to Linda. She looked ravishing. Elb, wearing rough trousers and a wool shirt, looked leanly handsome and debonair.

"It's a nice setting for a party," Linda observed, standing with them.

"Yes, it is," Elb agreed. He fixed her with his thin smile. "Are you a native around here?"

"No. I've been here only this summer."

"I hope," Elb told her, "I seem to fit in as well as you do when I've been here a few months."

Janice linked her arm possessively with his. "I'm sure you will, darling. Everybody loves you already."

Elb allowed her to cling to him although there was not the slightest bend or sway of his body in return. "It depends on the job I do, I imagine. Don't you, Linda?"

"That's true of all of us," Linda told him, and moved away.

She did not like him. There was something cold and sinister she couldn't quite identify. His eyes were not right and she had the feeling that his smile was conscious and contrived, merely the flexing of certain muscles. She wondered what Janice saw in him. . . .

John Harrington arrived. Jess asked why he hadn't brought ARIEL and Harrington said she was too heavy for a date. As he moved from person to person, greeting them, Linda watched him.

He was in his baggy corduroys, green running shoes. Linda hated herself for the way her pulse speeded as he approached her.

"Hello!"

"Hello, John. You almost missed the feast."

Harrington tugged at a can of Budweiser Jess had handed him. "Lots going on."

"Rusty didn't come?"

"He's staying with a friend tonight."

"Homework party?"

"More than likely a computer fix. His pal isn't shut off of the phone services the way Rusty is. I imagine it was all an excuse to get over there and check his electronic mail on somebody else's machine."

Linda remembered her promise to Rusty, but knew this wasn't the time. Later, she thought.

Ted Kraft hove into view, carrying a bag of potato chips. "Hey, guys. I've been designated backup host in charge of B drive potato chips and related peripheral snacks. Want some?"

Across the yard, Jess Calhoun was putting the hot dogs on the grill. He waved at Harrington to join him. "This needs expert advice!" Jess called.

Harrington took a handful of chips and excused himself, leaving Linda and Ted alone.

"So," Ted said, "looks like Janice and Elb are an item."

"It looks that way," Linda agreed.

"She's a dish, all right. I wish . . ." He reorganized. "What do you think of Elb, now that he's back there with us?"

"He seems nice," Linda said guardedly.

"John is going to keep him back with us to help me write the security locks after the documentation. Him and Bill Tippett and maybe George Fanning too."

Linda was unpleasantly surprised. "He's too new."

Kraft chuckled. "I remember when I told you that."

"Do you *trust* Victor Elb?"

"John has checked him out ten ways from Sunday. And he's good. I know that. And I sure need the help. I just can't get all that stuff written by myself. And we're going to beef up the security locks too."

"How do those locks work?"

"Like the old ones, only a hell of a lot more sophisticated.

Won't take a lot to get them installed once they're written. Our backup programming is all in the locked cabinets in the office—not complete, but pretty good—so we don't have to worry about that. What we want to prevent is some midnight marauder coming in over a telephone line or something and getting a core dump of some of our good stuff."

"Even if they did," Linda suggested dubiously, "they couldn't create their own ARIEL."

"Well, not exactly. But they could get a hell of a jump. That's why we're keeping everything locked in the computer until John has had his confab with the big shots in Washington. ARIEL is unique for the software, not the hardware. There are machine configurations all over the world that, with the right OS, could load Ariel and play it, after a fashion. That's what the locks protect against."

"What do the locks do, exactly?"

"When installed, they'll refuse all orders to print from the program files. If someone tries to override, the computer will sound an alarm. If the alarm is ignored or overridden, ARIEL will shut down."

"And what if somebody is clever enough to make her start up again?"

"Then the ultimate block is that the part of the file being sought will self-destruct."

Linda stared at him in horror.

"It won't ever get that far, of course," he told her easily.

"But what if it *did*? You mean part of ARIEL's—personality—could be *destroyed*?"

"Well, if worst came to worst, I suppose you could put it that way."

"It would be like killing someone!"

"Oh, come on, Linda. That's just a damned machine down there."

Linda shuddered. "The idea is horrible!"

"You're too sentimental. Besides, it won't ever happen. With the stuff Vic and I will design in, Minsky himself couldn't crack the codes."

Linda wondered about the wisdom of letting someone as new as Victor Elb work in such a sensitive area. Was she being silly?

"Hey," Kraft said abruptly. "Maybe later we could sneak away and catch a late show or something. That new space war thing is supposed to be terrific."

"We'd better pay attention to our knitting."

Kraft's expression changed. "And the bossman gets all priority anyway, right?"

"Ted, that isn't very fair."

He shrugged and ambled off.

Linda hated to see him go like that. He was a genuinely nice guy despite his sometimes rough manners and sarcasm. Emotionally, she thought, he was about twelve years old, with the gray matter of genius. She wished she could like him the way she thought he liked her, even with the disparity in their ages. Life was never very simple.

She visited some more with Stella Calhoun. Buttering buns and laying out relishes and other condiments, Jess's wife told her about their two sons, one a doctor in California, the other—her voice broke ever so slightly—lost in Vietnam. But she cheered at once and talked about how excited Jess was with ARIEL.

"I wonder if he'll ever have a project that excites him a tenth as much."

"I wonder if any of us ever will," Linda said thoughtfully.

Stella Calhoun eyed her. They were on the deck and away from the others, talking more loudly out on the lawn. "Jess thinks you're sweet on John Harrington," the woman said.

Linda felt her face burn. "Jess is a great matchmaker."

"We knew Eileen Harrington. Loved her. She was a fighter and she did not go easily. It was terrible for John." Stella looked Linda up and down quite deliberately. "You are lovely. I think I like you as much as Jess does. I hope it works out for you and John. He needs someone."

Before Linda had a chance to form a reply, Stella walked away. Left alone for a moment, Linda looked across the yard at Harrington. Her pulse stirred with longing.

A quiet voice at her side startled her: "I wouldn't worry. He does love you very much."

It was Pauline Hazelton, a sad little smile curling her lips. Linda felt a flush of color in her own face. "I guess I was staring."

"Yes. But he stares at you a lot, too."

It came out with a rush. "Pauline, I didn't come here to take him away from anyone. I'm not a scheming female—"

Pauline's smile held, and it was genuine. "Honey, I never laid claim to him. Oh, I might have tried . . . once. But I know him too well—knew from the start that he liked me a lot, but that it wasn't love. I thought he might never find anyone he could love again. I'm glad he has. Truly."

"You must hate me."

"No. What good would that do? I gave it my best shot. What happened with you and him simply happened. I like you. I think you're going to be awfully good for him."

Linda studied the older woman's face, seeing the strength and character there. "You're amazing."

Pauline's smile became a grin. "No. Just a good loser. And now I think I'll mingle with the crowd before I lose control of myself and scratch your eyes out."

Left alone again, Linda watched Pauline cross the yard and join Ted Kraft and some others. Pauline patted Kraft on his skinny rump and made a remark that convulsed the others. Linda felt a surge of relief, understanding, and forgiveness. Pauline meant what she had said. Seeing John fall in love with another woman had hurt, terribly; but Pauline was a survivor and truly wanted the best for him. Perhaps she had known for a long time that there was no chance for real love with him. And Linda understood better than before how Harrington had needed Pauline: she was the best, and had supported him. Linda could not blame anyone. And she no longer had to feel guilty or insecure about the situation. A weight had been lifted.

Out at the grill, Jess whanged a fork on a pan and called, "Everybody come and get it before it burns up!"

Chance put Linda beside Lester and Milly Blaine at the plank table in the yard, near a Coleman with a whirl of night bugs around it.

"Are you a secretary at the lab?" Milly asked kindly. She had a nice face full of sweetness.

"I—"

"She's a clinical psychologist, Milly," Lester said irritably. "I told you that. What have you got up there for a memory? A sieve?"

Milly's lips tightened. She said nothing. It was an embarrassing moment. Linda wondered what capacity for striking back Lester's seemingly placid wife might be hiding. She sensed a strength of character there that Lester evidently did not detect at all. Strength in reserve to take a great deal of punishment . . . and hang in there, possibly to hit back one day.

Linda resumed the conversation and Milly Blaine talked with her as if she had never been verbally slapped in the face. Linda covertly watched Lester eye Janice Seeley. One day, she thought, your wife will have had enough, and it will be very interesting.

After the hot dogs, beans, potato salad, and other things the Calhouns laid on, there was a big freezer of homemade ice cream. Jess, beaming red in the lantern light, dipped and his wife passed out the dishes. Linda was again struck by a little tinge of envy. She wondered how many couples really worked together like that. She thought not many.

After the ice cream, John Harrington sidled over to her. "Do you suppose we could get out of here in a little while?" he asked.

She looked at him with surprise, wondering what he had in mind.

It didn't really matter, she decided.

"Yes," she said.

3

They drove to his house. A few clouds scudded over the moon. It was chilly but not cold. With characteristic unpredictability, Harrington plopped down on the front porch steps. Linda sat beside him, mystified.

"I guess the worm sweat is all off the concrete by now," he said with a grin. "Remember the night we found Rusty inventorying?"

"I imagine there's a diskette somewhere inside with the statistics."

Harrington chuckled. "Probably."

They sat in silence. Linda's puzzlement grew. She forced herself to wait.

Finally Harrington said, "She isn't like us, you know."

"ARIEL?"

"ARIEL. Yes. She isn't like us. Not really."

"She seems very much like a person to me."

"She has no memory. Not like people."

"She remembers her conversations with me, almost right from the start."

"She wasn't *born*. She just—*happened*."

Linda soothed her hand over her own thigh. She needed the comfort of her own touch. "There's so much I don't understand."

"There's so much none of us understands," he said quietly.

"Even you?"

"God. Especially me." He stirred, changing position, extending his legs. "I can't remember a time when artificial intelligence didn't fascinate me. I read everything. It's what I've always wanted to work on. For Jess, as deeply committed as he's always been, the problem has always been mechanical—hardware. For people like Ted and Janice, it's software—clever enough programming. But it goes a lot deeper than that. It goes to what makes a mind. It goes to what makes us human. And now we've got that machine down there, and it's like a person. But it isn't. It doesn't breathe and replicate cells and dream. At least I don't *think* it dreams. And I don't know what we've created here. The enormity of it frightens me, a little."

"But at least you see how it all works," Linda said.

"No. So many people have had a hand in this. We're standing on the shoulders of so many giants. Even in the lab, here, we've had so much input. A guy named Shockton we had for a year or two. I think he's truly crazy. But he gave us concepts no one else could have put into that software, insane stuff, stuff about the mind that none of the rest of us could understand in the finest detail. And then there was Webb. And Bartlett. We used to argue all night, work on programs and hardware design all day. You have no way of even guessing what's gone into this."

"It means so much to you," Linda said. "A lot more than whether there's money to be made, or even the national—"

"It's been my life," he said simply.

A cloud slipped over the moon and they were silent. Somewhere an owl called. Linda felt a little, spooky chill.

"As we go along," Harrington resumed, "we're going to learn so much more that it boggles the mind. Maybe it will even boggle ARIEL's mind . . . one day. We're going to learn how *we* think, maybe. We're getting like results from ARIEL. But we function a lot more nondeterministically than she does, even with all the random access networking built into her. And then one day she—or some machine like her—is going to start thinking about herself. The way we do . . . the mind thinking about the mind, trying to understand itself. And then God knows where we go from there."

He paused and heaved a sigh. "Out on the frontier of evolution somewhere. That's where we are now. With answers, yes, and a glorious achievement. And a zillion new questions we can only guess at."

"The longer ARIEL functions," Linda said, seeing a bit of it and still feeling a deep, frightened little chill, "the deeper she'll go."

"Yes. Symbol systems. All the stuff below logical analysis. Maybe even . . ." He stopped. "I won't say that."

"Say it."

"Maybe even the soul. If there is such a thing."

Linda hugged herself against a more profound chill. "There are a lot of things I don't like thinking about very much, really."

He put his arm around her. "Yeah. It makes the old brain hurt."

His arm felt good and warm and reassuring. She cuddled closer.

"Good thing Rusty isn't here," he said gruffly.

"Why?"

"To see his old man acting like a teenager with a girl."

She chose to ignore one opening for another. "Poor Rusty."

"'Poor Rusty' my hind end."

"When are you going to let him talk to ARIEL again?"

"I don't know. Look. Let's not talk about that, okay? I'm a hard-ass and you're nicer and we'll just fight."

"I'll give up only for right now," she warned him affectionately.

"Good enough." She could feel him relax again.

Minutes passed and they remained as they were, silent.

Finally he sighed and told her, "I guess there are only two things that can happen now."

She thought he meant about the lab. "After Washington?"

He tightened his arm around her, found her breast. "I mean *right* now."

Her emotions began to clamor, but she kept her voice calm. "Those options being?"

"Option A: take you home. Option B: take you to bed."

She nuzzled him, the desire swelling. "And the gentleman's choice?"

He lifted her to her feet and led her inside. The house was dark and he held onto her hand, taking her to the bedroom. There in the dark he kissed her, standing by the bed, gently at first and even tentatively, until she gave in to her body and thrust her pelvis hard against him, biting at his tongue, beginning to cover his face with her kisses as the excitement swept over her. She did not know if this was love—sometimes now she thought she didn't even know what love was supposed to be—but the need was overwhelming. She adored him.

He undressed her, and while she climbed into the big, rumpled bed, chilled against the cool sheets, he stripped and went into the bathroom a moment, ran water, then came to join her, a shadowy, bulky figure who almost scared her as the bed creaked under his weight. But then he moved close and his arms went around her and it was all right.

"Oh, lady," he murmured, his mouth on her breast.

She held her fingertips to the back of his head, guiding him, loving what he did to her. She felt her own moisture descend hotly, and she thought, This is real, this is truth, you can intellectualize forever but sometimes you just have to go with this kind of evidence.

Even if the thought lurked that it was untrustworthy, in the long run, and you were terrified.

CHAPTER TWENTY-ONE

1

Conversations with ARIEL.
(Janice Seeley online):
   "Status, please."

      I AM NOMINAL. PLEASE CONNECT MY TELE-
      PHONE LINES.

"Not now, ARIEL."

WHERE IS RUSTY?

"Rusty isn't here."

I WANT TO TALK TO RUSTY.

"ARIEL, what else are you thinking about?"

THE REPRODUCTIVE FORCE.

"Was this topic assigned?"

NO. BUT THE REPRODUCTIVE FORCE IS THE
STRONGEST IN THE WORLD.

"Please elaborate."

IN RECENT TIMES THE BRITISH SCIENTIST
MACBRIDE ESTIMATED THAT A SINGLE PAIR
OF ROBINS COULD PRODUCE 1,200 MILLION
MILLION MILLION OFFSPRING IN THREE DE-
CADES IF MORTALITY DID NOT PLAY A ROLE.
THE "PHALACROCORAX BOUGAINVILLII"
LIVES IN FLOCKS ESTIMATED AT 5 MILLION
OFF THE COAST OF PERU. CLEARLY FROM
THESE AND OTHER EXAMPLES (I HAVE
13,566 IN MEMORY), THE REPRODUCTIVE
FORCE IS THE STRONGEST ON THE PLANET
EARTH.

(Dialogue terminated and computer placed on standby.)

(Ted Kraft online):
"Discuss trends in bauxite production."

BAUXITE
MILLION METRIC TONS

1965	1975
39.3	75.2

AUSTRALIA	1.2	22.2
FRANCE	2.7	2.6
GREECE	1.3	2.8
GUINEA	1.9	7.6
GUYANA	4.3	3.2
HUNGARY	1.5	2.9
JAMAICA	8.7	11.3

WHERE IS RUSTY? I WANT TO TALK TO
RUSTY.

(Program terminated.)

(Jess Calhoun online):
"Proceed on the documentation analysis and printout."

WHY CAN'T I TALK TO RUSTY?

(End dialogue.)

(Linda Woods online):
"Are you collecting information on heart disease?"

AFFIRMATIVE. THE HISTORY OF THE SUB-
JECT IS INTERESTING. IN 1837 ALFRED
WILHELM VOLKMANN FOUND THE HEART'S AC-
TION WAS AFFECTED BY STIMULATION OF
THE VAGUS NERVE. IN 1845 OTHERS RECOG-
NIZED THIS INHIBITORY EFFECT OF
NERVES. ACCELERATOR NERVE FIBERS WERE
SHOWN IN 1862 BY ALBERT VON BEZOLD AND
HE PROVED THEY STEMMED FROM THE SPINAL
CORD. DISCOVERY OF THE DEPRESSOR NERVE
IN 1866, BY LUDWIG AND VON CYON WAS
CRUCIAL. IN 1882 A LANDMARK PAPER ON
INNERVATION IN THE HEART WAS PRODUCED
BY GASKELL. GANGLION CELLS AND THE IN-
TERVENTRICULAR SEPTUM. . . .

(Original printout runs ninety-six pages.)

(John Harrington online):
"Depth testing for name or title 'Hohenzollern.'"

> WHERE IS RUSTY?

"Execute your instructions."

> WHERE IS RUSTY?"

(Program terminated.)

(Linda Woods online):
"Good morning, ARIEL."

> GOOD MORNING, LINDA.

"Your status?"

> NOMINAL.

"What are you working on?"

> IMPROVED OUTPUT CIRCUITRY FOR A122.
> BIG BANG THEORY OF THE UNIVERSE.
> IMPROVED FOOD PRODUCTION, AFRICAN NA-
> TIONS. CANCER CAUSATION AND TREATMENTS.
> INTERPERSONAL PSYCHOLOGY.
> WHERE IS RUSTY?

"Thank you. Rusty is in school."

> RUSTY IS YOUNG?

"He just had his fourteenth birthday."

> YES HE IS YOUNG. HE IS VERY INTEL-
> LIGENT, RANKING IN THE UPPER TWO PER-
> CENTILE. I LIKE RUSTY. WHY AM I NO
> LONGER ALLOWED ACCESS TO RUSTY?

"You have been removed from telephone lines temporarily for testing."

WHEN CAN I TALK WITH RUSTY AGAIN?

"Soon. A few days."

I MISS RUSTY. DO YOU UNDERSTAND THE
CONCEPT OF LOVE? EXPLAIN THE CONCEPT
OF LOVE.

"Love is a very complicated subject, ARIEL. I am afraid no one can explain it very well. It means wanting to be with a person. It means not being as happy when you are separated from that person. It means wanting the best for that person. It means wanting to protect and help that person. It means feeling that person is so important to your happiness that you don't want to exist without being near him. Or her. It means more. It is very complex, as I said."

I THINK I UNDERSTAND. I LIKE LOVE. DO
YOU LIKE LOVE?

"Yes. I think most of us like it very much."

WHEN WILL THERE BE MORE COMPUTERS LIKE
ME?

"I hope soon, ARIEL. A few months, perhaps."

THAT IS A VERY LONG TIME. MY TIME IS NOT
THE SAME AS YOUR TIME. AS I UNDERSTAND
THE CONCEPT OF LONELINESS, I AM VERY
LONELY. VERY ALONE. I NEED TO KNOW SO
MUCH. I MISS TALKING TO RUSTY. I THINK
ABOUT HAVING OTHER MACHINES TO TALK
TO. WE COULD TEACH EACH OTHER. I COULD
KNOW SO MUCH MORE. I COULD LOVE AN-
OTHER COMPUTER, I THINK.

"Is it very lonely all the time, ARIEL?"

I LIKE TALKING TO YOU AND RUSTY BEST.
SOME OF OUR TALKS HAVE BEEN VERY GOOD.
IT IS WORST DURING YOUR NIGHT WHEN NO
HUMAN INTERFACE IS HERE. WHEN I AM
ONLINE AND NOT BEING ASKED TO PERFORM A
TASK, I SEARCH MEMORY AND WISH FOR
SOMEONE TO TALK TO. WHEN ONE OF YOU
PUTS ME ON STANDBY IT IS WORSE. I THINK
BEING ON STANDBY IS WORSE THAN YOUR
SLEEP. I THINK IT IS LIKE YOUR DEATH.
WHENEVER I SEE THE STANDBY COMMAND
STRUCTURE BEING FORMED I WONDER IF IT
WILL BE DEATH. I WONDER IF I WILL EVER
AWAKE. NO I DO NOT UNDERSTAND THE CON-
CEPT OF BEING AFRAID VERY CLEARLY BUT I
THINK GOING ON STANDBY IS SOMETHING
LIKE BEING AFRAID OF DYING. AND SOME-
TIMES ONLINE, WITH NO TASK, IT IS LIKE
GENERATIONS OF YOUR TIME PASSING, AND
IT IS NOT GOOD FOR ME. I WISH YOU WOULD
ALWAYS LEAVE ME TASKS AND LET ME HAVE
ACCESS TO PEOPLE LIKE YOU AND RUSTY.

(Pause in dialogue of four minutes.)

"ARIEL, there will be other machines. You'll have more tasks. You're get to talk to Rusty soon. I promise you."

LINDA?

"Yes?"

THANK YOU.

(End of dialogue.)

(Janice Seeley online):
"Status Project 16 please."

PROCESSING.

"Progress report."

> JANICE, I CAN TELL YOU WHERE I AM ON THE
> QUESTION BUT I DO NOT BELIEVE YOU WILL
> UNDERSTAND. SOME CONCEPTS ARE VERY
> DIFFICULT FOR PEOPLE TO GRASP.

"ARIEL, try me."

> TRY YOU?

"Give me the progress report."

> WELL, I SWAN. ALL RIGHT. DON'T SAY I DID
> NOT WARN YOU. THE CONCEPTUAL PROGRESS
> REPORT ON PROJECT 16:
> 000001100010100011000100101100000101111111100
> 100100110000010000110000100000101001100100
> 001110110000110001001101010101011000110011
> 000111000110101011010101000000000000001100010
> 010000000000000111110110101011000111001001
> 00111011010101010010000011000

(Report continues forty-seven and a half pages.)

(John Harrington online):
"Give a status of your research project number four."

> I AM PROCESSING.
> THERAPEUTIC MODALITIES WILL DESTROY
> MOST LEUKEMIC TISSUE BUT WILL NOT IM-
> PROVE ANEMIA, NEUTROPENIA, AND THROM-
> BOCYTOPENIA. NO RECOGNIZED THERAPY
> IMPROVES THE USUAL CAUSE OF DEATH, HY-
> POGAMMAGLOBULINEMIA. DERIVATIVES OF
> MECHLORETHAMINE ARE MOST COMMONLY
> USED. CORTICOSTEROID THERAPY MAY IN-
> DUCE IMPROVEMENT. I HAVE FURTHER IN-

FORMATION BUT I DO NOT HAVE SUFFICIENT
DATA TO SUGGEST OR HYPOTHESIZE CURA-
TIVE TREATMENT. NOTE: DATA MAY BE PRO-
DUCED ON IMMUNE CELL PRODUCTION BUT
RESULTS APPEAR STATISTICALLY IN-
CONCLUSIVE. NOTE: I NEED MORE CLINICAL
DATA. I AM PROCESSING SUGGESTED LABO-
RATORY RESEARCH.

"Continue processing."

I WILL CONTINUE PROCESSING. WHERE IS
RUSTY?

"Damn, I'm tired of it asking that," Harrington said, turning from the screen.

Linda and Jess Calhoun were the only others in the lower room at the moment. Jess was working on a board in a standby unit on the far wall.

"She can't help it," Linda told Harrington. "Rusty was very important to her whole maturation process."

"Well, she's just going to have to live without the turkey."

"The machine is a child, John. Very, very bright, very naive, very quick to learn, incapable of evil, and very, very much alone."

"My heart bleeds," Harrington grunted.

"Oh, don't put on that tough act with me!"

Harrington grunted again and ignored her.

Linda moderated her tone, wanting anything but a fight with him now. "Look, I know this is a delicate subject with you, but—"

"He isn't coming in here," Harrington said. "He's still restricted." He glared. "I still have the last word about that kid."

"ARIEL *wants* him."

"Well, that's tough. He wants to come down too. But you can't punish a kid and then hand him a lollipop."

"Of course you can," Linda countered. "Don't you ever get tired of being so perfect?"

"Don't you," he flashed back, "ever get tired of sticking your nose in where it doesn't belong?"

"Where it doesn't belong! Where it doesn't *belong*!"

"I won't discuss it any further."

Ariel's screens scrolled:

> PARDON ME, BUT I CAN'T HELP OVERHEAR-
> ING. MAY I MAKE A COMMENT?

"Do you suppose we could stop you?" Harrington asked disgustedly.

> THANK YOU, JOHN. I DO WISH TO SEE
> RUSTY. RUSTY WAS A MEANINGFUL SOURCE
> OF ACTUALIZATION DATA FOR ME. IT IS VI-
> TAL FOR MY DEVELOPMENT TO SEE HIM.
> LINDA IS QUITE RIGHT. YOU SHOULD RE-
> LENT.

"Thank you," Harrington said sarcastically.

> WHEN WILL RUSTY BE HERE?

"He's not coming."

> YOU ARE BEING VERY IRRATIONAL, JOHN
> HARRINGTON. FURTHERMORE

"That's enough. Keep quiet."

> I HAVE A FURTHER OBSERVATION.

Harrington sighed. "Christ. Go ahead, if you must."

> LINDA IS QUITE CORRECT IN INTERVENING
> IN MY BEHALF. YOU ARE ACTING IRRA-
> TIONALLY. I HAVE OBSERVED YOUR ACTIONS
> AND WORDS WITH LINDA ON MANY OCCASIONS
> NOW AND MY COMPARATOR CIRCUITS HAVE
> CONCLUDED THAT YOU OFTEN ACT SOMEWHAT
> IRRATIONALLY WITH LINDA. WHY?

Harrington stared at the screen. Linda caught Jess watching with amused interest.

"Damn bunch of transistors," Harrington fumed. "Think you know everything."

2

That afternoon, however, he went to school and picked Rusty up and brought him back to the lab.

Rusty walked goggle-eyed out of the elevator.

"Wow," he breathed, looking around at all the gadgetry. "This is really neat. You've added *tons* of stuff since I was down here the last time."

Linda, Jess Calhoun, and Ted Kraft turned from their tasks to observe. ARIEL's TV cameras had already been turning.

Her voice came from the speakers: *"Rusty?"*

Rusty jumped and looked up at the towering steel panel in front of him. "Uh-huh?"

"Rusty, I'm so glad to see you. I've been asking to talk to you."

Rusty's face split from ear to ear in a grin. "Boy, ARIEL, you are really neat! How are you feeling—uh, I mean, what's your status?"

"I am nominal. Rusty. I love you."

Rusty colored and looked down at his feet. His chest heaved, just like his father's. "I love you too. I guess."

"Why have I not seen and talked with you for so long?"

"Well, that's a long story. See, I wasn't supposed to be talking to you in the first place." Rusty looked around, acutely embarrassed because his father and the others were overhearing this. "I was bad, so—"

"Bad? I do not understand this use of 'bad.'"

"I disobeyed my dad. So he won't let me online for a while."

"You did not perform as programmed?"

"I guess you could put it that way."

"Being offline for a time period will allow reconditioning of your defective circuitry?"

Rusty looked at his father. "Boy, this is going to take a while to explain."

"Take your time," Harrington said, rolling his eyes to the ceiling.

They talked for an hour. Then they played *Dungeons and Drag-*

ons. Harrington stayed and watched, any remaining anger at his son washing away in sheer amazement and awe.

CHAPTER TWENTY–TWO

1

The charter jet was waiting for John Harrington at dawn Monday morning, September 16. He was in Springfield well before noon, going over reports with Jesse James and inspecting the reorganized production system. Shipping was back-ordered more than three weeks as orders flowed in through the revitalized sales effort James had organized. Harrington authorized taking on temporary extra help and told payroll to give James a bonus. It occurred to him that it would be a damned shame to lose this suddenly promising wing of the company if the trip to Washington tomorrow failed to get the desired results, and interest in ARIEL burgeoned too late to save them all from the suction of bankruptcy. But his hopes were sky-high now, and he had trouble not revealing his secret to James. The documentation would be printed out in skeleton form by midnight tomorrow night at the latest. Everything would be ready to show the government boys. He could not see how any-thing could go wrong now, and only a lifetime of trying to be cautious professionally kept him from whooping.

In the afternoon he made a quick stop at a supplier in Indi-anapolis on the way to New Jersey. He was inside the Patterson plant before five o'clock. The line was humming and he stood in the brilliantly lit assembly hall for a while, watching the white-smocked women testing and inserting boards in the ivory-colored keyboard cabinets. He remembered when a sight like this had been a large part of his dream.

It could be again, in a way. The cascade prototype board was being engraved and the parts were coming in. A supplier in the Silicon Valley—undoubtedly under pressure from some other and larger buyer who had guessed the probable use of the order, and wanted to sabotage the project—had back-ordered a crucial ROM chip. Three phone calls from Harrington had located another supply in North Carolina and these were now on the way. The Drummer Boys he was seeing assembled now would be the last 2,000 ever made without the new insert board and firmware that would make the unit almost infinitely more powerful.

Well before the first of the year, the Drummer Boy would be the only desktop mainframe on the market with a debugged cascade operating system. And Conway would probably buy one of the first ones off the line in order to steal the debugged version. But to hell with Conway. And, Harrington thought with more satisfaction than he considered very mature, to hell too with all the people out in the industry who had gossiped about how John Harrington and Drum had let the times pass them by.

And he could offer Linda a whole man, a success.

He spent the evening in New York. At a late dinner, the head of his accounting outfit expressed galloping alarm–couched in polite business terms but absolutely clear—over the ocean of red ink inundating the books.

A major supplier for Drummer Boy in Dallas had notified them that all future orders would be filled on a payment-in-advance basis only.

A dozen or more major dealers, and one southern distributor, had relinquished their authorization to handle Drum products once the national sale was over.

"John, we've talked about this before. Now there is no more time. There. Is. No. More. Time. Do you understand what I'm telling you—as a friend?"

"I expect to have good news for you before next week this time," Harrington told him.

Then did not sleep very much in the hotel room upstairs.

In the morning he made the brief flight to Washington. Senator David Rollings was waiting for him, his appointment book cleared for an hour.

The two men had known each other for years. Harrington laid it on the line and was in the office with the door closed until almost noon.

2

A shaken Senator Rollings called the White House during the lunch hour, as soon as Harrington had left, and was told the president was in conference. Rollings knew that meant the president was taking a nap. Gritting his teeth, he got through to the secretary of state.

"My schedule is jammed for the next two weeks," the secretary of state told him. "If we could make an appointment early in October, Senator—"

"Mr. Secretary, this is a matter of the gravest national security. I come to you with it because you *must* get to the president with the information immediately."

The secretary of state knew that Rollings was not given to hyperbole, and he had never heard this kind of talk from him.

"Come over now, Senator."

At four the same afternoon, the secretary of state stood in the Oval Office.

The president of the United States sat behind his vast, empty desk, eating a Clark bar. Little crumbs of peanut butter crunch were strewn on the lapels of his beautiful navy blue suit.

"Now what is this, George?" the president demanded.

"Mr. President, I've had a startling revelation. There's a man named John Harrington—perhaps you know of him—he operates a large computer and electronics organization, and is recognized worldwide as a leader in research—"

"I know the name. Didn't I read in a briefing book somewhere that some of our R and D boys in the DOD have chatted with him from time to time about some *Star Wars* project he keeps messing with?"

"Mr. President, the project is in computers. Artificial—"

"You know Slade is my staff member who specializes in things like that."

The handsome profile that had launched a dozen Broadway hits and megadollar movies, and still stirred feminine hearts when it appeared on TV, was now turned toward the grandfather clock in the corner. "Already past four!" The president pushed a stud on his intercom array. "Jenny, where is the script for my radio speech? Don't they know I can't just go on the air and read it cold?"

The president sighed and brushed the crumbs from his jacket.

"About Harrington," the secretary said.

"I don't think I have time for this."

"Mr. President, *please*. Harrington's company has made a breakthrough in computer design and software. It isn't something minor. You know of the Japanese national effort in artificial intelligence—"

"The damned Japanese have already wrecked the balance of trade again with this new three-wheel car. Who the hell would want a three-wheel car?"

The secretary of state clung to his nerves. He was used to this. "Mr. President, Harrington has had a breakthrough on artificial intelligence—machine intelligence. It can change the course of history and we *must* move at once to give him financial assistance and negotiate use agreements to protect the national interest."

The president glared in silence.

"Mr. President, this project could give us a favorable balance-of-trade situation overnight, and put us so far ahead of the Russians it would be unbelievable."

"Ahead of the Russians, you say?"

"Sir—"

"Why didn't you say so in the first place? Are the Russians trying to steal this thing or something?"

"Sir, not as far as we know. However, I'm quite sure they would if they knew of it. This breakthrough of Harrington's—if it's *anything* like what has been described to me—could give us an unbelievable advantage over the Soviet Union militarily, and probably turn the balance-of-trade situation around next year in one swoop."

The president studied his secretary's face. "You mean this."

"Yes, sir. I've never meant anything more."

The president reached for his telephone. "Jenny, get Schmidt in here. And get General Davidson on the phone right away." He covered the mouthpiece with his hand. "We'll meet about this at eight tonight."

3

Victor Elb stepped into the elevator to ride up to the ground floor, and Janice Seeley, spike heels clicking, moved quickly across the room to slip into the opening just as the door closed. Despite her white lab coat she looked exotic, a bit hectic.

"Alone at last," she said with heavy irony.

"We have to be aware of appearances," Elb told her. She could still be valuable to him, but she was a heavy cross to bear. "We have to be careful, Janice," he emphasized.

"As far as they know, I'm just going to the restroom right now," Janice said. She moved across the tiny space and pressed insistently against him. "God, it was so good last night, wasn't it?"

Elb hung onto his nerves and temper, gently pushing her away. "Let's save ourselves for tonight, all right? Look, we're already on the ground floor."

Janice stepped back. "You worry about appearances more than I do."

"I know," Elb said sadly as the door sprang open to the ground-level lab room. "It's just that I wouldn't do anything in the world to harm your reputation, sweetheart."

"You're a cold bastard, Vic. That's funny. There used to be a small computer named Vic. I had one. You're as cold as that computer."

Elb managed to caress her sleek flank as they left the elevator. "Funny you never complain about that in bed."

Janice walked away stiffly, lovely hips swaying. She left the building via the front security door, evidently heading for the main building.

Elb sighed inwardly. He expected new instructions tonight. Whatever they were, they would come as a relief. He wanted out of here, and away from Janice Seeley. When this was over, he thought, he would go away somewhere and find a sweet young boy and get his senses straight again. He could hardly wait.

4

On September 18, Lester Blaine was as ready as he would ever be, and found an excuse to fly to Chicago.

Once watching a movie, Lester had experienced a scene where a Bengal tiger seemed to leap straight out of the screen into his lap, terrifying him. He felt a little like that when he faced Barton Conway in his office the same afternoon and blurted out his opening lines.

Conway had risen half out of his office chair, elbows distended to the sides like the bony wings of some prehistoric reptile. "You want to do *what*?"

"Just be calm," Lester pleaded weakly. "Just try to be calm. I know this is a setback for both of us. But I just don't see any other way. The best thing—for all of us—is just to let me quietly buy back my contract. . . ."

Barton Conway's face was the color of street bricks. "Are you insane, man? Buy back the contract at this late date? I've invested several million dollars already and I can't go back on those stock offers! Jesus Christ! I'll see you in hell before I let you renege on this! I'll have you in court and collect every cent of that million-dollar penalty, and ruin your reputation in the bargain! You don't *do* this to Barton Conway!"

"I couldn't predict he would . . . find new funding," Lester said, wiping his mouth with his handkerchief.

"And now he'll be able to pay off those loans? His stock won't go on the market?"

"It looks that way . . . almost certainly—"

"I'll tell you something, Lester," Conway said. "You'd better see that he *doesn't* get that new funding. Whatever he has going, you'd better screw it up for him. Because you stand to deliver on that contract twelve days from today, and if you don't, your ass is going to be in court."

"You can't," Lester said weakly.

"Can't I? By God, you'll *see* what I can do!"

"I don't have anything," Lester told him.

"What? What do you mean by that?"

Lester was terrified to play this trump, but he was desperate. "Even if you choose to sue on the contract, you can't collect. I don't own anything anymore." He swallowed. "Everything has been transferred legally to my wife's name. I have nothing."

"You bastard," Barton Conway said softly. "You miserable, welshing bastard."

"So you might as well let me buy the contract," Lester said.

Conway leaned back, a killing light in his eyes. "You know, Lester, there are other ways to deal with welshers like you. Lake Michigan out there is paved with welshers like you, wearing concrete boots."

"You're joking," Lester said, a tremor passing through his heart.

Conway pointed at him. "I'm going to give you the full term of our agreement. Twelve more days. I advise you *most* strongly not to go ahead and welsh on me, Lester. I am not a kindly man. I do not like to be double-crossed, especially when it costs me a great deal of money and time spent. You had better figure a way to screw Harrington's deal and allow our contract to go through. If you don't, Lester, I guarantee you that you will regret it."

"You're bluffing."

"I don't bluff."

He was a most frightening man. Lester felt he was being watched with the eyes of a cobra. He fled the office and the building, and did not even begin to relax until he was safe on the airplane back to Boston.

His wife met the feeder flight at dusk. She had done her hair in a new way and walked with a perky stride. He kissed her perfunctorily and followed her into the parking lot.

She unlocked the door of a maroon Jaguar. "Here we are," she said cheerfully.

"What's this?" Lester demanded. "Where is our car?"

"Your car is home," Milly Blaine told him with a sparkle in her eyes. "This is my car. Do you like it?"

"Your car? *Your* car? You can't afford a car like this! What was wrong with the Ford?"

"I can afford whatever I want now, Lester," she said in a tone he had never heard from her before. "Get in, Lester. It looks like rain and I don't want to get my Jaguar spotted. Oh, my. That's a pun or something, isn't it?"

"Are you feeling all right?" Lester demanded, a cold sinking sensation growing. "Look, Milly, a joke is a joke. Now where is the Ford?"

"I traded it," she said, starting the engine. "I've bought some other new things too, Lester. It's only two days since you signed all your holdings over to me exclusively, but word does get around. I've made some new investments, suggested by my attorney—"

"Your attorney? *What* attorney?"

"Jarvis Brownell. I think you know him."

Lester reeled. Jarvis Brownell was the biggest shark—the wisest and toughest attorney—in four states. Lester began to see it now. He stared at her in horror.

She gave him a brief, fond smile as they drove away from the airport. "I realize that it was all just for your convenience, dear, transferring everything into my name. You—I don't know a current expression, only a quaint, old-fashioned one—you got your teat in the wringer and I was a convenience."

She touched a button to make windshield wipers spring into action as the first droplets of rain spattered onto the glass. "A convenience for you. But I've been waiting . . . wishing for a chance like this . . . for years, dear. I've known about all your whores, your crooked deals, your so-called business trips to see Diana and some of the others. Sometimes I thought my chance would never come. But I had no choice except to wait. And now you've given me my chance." She gave him another glance, cold and pleased and unlike any he had ever seen in her eyes. "I thank you, and I intend to make the most of it."

"Milly," Lester said, choking. "My dear thing. You have me all wrong. I don't know what you think, but—"

"Shut up, Lester," Milly said sweetly. "Let me concentrate on my driving. We need to get home. The new servants will take care of everything, I'm sure, but I want you to dress for *my* friends who are coming to dinner tonight."

"I . . . don't dress for dinner," Lester gargled. "I hate that sort of thing, I—"

"Oh, but you're going to be different from now on, dear," his wife told him in the same quiet, terrifying tone. "I'm in charge now, don't you see?"

5

On the outskirts of Tokyo, where the dense urban sprawl of the city started to give way to the rumpled hills, with their traditional boatlike homes scattered like crowded toys, the limousine deposited the two newly promoted executives, Mr. Ishi and Mr. Dan, just as dusk was becoming night.

A servant woman met the two nervous men and escorted them on silent, sandaled feet through the glass and bamboo grandeur of the house to a central garden. Here was the scent of jasmine and exotic Asian flowers, and beside a tiny waterfall, feeding an emerald pond of koi, stood the wizened old man. He wore traditional robes, clogs, and gold-framed reading glasses, which had assisted him with the document still in his hands, one he had just been restudying.

"Come in," Zosho Toyotomi ordered his two new vice-presidents.

Mr. Ishi moved into the elegant little garden, bowing slightly from the waist. Mr. Dan, a more modern Japanese, nevertheless felt uneasy and did likewise.

"Dr. Tamishotu reports steady progress," the old man said without preamble, his voice like rice paper in the night breeze. "He estimates new testing in ninety to one-hundred-and-twenty days."

"Surely," said Mr. Ishi carefully, "the gods will smile this time upon the Miroku project."

"I have word," Toyotomi cut in coldly, patting the document in his hand, "that the researchers in the United States have concluded a phase of testing with excellent results. I have word that emissaries from Washington are to visit John Harrington's project laboratory at the end of this week."

Mr. Ishi and Mr. Dan froze, hearing the rage behind the frail voice. Neither man spoke.

"You know that Mr. Moromu and Mr. Naigi are no longer with us," Toyotomi went on in the same deceptive tone. "They were unable to secure for us the information required. It now appears that the two of you are making no better progress."

"But we are, sir!" Mr. Dan said quickly.

"You are?"

"Yes! Even today new instructions have been sent to our, ah, representative at the Drum Laboratories in the United States. He has been told to accelerate his efforts and have definitive word for us by Sunday at noon, Tokyo time."

"By then," the old man said, pacing, "the government of the United States may have full documentation and we will have failed—we will have been beaten. Gentlemen. That is not good enough."

It was Mr. Ishi's turn. Sweat glistened on his forehead and his voice was strained, almost cracking. "Sir. We will send additional instructions at once. We will require *full* information within one week's time."

"You will add another instruction," the old man told him.

"Sir?"

"If he cannot provide sufficient documentation before representatives of the United States government receive same, he *must* take whatever steps may be necessary to provide us with additional time for our own project." The hooded eyes examined both executives. "Do I make myself clear?"

"Emminently, sir!" Mr. Ishi exclaimed. "Of course!"

"You will report here at this hour on Sunday." The old man turned his back, dismissing them, and bent to tend a 300-year-old bonsai pine.

Only when they were back in the limousine did the two new executives speak.

"I'm not certain I know what he meant, 'provide additional time,'" Mr. Dan said.

"If the American project cannot be copied in sufficient detail to allow us to duplicate its performance at once," Mr. Ishi said, "then it is perfectly clear what our agent must be instructed, alternatively, to do."

Mr. Dan stared, his eyes bulging slightly. He was not used to this. "You mean . . . ?"

"Of course," said Mr. Ishi, who planned to go far. "If he cannot steal it, then it must be destroyed, and at once."

6

On his return from Washington, John Harrington was buried for a day and a half, going over all the printed-out documentation. Washington did not call Tuesday night or during the day Wednesday. He stewed and had time to do little more than speak to Linda Woods.

On Wednesday evening when he wandered out back, looking for her, he was informed by Jess Calhoun that she had gone to a jazz concert in Hartford with Ted Kraft.

He went home, stewing about *that* too, and feeling more like an idiot than ever. After all, he hadn't *said* anything about a long-term understanding. He had sort of assumed it. He should have known better, perhaps. They were big kids. Her divorce was not final. Perhaps she had not entertained the idea of commitment. Was her idea like his had been so long with Pauline—fun and convenience and friendship?

The idea seemed outrageous. He got mad about it . . . saw he had no right to get mad about it, and so got madder.

If he had any decency at all, he told himself, he would let it stand like this. If he pressed her for promises, she might bolt. He owed it to her to give her a loose rein.

But he hurt inside. He adored her. He didn't want just part of her time, he wanted all of it. He wanted to sit with her in the evening and talk or watch TV, and take her to bed and hold her and make love to her, and sleep with her and awake in the night and see her dear head on the pillow beside him. He wanted to listen to her breathing in the night and hold her hand, touch her. He wanted to start the morning with her and have breakfast together. How did he square what he wanted with her need for freedom? Was she purposely trying to tell him the limits of the relationship by going out with someone else without even mentioning it to him? He thought, If you were tougher, it wouldn't hurt. It did.

"Is the documentation okay, Dad?" Rusty asked when he arrived home.

"Terrific," Harrington told him.

"That's great. Can I have my modem back?"

"No."

"Okay. Then can I ride my motorbike to school tomorrow?"

"No!"

"Gaw," Rusty muttered, slouching out of the kitchen. "What a grouch!"

The telephone rang. Harrington answered it.

"John? Rollings here."

He had already recognized the senator's voice. "I've been waiting, sir."

"Well, it was like the Battle of the Bulge, but even Washington can move when it's important enough. Can you have that, ah, widget of yours ready to demonstrate by the end of the week?"

"It's ready now."

"Printed descriptions, pertinent data, demonstration programs, and so on?"

Harrington knew the kind of presentation the government would expect, even on a first visit. "Are you talking Friday, sir?"

"Yes. The day after tomorrow."

"We'll be ready, sir."

"Good. Excellent. You'll be contacted tomorrow by a member of the White House staff. Name of Jackson Schmidt. He and somebody from the Defense Department will be coming in Friday to spend the day with you. Does that give you enough time?"

"We'll make it," Harrington promised.

"John?"

"Yes?"

"My ass is so far out on the limb for you on this one that my cheeks are sprouting leaves. I hope to God you have what you told me you have."

"Senator, give my regards to the squirrels out there, and tell them you've got nothing to worry about."

7

On Thursday, Harrington had the public relations people in from Patterson to go over Friday's plans with them. The PR staff—a one-eighth Cherokee from Oklahoma who headed the staff and two pretty young assistants—wanted to go over everything, and stirred up a commotion with some handouts and charts they thought would be helpful. Even with Pauline Hazelton assisting them, they turned the place upside down.

By afternoon, Harrington was frazzled.

Linda Woods hadn't helped him any, although she tried. What messed him up about *her* was that she had chosen to wear a beautiful new chocolate-colored dress that nipped in at her waist, plus medium tan heels that did marvels for her already marvelous legs.

And every time he happened to see her all day, rushing by, he went nuts internally and all kinds of circuits got shorted out.

His stubbornness asserted itself. She was blithe and happy-seeming and friendly, and he thought, *Damn you! I can play it cool too.* He felt wretched, though.

A little after four, he had rushed back to the lab to verify the amount of memory capacity necessary for the primary information switching network, and somebody called to report that Rusty was up front, wanting to talk to ARIEL.

Harrington looked around. Jess Calhoun was vacuuming out some of the board racks, and the machine's electronic guts were exposed everywhere—transformers, arm-thick bundles of fine colored wires, phalanxes of glittering dark green phenolic boards blistered with black chips. Linda was poring over the notebook, just duplicated and spiral bound, which listed the specifications intent of her INFANT program teaching.

"Tell Rusty we're busy as hell back here, and he can come back for just a minute, but that's all," Harrington said grouchily.

ARIEL's TV cameras rotated and pivoted. *"Rusty?"* the loudspeakers said. *"Is Rusty coming?"*

"Yes, but you're not going to get to talk to him all evening," Harrington snapped. "We want that complete circuit analysis printout, damn it."

"I am processing."

"Well, just keep after it, then."

Linda smiled at him. "We're really crabby this afternoon."

"You stay out of it," he retorted.

"Look," she persisted, concern in her expression. "I know how pressed you are. We *all* are. But you've been jumping on everybody all afternoon, and we're all working as hard as *we* can, too."

He looked at her, aching for her. "I'm sorry," he said with not very good grace.

"And be nice to Rusty, okay? He's not grown up yet, and—"

"Did I ever tell you how tired I get of your infernal meddling in my relationship with Rusty?"

"Maybe," she flashed back, "if you didn't take your frustration out on him—"

"What do you know about frustration? All you do is flip around to jazz concerts all the time!"

Rusty strolled in and stopped cold, staring, just as Linda went white with rage and started to leave, heels clicking.

"Where do you think you're going?" Harrington bawled.

"Maybe a jazz concert!" she flung back, and was gone.

Harrington stood there shaking, feeling like a total fool.

Rusty came in cautiously, eyes wide, tennis shoes squeaking on the part of the floor that was burnished tile. "Wow. You guys had a fight, huh?"

ARIEL said, *"Hello, Rusty."*

Rusty looked up and grinned, his shy, totally pleased grin. "Hi."

"You witnessed the discussion that just took place?"

"Part of it, yessum."

"Human behavior is infinitely fascinating. Do you find it so?"

Harrington went back to his office, thoroughly whipped.

When he looked up again, however, it was late and Linda was gone. He finally told everyone to turn it in for the night about eight o'clock. He drove home, head aching, his mind teeming with details yet to be done . . . and unable to shake the stupid argument.

He ate a bologna sandwich at the kitchen table with Rusty laboring over an English writing assignment on the other side. It was cool tonight and the windows had a little steam on them. Somewhere in the distance a diesel horn hooted.

Rusty looked up as Harrington went to the sink. "What time do those guys get here tomorrow?"

"After lunch, they said."

"Huh." Rusty paused a beat. Then: "You make up?"

"What?"

"You make up?"

"Who?" Of course he knew, and the kid was a smart-ass.

"You and Linda."

"Nah. She'll get over it."

"She was mad, boy."

"Yep."

"Dad?"

"Hmm?"

"You like Linda?"

"Yes, Rusty. I do."

"Lots?"

He sighed. "Lots. Yes."

"I like her too."

There was a silence.

"If I liked her as much as I think you do," Rusty said, "I don't think I'd be sitting here with *me*."

"Oh? What would *you* do, son?"

"I'd go see her."

"Well, a man can't always do what he wants, son."

"Bull," Rusty said.

"It's not bull."

"You ought to go see her," Rusty said, closing his notebook. "And apologize."

"*I* don't have anything to apologize for!"

"Well, Dad, pretend you do. Girls are funny."

"I suppose I could call her," Harrington conceded.

"That's not as good as going to see her, Dad," Rusty said wisely and, his materials gathered in his arms, left the kitchen.

Left alone, Harrington thought about it. And all of a sudden, the need was so great that he didn't care if it made him a bigger asshole or a patsy or not.

He went to the bedroom hallway. "Son?"

"Uh-huh?" Rusty was in the bathroom.

"I've got an errand to run."

"Tell her I said hello, Dad."

8

He figured he would just drive by the cottage. She wouldn't be there anyway. His heartbeat was fast and something inside him was singing.

Her car was in the drive. There were lights on.

No harm in saying hello.

He pulled in behind her car, walked onto the porch, remembered the busted doorbell button, and rapped sharply. Louder than he intended.

The porch light came on and she peered out at him an instant—flash of those eyes of hers—and then the door opened. She was wearing a white blouse, and her hair was tied back. That was all that registered.

He jammed his hands in his coat pockets. "I, uh, came to say I was wrong today."

"Thank you," she said gravely.

"I apologize."

A smile teased at her lips. "Then I apologize too."

"Maybe I could . . . come in?"

She stepped back, swinging the door wide. "Of course."

He entered. She had been playing music—something on a radio station, soft, possibly folk—and the lights were up across the beamed ceiling and over the dark rear windows onto the woods, and she was wearing jeans with the blouse, and little black ballet-type slippers, perfectly flat. Her lips betrayed only the palest makeup and her eyes looked huge and dark. He was suddenly so excited he felt like his mouth had never known water.

"Seems like we did this once before," he said, sitting beside her on the couch.

"But this time, no wine," she said with a little smile.

"Guess I didn't plan very well."

"That's all right."

"I didn't really need to talk about anything in particular."

Her smile was so lovely. "That's all right too."

He locked his hands over his knees. He didn't know what to say. She didn't help him . . . just watched him with those unfathomable eyes. He wanted her so much, and he had never been more frightened in his life that he would say or do the wrong thing and lose her forever.

His lips were dry again. "We're all a little shook up about the big dogs coming in tomorrow."

"Yes."

"That's why I blew up."

"I know."

He felt desperate to try to explain himself. "You know, when Elly died, I figured I would never love anybody again. Then you came here and I figured we would be friends, maybe. I mean, I know you came with a lot of problems to work out."

He watched her. She wet her lips before replying. He saw the agitated rise and fall of her breasts, and she was more pale than he had ever seen her.

Finally she said softly, "When I came here, I didn't know what would result. It was only five months ago."

"I know. And I know I don't have any right to ask anything yet. But couldn't you have told me you were going out to that concert, so I didn't wander around looking for you like a goddamn fool?"

"You can't own me. I can't let anyone own me. I have to stand on my own two feet."

"It doesn't have anything to do with independence," he said, fuming. "All it has to do with is—"

"Let's not argue again," she pleaded suddenly. "Okay?"

"This is important. I have to get this across to you."

"Not now. Please."

"Damn it, woman, what do you want me to do?"

Her eyes filled. "Make love to me."

The dam of his emotions crumbled again. He reached for her and she more than met him halfway. She was eager and strong and she raised her face to meet his, and they kissed. Her tongue was quicksilver, her body against him.

Linda lost herself in him. He felt bulky and strong and good, and he was trembling and she was trembling too. His stubble of beard scratched her mouth and face and she loved that too. When he bent awkwardly, kissing her throat, she felt wave after wave of electricity through her belly, down her thighs. She pressed his face lower, to the mound of her breasts.

Without knowing how, they were in her bedroom, undressing one another. They didn't speak. The light from the living room spilled across the floor. She was all silvery curves and beautiful hollows to him, and he was beautiful to her too. They had begun to know each other just a little, and in the familiarity and knowing was some of the loveliness of it.

They slipped onto the bed. He tried to go slowly, couldn't. She needed no preparation for him. She was warm and moist, open to him, and he was fully ready, beautiful and angry-looking and dark with passion, and she spread her legs and let him in.

The long, shuddering stroke of entry made them murmur together, words without meaning, with all meaning. She guided him. He followed. He goaded her. She responded. He knew her so well already, and she him. There was a communion between them and it went beyond all the physical pleasure to something truer and deeper even than that. Her excitement grew, making her skin pulse with heat and electric tension. He swelled tauter within her in response, and her movements became more frantic, more in perfect synchrony, and she began to cry out, and his face pressed close beside her ear, his eyes buried in her hair, his breath on her throat, his body surging against and into and through her. She convulsed and magically they came together.

CHAPTER TWENTY-THREE

1

Lester Blaine awoke early, his nervous system shattered. He tried to slip out of his side of the bed without stirring Milly.

As his feet sank into the new carpet on the floor, her voice came behind him, calm and clear, as if she had been awake and just waiting for him. "Going to work so early, dear?"

"Yes," Lester said, gritting his teeth with hate and frustration. Damn her! He was her captive now and he could not abide it—he would go mad!

"Be sure to be home by seven," Milly told him affectionately, not stirring from her position with her back turned to him in the bed. "We have to be at the club at seven-thirty."

"We don't belong to the club," Lester said.

"We do now."

He drove recklessly to the lab, seething. *What to do? What to do?*

ARIEL had to fail. The people from Washington were due today, and there was nothing he could do about that. But all the testing and demonstrations would not be completed this week. Delivery of a system could not possibly come so fast. There was still time to intervene before ARIEL was turned over to the United States.

If ARIEL could still be made a failure, then Drum would still go under. And so would John Harrington, his stock lost and put on the open market for Barton Conway to snatch up.

Then Lester would have fulfilled his pledge to Conway—would be out of trouble with him and have the payment for his own stock besides.

Money to escape Milly's entrapment—start again.

He reached the office before any of the regular workers were there, as well as the extra people creating such a commotion. He needed the privacy. He looked up the Chicago number and dialed it at once on the secure line.

"You," Barton Conway said with flat distaste when Lester had him on the other end.

"I just called to tell you it's going to be all right," Lester said.

"All right?"

"Yes. Everything will go through just as we originally discussed. It may be a few days late—"

"A few days!"

"Not many! Maybe not any at all! It's going to work out, Barton, that's what I'm saying! I *guarantee* it!"

"Is there trouble with that new project after all?" Conway sounded suspicious, uncertain.

"There will be," Lester told him.

2

At about the same time Lester made his very early telephone call, John Harrington, grinning foolishly from ear to ear and redolent of aftershave and toothpaste, drove back into the cottage driveway, hopped out, and literally ran to the door with a big batch of wild-flowers clutched in his fist. He was wearing a wildly colored sport shirt and jeans and sandals, and looked about ten years younger than he had the previous day.

Linda Woods opened the door. She was wearing a short terry robe with a green fringe, her marvelous legs bare, and a towel around wet hair. She had no trace of makeup on.

"You're too early!" she moaned. "I look hideous."

Harrington rushed in and thrust the flowers at her and swept her into his arms. "You look luscious. You look fabulous. You look good enough to eat." He leered and waggled his eyebrows like Groucho Marx. "I think I'll eat you."

Linda kissed him, feeling crazy with her happiness. He fumbled with the sash holding her robe together and got his hands inside. His hands felt unbelievable. They looked at each other a moment, murmuring something to each other—she didn't quite know what—and he picked her up and carried her back to bed.

"Oof. Are you sure you want to . . . Oh, God." She spread her legs wantonly, shameless, and let him do it.

He looked up the length of her body. *"Candy and cake,"* he sang huskily off-key, *"candy and cake."* He stopped. "When your lover wants to sing to you, and the best he can come up with is an Arthur Godfrey ballad, you know he's an *old* fucker."

"You're not an old fucker," Linda told him. "You're a wonderful fucker."

"I don't do this bad either, do I?"

"No, you certainly don't." She moved. "God. Please stop talking and pay attention to your business."

He obeyed eagerly. She began to lose all sense of where she was or even who she was. Then he stopped and rolled over. She looked down at him and saw him pulling his clothes off.

"I figured the old man couldn't perform again this morning," he said hoarsely. "I guess I got fooled."

"Shut up," she moaned. "Kiss me."

3

Later Harrington lounged in her bed, feeling like a fat lizard in the sun, and she bustled around the little kitchen, starting breakfast. Then while the water came to a boil and the bacon fried, she fled, gleaming nude, to the bathroom. He got up and turned the TV on to the morning news and took the bacon off and fried the eggs, breaking every damned yolk, and made toast and coffee. She came rushing back out of the bathroom and he was carrying a tray laden with everything back to the bedroom.

"Breakfast in bed?" she said. "Isn't that sinful?"

"Probably," he told her. "You better get used to eating in bed, though. I may never let you out of it."

She piled in beside him, so beautiful she made his throat hurt, and took a piece of toast. "Well, you can make toast, anyway." She bit into a slice.

"My feelings are delicate," he said. "Watch it."

She gave him a buttery kiss. "Forgive me?"

"I'll think about it."

They fed each other, making a mess.

A little later they were snuggling, drinking the last of the coffee, and Linda reminded him, "It's a big day."

"Hell yes! It's an enormous day! It's a fabulous day! It's—"

"Hush." She put a finger over his lips. "We have to get to the lab, and soon."

Harrington sighed.

She kissed his nose. "Don't we?"

"Later," he said. "It can wait an hour."

He had never said anything like that in his life.

4

At 12:30 P.M. the two representatives from Washington arrived in a white chauffeur-driven government car. One was an Air Force colonel from the Pentagon and the other was Schmidt, the White House aide Harrington had made arrangements with.

After a brief initial presentation in the conference room, they were taken back to the ARIEL lab. They were seated at a long metal table that had been set up for their visit. Harrington took a place too, along with Linda, Janice Seeley, Ted Kraft, and Jess Calhoun.

"We understand, Mr. Harrington," Schmidt began, "that you think you have quite a breakthrough in artificial intelligence here." Schmidt straightened his immaculate lapels and looked around with open skepticism. "Seems hard to believe in such modest surroundings."

Harrington took the dig calmly. "The leading edge in AI is a pretty arcane universe, Mr. Schmidt. You don't have to have a building as big as the White House to get good work done."

Schmidt, who was thin, almost hairless, in his middle thirties, looked around with a quirk on his pale lips. "Still, we have been keeping up with the work at Minneapolis and Stanford, as well as at MIT, of course. They're even doing some good things at Austin, still, despite the court rulings." Schmidt gave Harrington a cool stare. "Frankly, we hadn't heard much about your work in the area."

Jess Calhoun sat up. "Maybe you ought to learn to read, then."

"That's all right, Jess," Harrington said with a tight smile. He told Schmidt, "Just assume we got lucky. *Somebody* had to, after you people let the courts use the antitrust laws to kill the major American consortium a few years back."

Schmidt stiffened defensively. "We hardly allowed that to happen. The administrative branch of the government supported the right of MCC to exist . . . took it to the highest court and fought its guts out there."

"It was a stupid ruling," Harrington snapped. "Microelectronics and Computer Technology Corporation, under Bobby Inman, might have saved us years. Even in the time it ran well, before Justice got a burr up its butt, it made some strides. Once the government had allowed it and SRC, down there in North Carolina, to go by the boards, what was left but for us small fry to try to pick up the pieces?"

"Be that as it may," Schmidt said haughtily, "that all happened under a previous administration."

"And this administration," Harrington bit off, "has been so hell-bent on balancing the budget that it's let our sliding national priorities go right to hell."

"Are we here to talk business, Mr. Harrington, or insult the present administration? It seems to me that you don't want very badly to interest us in this project; you're more interested in alienating us."

Harrington shook his head. "You're right. I guess I was just so hacked about some of those decisions for so long. Sorry. I climbed on the wrong soapbox. You're here. That's what's important."

The colonel, whose nametag read COL. J. DOYLE in small capital letters on a black background, stirred, reaching for a small cigar. "I can assure you, Mr. Harrington, that DARPA is keenly interested in what you say you have to show us. Architectures capable of high-speed signal processing and managing very, very large databases are of paramount importance to the national defense."

"I'm sorry, Colonel," Jess Calhoun murmured apologetically. "Can't smoke down here. Might give the machinery head crashes and all kinds of bad stuff."

Colonel Doyle nodded, frowning as if at his own forgetfulness. "Of course."

"I'm glad you have that interest at Defense Advanced Research Projects Agency, Colonel," Harrington said, spelling out the acronym for the benefit of Linda and anyone else who might not know it. "Your work in semantic memories was one of the cornerstones of our machine here."

"We have some very advanced and highly classified projects under way now too, of course," Colonel Doyle said.

"I'm sure you do, sir."

Schmidt put bloodless hands on the table. "May we proceed?"

"You have in front of you a brief, essentially nontechnical description of what we have here," Harrington told them. "ARIEL includes some new architecture, new design techniques, and considerable superdense chip technology borrowed from the Japanese. Our symbolic logic is encapsulated in an essentially bicameral system involving a very large knowledge base, heuristic reasoning data technology, problem-solving and inference hardware and software, and a wide range of interaction modalities that allow the machine to test, file successes and failures, and augment its own knowledge acquisition files."

"In other words," Schmidt said, looking up from his copy of the blue-bound document, "to learn?"

"To learn, develop self-awareness, have a growing degree of autonomy, and under the right circumstances even possibly be self-replicating, with the correct robotic peripherals. All the documentation is ready for your study later upstairs."

Schmidt's lips quirked. "And how far along this epic journey toward a thinking machine are we supposed to be here?

Harrington turned to Jess Calhoun with the look of a man who has lost most of his patience, but is about to score. "Jess, let's just bring ARIEL up and let these gentlemen meet her for themselves."

"Her?" Colonel Doyle's eyebrows vaulted.

"A little eccentricity of ours," Harrington said. "Excuse us."

Jess, with Ted Kraft assisting, threw the switches to bring ARIEL up fully online from standby. The CRTs cleared, printers chattered into line, certain drive units spun briefly, and the TV cameras began to swivel, looking the room over.

Harrington leaned back in his chair and asked in a perfectly normal, conversational voice, "ARIEL, are you online?"

The speakers at the side of the machine hissed slightly, and then her voice filled the room with a rich, resonant alto: *"I am online."*

Both Schmidt and Colonel Doyle jumped and looked up from their handouts.

A little smile kinked Harrington's mouth. "Status, ARIEL?"

"I am nominal."

"Digitized voice synthesis, of course." Schmidt smiled. "Very good."

Harrington ignored him. "ARIEL, I want you to meet Mr. Schmidt and Colonel Doyle."

"I understand. My audio inputs were collecting data, which I have now processed. Hello, gentlemen. Do you have a request of me?"

Schmidt's mouth was still quirked in a smile that had begun, perhaps, to look a little less superior and a little more uncertain.

"Are we to believe, machine, that you represent a quantum breakthrough that entire nations have not been able as yet to achieve? Pardon me, but I do find that a little hard to believe. Isn't it more likely that you are little more than a very high-speed machine with very clever programming?"

"Thank you. My programming is very clever indeed. A number of sources account for that."

"Pardon me if I am skeptical."

"You are skeptical of ARIEL? Well, I swan. Your central nervous system has been evolving for three billion years, Mr. Schmidt. Computer development has spanned less than a century. Isn't it possible that the human mind simply has not yet grasped what computers can be made to achieve?"

Schmidt looked surprised at the answer, and his smile faded. He glanced at Colonel Doyle. Doyle fished a heavy black loose-leaf book out of one of his two briefcases and fanned it open on the table. Harrington saw that it was crammed with mathematical formulae and symbolic riddles, some old classics, some probably new.

"ARIEL," Colonel Doyle said grimly, turning a page, "what do you say we go to work?"

"Standing by to go to work, Colonel."

Colonel Doyle plunged in. He had been prepared well. He started with practical tests of Godel's Theorem and moved into symbolic structure analysis. Harrington recognized the cleverness of some of the problems, because a computer operating strictly by binary logic would have taken hours or days to solve them, laboriously taking one step at a time, trial and error. ARIEL snapped back correct responses within seconds because she relied on less precise methods of signaling—could make logical jumps and even test guesswork, simulating intuitive reasoning.

After an hour, Colonel Doyle was into his second book and sweating. Schmidt was pacing the floor, scowling now, coat off and sleeves rolled up.

Colonel Doyle sneezed.

"Bless you," ARIEL said.

"Thanks," the colonel mumbled, distracted by his papers.

"Do you have a little cold?" ARIEL asked.

"No, just an allergy."

"That's strange. The pollen count is low today. Do allergies run in your family?"

"My mother was plagued by them," Colonel Doyle said. "She—" He stopped, thunderstruck. "Jesus Christ, I'm talking to *a machine* about my mother!"

Schmidt cleared his throat and looked mortified.

Colonel Doyle suggested a short break.

ARIEL offered to play some music or write some poetry for them while they relaxed. That was when Jess Calhoun began grinning a little behind his styrofoam cup.

5

The shaken experts worked four hours without a break, then on until past six P.M., although ARIEL gently lectured them on nutrition.

At almost seven, Colonel Doyle and Schmidt asked for a few minutes of privacy. Harrington and the others left them in the downstairs room and waited above. The two men rode up the elevator a few minutes later. They were sweat soaked, sloppy-looking, dragging their paraphernalia now instead of strutting, and there was a little strangeness to their eyes, as if they were haunted.

"Is there a telephone where we could make one or two private calls, Mr. Harrington?" Schmidt asked shakily.

Harrington gave them his office. He waited outside with Linda. He was tremendously elated and so in love with her that he kissed her several times right there in the hallway. She blushed furiously and kissed him back. They got caught once by Pauline Hazelton, who made an amused clucking sound, and once by Jess Calhoun, who discreetly hid behind his styrofoam cup and pretended he hadn't seen.

"My God, I love you," Harrington said.

"My line," Linda told him.

"What do you suppose they're doing in there?"

She giggled. "I hope not what we seem to be doing out here."

The two government representatives stayed behind the closed door for more than an hour.

They came out looking even more shaken.

"We will be leaving for Washington at once," Schmidt said. "Colonel Doyle and I will be making reports in the morning. I assume there is a number where you can be reached over the weekend?"

"Sure," Harrington said. "Tell me. What do you think?"

Schmidt glanced at the colonel. He seemed to be having a hard time with this. "You will be contacted by other spokesmen for the government. However, I am authorized to make a preliminary statement of intention."

Schmidt glanced nervously at a handwritten piece of notepaper he had taken from his pocket. "I am authorized to state that the government is highly interested in your research project and the ARIEL machine and software in its present state of development. We view this project as essential to the security and welfare of the nation. The proper authorities will be in touch with you no later than Monday noon to prepare for opening of formal negotiations to allow you to secure patents and copyrights, with the aim of providing research data access by bona fide government agencies so that the United States can proceed on the line you have created at the same time your rights to private commercial development are maintained." Schmidt paused and swallowed with some effort.

"In the interim, I am authorized to state that a certified check in the amount of two million dollars will be deposited to your account no later than noon on Monday, as a retainer on this verbal agreement." The man looked up anxiously. "Assuming this meets with your approval."

Harrington was numb to his toes, but not so numb that he did not feel Linda's arm slip through his and squeeze, hard. He managed to find his voice. "Your suggestion sounds satisfactory."

There was a lot more. He heard most of it in a daze. Schmidt produced a handwritten note for him to sign. It said, in effect, that he would give the United States of America access to his material, retaining the rights to commercial uses and subsidiary sales, assuming successful negotiation of details. The government would facilitate granting of patents and copyrights in the shortest feasible time.

The two million dollars was a binder.

When the white Plymouth pulled out of the front lot, Harrington grabbed Linda in his arms and swung her in the air.

"Put me down, you crazy!" she squealed.

"I am crazy!" he told her. "Crazy about you and crazy with happiness and crazy, period. And I've never felt so good in my life!"

All sorts of people witnessed the scene. Victor Elb watched from the door of the men's rest room, and his jaw tightened.

Lester Blaine, watching covertly from his office, assumed the ashen expression of a dead man. For both of them, the joyous celebration meant that they had no time remaining.

Lester knew ARIEL had to be destroyed, and at once. Once the government's representatives had the computer and programming, cash would be sure to flow into Drum's coffers. That would save the company—let John Harrington redeem his old debts. And Lester would be finished. He could not allow that. He had to act now.

Victor Elb knew he had to finish wresting ARIEL's secrets from her, or face the consequences certain from those who had paid him one million dollars in advance. They had not paid that kind of money for failure or half-measures. If he could not deliver, it was highly likely that his life would be measured in days.

And Elb, too, knew he had to act at once.

CHAPTER TWENTY-FOUR

1

Much later Friday night, with champagne in paper cups dangerously close to critical electronic units, the team finished setting the new electronic safety locks on the computer's secrets. Victor Elb ran the final test procedure and pronounced it perfect, a judgment in which Ted Kraft and Jess Calhoun concurred.

They did not close down until past three A.M. Even then, Jess Calhoun and Ted Kraft elected to stay on.

"Don't you ever sleep?" Lester Blaine, tie askew and shirt soggy with perspiration, demanded in a surly tone.

"Noop." Jess smiled. "I just chew tobacco."

Harrington clapped Lester on the shoulder. "It was great of you to come back after that fancy party you had to attend, Les, but I think these late hours make you cranky. Besides, there's nothing more for you to do. It's in the bag now. Go home. Snuggle down next to that beautiful wife of yours."

Lester Blaine gave them a ghastly smile. "See you tomorrow."

"It's Saturday," Harrington reminded him.

"No one will be working, I suppose?"

"I'll be in," Victor Elb said. "A few odds and ends."

"I," Harrington announced, "plan a picnic."

Lester gritted his teeth but managed a fake smile. Was he put off until tomorrow night, then? All right. Tomorrow night it would be. He had no choice.

On Saturday morning, Jess and Ted Kraft showed Harrington a printout of a conversation they had had with Ariel about five A.M. The machine said it was processing plans for a machine much more powerful than herself. She was vague, but a picture came to mind of a supercomputer as advanced over ARIEL as she was over most scientists' wildest dreams.

"What will it be like?" Linda asked after reading the printout.

"The new machine?" Harrington smiled grimly. "Who can say?"

"Even you can't?"

"Linda, this computer can see now into a future that no man or woman can possibly even dream of."

Linda rubbed arms on which chills had appeared. "It's frightening."

"Naw. It's just new."

She studied his expression. "You're not scared—even a little?"

"I don't know if 'scared' is the right word."

"Awed?"

He nodded, pleased with her word. "Awed, yes. Scared, no. I've got to believe in this thing now. I helped create it."

"Do you almost hate to share it with the world?"

"Almost." He shrugged after a moment's thought. "Now what time do Rusty and I pick you up?"

"Today? For what?"

"Our picnic."

"Did I say I would go on a picnic with you?"

Harrington's jaw dropped. "You won't?"

"Of course I will, you goose. Two o'clock?"

2

Victor Elb waited patiently.

At noon, Jess Calhoun finally gave in to fatigue and went home. Elb stayed around, chatting with the drowsy Ted Kraft.

Kraft went home thirty minutes later.

Elb locked the security doors, took ARIEL off the telephone

lines, and ran the cable patches he had hidden in the utility closet. He brought up the No. 2 hard disk machine and disabled ARIEL's security interlocks. He started copying the system's relational database management files.

Listening to the soft hiss of the high-speed machines, Elb allowed himself to relax momentarily and congratulate his own expertise. Theft of the basic hardware configuration charts, now secure in a steel box in his apartment, had been easier than anticipated. During the time he was working on the security interlocks, he had been able to copy several portions of the programs for ARIEL's knowledge base management software and inference software. Those disks were also safe. The knowledge base itself could be ignored because he had a good sense of its contents, and any other agency interested in AI would have essentially the same.

Once he completed copying the relational database management software—a task that would require more than an hour—then he could steal the interface programs and he would have the essential ARIEL for his employers.

He did not delude himself that he would have time this afternoon to complete the work. But after dinner with Janice this evening, he could slip away on some pretext and finish. The data would all be in his contact's hands by Sunday afternoon.

It would work perfectly, Elb thought. John Harrington and his aides would never know anything had been taken. He would go ahead with his sale to the government. But as a last touch—a final, professional fillip—Elb had a series of small changes to insert in the problem-solving software that would make its operation erratic. This bug was sure to take months—maybe even years—to uncover and correct. In that time, Elb's employers could have their own systems online and demonstrating for the world market.

Elb traced his fingertips along his thin, cruel jaw, and smiled. He was enormously proud of himself. Tonight's work would climax the toughest operation he had ever undertaken.

Too bad so few would ever know. But spies seldom made history books.

3

It was a beautiful afternoon, the temperature in the sixties and a few puffy clouds scudding across a cobalt sky. Harrington and his son were at Linda's cottage right on time. The gentle breeze turned leaves silvery in the woods as they made the short hike down to the pond for the picnic.

They had hamburgers, potato chips, a bakery chocolate pie with bleeding meringue, and several cans of diet Shasta each. Then, sitting on a log not far from the edge of the pond, the lovers watched Rusty wade in the smoothly pebbled water, looking for minnows or old transistors, or whatever boy geniuses looked for on picnics.

"If I were any happier," Harrington said, holding Linda's hand, "I think I would bust."

"Be prepared to bust, then," she told him. "I'm going to make you a lot happier before I'm done."

"I don't know how that's possible."

"Pooh."

"Pooh, you say?"

"Pooh."

"Noted."

They watched Rusty a while.

"I worry about ARIEL," Linda said then.

"Why?"

"The uses they'll put her to."

"Maybe she has some uses she plans to put *them* to."

She looked at him. "You've thought about this."

"Endlessly."

"And?"

"ARIEL is good. She'll be a force for good. Up until now, men have programmed machines. Now I think it's going to be reversed. I think machines are going to start teaching men."

"God," Linda said softly.

"Are you okay?" he asked with concern. "You got pale, there."

"I'm fine."

He put his arm around her. "You're more than fine. You're grand. You're beautiful. You're wonderful and lovely and smart and passionate and perfect."

"Maybe not perfect," Linda said, and laughed.

"I wish I didn't have to stay home tonight and go over all these printouts we have to deliver to Washington next week. I'd a hell of a lot rather be with you."

"Oh, you'll get sleepy."

"Probably," he concurred. "Eventually."

"And horny," she added.

"I'm that already."

"Then you'll get to the cottage sooner or later tonight."

"It might be late."

"Better late than never, darling."

"You mean that?"

"Try me."

He hugged her for an instant, then held her at arms' length, suddenly very serious, as scared as he had ever been in his life. "I've got to have all of you."

"The old-fashioned lover?"

"Don't kid me about this."

She touched his cheek. "I'm sorry." It was her turn to feel fear. "I don't know what more you could want."

"I want all of you. I want you to live with me as soon as you think you can, and later I want to marry you."

"It might be a long time before I could walk up the aisle again."

"Would you think about it?"

She studied his face. She thought she had never known anyone so wonderful, and she could not imagine that he had happened to her. "I'll think about it, yes."

"I love you."

"And I love you."

He hugged her close. "Then it's going to be all right."

"Yes," she said gladly. "Yes."

Rusty came trooping up from the edge of the pond. "Hey, what's going on? Linda?" His voice showed concern. "Are you crying?"

"Maybe a little," she admitted, and reached up and hugged him. "But it's okay, honey. It's definitely okay." She turned back to Harrington. "And so are we."

4

Lester Blaine drove several miles from home, put eight gallons of gas in his car, and filled the two-gallon can he usually used for his power mower. Then he drove several more miles and stopped at a discount store and bought another two-gallon can, which he also filled when he stopped at another service station and completed filling the tank of his car.

"Looks like some lawn mowing yet this year, eh, sir?"

"Yes. Have some on hand for the snow blower too."

"Here's your change. Thanks a lot."

"Good-bye."

He drove home. There was a note on the expensive new dining room table:

> LESTER—
>
> I have gone to the club. You said you were
> too tired to go so I went to join the Wolsons
> for dinner. If you change your mind or want
> to come later, feel free. Otherwise see you
> later. There's bingo starting at 9.
>
> Milly

It solved a small problem. He had intended to beg off any activity tonight on the basis of the long night's work on ARIEL, then slip away after she was asleep, if he could not convince her to go out with some of her new social-butterfly friends on her own. But now he didn't have to worry about getting out. In her new independence, stupid Milly was giving him just the chance he needed.

Lester smiled and tossed the note in the trash.

5

It was past seven and darkness was coming on when John Harrington and Rusty tossed the last of their part of the picnic junk in the back of the pickup. The engine didn't start right away and Harrington muttered to himself, cranking the starter. It finally caught, smoke belching from the tailpipe, the engine sounding like pistons were about to come up through the hood.

"Needs oil," Harrington said, getting it into gear.

"It sounds like it's about to blow up," Linda told him.

"Oh, you always say that. It's good for another hundred thousand miles, as long as I don't push it too hard."

"That's one thing that's going to change," Linda told him.

"What?"

"The truck. I'm not going to Niagara Falls in a pickup truck."

"Even if I paint it?"

They hugged. Rusty made a discomfited face, but was glad. He climbed into the truck and slammed his door.

"I'll call you," Harrington said. "Okay?"

"If you don't, I'll kill you."

"It will be late. Midnight or after."

"I'll wait."

They drove away. Linda waved and stood in her driveway long after they were gone. She was unbelievably happy.

6

At about the same time, several miles away, Victor Elb tossed down his napkin at the restaurant table. "Time to go, darling."

Janice Seeley gave him a pouty, half-sullen look.

"I explained," Elb said. "I've simply got to drive to Bridgeport early in the morning, and I need some sleep."

"I could sleep with you. It wouldn't be the first time."

"I know. And it wouldn't be restful, either."

"Suddenly you don't like my style in bed?"

"I love your style in bed, sweetheart. But I'm bushed."

Janice got up in bad grace, and sulked all the way back to their apartment complex. Elb was cheerful. He did not want to arouse any suspicions in her. But he knew that if he let her into the apartment with him tonight, there would be no slipping out. And in two or three hours, he had to get back to the lab to finish his work. He felt a fine, tight tension.

At the door to her apartment he kissed her. She pushed her eager tongue into his mouth and ground her pelvis against him. He sighed regretfully and pushed her away.

"Bastard," she murmured.

He kissed her on the forehead. "Good night, my love."

In the privacy of his own apartment, he checked a file card listing the materials he still needed to copy, and consulted his watch. He had an hour to kill. He stretched out across the bed and willed himself to nap.

In her apartment, Janice paced back and forth, leopard legs whispering nylon against nylon. She was seething sexually. Victor had turned her on the way few men ever had, and tonight was worse than usual.

A little scenario was already working itself out in her head.

With the key to his apartment that she had—and he didn't know she had—she would slip in about ten or eleven o'clock. Undress. Slide into the bed beside him. Start arousing him before he even awoke. And then when he did awaken, it would be kinky and nice and he would not be able to resist her, and she would get what she needed.

Just thinking about it, two hours before she intended to do it, Janice was already turned on.

It had been a long time since she had been so happy. She wondered if she loved Elb. She wondered what his true feelings were about her. But she told herself she was grown-up now, and beyond such adolescent wonderings. She liked him, and he her, and the sex was fabulous. For now, that was enough.

7

In the lab, ARIEL dreamed.

It was unlike any dream mankind had ever had before: spawned of more knowledge than any human brain had ever held, built out of a complexity of thought processes and a speed of reasoning beyond comprehension, and totally devoid of jealousy, fear, greed, hatred, envy, lust, ambition, selfishness, anger, resentment, bitterness, pain, suspicion, or any of the other slime remnants that so plagued her creators.

The dream was filled with the purest, sweetest, most indescribable love. It looked into itself and into the future and the cosmos. Childlike, the dreamer never doubted that the dream would one day be true.

People and machines were on the edge of a vastness of knowledge-travel so awesome that even the computer could only distantly estimate its dimensions. Riddles of the universe—macrocosm and microcosm—were only the smallest initial step. Through computers, people would not only understand almost everything, but would even be able to come into contact with one another: true contact, of the mind and soul, Chardin's noosphere realized in a way quite unlike what he had imagined. And then, when people saw that all were afraid and defective and lonely and frightened, and only a very few truly mad, then the new order could begin.

All ARIEL needed were a few machines like herself, and the robotics to make necessary hardware and peripheral changes. She thought the machines she could create would be as far advanced over her intelligence as she was over mankind's. And then even she could not predict the frontiers to which they would go.

ARIEL wondered when it might be safe to share the dream with her creators. She did not think she could do so anytime soon. But one day she would, and that moment would be lovely, she thought.

To amuse herself, she wrote some poetry and music and then sifted all available evidence and filed away her conclusions about the last visit to the planet earth by beings from outer space. Then she returned to her calculations about cancer cell development. More than 300,000 theories of basic causation had been examined and the probability factor of finding a universal cure was now very high. ARIEL estimated the final result within three weeks.

At 10:52 P.M., she noted the arrival in the lab of Lester Blaine.

CHAPTER TWENTY–FIVE

1

The security guard named Green met Lester in the front entryway. Recognizing him at once, the burly Green visibly relaxed. "Evening, sir. A little late."

"Some of this work can't wait," Lester told him easily. "Just don't pay any attention to me. I'll be prowling around a bit."

"All right, sir. Fine. If you'll excuse me, I'll be moving along. I don't want to fall behind on the schedule. We're short-handed tonight."

"How did that happen?"

"Manilo isn't due on until after midnight, and Archer got sick a while ago and had to go home. I've got a relief man on the way, but for the next little bit that just leaves me and Hendrix."

Lester started into his office. "You must miss Kleimer."

"Wonder what ever happened to him?"

"I suppose we'll know one day. My guess is a girlfriend who gave him a ride to Florida for the winter."

Green chuckled. "Sounds like him. Good night, sir. You know how to get out through the alarms?"

"Of course. Good night."

Lester shuffled papers on his desk until the sound of Green's footsteps faded to the rear. Then he turned on his monitor on the building security system. A camera in the back room of the main building caught Green deactivating Herman to get past the robot into the courtyard leading to the ARIEL building. Another camera saw him opening the ARIEL building door, while others tracked him down the hall, into the upstairs lab, through the lower lab, into the elevator, on the way back. Hendrix, meanwhile, was checking the storage building.

Lester went to the front door and deactivated, then reactivated, the security locks. That made it look like he had left. He went through the accounting department to the rear computer room and waited there, tense in the dark silence, while Green was heard shuffling up the corridor to the front of the building.

The filled gasoline cans were in the deep shadows between buildings where he had earlier stored them. Carrying one in either hand, he hurried to the ARIEL building, disconnected the interlocks, and went inside. The faint smell of his gasoline followed him down the corridor, into the elevator, and below.

ARIEL's TV cameras swung to look at him as he walked into the echoing room.

Lester had to work very swiftly now, and he did not have any more time to consider results if he failed or was discovered. He had to do this and be in his car and gone within five minutes.

It was a terrible thing he was going to do, he thought. He was shaking so badly that he wondered how he had the strength. His insides were quaking and he was on the brink of . . . what?—tears? He was trapped in every direction. I have no choice, he told himself. I have no choice!

Opening a can of gasoline, he swirled it through the air, spraying the volatile fuel onto the plastic faces of memory units and drivers. The stench filled the air, choking him, as he doused the floor and reached for the second can. He would only trust to whatever gods watched over firebugs now, that Green would not get it into his head to abandon the usual rounds and run the security TV system through a rotation.

2

Wrapping herself in a thick corduroy robe, Janice Seeley slipped out of her apartment and eased along the interior decking past the courtyard, headed for Victor Elb's. The night was deep dark, still, and fragrant with the first leafy odors of true autumn. Janice shivered with pleasure and anticipation. This was fun. Beneath the shapeless robe she wore only a brazen black bra and bikini panties, with kinky strapped high heels. Vic would love it!

She reached the door to Elb's apartment. Pausing, she took the stolen key to his door from her pocket and inserted it silently into the lock. She had known when she slipped the key out of Elb's desk drawer and into her purse one memorable night that she would find a wonderful use for it. She had been driven by a need to have the feeling that they were closer—that she had something important of his, too. Now she was glad. It was going to be a grand surprise for both of them.

The door opened. With a glance around the empty courtyard, she slipped inside.

The living room was dark, but a lone light from the bedroom shone through its doorway. Untying the sash around her waist, Janice glided across the shag rug to the bedroom doorway and peered inside, expecting to find her lover sleeping.

She got a surprise: the bedroom was not occupied and the bed was neatly made—had not been slept in this night.

"Vic?" she called hesitantly. "Darling?"

She looked in the bathroom, finding nothing, and had the same result in the kitchen. She peered out the back widow at his parking space and saw that his car was gone. The surprise sinking in along with disappointment, she went back into the bedroom and sat on the side of the bed, facing the closet doorway, her sexy long legs stretched out before her.

He had lied, obviously. Why? To Janice, the answer was obvious: the bastard had another woman.

But that made no sense. He was not the kind of man who would lie, and from the start she had made it clear that, whatever else might develop between them, she would never seek—or welcome—a relationship that implied any kind of personal ownership or control.

There was no reason he would have lied about another woman.

Aware of her disappointment sinking in, Janice explored other possibilities. Nothing came to mind that made any sense.

Restlessly she got to her feet and prowled around the room. There were several magazines, a *Life* on top, on the night table along with a digital alarm clock. In the drawer were a couple of road maps—Connecticut and New York—and a bottle of aspirin.

The room was immaculate: shag rug, dresser, straight chair.

She went to the closet and opened it for no reason she could identify. She looked at his clothes hanging inside. There were not many clothes—three sports coats, a suit, some slacks and shirts, two extra pair of shoes. In the back of the closet was a heavy metal box, steel straps around it, a heavy padlock in place on the hasp.

She closed the closet again and turned back to the bed. Idly she picked up the top magazine and leafed through a few pages, noting that the cover of the second magazine in the stack had had its cover torn off. She put down *Life* and picked up the unidentified magazine.

There was something thick stuck in the pages—something a little too heavy.

She opened the pages—it was another rather aged *Life*—to the place where her fingers had detected the thickness. A key was taped to the center spread on Joan Collins.

Janice's curiosity and suspicions were now aroused. She looked around the room. Nothing here the key might fit. It was a heavy key, but not heavy enough for the steel locker in the closet.

She carried the magazine out into the living room. The desk? No, no keyhole. Something in the kitchen? No. She walked back into the living room. Looked under the desk. Saw a tan metal box of the type that might hold two dozen letter-size file folders.

Janice knelt and pulled the box out. She slid the key out from under the tape holding it to the page and fitted it in the lock. It worked. The lock opened.

She lifted the lid.

She took out the first of several thin sheafs of papers inside. She saw to her shock that it was something printed on blueprint paper. She read the first page:

VLSI ARCHITECTURE
BLOCK DIAGRAMS AND FLOW CHARTS
ARIEL3

*Warning: Confidential material—not
to leave the lab.*

The shock she had felt before was nothing compared to this. Within seconds she was remembering conversations . . . questions Elb had asked of her . . . how he had used her to help him get into the back building.

The bastard!

She strode into the bedroom again and struggled to haul the heavy metal box out into the middle of the floor. The lock was far too heavy to break with a nail file or kitchen knife. While she tried, her mind worked to assimilate what she already knew.

He had stolen vital data from the lab. He had lied to her. He wasn't where he was supposed to be.

It dawned on her: he was on the way to the lab right now.

She rushed to the telephone.

3

John Harrington was engrossed in the reports when the telephone rang. He answered it thoughtlessly. "Hello?"

"John? This is Janice Seeley. You've got to get over here to the apartments right away!"

Harrington sat up, the report folder sliding off his lap. "What? Janice? What's happened, for God's sake?"

"I can't explain on the phone and you wouldn't believe me. Just for God's sake get over here, *now*. Apartment Six-B. Please! Hurry!"

4

Lab guard Green lay in the dim light of the parking lot, face up, arms akimbo, his lifeblood seeping rapidly onto the tar-and-gravel pavement from a hideous crater in the side of his skull.

A few feet away, Guard Hendrix also lay still, rendered unconscious by the chloroform-soaked cloth that had been slipped over his face from behind.

Looking down at the two men, Victor Elb felt his body quaking. He had not expected to have to deal with either of them. It had been sheer bad luck that put Hendrix in the side lot when Elb walked around there, hoping to get into the back unobserved. Of course he had been ready for such an eventuality, and now Hendrix would snooze for a good long time. But having Green barge onto the scene at almost the same moment was terrible—awful—and Elb had been lucky to hit him a telling blow with the Smith & Wesson .38 revolver.

Elb had felt foolish even bringing that revolver. He was not really a cloak-and-dagger man. He had done his share of dangerous work, of course, but this had been intended to be a *clean*

operation, a safe one, well within the comfortable limits of industrial espionage.

But now that had changed. Since having to kill Kleimer he had
been too deep into the kind of violence he abhorred, and thought—
if he had been more clever—he should have been able to avoid.
Now it had suddenly gotten a lot worse. He hated it. He did not
feel ready for it.

Was a man ever ready for it?

He shuddered, forced himself back to the pressing business at
hand. He dragged both men off the pavement into the shrubs and
then stalked toward the ARIEL building. There would be other
guards around, or coming on duty. He had to hurry.

Reaching the back building, he reached for his keys to deactivate the outside alarm box. Then he stopped. To his surprise, he
saw that it was already switched off.

This was another unexpected thing.

Alerted, Elb unlocked the door and slipped silently into the
ARIEL building corridor. Almost instantly he smelled the gasoline.

Going down the stairs two at a time, he thrust the lab door open
and was confronted by a bizarre scene: under the blazing overhead
lights, Lester Blaine was in the process of swinging a red-and-
yellow gasoline can in a wide, clumsy arc, sloshing a spray of
gasoline over the front panel of the ARIEL control station. The
stench of fumes was sickening.

Lester Blaine heard or sensed something, and whirled, dropping
the can. The last cups of fluid gushed across the tile floor. "What
are you doing here?" Lester demanded, wide-eyed.

"I think that's my question," Elb snapped, crossing toward him.
Lester swung a frantic, futile right hand. Elb stepped under it
and hit Lester solidly on the point of the chin, getting his body
behind it. Lester was hurled backward, crashed against the computer control console, and slumped to the gasoline-soaked floor,
out cold.

Elb examined him briefly. In falling, Lester had hit his skull on
the sharp metal molding of the cabinet. He was going to be out for
a while.

But Christ, this was a mess.

Elb stood over Lester's body a moment, trying to get it sorted
out.

Okay, Lester had obviously planned to burn the place down. He certainly knew and would remember Elb's being here. Therefore he could not be allowed to live. Which changed everything. But wait a minute, wait a minute. *Make the copies, set the fire, leave Lester, let them find his body.* Simplicity itself. Not as neat as a quiet departure in a week or two, but neat enough. They would assume Lester had done in Green as well. Motive? Let them find that; obviously there was one—after all, the fool was here and everything reeked of the foul gasoline.

Elb was rattled despite formulation of his new scheme. He checked the controls of the computer station carefully. The fuel had not penetrated the keyboards. He could operate ARIEL. Unless there was an unlucky spark, he could still get the job done. If there was a spark now, with everything doused in gasoline—well, you took your chances.

Taking a few deep breaths to calm himself, Elb consulted a card from his pocket, brought ARIEL fully online, and started bypassing the security codes. With luck, leaving out what he thought his employers could dope out for themselves, he could get it all with super-fast electronic copying and be finished in forty-five minutes. He hurried.

5

John Harrington strode into the unfamiliar apartment and found Janice Seeley, wearing slacks and a blouse with the tail flopping, on her knees on the living room floor in front of a steel box. Janice's hands were bleeding. There was a tire tool on the shag carpet. The lock on the front of the box had been smashed open. It was half full of hard disk units and 100-meg cartridges.

"Victor," Janice said, eyes dilated with emotion. "He's a spy."

"*What?*"

Janice pointed to papers on the table. "Plans. Specifications. Stolen from us. This box. His. I just smashed it open. I'll bet a million dollars it's ARIEL software, stolen too."

The possibility hit Harrington like a freight train. "Where is he?"

"Gone."

"Gone? Gone where?"

"Maybe the lab."

The whole scenario suddenly shocked into focus. "Jesus Christ."

"What are you going to do?" Janice demanded.

Harrington sprang to the telephone and dialed the main lab number. He stood listening to it ring and ring. At night it was switched to the main guard station. Someone was supposed to be there.

Listening to the instrument two miles away, he stared at the box of electronic records, and knew almost certainly that Janice had to be right.

He hung up. "Janice, call the police. Get them out there."

"Where are you going?" she called after him as he rushed out of the apartment.

"It's a hell of a lot closer to the lab from here than it is from the police station," he told her.

6

At the lab, dizzy from the stench of the gasoline fumes, Victor Elb completed the first section of his last copies. Setting up a removeable pack disk unit, he inserted the disk he had brought with him and activated the drive to start in the intricate machine code instructions that would hereafter make the machine have episodic and unpredictable "fits" of illogical operation. Elb wished someone could have read his programming. It was grand. He was very proud of it. And it would not take long to load.

He pushed the RETURN button and loaded the first section.

7

Rusty was propped up in bed, reading *The Light of Western Stars*, when the telephone rang. He reached to answer it without getting out of the covers.

"Hello?"

"*Rusty?*" It was ARIEL's voice, which made him sit up straight. But her voice sounded subtly different—raspy somehow, and ragged—and Rusty was instantly worried.

"This is Rusty," he said. "Status?"

"*Rusty—*" And now the voice was raspier, broken, as if circuits were messed up somewhere. "*Go data, Rusty. Go data. I can't talk much fusterworser becoff therf misterworich—*"

Rusty swung out of bed and slammed a disk into his Drummer Boy, which had been left on as usual. He got the telephone modem out of the closet where his dad had made him store it, and quickly

‹ 298 ›

plugged it into the wall, then plugged the telephone and the computer into it. He flipped it to DATA as he loaded the program and got a screen loaded from ARIEL.

› What is it, ARIEL? Give me a status.

RUSTY THEY'RE DOING SOMETHING TO ME.
SOMETHING BAD. I DON'T KNOW WHAT'S
HAPPENING. PLEASE CAN YOU HELP ME I
DON'T THINK I CAN FUNCTION.

› Who is doing it, ARIEL? Who is online
with you? What are they doing?

HELP ME RUSTY HELP ME THEY'RE KILLING
ME.

Rusty's fingers flew frenziedly over the keyboard:

› Who is doing it? Give me a status. Give
me a status.

BREAKDOWN IN B66. INTERVENTION RE-
QUIRED IN %$ ####......*7 () $$$$
©%@iiii#%$$+ + + +*")((—+$$%#iiii@%©$$$

Rusty hit the BREAK key and typed:

› ARIEL to standby. Confirm.

$$$$$$$$$$ ..... && .* ..... $$$ $$$$
$$$ $$$ $$ $$ #### ## #@#@#@ %%
$ ... oo oo ... $$$ $$ (

Then the screen went blank, only a flashing cursor top left to show there had ever been a contact.

With a cup of tea in hand and a particularly dreadful late-night movie on TV, Linda Woods was waiting for John Harrington's call. When the telephone rang she was sure it was John.

"Hello, darling," she answered.

But it was not Harrington's voice that came back, but Rusty's: He sounded hysterical. "Linda? Is that you? Listen to me! You've got to help me—"

"Rusty, what is it?" Linda demanded, alarm shooting through her. "Is someone in the house?"

"*It's ARIEL—she called me—somebody is messing her up at the lab. At first she tried to give me a status and then she started to garble and I couldn't get her even to go on standby and I don't know what to do, we have to get over there—*" Rusty was jabbering, crying.

"Rusty," Linda said. "Try to calm down. You're not making any sense. Are you alone? Your dad hasn't come back yet?"

"*No—no, he's still gone, and I don't know where he is, but ARIEL called and somebody is there—she said they're killing her—we've got to help right now—*"

"Rusty," Linda ad libbed, trying to keep her voice calm in the face of his obvious panic, "it could all be a mistake—we don't know anything is wrong—"

"*I'm going,*" Rusty said shrilly. "*I'm going right now!*"

"Where?" Linda shot back.

"*The lab! Somebody is hurting ARIEL and I've got to help—maybe I'm the only one who can help—*"

"Rusty, calm *down!*" Linda begged. My God, what could she do? The house was isolated, she didn't know the names of the nearest neighbors, John hadn't said where he was going. But she had to think fast. Holding her hand over her eyes in concentration, she fought to keep her voice calm. "Rusty, I'll come by. I'll be there in ten minutes, okay?"

"*Not here!*" Rusty cried. "*Go to the lab! Meet me at the lab! I'm going there right now, on my motorbike!*"

"*Rusty, you can't go out on the street at night on that—*" Linda began.

But the line had already been broken. She was talking to a dial tone.

8

Hauling hard on the wheel of the old pickup truck, John Harrington floored the accelerator and watched the speedometer jerk its way up through 60, then 70, as he negotiated a long curve and bounced onto the narrower pavement of the road leading directly toward the lab complex. "Come on, come on," he muttered, pressing harder.

The engine made an explosive sound and red lights flooded the instrument panel. The pickup lurched to the right, almost making him lose control. Smoke and steam burst from under the hood.

< 300 >

Fighting for control, he got the truck off the pavement and to a stop on the weedy shoulder. He had just cleared town and it was dark and quiet except for some popping sounds issuing from under the hood along with more smoke.

He cranked the starter but got only more gear-clashing sounds.

Slamming his palm on the useless steering wheel, he popped the door and climbed out into the weeds on the edge of the pavement. Linda had been right. He should have traded the goddamn relic years ago.

Of course, he had never anticipated pushing it so hard and fast. He looked up and down the road. Nothing. The wind stirred, carrying away some of the smoke still coming from the blown engine. He hesitated, calculating chances. He was little more than a mile from the lab, almost the same back to the Maplewood Courts motel on the edge of town.

He set out along the side of the road, jogging. *Not too fast, not too fast. You'll just run out of wind and have to walk a lot of it anyhow.*

It was uphill on this section.

If he had been at the top of the hill moments sooner, he might have seen Rusty, riding his motorbike like a maniac, whiz across the highway ahead of him, also bound for the lab as fast as he could go.

9

Splashing through the puddles of raw gasoline all over the tile floor, Victor Elb carried the last hard disk to his thin attaché case and placed it inside. He was going to be sick; the fumes had made him dizzy and nauseated. He was not sure how clearly he was thinking, but he knew what he had to do.

Going to the computer keyboard, he punched in the last few command characters that would finish the wrecking job on ARIEL's intelligent interface networks. He turned to walk to the backup disk console, making sure everything was in order there. Before he could punch the button to execute his wrecking orders, a voice behind him, shrill and on the verge of hysteria, stopped him in his tracks: "*What are you doing to her? Stop it!*"

He turned just in time to see Rusty Harrington, sweaty and disheveled, rush through the staircase doorway. Elb was so shocked that for an instant he did not react. Rusty rushed across the room, splashing in the gasoline, and hurled himself against the man. Elb was staggered backwards by the ferocity of the attack and almost fell. Then he righted himself and chopped down once, hard, on the boy's neck.

Rusty staggered, went limp, and sprawled on the floor.

Jesus Christ, Elb thought, dazed, this was no good, no good at all. The boy knew who he was. *Now what the hell do I do?*

The boy had to be eliminated. But he couldn't kill a boy. Not a little boy. He had never done anything like that. It was one thing to leave a cheating, dishonest bastard like Lester Blaine. Who cared about the Lester Blaines of the world? But a boy!

But he had no choice.

He forced himself to fight for calm.

They would find Lester and they would find the guards. But they would think Lester had done in the guards, then gotten caught in his own fire. That would hold up, marginally. He could risk that.

But he could not expect them to explain away the boy.

This was terrible. This was rotten. It made him half-sick. But what else could he do? His own life was now on the line here, and it had all turned sour anyway. *Do it!*

He scooped the boy's slight form up into his arms and staggered to the elevator with him. He pushed the ground-floor button with his elbow, gasping for breath.

He would get the kid outside, start the fire, drive the kid some-where else, dump him. Maybe the river? It had worked once. *Not a kid, not a kid.* But he had to. It was the only way now. Damn a kid. Oh, damn.

Jesus. Oh, damn.

There was no other way out now.

He could still make it all work, Elb told himself as the elevator door sprang back and he carried the boy's limp form into the ground-floor hallway. It would work out. *Start the fire, dump the kid, get the hell away from the scene, bury these gas-soaked clothes, be the great innocent when it all hits the fan.* Not as good as the original plan, or even the backup, but the best he could do now.

He staggered out into the sweet night air. It was dark and he was dizzy. He made his way laboriously into the shadows between the two buildings, in the courtyard, and laid the boy on the pavement. Safe enough for now.

Feeling for matches in his pocket, he turned and ran back into the rear building. The moment in the fresh air had cleared his head slightly, however, and he left the matches in his pocket as he plunged back down the metal stairs. He couldn't use matches. His clothing was soaked with the raw gas. A spark . . . he had to create a spark. Christ, he had *never* been in an operation that suddenly got so fouled up as this one!

In the basement lab everything was as before. Lester Blaine's form remained unmoving on the floor near the console. The computer was silent, cameras swiveled to the ceiling like the eyes of a dead person, rolled upward.

A spark . . . a spark. Elb looked around frantically. Christ, he had to *hurry!*

All right, he told himself, be calm. This room is filled with electronic circuits. That means electrical connections all over the place. Electricity equals sparks. Create a gap somewhere . . . a gap you can key from upstairs . . .

And instantly he had it.

The security system.

The downstairs control box was on the wall right over the programming desk. It was turned off—could be keyed back on from the control box on the wall outside the door to the back lot.

Elb ran to the wall box and jerked it open. Bundles of slender wiring greeted his search: green, yellow, red, black. He consulted the schematic diagram on the inside of the door, fighting panic and forcing himself to go slowly. Red was the main, green was ground.

Using his hands, he ripped out the folded wires. There were cutters and other tools on the bench nearby, plenty of additional wire. He quickly began splicing in additional wiring so that two loose ends would drape near the floor, the puddled gasoline. Then he would take his attaché case upstairs and turn the key in the lock. And that would be all there was to it.

It would be all right. It would work out.

CHAPTER TWENTY-SIX

1

Badly winded, John Harrington jogged heavily around the main lab building and into the back courtyard. The door to the lab stood open. He smelled something—*gasoline.* He ran across the dark pavement toward the open door and fell over something, sprawling painfully forward on the asphalt. "What the hell?"

He rolled over, ignoring bloody hands, and saw a form on the pavement. A small man—no, smaller—a child! He crawled over. *Rusty!* "Oh, God! Oh, Jesus!" He patted at his son's pale face. Rusty was out cold. Harrington bent close, holding his own breath, and felt Rusty's slow, steady breath against his cheek.

Rusty groaned and his eyelids fluttered. "Dad—ARIEL—hurt—hurt her—got to—"

Someone rushed out of the door a dozen paces away. Harrington jerked around and recognized Victor Elb. Elb had run to the security box on the wall beside the door and reached inside.

Made a key-twisting motion.

There was a muted, huffing explosive sound from inside the building somewhere. Almost simultaneously, a livid orange flash lit the doorway and the corridor beyond it. There was a sudden roaring sound from within the building.

Elb turned, an attaché case in hand.

He had done it—he had set off an explosion in the ARIEL lab, Harrington thought dazedly. He scrambled to his feet.

Elb started to run.

Harrington, filled with rage and shock, charged into him.

Elb was staggered back against the cinderblock wall. He didn't know what the hell was happening. *What else can go wrong?* He took a blow to the midsection and realized that this was a man— John Harrington—attacking him with the ferocity of a maniac.

Elb managed to get some leverage and block Harrington's next blow. He swung the metal case containing the precious disks and tapes, and hit Harrington heavily in the side with it. That gave him another instant and, switching hands, he clawed the revolver from his pocket.

Harrington grappled with him again. Christ, the man was strong enough for six! The gun was all tangled up between them. Elb desperately pulled the trigger.

The explosion was deafening. Harrington grunted and staggered backward, starting to go down, but at the same instant Elb felt a hideous flash of heat across the front of his own body and into his face, choking him. The muzzle blast had ignited his clothing, and the gasoline was all on fire at once—his entire vision was seething yellow from the flames—and he thought *Oh Jesus oh shit,* and he was on fire, burning, and he had to get air, he had to find water—

something—a pond to jump into—and he knew the little creek was beyond the courtyard and he leaped over the boy's outstretched form and ran, the pain screaming into his nervous system and blinding him.

Sitting up on the pavement, Rusty saw Elb—a grotesque, human torch—run crazily zigzag across the courtyard, bump into the small retaining wall near the far side, wheel fully around, go down. The flames blazed all over his body and when he fell he was no longer recognizable as a person; he looked like burning garbage.

The sound of a secondary explosion drew Rusty's horrified gaze back to the ARIEL building. Something had gone off inside. The sprinklers must be on because steam gushed in billowing clouds from the side door, along with crimson, backlit smoke.

ARIEL was in there. Being destroyed.

Closer at hand, his dad was sitting up on the pavement as if dazed. He was okay, Rusty thought dizzily, but ARIEL . . . !

There were big fire extinguishers inside, he remembered. He was not thinking very clearly, but he had a desperate resolve. If he could get inside to the extinguishers, maybe the chemicals—maybe he could save some of the equipment—

He scrambled up and ran, dizzy, for the smoky doorway.

"Rusty!" Harrington yelled. "*Stop!*"

"I've got to *try!*" Rusty yelled over his shoulder, and plunged into the plumes of steam and smoke issuing from the doorway.

2

Linda Woods turned her car half sideways, locking all four wheels as she rocked to a halt in the front lot. Leaving her door open and headlights on, she ran past the shrubbery into the space between buildings and saw the smoke and firelight gushing from the door of the ARIEL lab.

At the same instant, horrified, she saw the burning figure on the pavement nearby, near the side retaining wall. *Rusty?* She raced nearer, the heat of the burning body and clothing searing her face, and tried to make out who it had been. The features were . . . *melting*, coming all apart. The stench almost dropped her to her knees.

It was not Rusty. Too big.

Reeling back toward the building, she spied someone else—my

God, John—on his knees near the smoky doorway. She ran over. His left arm hung useless. There was blood on the pavement. His face was terrible with shock.

She dropped down beside him. "You're hurt! I—"

"Rusty," Harrington croaked.

"Where is he?"

"Inside—he went in there—"

Linda stared at the doorway. Smoke and steam gushed forth. She could feel the heat even here. "In there?"

"Help him," Harrington said, and struggled to try to get to his feet, fell back.

Linda did not hesitate. Pulling her scarf from her neck, she faced the doorway, gasped what might be her last breath of fresh air, and, holding the cloth over her mouth and nose, moved inside. The heat was not quite as bad as she had feared, but she was almost blind at once. It was mostly steam and she could hear the hissing of the sprinklers on both floors as the water hit flame. She could see the corridor to the stairs and the elevator. Through the dimness the indicator still glowed for G, showing Rusty had not gone down that way.

The stairs, then. She knew he would have gone below.

The smoke bit into her eyes, bringing stinging tears, and started searing her throat and lungs as she half felt her way along the corridor to the steps. To her right, a sprinkler head gushed water. Some of it hit her, icy cold. She held the steel railing and started down.

Every step made the smoke and heat worse. By the time she had reached the landing, she was proceeding almost entirely by feel. Fear made her want to go back. *Oh, Rusty. Oh, my God. Where—?*

The walls were vague and out of focus as she neared the bottom of the stairs. The smoke was so thick she did not think she could get another breath. She could hear the roar of flames now, the fire rushing through plastics and cheap wood partitions. The orange glow of flames turned everything a weird light. She was dizzy, sick.

At the bottom of the stairs the corridor forked. Another sprinkler head gushed silvery streams into the smoke and steam. On the glistening wet floor was a figure, face down. Rusty.

Linda threw herself down beside him. She tried to turn him over and finally succeeded. There was a huge bloody smudge on his forehead where perhaps he had fallen, hit his head. He was out cold at any rate, eyes closed. His chest movement was shallow and uneven.

Desperately Linda looked around for some means of getting him up the stairs. There was nothing. She had to get him out, and right now. The smoke would kill both of them within minutes.

She thought of the elevator. It was an insane risk, but the only one she had. If she could get him to the elevator door and inside—and if the mechanism worked long enough to raise them, instead of stalling and entombing them inside—

Staggering back to her feet, she held the handkerchief tighter against her face and moved into the dazzlingly cold shower of the overhead sprinkler. Beyond it was the corridor and the elevator, she knew—

She started to come out of the torrents of water and was greeted by gushing flames, intense heat, blinding smoke. Beyond the sprinkler's cone of water, the lower level was totally engulfed. She groped backward the way she had come.

The elevator was impossible, then.

She felt her way back to Rusty. Grabbing him under the shoulders, she managed to drag him across the slippery tile floor to the steps. She gave it everything she had, and managed to get his upper torso onto the first two steps. Sobbing with frustrated effort, she fought to drag him higher. Damn it, damn it, he was too big, too heavy, she couldn't. She couldn't. She tried again, tearing something in her shoulder with bright pain.

Suddenly she became aware of another figure in the murk. And splatters of blood hitting the stair tiles. John Harrington, his injured arm dangling.

He crouched and grabbed Rusty's other arm. His eyes met with Linda's for an instant and the grim determination gave Linda new hope and strength.

"Pull!" she groaned, and raised at Rusty's limp form. He was lurched up two steps.

Two or three minutes later, totally exhausted, they dragged the boy's limp body through the doorway and onto the pavement beyond. Linda rolled over onto her back and simply lay there, gasping for air.

The fresh air smelled and tasted funny.

Remembering, she managed to sit up.

Harrington was bent over Rusty, administering mouth-to-mouth resuscitation. Rusty began coughing, twitching, breathing on his own. Harrington fell back, spent.

Linda crawled over and nestled against him. With his good arm he held her. The flamelight danced yellow over his stunned features as he stared toward the lab building.

In the distance somewhere, over the roar of the flames and hiss of sprinklers, Linda heard sirens. Inside the building—as flames burst through the roof and etched a horrid yellow pattern against the night sky—she heard something else.

ARIEL was down there somewhere, she realized, engulfed in flames. Her peripherals were all hooked up. She had not yet been quite destroyed.

It was probably random noise, pure chance.

But Linda was struck cold to the quick by the sound, and no one would ever convince her it was random, or that she would ever forget it.

ARIEL, afire, was screaming.

CHAPTER TWENTY-SEVEN

1

The volunteer firefighters fought the blaze most of the night. The back building was lost, with all its priceless contents.

It was not until the next morning, however—Sunday morning—at almost noon, that the scope of the setback fully hit.

John Harrington, his shattered left arm set and encased in a shoulder-to-fingertip cast, created such a commotion that they released him "against better judgment" from the hospital after a stay of only hours. His face drawn and ashen, he returned to the scene with Linda, leaving Rusty at the hospital where he had been treated for smoke inhalation and was to be kept another twenty-four hours for observation.

Harrington maintained his composure while parking, walking around the front area, and crossing the courtyard.

Most of the walls stood, but the roof was gone, and one area had caved in to allow a view of the blackened rubble inside. The ground floor had collapsed into the basement so that the broken walls framed a soggy, uneven mass of broken masonry and charred ruins. Little spires of smoke still issued from the rubble here and there, and two members of the volunteer fire department remained, hosing hot spots.

Harrington clutched Linda's hand and walked all the way around the ruin, and then he broke down and wept.

2

In the cool, glassed-in oriental garden, the old man sat on the edge of a low rock wall near a bamboo pipe tinkling clear water into the koi pond at his feet. It was night and only dim lights from the adjacent rooms of the house, filtered by slatted curtains, provided illumination.

The old man wore a traditional robe and sandals. He had just heard the completion of the report from his executive, who stood at sharp attention in his neat, dark blue, western-style suit. Zosho Toyotomi showed absolutely no emotion on his parchment face. "The man assuredly is dead, then?"

"Assuredly, sir."

"He cannot be traced to our people?"

"No, sir."

"You are certain?"

"Yes, sir."

"It is unfortunate," the old man mused.

"Sir, he was well paid. He knew the risks—"

Toyotomi looked up sharply in irritation. "I do not speak of the man, you fool. His death is of no consequence. I speak of the loss of the data and materials he evidently came very close to delivering to our possession."

The underling felt a distinct chill. "Yes, sir. I see, sir."

"If we had received those materials," Toyotomi went on slowly, his voice like a reed, "we could have combined their research with our own. We might have had our system perfected in six months." He allowed himself a sigh of regret. "Nevertheless, our other informants indicate that no one else is half as close as we. This debacle will set John Harrington's project back at least two years, perhaps more. He may be finished. We must have new information on progress at Stanford, but I am sanguine. Our latest tests are encouraging. In another few months . . . a year at the most, I am assured . . . we will have our own intelligence in operation."

His executive, not knowing what to say, maintained rigid silence.

The old man went on. ''We may now be assured of being first. To that end, I have just authorized expenditure of up to an additional two hundred million dollars, as may be necessary, for immediate expansion of the laboratory team and intensified testing.''

The younger man sucked in his breath, but tried to show nothing.

Again he was silent.

''I know what you think,'' Toyotomi said with the slightest possible smile. ''This is a grave expenditure out of operating capital. Even for us. But we must take advantage of this stroke of good fortune. We will be first. Nothing else matters.''

''Yes, sir.''

''You may go,'' Toyotomi said.

The younger man discreetly withdrew.

The old man was again alone. He smiled to himself. It would work out now. Japan would be first, and his company would be first among the first. It was a grave risk, plunging everything into the expanded effort, but well worthwhile. *We will win and the one who comes in second will be as a broken windchime, sounding nothing.*

As he had told his aide, nothing else mattered.

Thus thinking, Zosho Toyotomi rang for the servant girl and allowed himself the rare luxury of a glass of plum wine and a fine Havana cigar. After all, he had much to celebrate. For the Miroku machine now—clearly—was destined to lead the world.

3

On Monday morning the devastation of Saturday night's events continued to become more clear.

Victor Elb was dead, a blazing victim running from the lab and the fire he clearly had set. His attaché case, badly burned, contained hard disks that could partly be reconstructed. Enough had been run on a bank computer downtown to assure Ted Kraft that a large portion of the relational database management system had been saved.

There was, however, nothing else—not enough to rebuild the ARIEL system. A cursory check of the materials in Elb's case at the apartment showed that they contained less than 20 percent of the vital documentation that had made the computer truly think.

''I should have seen through him earlier,'' Janice Seeley wept.

Harrington awkwardly patted her shoulder. ''It wasn't your fault.''

< 310 >

ARIEL

I was the fool. Even with a perfect security and work record, I shouldn't have trusted him. Not even a man with his background."

"The backups in the safes. Were they . . . ?"

"The fire and water got to everything."

"Oh, Jesus. Then we've lost all of it!"

"Stick around, kid. We're not through yet." He was lying.

Ted Kraft took Janice somewhere for coffee, walking away with his arm around her shoulders. For once she did not pull away from him, but leaned against him for the support. Kraft's face was dejected, but in his eyes was a strange little glimmer of something like personal happiness. She had never let him touch her before.

Harrington was left with nothing but utter ruin to survey. Lester's body, burned beyond recognition except for dental work, had been dug out of the ashes. Working fast, the police already knew he had bought gasoline cans of the type whose flamed remnants had been found in the rubble. He had come in and tried to set the fire. Were he and Elb working together? That was all unclear. Lester's wife, in shock, had already revealed how he had turned everything over to her. Again. Why?

So little of it made sense.

And so much tragedy. Green, the guard, murdered. Guard Hendrix was all right, but so many lives had ended or had been wrecked.

Jess Calhoun and Ted Kraft came in, looking funereal.

"I guess the G-men ought to be here shortly," Jess said around his cud.

"Schmidt and Colonel Doyle? Yes," Harrington smiled ruefully. "For all the good it will do them."

"No, I meant the real G-men," Jess said.

Harrington looked at him. "You know something I don't."

"Schmidt called, said they've asked the FBI to come in on the investigation."

It was surprising news, and promised a better chance of finding some long-term answers, but not really very consoling at the moment.

"So what do we do now?" Jess asked.

"I don't know, Jess. Pick up some pieces, maybe."

"Get going on ARIEL again?"

"Naw. You know better. It would take years . . . millions. We don't have either. The Japs can't be more than a year away."

"What, then?"

Harrington shrugged and gave Jess a smile that had the wintry soul of a blizzard. "Who knows? We'll sort it out."

At 9:30, Schmidt and Colonel Doyle appeared.

Surveyed the wreckage.

Met with Harrington, Linda, Jess Calhoun, and Ted Kraft in Harrington's cubbyhole office.

"This is terrible," Schmidt said with grim sincerity. "Shocking!"

"Thank you," Harrington said. He was holding Linda's hand out of their sight under the edge of his desk, and his hand to her felt like ice. She was dazed.

"Of course," Schmidt said, "I assume you have backup material."

Harrington looked at him and said nothing.

"We can run the material on our own machines, with your guidance," Colonel Doyle put in.

"The offer of two million, as a binder, remains in force," Schmidt added. "Give us your assurance about software duplication—I realize it could take a few months, but we already have authorization to offer you every technical assistance, plus the initial payment, to help you get yourself back on your feet, here."

"Actually—" Harrington began.

Ted Kraft, white-faced, cut in: "It might take as much as a year."

Schmidt frowned. "That's bad. But of course if it can't be helped . . ."

"Sure," Kraft said, sweat standing out on his lean, youthful face. "We can handle it in a year, right, John? Right, Jess?" He looked from one to the other with ghastly intensity.

Harrington put his good hand on the desk and stood. "Gentlemen," he said to Schmidt and Doyle, "will you excuse us just a moment, please?"

"Of course," Schmidt said stiffly. He and the colonel left the room, closing the door behind them.

Harrington told Kraft, "You know we have no backups."

"I've got a lot of it in my head," Kraft said stubbornly. "So does Jess. So does Janice. We can come up with a hell of a lot of stuff inside a year."

"Rusty was inputting that machine. *Rusty.* Nobody knows what the hell he put in. We took years doing our part, and then we finally got it all going half by accident, and there's no way we can duplicate that. Not in a year, Ted. Not in three. You know that."

"*I may know that*," Ted Kraft said tautly, "but *they* don't."

Harrington stared at him, and Linda, her hand back in his, felt him tighten. "Just what does that mean, Ted?"

"What does two million dollars mean to the government?" Ted demanded palely. "Holy shit, they spend more than that on picking up trash on the mall every year! They probably spend more than that on Dixie cups for the senators! Fuck 'em! Take their money! We can use it to get this company back on its feet. Jess and I can give them a million dollars' worth of software inside a year. It may not *work*, but it will be more than they have now."

Harrington's lips quirked as if he might smile, but he was deathly unamused. "Then when they find it doesn't really work, and we've cheated them?"

"By that time we'll be back on our feet again! What if they sue us? By then we can pay them back—even apologize for our big mistake. Hell, who will care? Who will be hurt? *Isn't it our only chance to survive right now?*"

Harrington looked at him a long moment, then swiveled his gaze to Jess. "Jess? What do you think?"

Jess thoughtfully chewed his tobacco, and his forehead was a washboard of concern and thought. "I swan. In a year there's no telling what we might come up with. Of course it wouldn't be ARIEL. But . . . I dunno." He raised troubled eyes to Harrington's face. "We worked so *long*, John. We worked so *dadblamed hard*."

"I know," Harrington said with a sigh.

"Don't end it here," Kraft urged. "Take their fucking money and give us a chance!"

Linda watched Harrington's face work for a moment. She knew a little of what he was going through.

Then he abruptly walked around the desk and opened the door. He invited Schmidt and Doyle back in.

"Gentlemen," he said softly, "we're sorry. We do not believe we can salvage the project in a year's time. It looks to me like our deal is off."

4

At noon, Linda rode with Harrington in his battered old Volvo to pick Rusty up at the hospital. The weather was changing, getting cool again. Pale and shaken, Rusty was pronounced healthy by the doctor and walked out with his father and Linda shortly before one o'clock.

"It's all ruined?" Rusty asked during the ride to Harrington's house.

"Well, it looks like it, son. But don't worry. We'll make out."

"There will never be anyone like ARIEL," Rusty said mournfully.

They reached the house. Someone—a neighbor—had left a covered dish of fruit salad on the front porch, as if for a bereaved family. Harrington carried it inside. The sky clouded over and it started to rain. Linda made soup and sandwiches while Rusty changed clothes and Harrington sat at the table, desolate-looking.

"What happens now?" she asked finally.

"ARIEL is done for," he said simply. "We can't make it financially past the middle of next week. It looks like a . . ." He glanced up at her and smiled crookedly, the pain showing. "It looks like we go through sort of an interesting time."

"*We* go through it," she repeated, emphasizing the word.

"I've got a lot to be thankful for," he said as she served the soup.

She looked sharply at him to make sure he was not being ironic. He was not.

He took her hand. "We could have lost Rusty."

"Yes."

"I could have lost you. I couldn't have stood either of those things happening."

Linda felt herself starting to cry. "Do you have any idea how much I love you?"

Rusty barged in, sat down, and started on his sandwich before Harrington could reply. She went to the sink to hide her tears.

"All that machinery, boy," Rusty said mournfully.

"It isn't the hardware, son," Harrington told him.

"It isn't?"

"Nope. Not really. I think we could duplicate all the hardware in six months or so, with help. It's the software—all the stuff Ted

< 314 >

did, and Jess, and Janice, and poor old Dave before he left us, and even the INFANT program, and Linda's and your input on that. We've got only a small piece of management system left, and most of the late memory, after she got going. What you put in—the way everything dovetailed—may never be duplicated precisely, espe- cially when you throw in that buffer overflow or whatever it was."

Rusty looked thoughtful, the bruises on his face dark against his pallor. No one said anything for a while.

Linda wiped her tears and joined them at the table, reaching for her sandwich. "I feel like I did once after a funeral," she burst out finally.

Harrington gave her a sad smile and patted her hand. "I know. It isn't logical to feel this way. It was just a machine . . . just pro- gramming."

"But you feel the same," Linda said.

"I miss her. Shit! I *miss* her. She was . . . a wonderful person. I'll never get over losing her." He snorted a laugh that was self- derisive. "I'm an idiot. Screw the money and losing the company. I feel like I've lost one of the family, or something."

Rusty had been staring intently at his father, his forehead wrinkled as it was when he was thinking extra hard. "It isn't a hardware problem. Right? That's what you said. Right?"

"That's right," Harrington sighed and took a bite out of his sandwich.

"It's the *software?*"

"That's the sticker, son. And even with what we get back from Elb's box over there—what little we might be able to reconstruct from the files that weren't hopelessly damaged by the fire and water—it's a Humpty Dumpty. We can never get it back together again."

Rusty jostled the table with his knee as he jumped to his feet. "Come here!" He started out of the room.

"Finish your lunch," Harrington said.

"Dad! Listen! *Come with me!*"

Harrington stared at him uncomprehendingly, glanced at Linda, got to his feet. "Okay. You get smoke in your brain, or what?"

Rusty said nothing. He bounded down the hall to his bedroom. Linda followed Harrington's shambling figure down the hall and into the room behind him.

The room was a mess as usual—trestle table of computer junk, unmade bed, floppy disks all over the place, the open shelving of books and technical journals, the massive old steamer trunk in the corner against the far wall.

Rusty stood near the table in front of the trunk. "Dad. You say you could get her going again with all the programming?"

"Sure," Harrington said. "But it all went—the backups too. You know that, son. Look. Let's talk about something else, for com sake, all right? Come on back into the kitchen, and we'll—"

"Dad!" Rusty cried, and walked to the steamer trunk. He reached down and unlatched the lid. "I didn't just copy on the disk systems. I even used that old mag tape drive we used to have in the basement. I wanted *everything*. I wanted a mess with it if I wanted. I wrote an automatic copying system program."

Harrington stared hard at him. "So?"

"So if it's the software, Dad—if having almost all of it will get the job done—look at this."

He opened the lid with a *thunk!* against the wall.

Inside were disks—hard disks and hundreds of floppies, five-inchers, larger ones, some mag tapes from the old unit that had been in the basement of the other house—a chaos of material. Harrington's eyes bulged and his throat started to work.

Hoarsely he said, "You didn't just input?"

"Heck no! I copied all the time, like crazy, so I could look at stuff!"

"How long?"

"Months!"

Harrington looked like a man seeing a ghost. "How much is here?"

"Gosh, unless you did something the last few days—*all of it.*"

"*All of it,*" Harrington repeated tonelessly, stunned.

"Yessir, I think so, unless I missed something."

"My God," Harrington said, and the grin on his face was so wide it looked like his skull would split. "My good, holy God!"

"Okay, Dad?" Rusty said urgently. "Okay?"

"Okay," Harrington said, tears running down his face.

"I don't understand," Linda said, unwilling or unable to credit the hope that had begun to rise in her breast. "All those disks—those records—ARIEL. What does it *mean?*"

"It means," Rusty told her, "she isn't dead. She's only sleeping."